"Revved up and red-hot sexy, ~~Roni Loren~~ delivers a riveting romance!"

—Lorelei James, *New York Times* bestselling author of the Blacktop Cowboys series and the Rough Riders series

"Hot and romantic, with an edge of suspense that will keep you entertained."

—Shayla Black, national bestselling author of *Mine to Hold*

"A sexy, sizzling tale that is sure to have readers begging for more! . . . I can't wait for Roni Loren's next tantalizing story!"

—Jo Davis, author of *I Spy a Dark Obsession*

"Sexy as hell, gutsy as all get out—*Crash Into You* has balls! Watch out. Roni Loren, just like the men in her books, knows how to keep you up all night. *Crash Into You* is sexy as hell and goes into the dark places other writers shy away from. Loren understands the dark beauty of D/s and treats her characters with respect even as she takes them to the very edge of what they and the reader can handle. I can sum this book up in one word: Damn!"

—Tiffany Reisz, author of *The Siren*

"This steamy, sexy yet emotionally gripping story has the right touch of humor and love to keep readers coming back for a second round."

—Julie Cross, author of *Tempest*

"A stunning first work. I read it straight through in one sitting, and I dare you to even attempt to put it down."

—Cassandra Carr, author of *Talk to Me*

Titles by Roni Loren

CRASH INTO YOU

MELT INTO YOU

eSpecials

STILL INTO YOU

melt into you

RONI LOREN

HEAT | NEW YORK

THE BERKLEY PUBLISHING GROUP
Published by the Penguin Group
Penguin Group (USA) Inc.
375 Hudson Street, New York, New York 10014, USA

Penguin Group (Canada), 90 Eglinton Avenue East, Suite 700, Toronto, Ontario M4P 2Y3, Canada (a division of Pearson Penguin Canada Inc.) • Penguin Books Ltd., 80 Strand, London WC2R 0RL, England • Penguin Group Ireland, 25 St. Stephen's Green, Dublin 2, Ireland (a division of Penguin Books Ltd.) • Penguin Group (Australia), 250 Camberwell Road, Camberwell, Victoria 3124, Australia (a division of Pearson Australia Group Pty. Ltd.) • Penguin Books India Pvt. Ltd., 11 Community Centre, Panchsheel Park, New Delhi—110 017, India • Penguin Group (NZ), 67 Apollo Drive, Rosedale, Auckland 0632, New Zealand (a division of Pearson New Zealand Ltd.) • Penguin Books (South Africa) (Pty.) Ltd., 24 Sturdee Avenue, Rosebank, Johannesburg 2196, South Africa

Penguin Books Ltd., Registered Offices: 80 Strand, London WC2R 0RL, England

This book is an original publication of The Berkley Publishing Group.

PUBLISHING HISTORY
Heat trade paperback edition / July 2012

Library of Congress Cataloging-in-Publication Data

Loren, Roni.
Melt into you / Roni Loren. — Heat trade paperback ed.
  p.   cm.
ISBN 978-0-425-24771-6
1. Open marriage—Fiction.   2. Triangles (Interpersonal relations)—Fiction.   I. Title.
PS3612.O764M45   2012
813'.6—dc23
2011051846

PRINTED IN THE UNITED STATES OF AMERICA

10 9 8 7 6 5 4 3 2 1

To Mom and De.
Your wholehearted, unconditional support
is the best gift a girl could ever receive.
I love you.

ACKNOWLEDGMENTS

Thank you to my husband, Donnie, who can always make me laugh and brighten my day no matter what's going on. You're my rock star. I love you.

To my kidlet: you amaze me daily with your awesomeness. And though you don't realize it now, Mommy wouldn't have had the chance to be a writer if you hadn't come into my life and inspired me to give my dream a go. I love you.

To my grandfather, Ron: your drive and enthusiasm for all that you do have always been an inspiration to me. I'm proud to be named after you. Love you.

To my writer friends, Julie Cross and Jamie Wesley, who keep me sane and talk me off ledges.

To my agent Sara Megibow and editor Kate Seaver: you ladies make it a joy for me to "go to work" every day. Thank you.

To my online writer friends, who amaze me daily with your brilliance, your humor, and your kickass support for your fellow scribes. Y'all are definitely the coolest kids in the cafeteria.

And to anyone who picks up one of my books to read: I appreciate you more than you'll ever know. Thank you.

PROLOGUE

twelve years ago

Most of the time temptation climbs into your lap and straddles you, demands you deal with it immediately. Give in or deprive yourself. Choose your adventure.

Jace's general stance: Deprivation was overrated.

But he'd never faced this kind of temptation. The kind that seeped into your skin so slowly you didn't even notice until you were soaked with it, saturated. To the point that every thought, every breath, seemed to be laced with the desire for that thing you shouldn't have.

And right now that thing was nibbling flecks of purple polish off her fingernails.

Jace shifted on the rec room couch, pretending to look for the remote control, even though he could feel the damn thing digging into his hip. He had to do something to get her calves off his lap. Otherwise, she was going to feel exactly how much he hadn't been concentrating on the horror movie. Or she'd assume he'd gotten the monster hard-on watching the teens get butchered on the screen. Although, thinking he got off on blood and guts might be preferable to the real reason he was sporting wood.

She tucked her legs to her chest and set her chin on her knees, staring at him with eyes so pale blue, they looked like silver dimes in the flicker of the television. Thunder rumbled outside and her gaze darted to the window behind him. Wary. "Maybe we should've watched that Jim Carrey movie instead."

He hit Stop on the VCR, cutting off the eerie music to the closing credits, and resisted the urge to scoot closer to her, to curl around her lithe body and slay her fears like the dude in the movie had done for the heroine. Well, up until the guy's head was lopped off. That he could skip. "See, I warned you it would freak you out. I shouldn't have even let you watch it. It's rated R. Too old for you."

She snorted and shoved his thigh with her foot. "Said the nineteen-year-old who just finished his third beer."

He glanced at the empty bottles on the side table. Yeah, he was batting a thousand on the responsible adult thing tonight. Good thing his parents had left him in charge. "I'm in college. Beer is part of homework."

"Whatever. I'll be rated-R approved in three months anyway." She grabbed her Coke off the coffee table and sipped, drawing his attention down to her heart-shaped lips and the way they drew the liquid slowly from the bottle. "Hell, I'll be porn approved."

Fuck. That's the last image she needed to paint on his brain. "No, you won't. Gotta be eighteen for that."

Lightning reflected off the silver ring in her arched eyebrow. "You would know, I'm sure."

"I'm a guy." Which should be enough of an explanation. "And don't you dare watch any of that shit until you're like thirty."

"Oh, please. I'm not that innocent, Jace," she said, yawning and setting down her drink. She rubbed her eyes with the heels of her hands, smudging her heavy kohl eyeliner until she looked like some gothic angel. "The couple I was placed with last time had a huge stash that their idiot sons always raided. I've seen my share of *bom-chicka-wah-wah*."

"Oh, terrific. Glad you were supervised so well."

"It was stupid. The guy actors were ugly and the girls were fake-looking." She bumped his thigh with her bare foot again. "Kind of like those chicks you always date."

He almost jolted when she touched him. He felt like that game Operation where any slight nudge sent a loud buzz through his system—only this buzz went straight to his dick. Every time he was around her these days was like this.

He'd almost gotten used to it, had accepted the painful state as part of his daily existence. Then two weeks ago they'd been goofing off in the pool. She'd sprayed him in the face with the hose, and he'd grabbed her by the ankle and pulled her into the water with him. When she'd surfaced, she'd been laughing—something as rare as a unicorn sighting.

He'd pushed her hair off her face, intending to dunk her again, but had gotten caught in the net of her laughing eye-lock. He'd hesitated. And in the space between blinks, she'd glided in closer to him, invaded his space, and kissed him.

And dammit, he'd kissed her back. Had let all the pent-up desire he'd harbored for her over the last few months pour into the kiss. So stupid.

He knew having someone live in his parents' house for a year didn't make her his sister. But he wasn't dumb enough to think kissing her was okay either. Especially when she was still in high school. Man, if hell existed, he was going straight there.

He'd stopped the kiss when she'd pressed her body against his, her one-piece bathing suit not thick enough to insulate him from her every peak and valley beneath it. She'd swum off without a word and hadn't mentioned it again, apparently voting to pretend it never happened. He'd seconded that vote.

But now he realized they were probably going to have to discuss it. Draw a nice little chalk line between them. He'd drunk the beer, hoping to get some liquid courage, but no such luck.

He scooted more toward the arm of the couch, away from contact with her feet. "The girls I date aren't fake-looking." *Not totally.*

"They sure as hell don't look like me."

Fuck no, they didn't. They didn't smell of cherry shampoo like she did either. Or smile at only his good jokes, not the lame ones. Or make him feel like he was worth hanging out with—not because of his money, or his rank on the college swim team, but just because. "No one looks like you."

Her gaze shifted back to her chipped nail polish. "Yeah, well, not all of us can be supermodels."

"Hey, that's not what I meant."

She swung her legs from the couch to the floor and stood. "I'm going to go clean this polish off and go to bed. Thanks for renting the movie, even though I think I'll be sleeping with the lights on and the closet doors open tonight."

"Hold up." Jace grabbed her hand before she could escape, knowing he shouldn't say what he was about to, but not okay letting her walk away feeling like she was somehow less than. "I'm serious. Those girls only wish they looked as great as you. Really."

"You're so full of crap I bet your eyes have turned brown with it." She slipped her fingers from his grasp and hugged her elbows. "Don't do this because of what happened in the pool. I have enough people doing the let's-lie-to-make-her-feel-good thing. You're the only one I've been able to count on to not bullshit me."

Thunder rolled outside as if gathering energy off her building anger.

He leaned back on the couch, his hands out to his sides. "Chill, I'm not lying to you, okay?" *I haven't really been sitting here all night watching you instead of the stupid movie. And no, I haven't spent the last two weeks replaying how good it felt to kiss you that day. Or wondering what would've happened if I hadn't stopped things.*

She stared at him for a moment, eyes narrowed, like she was determining results on some internal lie detector.

He knew more discussion in this direction wasn't going to lead anywhere good. If she kept prying, his feelings were going to slip out, especially with his tongue loose from beer. "You should go to bed."

Her lips parted as if she was going to push the issue further, but then—thank God—clamped them shut and turned her back on him. "Good night, Jace."

After he was sure she'd be done in the bathroom and tucked into her own room, Jace trudged upstairs to get ready for bed. He should've skipped brushing his teeth. The minute he stepped into the steamy, cherry-scented bathroom, his hard-on returned full force. She'd showered.

He groaned as images of her slipping out of her clothes right where he stood assailed him. Water sluicing down over her every curve, washing away all that makeup and leaving behind that natural beauty so few girls seemed to have. Her hands sliding soap over her naked body, touching, exploring. *Fuck.*

He brushed his teeth with brutal force and shoved his toothbrush back in its holder, fighting the temptation to climb in the shower and let the fantasy run wild while he stroked himself. He'd done it before with her on his mind. But he knew it wouldn't provide any real relief. It'd only key him up more, and all he wanted to do right now was fall into bed and crash. At least if he was sleeping he didn't have to think about the girl two doors down.

He made his way to his bedroom and flipped on a lamp. The room flooded with warm light, but then flickered off, the distinctive sound of everything electronic in the house going from a whir to dead silence following it. *Ah, hell.*

He crossed to the far side of the room and pulled back the curtains on the pair of large windows, lighting his room with the flashing of the storm. With wind like this, losing electricity had been inevitable. Now he wouldn't even be able to distract himself with TV to help get to sleep. He stripped down to his boxers and slipped between the cool sheets.

Stared at the ceiling.

This was going to be a long night.

He counted the seconds between the bolts of lightning and the boom of thunder—the space between getting less and less. The worst of the rain would pass over them soon. But he feared his throbbing hard-on wouldn't fade quite as quickly.

He tossed from one side of the bed to the other, trying to think of something—anything—besides the girl down the hall. Even re-playing some of the gory scenes from the movie they'd watched didn't help. Nothing could shake the image of her standing there—smudged eyeliner, faded sweatshirt, and a jaded smirk that told him she really didn't believe she was beautiful.

Didn't realize he couldn't even concentrate when she was near.

He flopped onto his back with a strangled sigh. He would never fall asleep at this rate. Not with his brain on an endless loop and his body staging the boner from hell. Resigned, he let his hand track down his abdomen and below the waistband of his shorts, imagining that it was her delicate, purple-polished fingers wrap-ping around his cock instead of his large hand.

He groaned as he stroked up the length and ran a thumb over the tip. God, how many times in the last few months had he thought of her this way? He couldn't ever remember aching for someone like this. Sex was sex. Girls were girls. Both had always come easy to him. Neither was something to get all knotted up about. Why was she so different?

Her name whispered off his lips as he brought himself closer to release, and the windows rattled with the next roll of thunder. Jace almost missed the faint *tap tap tap* sound mixed in with it. The noise came again. He tilted his head, listened. Another knock and then his door cracked open a sliver, a beam of light peeking through. "Jace?"

Fuck, fuck, fuck. He pulled his hand from his shorts and squinted in the glare of the flashlight. "Yeah, I'm here. What's up?"

"Can I come in?" she asked, her voice swallowed by another rumble outside.

Hell no! He sat up on his elbows, making sure he had enough blankets over him to cover what was beneath the sheets. "You okay?"

She stepped fully into the room and clicked off the flashlight. "Do you have any matches or a lighter? I . . . I know it's stupid, but the dark still freaks me out and I want to light a few candles."

He frowned. "No, sorry, I don't. I could go look downstairs. There may be some in the kitchen."

"No, don't get up." She took another step toward him, the flashing from the windows lighting her in strobe effect, each blink giving his eyes something new to torture himself with. Bare legs. Short gym shorts. Damp hair. A tank top so thin he could see the shadow of dusky pink nipples beneath it.

But where he lost it was when his eyes locked with hers. The longing he felt in his own chest reflected in her pale blue stare. He tried to clear the knot that lodged in his throat. "It's fine. I don't mind."

"I don't want to go back to my room, Jace," she said, something very different from fear lacing her words.

His tongue grew thick in his mouth. "Well, you can't stay in here."

Another step closer, now within arm's reach of him. "Why not? No one will be home until tomorrow."

He groaned and raked a hand through his now sweat-dampened hair. "Because . . . Jesus, you know why."

"Because you think I'm pretty." The corner of her mouth lifted despite the obvious nervous edge tracking through her tone.

"Don't do this," he said, not sure if the words were directed at her or himself.

"Come on, I want to know."

"Yes, because I think you're pretty." He looked toward the windows, breathed. "Because I damn near lose my mind every time I'm near you lately."

Her breath escaped in a sharp little puff, and the thunder rolled between them, electrifying the air.

He hardened his tone, hoping she'd run for the door. "Go back to your room. We're playing a dangerous game and doing the right thing has never been my strong suit."

"That's what I love about you," she said, sitting down on the bed, ignoring his warning. The curve of her hip brushed against the back of his hand. "You're the only one in this family that seems to live in the moment, to take risks."

Yeah, and his family hated him for it. He closed his eyes, trying to shut out the vision of her, but her scent wrapped around him just the same, awakening every nerve in his body.

Soft skin slid across his palm as she gripped his hand. "Take a risk on me, Jace. Please. I need . . ." She paused and he opened his eyes to find hers going shiny. "I need you."

The stark ache in her voice sank down into his bones, eclipsing even the sexual attraction he had for her and fueling something deeper, some longing to connect with her. Hold her. Soothe whatever made her so sad beneath that tough girl façade. To be that guy to fight off her demons.

To be what she needed.

So he squeezed her hand and pulled her down against him, taking her lips in a slow, savoring kiss and letting himself fall to the desire that had choked him these last few months. Her body melted along his, her hands exploring his bare chest, threading though his hair, touching and testing. Both brave and timid.

Jace held back his need to run his hands over each inch of her, afraid he'd overtake her with his own wants and urge her farther than she wanted to go. He settled for laying gentle kisses along the curve of her neck, tasting the sweet salt of her skin and breathing in her heady scent. He could spend all night relishing every nuance of her. Each flavor. Each texture. Each breathy sigh.

Her fingers traced down over his hip, pausing when they brushed the waistband of his boxers. Tentative.

He eased back from kissing her neck and tucked a stray hair behind her ear. "Hey, we can just kiss. This doesn't have to be anything more than that."

She bit her lip and looked down at her hands. "But what if I want it to be?"

The sweet plea in her tone undid him. Completely and totally decimated the last of his resistance. He put a knuckle beneath her chin and lifted her face to him. "Tell me what you want, baby."

The lightning flashed outside, revealing the color staining her cheeks. "I want everything with you, but . . . can you take the lead?"

He eased her off him and onto her back, kissing the corner of a mouth that smirked too often and stared into eyes that had seen too much. "Yeah, I think I can do that."

And he did.

Tasting her, touching her. Loving her.

Breaking every rule he'd set for himself and breaking the goddamned law.

But in the beautiful perfection that filled the next few thousand breaths, he didn't care.

Because sometimes doing the wrong thing was the only thing that felt right.

ONE

Evan Kennedy swigged the last of the tequila from the mini-bottle as her fiancé's moans of pleasure drifted through the wall behind her. She set the bottle down and sank back onto the bed, curling her pillow around her ears. This was torture—absolute Geneva Convention–worthy stuff. Next time they stayed in a hotel, she would make sure the suite had two bedrooms that didn't share a wall.

How was she supposed to sleep with that kind of erotic soundtrack in the background? Especially when the only company she had in her room was the hotel's mini-bar and a subpar selection of cable stations.

The heavy thudding of a headboard banging against the wall started up, rattling the three empty bottles on her bedside table. Oh, the guys were on their game tonight—obviously celebrating the good news they'd all gotten earlier in the evening. No telling how long their show would go on. With a heavy sigh, she threw the comforter off her legs and climbed out of the bed, happy to find she only wavered slightly.

She needed air. Or at least some place where two happy lovers weren't sharing passionate, wall-rattling sex while she lay in bed alone.

She yanked on a pair of jeans and a T-shirt, then tucked the last mini-bottle of tequila into her pocket. The bars downstairs would be closed by now, and although she rarely drank, tonight she had the urge to get comfortably numb. She just had to make sure not to run into any of the people here for her and Daniel's couples' seminar. That certainly wouldn't reflect well on the company. And the last thing she felt like doing was getting into a row with Daniel about "professional image."

After running a brush through her hair, she stepped out of her bedroom and threw one last glance at Daniel's closed door. The moans had turned to dueling male grunts. Clearly both parties were having a good time. An unexpected pang of sadness hit her in the gut, and her eyes burned as if tears were going to flow.

What in the world? Her hand went to her cheek, but of course no actual tears were there. She never cried. But that burning was the first sign she'd had in years that she was still physically capable of tears.

She shook her head. Maybe it was the tequila.

And the close quarters.

A walk would help.

She shut the door with a soft snick and made her way down to the lobby. As expected, things were quiet. The overnight desk clerk glanced up at her with disinterested eyes. She gave him a quick smile and turned in the opposite direction to head toward the pool and the beach beyond.

She slipped through the exit door, and the warm Gulf breeze wrapped around her, lifting her mood a bit. She closed her eyes and inhaled the salty air, letting it fill her lungs and hoping it would clear her head. But as soon as she opened her eyes again, the glowing swimming pool seemed to tilt in front of her. Whoa. Maybe she had overestimated her liquor tolerance. Three shots of tequila might have been two too many. She grabbed on to the back of a nearby lounge chair to steady herself.

Evan focused on the dark expanse of the Gulf of Mexico in the distance, waiting for the spinning in her head to stop. She just needed to make it to the beach, sit down in the sand, and get her normally iron-clad defenses back in place so she could return upstairs with a smile on her face. She didn't need the guys seeing her this way. They'd want to sit down and talk about feelings and shit. And really, she just didn't want to go there. The last thing she needed right now was for Daniel to put on his therapist hat with her.

After a few more fortifying breaths, she straightened her spine and made her way slowly around the edge of the pool and to the wooden stairs that led down to the beach. *Almost there.* But when she reached for the gate, the latch didn't give. "What the—?"

She looked down and sighed at the sign attached to the weather-beaten wood. *Private Beach—Closed: midnight to 6 a.m. No lifeguard on duty.*

"Dammit."

She stared longingly at the crashing waves, the peaceful solitude of the beach calling to her like a siren song. She peeked over her shoulder at the hotel's main building. There weren't any security cameras out here. Who would know? And Daniel had brought a hell of a lot of business to the hotel this weekend with the conference, so even if someone caught her, she doubted they would do more than politely direct her back to her room.

Without giving it more thought, she planted a foot on the lowest railing and draped her other leg over the top, making sure to keep two hands securely on the fence so her head wouldn't start whirling again. She hoped no one was watching because she was sure she was executing the maneuver with the grace of a walrus, but at least she didn't topple down the stairs. Score.

After a careful walk down the steps, she kicked off her flip-flops and curled her toes into the cool sand. Ahh, yes, *so* worth the rule-breaking.

Thunder rumbled in the distance, and the clouds far off on the horizon blinked with lightning. Damn, she should've brought her camera. The new lens she'd bought would've been perfect to catch the display. She moved closer to the water, stepping past the rows of hotel lounge chairs and closed umbrellas and not stopping until the spray from the crashing waves hit her face and the taste of salt alighted on her tongue.

The tide pooled around her feet, soaking the bottom of her jeans and sending a little chill through her. She rubbed her arms and glanced down the beach, taking in the deserted shoreline that stretched along the length of South Padre Island. The moonlight had turned the normally colorful view into silver sand and black water, but even in the darkness, she could tell she was alone on her three a.m. adventure.

No surprise there. People didn't come on vacation to wander around alone half-drunk in the middle of the night. No, the people in those beautifully appointed hotels lining the beach were cuddled up to their loved ones right now, sleeping off a fun day. Or, like Daniel, having crazy monkey sex with their lovers. Lucky bastards.

Normally, that knowledge wouldn't bother her. She'd made her decisions, had created a good life for herself. For the first time, she was with someone who loved her—even if that love was only platonic. But for some reason, a hollow ache had rooted solidly in her chest tonight. And paired with the heated need that had settled between her thighs after listening to an hour of lovemaking, she was dangerously close to feeling sorry for herself.

Her fists balled. No way. Screw that. The alcohol had to be what was making her feel this way. She just needed to sober up.

She looked down at the water swirling around her ankles. A dunk in the surf would probably snap her into sobriety pretty quickly. But walking back through the hotel in dripping-wet clothes wasn't exactly wise, especially when she wasn't supposed to be on the beach in the first place.

She gave the shore another quick scan, then shrugged. *Oh, what the hell.*

Evan stepped back from the water long enough to shimmy out of her jeans and T-shirt and tossed the clothes where the water's edge wouldn't reach. Despite the warm night breeze, her nipples beaded beneath her bra and goose bumps rose on her skin. A little zip of adrenaline went through her. Man, how long had it been since she'd done something like this, stepped outside the lines a little? She'd almost forgotten what it felt like.

To hell with the pity party. She was on a gorgeous beach and had the whole damn thing to herself. No more whining. She made her way back toward the waves and took her time submerging herself, determined to enjoy the luxury of owning this little piece of ocean for the night.

The water lapped at her as she moved further into the surf— bathing her legs, sliding up her thighs, soaking her panties. *Mmm.* The gulf was deliciously warm against her skin, caressing the dormant parts of her to full sensual awareness. Her hands cupped the water and drew it up and over her breasts, soaking her bra and the tightening buds underneath. A shudder went through her.

She wanted to sink into the salty depths and allow the sensations to take over, to wash away the dark emotions that had claimed her tonight. But even in her buzzed state, she knew tequila and swimming weren't good bedfellows. So, she stopped when the waves crested at her chest and settled in to watch the light show on the horizon.

The distant storm had moved a bit closer, and though it still wasn't near enough to be a threat, the view of the flashing sky was breathtaking. She wanted to kick herself for not bringing her camera. She'd had so little time for her photography since she'd gone on this seminar tour with Daniel she was beginning to worry she'd forgotten how to do it. Hopefully, when they returned to Dallas after this last stop, she could dedicate some time to her neglected studio.

With a sigh, she tilted her head back, closed her eyes, and dipped her hair into the water. Maybe that's why she was in such a funk. She'd spent the last few months supporting Daniel's passion and ignoring hers. She'd signed up for it, and the venture had turned out to be lucrative for them both, but it definitely didn't feed the part of her soul that slipping behind a camera did. That part was downright starved.

Thunder rumbled closer this time. Reluctantly, she drifted back a few feet. It was probably time to get out. The alcohol-induced fog in her head was clearing, and based on the sudden uptick in wind, the storm would be on top of her in the next few minutes. But before she could take another step, pain—sharp and sudden—shot up her thigh.

She yelped and jolted backward, her arms flailing before she crashed into the water and went under. Saltwater filled her mouth, silencing her shout, and a burning sensation wrapped around her thigh and radiated outward.

Disoriented, she scrambled for solid footing, trying to get back to the surface. She knew she couldn't have fallen into deep water, but the writhing pain and the knowledge that she was out there alone had panic edging in. She spread her arms in an attempt to tread water and finally felt sand against her toes. But just as she tried to push off, twin bands of heat wrapped around her upper arms and her entire body was propelled upward.

When her face broke the surface of the water, she sucked in a large gulp of air, half-coughing, half-choking. She kicked frantically, trying to make sure she didn't get dragged back under.

"Stop fighting or you're going to drown us both." The rumbling

male voice came from behind her, and the grip on her arms tightened. "We've got to get out of the undertow."

Her heart jumped into her throat, but she forced herself to stop
struggling so the stranger could help. His breath was warm on her
neck as he pulled them both backward, but he didn't say another
word. The water seemed to be fighting their progress, and the man
adjusted his hold until he had his arms hooked beneath her arm-
pits. She wanted to tell him to let her go, that she knew how to
swim, but her thigh was burning like a swarm of wasps had at-
tacked it and her head was spinning again.

A few hard-fought minutes later, packed sand scraped against
her heels, and she sucked in a deep sigh of relief. The man dragged
her another few feet until they reached dry land, then set her down
and kneeled next to her.

"Are you okay?" he asked, his broad chest heaving beneath his
soaked T-shirt.

She lifted her gaze to the concerned eyes staring down at her, an
odd sense of déjà vu washing over her. "I, uh . . ."

"I heard you scream. Are you hurt?" He touched the side of her
head, evaluating her.

She wet her lips. "My leg . . . Something stung me . . . I lost my
balance."

He glanced down the length of her—the mostly naked length of
her. *Shit.* She shot up into a sitting position and scooted backward,
but his hand locked over her knee as he stared down at her upper
thigh, which was still burning like she'd roasted it over an open
fire.

"Damn, it got you good."

"What are you talking about?" She tried to jerk her leg from
beneath his grip, but he held her firm as he examined her.

"Jellyfish," he said, frowning at her. "Your whole thigh is
striped. That must hurt like a sonofabitch."

She stared down at the red tentacle-shaped lines around her thigh. "Well, it doesn't feel awesome."

He chuckled, the rich sound seeming to vibrate from deep within his chest, and something stirred in the back of her brain. He climbed to his feet. "Here, let me help."

"Don't you dare pee on me," she said, the words slipping out before she could rethink them.

He tilted his head back in a full laugh this time, the sound echoing down the beach.

She cringed. "I'm sorry, I—"

He raised a hand, his eyes still lit with humor. "Don't worry. The urine thing is just an urban myth. And I'm definitely not going to ruin my 'just saved pretty girl from drowning' hero status by taking a leak on you. I'm not that stupid."

She couldn't help but smile. "Oh, a hero, huh? So this is all a big pick-up routine? Find drowning girls and ride in on your white horse?"

"Absolutely." He grabbed the hem of his T-shirt and pulled it off, revealing miles of taut skin, sinewy muscle, and tribal-style ink running across his shoulder and down one arm, rendering her momentarily speechless. Water dripped off his soaked hair—which looked to be blond, though it was hard to tell in the moonlight— and slipped down his now bare chest. Her gaze locked on the tiny droplets, tracking their path down to the band of his shorts until they disappeared. *Oh, blessed Lord.*

He cleared his throat, no doubt catching her in her perusal, and squatted next to her. His hand slipped under her knee. "Here, seawater actually helps the sting. Let me wrap this around your leg, and then we can go to my room. We'll get you feeling better."

She cocked an eyebrow at him. "Oh, really. Might want to tap the brakes there, Rico Suave. Despite my state of undress, I don't just go to strangers' hotel rooms. I'm not quite that easy."

Dimples appeared as he fought a smile. "Oh, not quite *that* easy, but easy. Duly noted."

She shot him a withering look.

"For the record, that's not why I was inviting you to my room. Although, I promise *that* certainly would distract you from the pain. But all I mean is my roommate is Mr. Prepared. He keeps a first-aid kit for the beach and always has a bottle of vinegar in it. It will help deactivate the venom."

She frowned. Two grown men on a beach vacation together? Great, not another good-looking guy who preferred other good-looking guys. Not that she was looking for anything to happen anyway. He was a stranger. An extremely pinup-worthy stranger. But still. In her sexually deprived state, a little flirting could be almost as satisfying as an orgasm. Almost.

With gentle hands, he bent her leg and wrapped his wet T-shirt around her thigh. His focus was on the task at hand, but she didn't miss the sneaky sidelong glance toward her open thighs, where her wet panties were probably revealing every detail of what lay beneath.

She cleared her throat, and his gaze darted back to her leg, but the corner of his mouth tugged up a bit.

Well, well, maybe not so gay.

Her body heated at the thought, even though her brain knew that, straight or gay, she wasn't going to do anything with her rescuer. "So how long were you out here? I thought I was alone."

He glanced up as he draped the shirt around her leg a second time. "I was here the whole time." He crooked a thumb behind him. "Was sitting in one of the lounge chairs on the far end. I thought you saw me when you looked down the beach, but I guess not."

"You could've said something, you know."

He gave her an unrepentant grin. "If a beautiful woman wants to go for a naked swim, who am I to intervene?"

"Very gentlemanly of you."

"Hey, never said I was a gentleman. Just a hero."

"Right," she said, her tone dry.

He tucked the end of the shirt underneath the first layer, securing it. "Is that too tight?"

"No, it's actually helping the burning a little."

"Hold on." He climbed to his feet and jogged a little ways down the beach, grabbed something from one of the lounge chairs, then walked over to where she had left her clothes and picked up those as well. When he returned he held out her T-shirt. "Go ahead and put this on. You're not going to be able to put on the jeans, but you can wrap my beach towel around your waist."

"Thanks." She took her shirt and towel from him, pulled the first over her head, then got to her feet and knotted the beach towel around her hips. She tilted her head up to smile at him. "So, Mr. Humble Hero, you have a name?"

He stuck out his hand. "It's Jace."

Her body froze, the world seeming to tip off balance for a moment. Had she heard right? She stared at him for a moment, taking in every nuance of his face, the earlier whispers of déjà vu now becoming shouts.

Was it really him? His hair was longer, his body harder and more mature, the green in his eyes more wary, but the resemblance was there. It'd been years—twelve actually. The nineteen-year-old boy she'd known had become a man. "Jace *Austin*?"

―――――

Oh, shit. The recognition that flashed in the woman's blue eyes had Jace dropping his hand. This chick knew him? He frantically flipped through his mental Rolodex, starting with the girls-I've-slept-with file.

When they'd locked gazes earlier, he'd felt a nudge of familiarity but had dismissed it. Surely, he'd remember this dark-haired beauty, especially if he had gotten the privilege of touching that lush little body. But something about her was poking at the recesses of his mind.

He rubbed the back of his neck and offered an apologetic smile. "Uh, yeah. Jace Austin. I'm sorry, have we met?"

She flinched a bit—the move subtle, but not lost on him. Damn, well now he felt like a jackass. *Had* they slept together?

She recovered quickly, the corner of her mouth tilting up. "Don't worry. I'm sure I look a little different than I did at sixteen. Especially without that god-awful bottle red hair and eyebrow piercing."

Sixteen? Red hair? The flashing list of names in his head suddenly flipped back over a decade and landed on one he hadn't thought about in years. One he'd purposely tried to block out. No, couldn't be. *"Evangeline?"*

She shrugged and looked out at the water, the wind whipping her hair around and disguising her expression. "It's Evan now. I stopped using my full name a long time ago."

"Wow, I don't even know what to say," he said, shaking his head. "You look great. I'm so glad to see that you're . . ." *Okay. Alive.* "Here."

She turned back toward him and smiled, though it didn't light her face the way the earlier smiles had. "It's good to see you, too. But, if you don't mind, before we go down memory lane, how 'bout that vinegar?"

"Oh, right," he said, his mind still whirling. "Follow me."

And she needn't worry. The last thing he was going to do was initiate any reminiscing. No, some things were better left buried. And how he'd destroyed the girl he'd sworn to look out for was A-number-one on that list.

TWO

Evan leaned against the back of the couch in Jace's hotel suite and clasped her hands in front of her to keep them from shaking. She'd thought about Jace so often over the years, despite her best efforts not to. She had wondered how he was doing, but she'd never allowed herself to look him up and check. She'd been a coward—afraid of how she'd react seeing him all grown up, possibly with a wife and kids or something.

When she was a teenager, Jace had been the perfect boy in her eyes. The only guy who'd been able to make her smile during those dark years. She'd stupidly assumed his attention had meant more than simple friendship, more than pity for a screwed-up foster kid. But God, how wrong she'd been. Of all the disastrous mistakes she'd made in her life, falling for Jace had been her biggest. She'd paid dearly for that error—still paid for it—but he would never know that.

And now he'd seen her moping alone on the beach and going skinny-dipping drunk. Stellar. If she'd wanted to show him how far she'd come, how put together she was now, she'd certainly gotten off to a shining start.

"I'm going to go grab the vinegar from Andre's room," Jace said, pulling her from her thoughts. "Why don't you go in the bathroom and unwrap your leg? I'll bring you the bottle."

"Yeah, okay," she said, proud her voice was steady despite her jangled nerves.

She made her way to the restroom and sat on the edge of the tub, arranging the towel to cover her lap. The burn of the jellyfish sting had lessened a bit from its five-alarm status, but still made it hard to sit still. Or maybe it was the fact that Jace was here that had her ready to jump out of her skin. Even after all these years, simply being near him had her stomach doing silly flip-flops. She needed to get it together.

She unwrapped the makeshift bandage and laid it over the edge of the tub right as Jace poked his head into the bathroom. "How's it looking, Ev?"

The affection lacing her old nickname poked at something she'd long since buried. She forced a casual shrug. "Looks like I got in a fight with a jellyfish and lost."

"Here." He stepped inside and the room seemed to shrink as his tall, still shirtless frame filled up the space. He squatted next to her and uncapped the bottle of vinegar. "This should neutralize the sting. Might be a little cold."

She winced when he poured the liquid over her thigh, but despite the shock of the contrast in temperature, the sting started to ease. "Ooh, that's better."

His hand cupped her knee and he ran a thumb over the curve of it, causing her breath to hitch. He glanced up from his crouched position, his eyes seeming to see right through her this-is-no-big-thing façade she was working so hard to maintain. "You okay, Ev?"

She could tell by the somberness of his expression, the edge of concern in his voice that he wasn't asking about the sting. The combination of his touch and the sentiment almost undid her, almost brought forth the tears she'd hadn't cried in a decade. She looked back at her leg. "I'm fine, Jace. Really."

He blew out a breath and stood. "Pat your leg dry. I'll be right back."

A few seconds later, he returned—thankfully with a shirt on. God knows she was having enough trouble concentrating around him without the added distraction of his bare chest. He tossed a ball of blue fabric to her.

"What's this for?"

"It's a pair of track shorts you can use. They'll be big, but hopefully the drawstring will help. You're not going to want to put your jeans back on over that sting."

"Oh, right. Thanks." She stared down at the shorts.

He cleared his throat. "Uh, why don't you go ahead and get changed. I'll be in the living room."

He'd already seen her in her underwear on the beach, but she knew why he was giving her privacy. Now that they knew who each other was, the wall of the past was firmly erected between them. There would be no more lighthearted flirting. Certainly not from her end.

Regardless, she appreciated the few minutes of alone time. It gave her time to regroup, pull her shoulders back, and slip back into the woman she was now—instead of the teenager she'd regressed to as soon as Jace had appeared.

When she stepped back into the living room, Jace was leaning over the small refrigerator, clanging bottles around as he searched for something. He glanced up from his task when she cleared her throat and sat on the couch.

"I was trying to see if we had any soda, but it looks like all we have is beer and water."

She smirked. "I think I've had enough alcohol tonight. Plus, I need to get back to my room."

A squeak from the other side of the room caught her attention. She turned her head just as one of the bedroom doors swung open on whining hinges. A drowsy-eyed man wearing only plaid pajama bottoms filled the doorway and leaned against the doorframe. "J, what the fuck are you doing in here? I'm trying to sleep."

Jace frowned in the man's direction. "Watch the language, Andre. We've got company."

Jace's roommate turned his head, his dark eyebrows lifting when he spotted her. "Oh." His gaze traveled down the length of her, pausing at the borrowed shorts, and a sleepy smile crossed his face. "Well, hi there."

Evan heated beneath Andre's attention, the hint of Spanish accent and the flare of interest in his eyes singeing her. No worries about the two gorgeous men in the room being gay. That was for damn sure.

Jace snorted. "Back off, Romeo. Evan's an old friend of mine and is only here because she has a wicked jellyfish sting. So you can dial down the flirt."

"Wait a second." Andre scrubbed a hand over his face and stepped closer, his eyes narrowing as if evaluating her closer. "Evan? As in Evan Kennedy?"

"No, Evan Litch—" Jace began, but she interrupted.

"Yes, Evan Kennedy." She stuck out her hand. "Nice to meet you."

Andre sauntered forward and took her hand, bringing it to his mouth and planting a kiss on top of it instead of shaking it. "Pleasure."

Jace walked up behind him, his brows knitted together. "You changed your name? Why does your new one sound so familiar?"

Andre laughed and sank into the armchair next to her. She

would've answered Jace, but she had a hard time drawing her attention away from Andre's lean, tan chest and the silver nipple rings glinting in the lamp light. *Oh, my.* Not to mention Jace's well-built form in her peripheral vision. Man, she was like a starved woman at a buffet. Beyond getting away from her past with Jace, she needed to get away from all this testosterone.

Andre answered for her. "Because this lovely lady is engaged to the guy who's running the whole couples shindig this weekend. She'll be Mrs. Doctor Dan in a few months."

She nodded. "Yes, November."

"Hold up," Jace said, drawing her attention back to him as he crossed in front of her and sat on the couch opposite her. "You're *engaged?*"

She cringed inwardly. Why had she let herself flirt on the beach? She knew better than that. Now she looked trampy on top of flighty. Fabulous. "Yes."

"To *the* Dr. Dan?" Jace eyed her in a way that made her want to shift her gaze to the floor. Like if she met his stare, he'd see every bit of the truth written on her face.

"Yes, the very one." She stood and forced a brief smile. "And I doubt he'd be happy knowing I was half-dressed in someone else's hotel room in the middle of the night. So I better head back."

"You didn't tell him you were going to the beach?" Jace asked, the frown lines around his mouth deepening. "That's dangerous, Ev. You should've told someone you were going out there. What if that undertow would've kept you under and I hadn't been there?"

Her jaw flexed. "I would've been fine. The jellyfish sting distracted me, but I would've been able to swim to shore. And I don't need to report where I'm going every second of the day to anyone."

"You do if your plan is to go skinny-dipping drunk in the middle of the night," he said, his voice rising.

Andre looked back and forth between the two of them, but was obviously smart enough not to jump in the conversation.

Her cheeks heated with a combination of shame and anger. "I don't need a keeper, Jace. I didn't need one when you knew me before, and I don't need one now."

Jace looked ready to argue the point, but then his shoulders sagged and he released a breath. "You're right. It's none of my business. I'm sorry."

Her fists, which had clenched during the exchange, loosened. This was ridiculous. Why was she arguing with someone she had no intention to lay eyes on ever again? Jace was her past. She'd spent a decade burying her old life and that version of herself. No good could come of dredging up any of those memories. She needed to keep Jace locked away in that "mistakes" box and get out of here.

"Look, I appreciate your help tonight. Really." She turned to Andre. "And thanks so much for the vinegar. It really helped."

"No problem, sometimes my Boy-Scout-like preparedness comes in handy." Andre gave her a little mock salute, but she had a hard time believing the wholesome routine when he was so busy looking like Latin-flavored sin.

Her gaze strayed to the door. "Um, well, I'd better get going."

Jace ran his fingers through his still-damp blond hair and sighed. "When are you leaving the resort?"

"Today. We have workshops until five and then we're headed back to Dallas."

"Let me buy you lunch," he said, standing in her path when she took a few steps toward the door. "We can catch up."

She didn't stop walking. "Jace, I don't think so. I've got a lot going on and am so busy with all this—"

"Hey." He laid a hand on her forearm when she tried to move around him, halting her. "I want to hear how you're doing. How your life has been. What happened after you left."

He meant after she'd run away. And what had happened was that her life had fallen completely the fuck apart. Not exactly fun conversation to share over burgers. And not a story she could ever tell him. She shook her head. "I just can't, Jace. I'm sorry. Thanks again for your help tonight. It was good to see you."

Without warning, he tugged her against him and enveloped her in a bear hug. Her cheek pressed against his solid chest, and the intoxicating scent of male wrapped around her. No, not just male scent, Jace's scent. A warm, familiar smell that yanked her back through time, back to the last moment she could remember feeling truly content.

He kissed the crown of her head. "Take care of yourself, Ev. I'm glad to see you're okay."

She pulled out of the embrace, swallowing past the tightness in her throat, and gave him what she hoped was a convincing smile. "I'm doing great, Jace. Just terrific." *Fan-fucking-tastic.*

There was a storm behind his green eyes as he stared back at her, but after a moment, he returned her smile and stepped past her to open the door. "Glad to hear it. Now get back to your room before your fiancé comes hunting us down in a jealous rage."

"Right." She glanced at Andre, who was watching her and Jace's exchange intently. "Nice to meet you, Andre. Y'all have fun on the rest of your vacation."

He lifted a hand in good-bye and after one last look at Jace, she walked out of the room, holding her breath until she heard the door click shut behind her.

———

Jace let the door close and then dropped back onto the couch with a groan.

"Whoa, what was *that* all about?" Andre asked.

Jace pressed the heels of his hands to his brow bone to stave off the fierce pounding that had started there. "Which part?"

"Um, not sure what to start with—Dr. Dan's woman being here

at all or the fact that you totally jumped her shit like you had some right to her."

Jace shook his head. "We have history. It's been twelve years, but I know her well enough to see that she's feeding me a platter of bullshit about being great."

Andre stretched his legs out and propped them on the coffee table as if ready to settle in for a great story.

Too bad this story sucked.

"She seemed fine to me. You sure you're not reading too much into it?"

"No, I watched Evan on that beach. She was sad—and drunk. I didn't know who she was at that point, but I almost got up to talk to her to make sure she was all right. But then she started taking off her clothes, and well, I got a little distracted."

Andre sniffed. "Can't blame you there. The girl's smoking. I saw her in the lobby yesterday and definitely conjured up some mental pictures her fiancé wouldn't have appreciated."

Jace tilted his head back and stared at the ceiling. "Believe me, I had the same thoughts down on the beach. I flirted with her and, up until she realized who I was, she was giving me all the positive signs—like she was interested."

"Huh. That's surprising. She and the doctor are supposed to be some power couple. She stays behind the scenes but he talks about her all the time on his radio show. Their whole image is based on that 'we're the super happy All-American couple, so let us help you be that way, too.'" Andre's snide tone made it clear how he felt about that sentiment.

Jace released a frustrated breath and lifted his head. "See, that's what I don't get. If things are going that awesome for her, why was she out there alone at three in the morning looking so lost? And where the hell was her fiancé? He should be looking out for her. She could've drowned."

"She seems pretty tough to me. I doubt she needs anyone watching out for her."

"Trust me. Evan always needed someone to do that even if she thinks she doesn't."

"Maybe, maybe not. Twelve years is a long time. People change."

He grunted. "No one changes that much."

"You should let it lie, man. She obviously doesn't want to reminisce with you and if you push it, you're going to piss her off and risk her saying something to the doctor. Stay focused on why you're here."

Jace stood and stalked over to the mini-fridge to grab a beer. Yes, why he was here. That's what he needed to concentrate on. Dr. Dan Witter could be the key to dragging Jace's sales numbers out of the drastic decline they'd been in over the last year. Between the struggling economy and the financial hit he took from his divorce, Jace's once thriving business was on shaky ground.

If the good doctor agreed to feature Wicked as the best adult store and website for couples on his sure to be a hit new TV show, *Reignite the Flame*, Jace could almost guarantee that he'd get enough of a bump in business to stabilize his current location and expand the chain.

It was make it or break it time, and make it was the only option he'd consider. He would rather die than admit to his parents that he'd fucked up yet again, that he'd made the wrong decision walking away from his lucrative financial planning job to pursue his passion.

He tipped back the beer and took a long swallow. He just needed to steer clear of Evan. That's what he should've done when he was nineteen and that's what he needed to do now. He wasn't the guy looking out for her anymore. If there were things amiss in her life, it was none of his business. And even if he had wanted to make it his business, she'd certainly made it clear she had no intention of talking to him about it.

He turned back to Andre. "You're right. No use dredging up the past with her anyway. I just wanted to make sure she was doing okay, and I guess she is."

Andre sat forward, setting his feet back on the floor. "So what's the deal with you two anyway? How do you know her? Old flame?"

Jace leaned against the wall, feeling his lack of sleep. He didn't want to talk about this right now—or ever really—but he knew Andre would put on his police interrogator hat if he tried to brush him off. Jace drained the last of his beer. "She lived with my family for a little over a year when I was in college. She was sixteen the last time I saw her. My parents fostered her."

"What happened at sixteen?"

"She ran away. Without a goddamned trace." He tossed his bottle in the trash can. "Seeing her again is like seeing a ghost."

Andre's forehead wrinkled. "So you were her foster brother? Man, the way she was looking at you, I would've bet money that you two had something more than that between you."

Jace's stomach knotted—the word *brother* stirring the old guilt into a maelstrom. His gaze shifted to the sliding glass doors and the darkened beach beyond. "Yeah, well, I'm not done with the story yet."

THREE

"Sweets, you okay in there?" Daniel tapped on her door. "We missed you at the meeting this morning."

"I'll be right out." Evan twisted her arm behind her, trying to reach the zipper on the back of her sundress. She'd slept through her alarm and had woken up right when she was supposed to be in the middle of a breakfast meeting with Daniel and a potential vendor. Not good.

After one more yoga-like move, she gave up and yanked open the door, finding Daniel leaning against the wall in the hallway, tapping out a text message and looking like an Armani model in his perfectly tailored slacks and dress shirt.

"Can you help me with this?" she asked.

"Hmm?" Daniel looked up from his phone, then pushed off the wall. "Oh, sure."

"Thanks." She turned around and waited for him to zip up the dress. "I'm sorry about this morning. I must've slept through the alarm."

"Yeah, I was going to wake you, but you were dead to the world when I peeked in. Guess we all need a lazy morning every now and then, right?"

She shot him a pointed glare over her shoulder, then turned and breezed past him into the suite's living area.

"What?" he asked, his tone innocent. "Did I say something wrong?"

Marcus, Daniel's business manager and boyfriend, looked up from his *USA Today* as she sank onto the couch across from him. He smirked. "Hey you, rough night?"

Her gaze narrowed. "I don't know, Mr. Yes-Please-Oh-God-Just-Like-That, what do you think?"

Marcus gave her a sheepish grin. "Oh, you heard that?"

She threw a pillow at him, and he ducked behind his newspaper.

"You guys are killing me. I know you're happy and in love and apparently rock each other's world, but take pity on the girl in the other room who doesn't have some sexy man heating up her sheets."

Daniel sat next to her and put his arm around her. "I'm sorry, sweets. We drank a little too much celebrating the TV deal and got carried away. We didn't mean to keep you awake."

"But look." Marcus lifted a steaming cup from the side table. "I went out and got your favorite fancy coffee for you. Does that help?"

"Marginally." She sighed and let her head rest against Daniel's shoulder.

"Is everything else okay?" Daniel asked. "You never miss a meeting, even if you didn't get a lot of sleep."

"I'm fine."

Daniel rubbed her bare arm and looked down at her, his all-knowing brown eyes evaluating her. "Are you sure that's all? You know if that new medication isn't working, I can talk to Dr. Barnes about getting you something different."

Oh, great, here we go. Daniel had been her best friend for too long, and paired with his psych degree, he was a formidable force at poking past her shields. "I don't need a different medication."

She didn't want any medication, for that matter. She'd weaned herself off those horrid antidepressants three months earlier. But she hadn't quite told Daniel that part yet. She'd planned to first prove how well she was doing off them before breaking the news to Mr. Overprotective. Unfortunately, her behavior last night wasn't exactly a billboard advertisement for mental stability.

"We saw the empty tequila bottles," Marcus added, his tone gentle. "It's not like you to drink like that."

"Oh, my God. Would you two just stop?" She shrugged from beneath Daniel's grasp with a huff and rose from the couch, grabbing her coffee from Marcus on the way up. "Seriously, guys, I'm not in the mood for Freud and his trusty sidekick. I couldn't sleep and listening to you guys had me all keyed up. So I had a few drinks and took a walk on the beach in lieu of a cold shower. That's all."

She walked to the glass doors that led to the balcony and stared out at the beach. The stretch of sand that had been so deserted just a few hours earlier was now filled with families and children, happily playing in the surf. She pressed her fingers against the glass, feeling so far removed from that world that the glass may as well have been made of impenetrable steel.

"Ah, the truth reveals itself," Marcus said from behind her, his tone playful. "That ridiculous vow of celibacy is finally getting to you, isn't it? I told you it was unnatural."

She ignored him. Blatantly.

"Is that it, Evan?" Daniel asked. "Are you lonely? I know things have been crazy with this seminar tour and we haven't been able to spend as much down time together."

She didn't turn around, just spoke to her own reflection in the window. "How can I be lonely? I'm always with two men."

"That's not the same," Marcus said.

"He's right," Daniel agreed. "We both love you and are so happy you're with us, but maybe you need to think about finding some physical outlet. It would be good for you."

She shook her head and turned around. "You want me to get a lover?"

Daniel frowned, his dark eyebrows dipping low. "You know you have that option. When we agreed to this arrangement, I never intended for you to give up sex. That's been your choice."

The *arrangement*. She guessed that was what they were calling it now. Daniel had saved her life and her sanity when they were on the streets. She owed him everything. And she'd never had someone she could count on so wholeheartedly in her life. So she'd readily agreed to do whatever it took to help him with his crazy business idea. But she hadn't known at the time she'd been signing up to live a lie.

The first radio station manager who'd considered Daniel for a job had told him he couldn't put Daniel on the air as a relationship guru if he was openly gay. He said—right or wrong—there was no way people in Fort Worth were going to take marriage advice from someone who couldn't even legally marry.

Evan had wanted to flip off the whole system and move to someplace more open-minded like Austin or maybe even California. But they hadn't had the money to do that then, and Daniel had been so desperate for a break that he'd come up with the *arrangement*.

Most of the time she was perfectly content with the decision. She'd never had so much stability in her life. And she was with a man she loved and could trust—even if she would never sleep with him.

Or anyone the way things were going.

"Yeah, well, I'm sorry if it's not exactly tempting to go jump in bed with some guy who's totally cool with me cheating on my fiancé." Evan shuddered. "The kind of sleaze ball who would be okay with that kind of thing is not someone I'd want to get horizontal with."

Daniel sighed. "I know it's not ideal, but you have to work with us here. I can't risk you telling someone the truth. The minute the relationship goes wrong, the guy could blow the whole thing open. Then, all three of us are screwed."

She groaned. "I get it, okay."

"Do you? It seems like over the last few months you've lost sight of why you agreed to do this in the first place. Don't forget what it was like before all this, Evan. What it could be like again if we're not smart."

She scoffed. *Forget?* Yeah, right. She'd love to fucking forget. But being on the streets and not knowing if you'd eat from day to day wasn't something that easily left the memory. "Don't be an asshole. Believe me, I know why I'm here."

Daniel's expression softened. "Sorry, I didn't mean it that way. It's just, we've done all this work and now it's really happening—national TV. I want you to be happy. Just think, a few more years and you'll never have to worry about money again. Then, if you want to walk away and do the traditional marriage and kids thing, you'll still be able to do that."

Her chest tightened, an invisible band squeezing out all of her air. No, she didn't think she'd ever be able to do that. Especially the kid part. But she'd never tell Daniel that. She sipped her coffee and turned back to the window. "I'm fine, okay? I think I'm just tired of being on the road. Let's drop the whole thing."

"You sure? You know you can talk to us about anything," Marcus added.

"Then talk to me about today's agenda," she said, desperate to redirect the conversation. "Isn't the first workshop about sex toys?"

Daniel snorted. "Well, that's not exactly how we labeled it, but yeah, it's for couples who are looking to spice up their sex lives.

The guy we met with this morning is leading it. Should be a fun workshop if the couples can relax a little."

"Hell, I'm only going so I can stare at the speaker," Marcus said, the sound of him folding his newspaper half drowning him out. "It's a damn shame that beautiful man is straight. Even if he hadn't presented such a great proposal, I would've given him our business."

She rolled her eyes. "Well, maybe I'll put in an order for a few toys for myself. Get myself a new battery-operated lover and solve all our problems."

"And no sleeping alone tonight," Daniel said, coming up behind her and wrapping his arms around her waist. "You can share our bed. We promise to behave."

She turned around in his arms, taking care not to spill her coffee on him, and smirked. "Thanks, that's sweet, but last time we did that, Marcus snored like a chainsaw the whole night."

A loud scoff came from behind Daniel. "I did no such thing."

Daniel chuckled and pressed his forehead against hers. "We're here for you, sweets. We're all in this together." He lowered his voice. "And all we need to do is roll him on his side after he nods off to shut him up."

"I heard that," Marcus called.

She couldn't help but smile. "I do love you guys, you know?"

"Back at ya, buttercup." He lifted his head and grinned. "Now let's go learn how to spice up our sex lives and try to keep Marcus from ogling our guest speaker."

———

Evan fiddled with the wire on the PowerPoint projector and cursed the damned machine under her breath for a second time. A few couples had already drifted into the meeting room, and she knew the speaker would be right behind them. Usually, she was pretty good at the technical stuff and had been successfully setting up the meeting equipment for all the workshops this weekend, but her pounding headache and lack of sleep had pureed her brain.

Plus, she'd discovered that the hotel's wiring was a bit temperamental, so she didn't want to overload the circuit again. Yesterday she'd nearly plunged the windowless room into darkness when she'd plugged the computer and the projector into the same power strip. For a few seconds the room had looked like a nightclub with all the blinking lights.

She kneeled down and scooted under the table to check that the surge protector was plugged in, making sure not to flash her backside to the audience while doing so. She never wore dresses to these things because she inevitably ended up doing dirty work of some sort, but the welts on her thigh were still too tender to have pants rubbing against them.

"Need some help with that?"

The sound of the familiar voice had her jolting upward, and she banged her head against the table's underside. "Son of a—"

"Oh, hell," Jace said, squatting down and peeking at her. "Sorry. I didn't mean to startle you. You all right?"

"I think so." She rubbed her head and took his offered hand so she could climb out from under the table, wondering for a second if she'd actually knocked herself out and was only imagining him here. Imagining him looking this dazzling in crisp black slacks and a polo shirt that perfectly matched his green eyes.

He smiled. "Do I need to render first aid again?"

She shook her head, still a bit dazed, although she was sure the lightheadedness had nothing to do with hitting her head. "What are you doing here?"

"You left before we had a chance to chat last night." He crooked his thumb at the projector. "I'm today's speaker."

The words took a moment to line up in her head. "Wait, what?"

He reached into his back pocket, pulled out his wallet, and handed over a business card. "Jace Austin at your service. Owner of Wicked which, as of this morning, is the recommended adult boutique and website for Dr. Dan's loyal fans."

Daniel stepped up behind Jace and clapped a hand on his shoulder. "Jace, I see you've met my lovely fiancée. Evan was so disappointed that she missed our meeting earlier. Something came up that she had to take care of."

Jace's gaze met hers. "No worries. I'm sure she's a very busy lady. I'm just happy that the both of you are staying on for the workshop today. Hopefully, I don't disappoint."

Daniel smiled. "Ah, I don't doubt you'll do great. Just be aware that some of these couples haven't so much as touched each other in months, sometimes years. So, they may need to be eased into the topic in order to feel comfortable."

"I understand. My plan is to have them do some non-threatening, sensate exercises with each other, make it fun and just a little sexy. Then hopefully they'll be relaxed enough to ask questions after that."

Daniel nodded. "Sounds good. I really want it to be a safe place for them to have an open dialogue. Plus, I want to normalize some of your products so that they feel comfortable to explore. I think beyond the emotional issues, a lot of couples just get bored with their routine in bed."

"Well, we definitely have a lot of things to alleviate that last problem." Jace smiled as he looked at her, then back to Daniel. "Hey, would you and Evan want to participate in the couples' activity? It may help the group feel more comfortable if they see you guys are willing to do it as well."

Daniel's gaze drifted to Evan, and she gave a slight shake of the head. He tucked his hands in his pockets, a mischievous glint flickering behind his brown eyes. "Actually, I'm going to be in and out. I have a conference call I have to take in the middle of it, but Evan can help you out. You can do the activity with her."

She clenched her jaw so it wouldn't drop open and sent Daniel a what-the-hell-are-you-doing look. "Daniel, I don't think—"

"I don't want to put anyone in an awkward position," Jace said, his eyes shifting toward Evan, his own discomfort evident. "I don't mind managing on my own."

"Don't be silly," Daniel said. "Evan will be glad to help, won't you, sweets?"

She pasted on a smile and vowed to kick Daniel's ass later. "Sure, no problem."

He probably thought he was doing her a favor—letting her have a little fun with a hot guy, but he had no idea how hard it was for her to even stand next to Jace without stirring up an old ache she'd rather keep dormant.

Jace eyed her in that way he'd done the night before, like he wasn't buying her bullshit, but his tone was bright when he spoke. "Great. We'll get started in a little while."

Twenty minutes later, Evan was ready to slip out the back door and bail on the whole thing. After introductions and a general overview of what he hoped to accomplish in the workshop, Jace had instructed the couples to ditch their chairs and get comfortable on the floor. The attendees were murmuring among themselves as everyone got settled—a little edge of anxiety zipping through the group.

Jace had assured them that these would all be simple exercises, but as he handed out gift bags that contained a number of sexy items—blindfolds, feathers, scarves—the mellow energy of the room had shifted into nervous anticipation.

Jace finished distributing the bags and circled back to the front of the room where she sat on the edge of the stage, bumping her knee up and down in time with her out-of-control heartbeat. He gave her a wary smile before hopping up on the stage and turning toward the audience.

"All right, guys and dolls, the lovely Ms. Kennedy has agreed to be my willing victim to demonstrate the exercise, so I'd like to thank her for her bravery. And hopefully we won't make the good doctor too jealous." Jace winked in Daniel's direction and the audience laughed.

Jace put out his hand and helped Evan to her feet. "Now since Evan's up here on stage and has a dress on, I'm going to have her sit in a chair for this, but for everyone else, I want one person lying on the ground and their partner sitting next to them. So first I need each couple to decide who is going to be leading the exercise and who is going to be the recipient."

The crowd began to hum with conversation again as each couple decided who would play what role. Jace turned to her and lowered his voice. "You sure you're okay with this? I know your fiancé over there kind of threw you to the wolves—or me, in this case. If it's weird that—"

"It's *fine*," she said, probably a bit too emphatically, then shrugged in an attempt to appear casual. "I'm a big girl, Jace. I can handle a blindfold and a feather."

His eyes darkened, an unreadable expression crossing his face. "Right."

He left her alone for a moment, giving her a chance to catch her breath, and headed to the far side of the stage. The lights dimmed slightly and for a moment she thought they'd tripped the circuit again, but then soft music started playing and she realized Jace was setting a relaxing mood for the group.

When he returned to her, he had a chair in tow. She sat down and faced the very attentive audience. Her tongue darted out to wet her lips as a paradoxical combination of dread and anticipation came over her.

Jace circled her chair and braced his hands on the back of it, his knuckles grazing her bare shoulders. "All right, everyone, the first thing we're going to do is establish a safe word. This is something that's typically used in more serious sexual play, but I think it's useful in this context as well. If your partner does anything that you are not comfortable with, you say 'red' and everything will stop. Understand?"

The audience members bobbed their heads, and Evan resisted the urge to bite her nails.

"This is all about establishing trust with your partner. Once you feel safe with him or her, you'll find you're able to let go and have more fun in the bedroom. So, let's get started by taking out your blindfolds." Jace bent and grabbed the little black mask from the bag next to her chair. "You want your mate to focus on the sensation of your touch, not everything else going on around them. So slip this over his or her eyes."

Jace touched her shoulder, and Evan nearly jumped out of the chair.

"Easy, Ev. I'm just going to put this on you." He walked around the front of her chair, blocking out her view of the audience, and leaned toward her. His hulking presence hovering over her should've made her more nervous, but it somehow eased her hopping nerves instead. Their eyes met for a moment, and she thought she saw worry flickering in his. But before she could examine his expression further, he slid the black material over her eyes and blotted out the view.

She took a deep breath, the loss of vision disconcerting her. Darkness was *not* her thing. She gripped the arms of the chair and strained her ears to get an idea of where Jace was moving. As if sensing her need, Jace laid a hand on her shoulder and squeezed, grounding her. The tightening muscles in her body loosened.

His voice was soothing when he spoke again. "Now, the only rule is that you can't touch the person anywhere overtly sexual— arms, legs, head, and face are all in play. Start with soft, easy touches above the neck. Like this."

Jace's hand left her shoulder and soon gentle fingertips threaded in her hair and moved in a circular motion against her scalp. A hard shudder of pleasure went through her, and she had to work hard to hold in a sigh.

"Feel free to use your hands or the feather we provided. The person receiving the touch shouldn't speak unless it's to use the safe word."

Evan could hear the shuffling in the room as people adjusted and started the exercise, but all her focus remained on the lovely pressure of Jace's fingers against her skull.

"Mmm," she murmured low enough so no one but Jace would hear. "You missed your calling as a salon shampoo girl."

"I didn't say you could speak," he said, his voice low, commanding.

The authority in his tone sent an odd zing through her. *Whoa.* She shifted in her seat, feeling warmer than she had a second before. She nodded, not sure if an apology would break the no-speaking rule as well.

His fingers halted as if he'd been surprised by something. Breath tickled her ear. "Sorry, Ev. That just slipped out. You can talk if you want."

She shook her head. "It's okay. I'll follow the rules you set for the activity. I can take direction."

She couldn't tell if the noise he made was an under-the-breath groan or a grunt of approval, but he returned to the exercise. His fingertips slid down the side of her neck and marked a whisper-light path across her throat that had her holding her breath and squeezing her eyes shut beneath the blindfold. Without consciously deciding to do so, she tilted her head back, giving him better access.

He traced over the line of her collarbone, ever so softly, but so damn effective. It was as if each brush of skin pressed a button on her circuit board, lighting up places that had long gone dim. Delicate threads of warmth traveled down from the press of his fingers to the curve of her breasts, settling right into her quickly hardening nipples.

Dark thoughts of Jace moving his hands lower, slipping beneath the neckline of her dress and cupping her breasts in front of all these people had liquid heat gathering between her thighs. His touch would be firm, confident. He wouldn't even care that others were watching. He'd just touch her however he pleased. And she'd let him.

She bit her lip. *Stop. This is Jace.*

She crossed her legs more tightly together.

Even if she could forgive him for how he'd treated her all those years ago, she definitely could never risk being around him again. Not as a friend, and certainly not as anything more. When he'd pushed her away, her entire existence had folded in on itself. Not before or since had she ever fallen for anyone that hard—let a person's place in her world define if life was worth living or not. It had been stupid. And dangerous. She'd spiraled into the pit of her depression so fast, she'd gotten whiplash.

She knew she wasn't that bad off anymore. She had taken steps to work with those damaged parts of her makeup. But she also knew Jace being near was like setting heroin in front of a recovering addict. She needed to run in the other direction.

Now if she could just convince her hormones of that.

Jace's voice broke through the quiet of the room. "If you feel comfortable doing so, you can use the silk scarf to bind your partner's hands above their head, so they can experience letting go of even more control. Then, you can move to touching the lower half. Keep the touch light and easy."

Evan could see a bit of movement through the shadow of the mask, and a warm hand grasped her wrist. "Evan, sit up straighter. I'm going to bind your hands behind the chair."

"Yes, si— I mean, sure."

Sir? Where the hell had *that* come from? It'd slipped off her tongue like it was the most natural thing in the world to call him.

Must've been that authoritative tone he kept using with her. Man, she needed more sleep. She was getting loopy.

Jace made quick work of securing her hands behind the chair. The binding was loose, but the effect potent nonetheless. Her heartbeat picked up speed. She'd never considered herself a control freak, but she'd also learned very early on not to trust anyone but herself. She wet her lips, reminding herself that they were in front of an audience. That this was completely harmless.

A warm palm ran along the back of her calf as Jace lifted her leg from the crossed position and set her foot on the floor. Goose bumps prickled her skin. Okay, maybe not completely harmless. Her libido was under a full-frontal assault.

She could picture him there, kneeling in front of her, knowing he could do whatever he wanted because her hands were tied. He could nudge her knees apart, slide her dress up her thighs, and run his tongue along the outside of her already damp panties. She sucked in a ragged breath. Shit. She needed to stop the fantasy reel before she started panting.

A new vibrator was definitely coming home with her tonight. Depriving herself this long had her on the verge of doing something stupid, like whispering to Jace to meet her in the maid's closet after the workshop.

And making that kind of mistake would ruin everything she'd worked for.

Not. An. Option.

Jace was going to fucking lose it. He hadn't planned for this exercise to go on very long, but there was no way he could turn around and face the audience at the moment. Evan's lightning-quick physical responses and eagerness to follow instruction had his cock swelling painfully against the zipper of his dress pants.

She'd almost called him *sir* for the love of God. What was she trying to do? Kill him?

He'd known immediately that doing this exercise with her would be tough, but he thought it'd be because of the old guilt of knowing what had happened the last time he'd really touched her. But hell, he couldn't even spell the word guilt if he tried at the moment.

All he could think about was how tempting those hard little nipples looked pressed up against the pale blue cotton of her dress. How silky the skin of her legs felt against his hands as he slowly drew his fingers up and down her calves. And how fucking hot she looked blindfolded and bound for him.

No. Not for him. She was someone else's. He needed to keep that at the forefront of his mind. *Shit.* He closed his eyes and tried to block out what was happening—focus on something else. War. Sick puppies. Female bodybuilders. Anything that would get the blood flowing back to his brain and out of his throbbing dick.

Because he could not tread in this territory. This was Evangeline— not some chick he could haul off to his hotel room, fuck, and leave. And beyond that, he didn't mess with other people's women—not without permission. He'd been on the receiving end of that equation before and refused to inflict that on someone else.

He moved his hands to her knees, hoping those wouldn't be as tempting as the soft flesh on her legs. But when he grasped them, he felt the little give of her thighs, the slight parting, and he had to bite back a deep groan.

He tried to picture Evan the very first time he'd met her when she was all bones and wide eyes—eyes way too jaded for a fifteen-year-old. But the image wouldn't appear. All he could think about was the gorgeous woman who sat before him. A woman who probably hated him, who couldn't even bear to have lunch with him.

He swallowed hard and, using his thumbs, drew tiny circles on the sides of her knees. Counting the rotations as he went, praying it would refocus him. Evan adjusted in her seat a bit and her knees parted enough for him to glimpse the lacey white panties underneath. And *holy shit*—the view was only half the torture. The sweet, hot scent of female arousal wrapped around Jace like a fist.

He sucked in a sharp breath, and his grip tightened on her. *Get up, moron! End the exercise.* But instead of listening to the shouting voice of reason in his head, he found his hands inching higher, brushing the tops and insides of her lower thighs, careful not to hit the jellyfish stings. Her legs quivered beneath his touch.

"Oh, God." The words were so quiet, so full of . . . need, he'd thought for a minute he'd only imagined he'd heard them. But when he looked at her face and the way her teeth were biting into her full bottom lip, he knew she'd said them.

Every nerve in his body seemed to electrify. *Christ.*

However, before he could figure out how to respond, the lights flickered and blinked out, blanketing the room in darkness. A few sounds of surprise came from the audience behind him.

"What happened?" Evan asked, stiffening beneath his touch, her voice higher than normal.

Before Jace could answer her, Dr. Dan's voice rang out through the pitch-black space. "Just stay put, everybody. Nothing to worry about. I'll go tell them to flip the circuit breaker, and we'll be up and running again in a minute. Relax and stay where you are for now. Don't want anyone tripping over anyone else."

Jace started to pull away from Evan, but the sound of her quickening breath gave him pause. "You okay, Ev?"

"Can you see enough to untie me? I . . . It's hot in here, and I'm feeling kind of . . . claustrophobic."

"Oh, yeah, no problem." He hopped to his feet, thankful for the lack of light. Otherwise the audience would see just how effective the exercise had been for him. Reigniting the flame was an understatement; he could set off a fucking forest fire right now.

Carefully, he moved around the back of the chair and felt around until he found her wrists. He hadn't tied her tightly, so it only took a second to loosen the bindings. Once she was freed, he heard her rustling around—probably taking off the blindfold. He wondered if Evan still had a fear of the dark like she'd had when she was a teenager. His fingers flexed, wanting to reach out and touch her again, make sure she was okay, but he held back.

"Ev, stay in the chair, okay? I don't want you to fall off the stage."

No response came.

A few seconds later, the bank of overhead lights flickered back on, and he shielded his eyes from the sudden brightness. He blinked, letting his vision adjust, and found the chair in front of him empty. He looked around the room.

The back exit door was clicking shut, and Evan was nowhere to be found.

Awesome. He'd stepped over the line again, and she'd done exactly what she'd done the last time.

Bailed.

God, he was a jackass.

FOUR

Evan's muscles ached as she unlocked the front door of her photography studio and went inside. She'd planned to come in earlier to get things in order for re-opening next week. But after the restless night she'd had, she'd decided to go to the gym first for Janice the Evil's advanced spinning class, hoping the punishing workout would beat her agitation into submission. No such luck. She'd almost puked thirty minutes in and now she just had embarrassment and a sore ass to add to the restlessness.

God, if she could just get some sleep, maybe she could get herself back on track. Since they'd returned from South Padre, she'd tossed and turned every night, her mind racing and her body craving things she couldn't have. It was as if seeing Jace again had knocked her whole system out of alignment.

Ugh. She dropped her bag and sank into her desk chair. What was the deal? She was the freaking master of blocking things out, of centering herself and focusing on the tasks at hand. But now she just felt . . . scattered. And all the things that usually kept her calm and content weren't doing a damn thing.

Part of it could still be her body adjusting to being off the medication, but there was no way she was going back to those pills. After so many years on them, she hadn't even noticed when the healing effects had switched from therapeutic to numbing. Until one day a few months ago when she'd seen her neighbor's sweet little dog dart across the street during her morning run and get hit by a car. The whole thing had happened in the space of seconds, and her neighbor had immediately rushed to the injured dog's side. But as Evan had stood there on the curb watching the horrible scene, she'd realized that all the things she should be feeling— sympathy, concern, sadness—were just . . . absent. Like her heart had gone hollow inside her.

That night she'd vowed to work her way off her prescription. She didn't want or need that crutch anymore. At one time her depression had been dangerous, but she was no longer that girl, and she had no intention of living the rest of her life on deep freeze. But the change hadn't come without consequences. Her whole system now seemed to be on the fritz.

So she was down to her last resort—the one outlet that had never let her down. Her photography. Maybe if she threw herself into her work, she'd find her way back to the stable existence she'd created before Jace's reappearance had knocked her off balance.

"Hey, stranger."

Evan yelped and nearly toppled off her chair. She glanced to the back of the studio where her part-time intern had stuck his shaggy head out from the storage room.

Finn grimaced. "Sorry, I thought you knew I was here. Didn't you see my motorcycle parked out front?"

She put her hand to her chest, her heart pounding beneath her palm. How had she not even noticed his bike? She really was in a freaking daze. "No, I didn't."

"Classes are out this week and I'm not scheduled at the restaurant until late, so I thought I'd come in and help you get things ready to go for Monday. Plus I wanted to experiment with a technique for a still life project I have coming up. I should've asked first, I—"

She shook her head. "No, it's fine. I'm sorry. You just startled me. I'm a bit of a space cadet today. No sleep."

He locked the storage area behind him and gave her a mock pout. "Poor thing. Traveling the country with your totally tasty fiancé. Must be a real hardship. I could take over for you, if you'd like."

She rolled her eyes. "Though you are prettier than me, Daniel's too old for you. You're what? Twenty-two?"

"Twenty-three." He smirked and tucked his inky black hair behind his ears. "And age I can work with. But that whole him being straight thing might get in the way."

She sniffed. If Finn only knew how wrong he was on that one. "So how'd the Allen shoot go last week?"

Even though she'd shut the studio down for the most part while she was out, she had let Finn take on a few simple jobs to get in some practice. He'd been with her six months and had proven to be more than reliable despite the fact that he was balancing community college classes and a waiter gig along with his internship. The eager desire to learn reminded her of how she'd been when she'd first discovered photography. And his talent behind the camera was so innate that she had full trust that her clients would be happy—especially with the intern discount she'd given them. She was already feeling awful that she'd have to let him go when she, Daniel, and Marcus moved to L.A. in a few months.

He shrugged. "It was cake. Just a couple of business headshots. She didn't want anything too"—he did air quotes—"out there."

"Oh, Lord."

"Yeah, so nothing fun. She wouldn't even do outdoor shots. I gave her what she wanted—boring pictures in front of a bookcase." He shook his head sadly. "A little part of my creative genius died on the inside."

He stepped to the file cabinet behind her desk and pulled out a folder. He tossed copies of the black-and- white proofs on her desk.

She picked them up and scanned through them. Even with the ho-hum background, Finn had captured the spark in the elderly executive's eyes and her take-no-shit smile. "These look great—excellent lighting. You made her look a decade younger." She handed the sheets back to him. "I appreciate you accommodating her wishes. Hopefully we can get something more fun for you to shoot next time."

"No worries. I'm just glad you're back so we can start booking some bigger stuff again."

"Me, too." She choked down the little pang of sadness that hit her at the thought of only having a few months left in this studio. Yes, she planned to get something new set up in California, but nothing would ever be like this little place.

It was located in what her real estate agent had called a "transitional neighborhood" when she'd first leased it. Evan had learned that this basically meant the little cluster of historic buildings was starting to be restored and inhabited by an eclectic blend of artists and other start-up business owners. But it also meant that if you hung around the area too late at night, your chances of getting mugged were pretty solid.

Finn shut the file cabinet and crooked a thumb at the door. "Hey, I was just about to go pick up a sandwich. You want me to grab you something?"

"Sure. Roast beef sounds good. Might as well completely negate my spinning session from this morning."

He laughed. "Got it. Be back in a little while."

After Finn headed out, she booted up her computer and checked the list of messages he'd stacked on her desk, grimacing a bit at the painfully low number of inquiries that had come in while she'd been out. Even with Finn covering the occasional headshot and family photo session, the workshop tour and her absence had delivered a serious blow to her business.

This kind of business was based on word of mouth and being available right when someone needed you. People planning weddings, children's portraits, and senior high school pictures weren't going to wait around for a photographer to call them back. They would just call the next one on the list. She'd once had a steady business building and now it was dying a slow death.

Well, no more. She refused to let her involvement with Daniel's business hamper her own dream any further. She'd work as much as she could these next few months before closing the doors here, but she also would dedicate herself to building contacts in California. Los Angeles was going to be a nightmare to have a start-up—a place where everyone needed headshots but no one wanted to work with an unknown. She'd have to be dogged in her pursuit of business once she got a location up and running out there. Because giving up her photography was not an option no matter how successful Daniel became.

She was thrilled with everything he was accomplishing and the money it was bringing in for all of them, but that didn't fulfill her like getting behind the camera did. There was something about capturing a person's emotions on film that spoke to the deepest part of her. She had accepted that she probably wouldn't get a chance to marry her soul mate or show off a new baby to the world. Hell, she hadn't even had a high school graduation, just a GED sent in the mail. But somehow, documenting other people's happy milestones helped fill the space inside her where she should've been storing her own. And it was time to start filling it again.

She picked up her phone to return the first call, but the bells on the studio's front door jangled, halting Evan from her task. She looked up from her desk with a frustrated huff to find her friend

Callie sweeping through the door, her mass of blonde curls staging a riot against the clip fastened at the back of her head. Callie pushed the offending locks from her face and beamed at Evan. "You're here! I thought you weren't coming back to work until Monday. I was just about to call you to wish you a happy early birthday when I saw your car parked out front."

Evan smiled as she hung up the phone and stood. Callie dropped her overstuffed purse to the floor and rushed toward her to give her a hug. Evan laughed while the taller woman squeezed her for dear life.

"Wow, I . . . uh . . . missed you, too."

"What are you doing here? I thought Daniel was going to keep you all to himself this week."

"I just stopped in for a few minutes to return some calls before I reopen next week."

Callie finally released her and put her hands on her hips. "For the record, you are not allowed to take this much time off ever again. I swear if I have to have one more lunch with Flower Shop Trisha, I'm going to keel over. She's so prim and proper, I feel like I'm having soup with the queen or something. I know she's probably lighting candles for me at church after some of the stuff I've slipped up and told her."

"Well your immortal soul could probably use all the help it can get."

Callie plopped into the chair in front of Evan's desk. "Amen, sister. Though I just finished a weeklong cayenne and lemon juice detox. The way it's been going, I think even my soul is cleansed."

Evan snorted. "Why on earth are you doing that?"

Beyond the fact that Callie bashed diets regularly for cutting into her profits at her bakery across the street, she'd always seemed comfortable with her curves.

Her grin turned sly. "Well, a lot has happened since you went gallivanting around the country with that man of yours."

"Oh, really? Do tell."

"I have a new boyfriend," she said in a singsong voice. "A new, devastatingly handsome, completely wonderful boyfriend. Even Finn gave him the thumbs-up in the looks department, and you know how picky that kid is. So I don't want to look like a dumpling next to him when we go out."

"Hold up. A new boyfriend? Cal, I talked to you at least once a week. You didn't even mention you were seeing someone."

"I didn't want to jinx it," Callie said, crossing her arms with a huff. "Every time I tell you about how great some guy I'm seeing is, I find out the next week that he has some catastrophic flaw—like he has an addiction to hookers or is a diabetic and can't eat cake. You're bad luck."

Evan shook her head, amused. Her friend *did* have abysmal luck when it came to men, but somehow she doubted it had anything to do with a jinx. Cal had a tendency of falling fast and asking questions later. Evan had learned that warning her to slow down was like talking to a coffee table. And hell, who was she to give relationship advice? She was marrying her gay best friend.

She leaned forward and placed her chin on her hands. "All right, so dish. Who is he? What's he do? And, more important, does he like baked goods?"

Callie sat up straighter, obviously bubbling over after holding back the secret so long. "His name is Brandon. He's a nurse over at the cancer center. And he's a total slut for chocolate cupcakes."

"Sounds amazing."

"Totally," she said, her eyes getting a little starry. "He's picking me up for my end-of-diet lunch. I texted him to meet me over here."

"Great."

"He loved the photos you have hanging in the shop, by the way. Said you knew how to make a piece of pie look downright seductive."

Evan laughed. "My claim to fame—sexy cherry pie."

"Hey," she said, pointing at her, "don't underestimate yourself. I sell more of the products you photographed than any others. Seriously, you have a gift of making things look irresistible on film."

Evan's stomach clenched a bit with that last part. A gift. Yes, once upon a time she'd made someone a whole lot of money with that innate talent. She rubbed her arms through her sleeves, trying to fight off the creeping chill that always came with those horrid memories.

"Hey now, there's an idea," Callie said, completely oblivious to Evan's sudden discomfort.

She took a deep breath and tried to refocus on the conversation. "What's that?"

"I should get you to take pictures of *me*."

"Huh?" Evan's eyebrows knitted.

"Don't look at me like that." Callie waved her off. "I'm serious. I've been trying to come up with something to get Brandon for his birthday, and I bet he would totally be into some sexy boudoir-style pics. We haven't, ya know, done the deed yet, so maybe that would get the ball rolling. He's that gentlemanly type and his slow approach is kind of driving me crazy."

Evan frowned. "Maybe slow isn't a bad thing."

"*Pfft!* I'm not getting any younger. No use burning daylight. So do you think you could make me look as sexy as that cherry pie?"

Evan pinched the bridge of her nose, Callie's question only bringing the past farther to the front of her mind—the haunted eyes of the women who'd posed before her camera. The sick feeling that came along with knowing you were sacrificing someone else's dignity to save your own ass. "I don't really do that style of picture, Cal."

"Oh, come on. Don't be a prude."

She sighed. "It's not about that. It's just, are you really going to trust a guy you just started dating with half-naked pictures of yourself? What happens when—"

She held up a finger. "Nope. Don't finish that sentence. I'm doing that whole putting positive energy into the universe thing. I'm not even considering that this guy isn't going to work out. Now will you take photos for me or not?"

"Cal, I—"

Callie's phone dinged and she checked the screen. Her smile turned florescent. "Oh, he's so sweet."

Evan hated that Callie already had that smitten-beyond-repair look. Even if this Brandon was a nice guy, giving your heart to anyone that easily had disaster written all over it. Evan had first-hand experience on that one.

"He's waiting outside. Sorry to stop by and then run off," Callie said. "But I only have a little while for lunch. We're shorthanded so Jessica will probably go on strike if I'm not back by one to help her."

"No problem," Evan said, ready to get back to her own work anyway. "We'll catch up next week."

Callie pointed a finger at her and arched an eyebrow. "And you are so doing those photos for me. I'll withhold *petit fours* otherwise."

"Hateful bitch."

She laughed. "Ta for now. Don't work too hard."

Yeah, right. That was exactly what Evan planned to do. Work so hard that she had no space left in her mind, her bed, or her heart for anything else.

FIVE

Jace straightened the display of erotic novels as his best friend, Reid, selected one of the paddles from the rack on the other side. Reid flipped it around in his hand, testing the weight and feel of it. He held it up to Jace. "Really?"

Jace shrugged, the sight of his suit-clad friend holding up a paddle with the words "bad girl" scrawled in pink a comical picture. "The newbies like that kind of thing. Makes 'em feel scandalous. It's got great thud, though."

Reid smacked it against his own thigh. Frowned. "Brynn needs more bite than that. Plus, she may laugh herself right out of the scene if she sees what's on it."

Jace grabbed a utilitarian black paddle with holes in it from the shelf. "Try this one. The holes lessen air resistance and give you more impact."

Reid took it from him to examine it. He sliced it through the air, the whooshing sound making Jace's skin itch. God, he loved that sound. Even better was the noise the sub made when it smacked against her bare skin.

"Mmm, better," Reid agreed.

"So how is that beautiful blonde of yours? You haven't brought her by in a while. Still afraid she's going to realize the error of her ways and come sub for me instead?"

Reid shot him a deadly look. "Don't make me test this paddle on your skull, smartass."

Jace laughed. A more tactful friend probably wouldn't make a point to remind Reid on a regular basis that Jace had shared Reid's soon-to-be-wife with him one night. But Jace had never claimed to have tact. Plus, he'd never been able to resist getting his oh-so-calm friend ruffled.

"You don't need to be worrying about my woman," Reid said, tucking the paddle under his arm and moving on to the vibrator section of Jace's store. "Worry about your own women. I ran into your mother the other day at the grocery store, and she said you never come when she invites you to family dinners. That ain't right, man. I ended up agreeing to stop by for one because she looked so damn sad about it."

Jace sighed. "Family dinners involve having conversation with my dad. And by conversation, I mean me listening to him talk about what a failure and a fuckup I am. They'll probably appreciate your company more."

"Look, your dad's a dick, but you need to tough one out for your mom. She's looking worn down with all this. Maybe having you there will give her a boost."

Jace grimaced. He loved his mom and felt like a dirtbag for contributing at all to her being upset, but he hadn't made it through a family meal since he opened up Wicked without having a knock-down, drag-out fight with his father. Seeing that wouldn't do his mother any good. "I'll try to make it over there for one."

Reid nodded and turned down the next aisle. "So how's business looking?"

Jace shrugged. "It's been better. It'd help if I could get Diana to stop drawing alimony."

"I petitioned the court to relieve you of that obligation. Diana's still maintaining an apartment address, but I had that PI I know follow her for a couple of weeks. She's living with Greg full time like you suspected." Reid grabbed a few more items off the shelf. "It's still a long shot."

"Un-fucking-believable." He'd already given her half of everything when they divorced and had paid a monthly stipend for two years. It'd been more than she deserved since she'd been the one to walk out on him. But he'd been so numb after she'd left that he'd just agreed to whatever instead of going through a nasty court battle.

Reid grabbed a G-spot stimulator and a pack of nipple clamps then handed all of the items to Jace. "I know, man. I'm doing the best I can. But it might be worth it to try and talk with her. Nicely. Appeal to her reasonable side."

Jace scoffed as he walked to the front of the store and dumped Reid's selections on the counter so his cashier could ring them up. "Diana doesn't have a reasonable side."

Reid tossed his credit card on the counter. "You better find one. Otherwise, she's got a decent shot of syphoning more money from you."

"Dammit. Isn't there a point where I stop getting fucked over? You've barely lost a case in your life. Can't we win?"

Reid frowned as he took his bag from the cashier. "Look, I'm going to do everything I can, but it hurts that you didn't take her to task during the initial divorce. She doesn't look like the bad guy in the court records." He laid a hand on his shoulder. "Talk to her, Jace. And I'll do what I can on my end."

Jace walked Reid out then stalked into his office ready to breathe fire. Fucking Diana. Just what he needed. Hadn't it been enough that she'd ripped his heart out and made him look like a god-damned fool? Now she wanted to suck his bank account dry, too?

Jace stared out the second-floor window and the darkened shops across the street. Wicked was one of the few stores open this late on a Thursday night. He'd landed a prime piece of real estate tucked between high-end clothing stores, a gourmet chocolate shop, and a salon. It was the perfect shopping spot for women and couples who may not feel comfortable venturing into the seedy part of town and going to a windowless dive with an *Adult Videos* sign flashing above.

But the tradeoff for having such a swank spot was that he also didn't get the cheap and easy business—the guys just coming in to grab a porno or some skin mags. He didn't sell either. Well, unless you counted some of the how-to videos they had in stock. So he had to count on the customers who weren't afraid to spend decent money on quality products. And with the economy the way it was, those customers were getting fewer and farther between.

The money he hoped to get through the deal with Dr. Dan would allow him to beef up his stock and Internet presence and offer more variety in price point. But if Diana kept milking him for alimony, he was going to run out of capital before the Dr. Dan thing even bore fruit.

He flipped the blinds closed just as his office door opened. Andre stepped in and leaned against the doorjamb, looking every bit the pissed-off cop. "She's a leech. Have I mentioned that?"

Jace snorted. "Guess you saw Reid."

"What's her deal? She's had years to get on her feet. Feet that I'm sure get a weekly pedicure and massage using your money."

Jace sank into his desk chair and rubbed a hand over his face. "This is the last thing I need. I've been crunching numbers all night. If it weren't for my contract with The Ranch, I'd be in some serious shit right now. I was counting on freeing up the money I was paying her each month to put toward the website and building stock. Now I've gotta go play nice and hope she grants me mercy when all I really want to do is ring her neck. And Greg's. What kind of asshole stands by and lets some other dude support the mother of his kid?"

Andre's shoulder radio squawked, and he pressed the button to respond. He looked up when he was done. "Don't go see her or Greg yet. You need to take a break and get away from that desk and those P&L statements. You go see them while you're like this, and I'll be arresting you for bodily assault."

Jace grunted. He'd never lay a hand on a woman without her consent, but Greg was a whole different story. Bodily assault was starting to sound real tempting. Or maybe just massive intimidation and threats to relocate the guy's nuts. Could he get arrested for that?

Andre's frown deepened. "See, I can already see you contemplating maiming and dismembering."

"Killjoy."

Andre pushed off the doorframe. "Look, we both need to blow off steam. I've been busting my ass to get that promotion. They have me shadowing the detectives on this huge case *and* still covering my regular beat. I've switched from days to nights so many times these last two weeks, I don't even know what time it is. Plus, you've been a miserable fuck since we got back from South Padre."

"You know your lease is up this month, so you're more than welcome to move somewhere else."

Andre flipped him off. "All I'm saying is that we should go have some fun this weekend. Recharge."

Jace perked up. A fun weekend?

Andre was right—that was exactly what he needed. Since they'd returned to Dallas, Jace had felt off, like he couldn't quite get back into the groove. And it had nothing to do with Wicked's bank account. The moment that had passed between him and Evan had replayed in his mind one too many times. And getting hard night after night thinking about a girl who was off limits was getting him nowhere. He knew just the kind of weekend he needed.

"Andre, I think that's a genius plan."

He grinned. "Of course it is. That's the only kind of plan I come up with."

Jace smirked. "I'll deal with Diana next week. There's no way I'm letting her earn any more money off my back. And I'll figure out this mess with Wicked. I have some new radio and print ads going live this weekend, so maybe that will drum up some new business."

"You could always ask your parents to release the rest of your trust fund. The money's supposed to be yours."

"I'd rather live in a box than give in and ask them for a penny of that damn money. That shit is so laced with strings, I might as well sign up to be a marionette."

"Well, if they ever want to send any of it over my way, I'll happily join the family financial business and toe the line. I'd at least get to sleep sometimes."

Jace chucked a pen at Andre, who deftly ducked out of the way.

"Kidding." Andre checked his watch, his break probably over. "I'll set things up for the weekend. Any requests?"

Yes. A dark-haired beauty with ice blue eyes and a mouth that begged to be tasted. A woman who clearly had never been under a master's hand, but whose body had responded the instant her hands were tied—in front of a live audience no less. He shoved Evan's image from his head. "See if there are any new members."

He quirked an eyebrow. "You want a newbie?"

"Yes." Anything to make him forget an oldie.

SIX

This was not how Evan had anticipated spending her birthday. She folded her hands in her lap and tried to keep an interested look on her face as one of the reporters asked Daniel another question about the planned television show.

She thought she'd have some time to get her head wrapped around the idea that they—well, Daniel—was going to have his own TV show. But two weeks after signing the deal the word was out, and the Dallas papers wanted to know all the details. The glare of the spotlight was already dangerously close to making her break out in hives. She much preferred being the one behind the flashbulb.

"Ms. Kennedy, are you going to be part of the show?" the female reporter asked, turning her head toward Evan.

She sat up a little straighter on the couch. "I plan to stay in more of a behind-the-scenes role."

Daniel put a hand on Evan's knee. "Evan's going to be in the audience most days, and I plan to call upon her when we need a woman's perspective. Hopefully, we can get her over her stage fright so she can become a bigger part of the show."

Evan tensed beneath his grip. What the hell was he talking about? They had never discussed her stepping into that kind of role. She bit the inside of her cheek to keep from blurting out the question for him. She gave the handful of reporters a tight smile.

After a few more questions were lobbed at Daniel and more photos were taken of the both of them, the group finally filed out of the house. Evan barely waited for the front door to click shut behind them before whirling around and pinning Daniel with a deadly glare. "Have you been drinking? Hit in the head with a blunt object?"

His eyebrows knitted. "What's the matter?"

She put her hands out to her sides. "Get over stage fright? Since when am I supposed to be on camera? That's not part of the deal. You know I don't want that."

He gave a put-upon sigh and placed his hands on her shoulders. "Calm down, sweets. It's just something the producers mentioned would be a good idea. You're beautiful and smart. They think you'll add to the brand better if you're not hiding in the background."

She groaned. "I'm not hiding, Daniel. I'm working my ass off with all the detailed stuff you don't like to deal with. The limelight is your dream, not mine. And how am I supposed to be at all the show tapings and still get my new studio off the ground?"

He frowned. "Evan, you don't have to worry about turning a profit with your photography. The money from this deal will be more than enough to support all of us."

She stared at him in disbelief, then wriggled from beneath his grasp. So her photography business was expendable—a little hobby that didn't bring in enough cash to count for anything. She stormed past him before she said everything that wanted to spill out of her mouth. "Whatever, Daniel."

Evan ignored the soft knock on her door as she finished putting on her eyeliner. An hour of alone time had eased her down from her boiling point, but she was still at a steady simmer. She had half a mind to go to her birthday dinner alone.

"Evan, it's Marcus. Can I come in? I have mail for you."

She blew out a breath and capped the eyeliner. "It's not locked. And you could've come up with a better excuse than that."

He cracked open the door and stuck his head in tentatively, like he was afraid she was going to chuck a shoe at him or something. It would've been tempting had it been Daniel. "You doing all right in here?"

"Peachy," she said with a saccharine smile.

He opened the door the rest of the way and stepped in, frown lines marring his smooth complexion. "Don't mind Daniel. His mouth is just moving too fast for his brain. He's so excited about finally reaching his dream that he hasn't slowed down to really consider how everyone else might feel about it."

She sighed and clicked off the light on her makeup mirror. "Look, no one is happier for him than I am. You know that. I know where he came from and how big of a deal this is. I just need him to understand that it's not *my* dream. I'm dedicated to making this work for all of us, but my financial interest is so that I can run my studio, not have to stress about money, and be able to . . . take care of a few things. The fame part is not my deal."

The corner of his mouth lifted. "Fame might not be that bad, you know."

Fame. Her stomach did a flip. She'd spent a lot of time honing this new life—changing her name, refining her look, sloughing off her old life—not just to get a fresh start but to escape the demons lurking in her past. Having her picture splashed across the papers or television wasn't exactly lying low.

"I'm not going to be on camera, Marcus. Get that through Daniel's head and we'll all be square."

He stepped behind her and set the stack of mail on the vanity table before giving her shoulders a little squeeze. "He won't make you do anything you don't want to, okay?"

She nodded. "I know."

"Now, why don't we drop this whole thing for now and focus on going out and celebrating your birthday?" He waggled his eyebrows at her in the mirror. "We have a gift I promise will put a smile on your face."

"Oh, Lord. Now you have me nervous."

He laughed. "Come on, hot stuff. We don't want to miss our reservation."

By the time dinner wrapped up, Evan found herself without the energy to hold her grudge. Sulking was hard to maintain when so much fabulous food and wine were being consumed.

"If your evil plan was to stuff me with buttered scallops and cheesecake so that I wouldn't be mad at you anymore, it's working," Evan said, licking a bit of strawberry sauce off her fork.

Daniel laughed. "I would never stoop so low as to prey upon your food-whore tendencies."

She tossed her cloth napkin at him. "Liar."

Marcus stole the last bite of their shared dessert and pointed his fork at Daniel. "Tell her what's next while she's still on her sugar and champagne buzz."

She eyed the two men, a little twinge of anxiety going through her. "What are you two up to?"

Daniel grasped her hand across the table. "Sweets, I know we haven't brought it up since our little discussion in South Padre, but Marcus and I have noticed you've been on edge for months."

"Oh, come on, not this again," she complained. "I told you I'm fine, *Doctor*. Totally stable."

He shook his head, amusement dancing in his eyes. "Chill out. I'm not psychoanalyzing you. You've just been a tad bit . . ."

"Bitchy?" Marcus offered before sipping his drink.

"Hey," she said, shooting him an offended look.

"I was going to say tense," Daniel said, bumping Marcus with his shoulder. "I really do think it's this whole celibacy thing getting to you."

She blinked in surprise, the subject catching her off guard. Now they were discussing her lack of a sex life at dinner? Her earlier hint of nerves ratcheted up to dread. "Wait a second, what does that have to do with what's happening next?"

"Well, we thought for your birthday we'd help you with that little issue," Marcus said, obviously fighting a smile.

"My issue?" Her mind took a moment to fully process the words. "Wait, with my *celibacy* issue?"

Daniel grinned. "Exactly."

She pulled her hand from Daniel's and stared at the two of them in disbelief. How in the hell could two gay men help her with her celibacy issue? They surely weren't going to volunteer to go bi or straight for the night. She almost laughed at the notion, but then a disgusting thought hit her, making her choke. "Oh, no. No way."

"What?" Daniel asked in a tone worthy of a halo and wings.

"I swear to God if you paid for some escort or something, I'm seriously going to kill you two right here at the table."

Daniel leaned back in his chair and sipped his coffee with a casual elegance that had Evan ready to throw something more damaging at him than her napkin. He set down his cup. "Evan, we would never do that to you. You deserve better than that."

"Definitely," Marcus said, sliding an envelope onto the table. "Like a membership to The Ranch. Three months fully paid."

She stared down at the little white envelope and the red *R* emblazoned on its wax seal. The thing looked innocuous enough, but she had a feeling the gift inside was far from innocent. She raised her gaze, hoping she was wrong. "Is that some sort of spa or something?"

Daniel's lips curled into a mischievous smile. "Not exactly."

"Jesus, Daniel, tell me it's not a brothel." She had no idea if they even had brothels with dude prostitutes, but she wasn't putting anything past her two friends. They were kinky bastards.

Marcus rolled his eyes. "Stop messing with her, D. You're freaking her out."

"Oh, neither of you are any fun," Daniel said, motioning to the waiter for a coffee refill, then looking back to Evan. "It's not a brothel, for God's sake. It's a resort where people go to live out their fantasies, explore their . . . inclinations with each other."

"Inclinations?" she repeated. "Like figuring out if they're gay or straight? 'Cause, no offense, but I don't have any doubts there."

His eyebrow arched. "I'm sure some go there for that. But this is more about venturing into things you may not have access to in your day-to-day life. Fantasies. Role-playing. Multiple partners. Bondage. In your case, maybe just a confidential sexual partner."

Her hands turned sweaty against the booth's leather seat as she replayed his list in her head. *Role-playing. Bondage.* She parted her lips, but the words stuck to her tongue.

Marcus pushed the envelope closer to her. "I've been a member for a while. The place is top notch—safe, exclusive, uber private— and has very strict membership requirements."

Her brain began to spin. A sex club? They wanted her to go to a *sex club*? The boys were out of their freaking minds.

"It's all very confidential," Daniel added. "I don't want you to reveal our situation, but members will know you're engaged and that your fiancé approves of you being there. People there won't blink an eye at that. They're used to unique situations."

She looked back and forth between the two of them as her ability to form sentences returned in a rush. "You seriously expect me to just go there and have sex with strangers? Are you nuts?"

Marcus gave her a sympathetic look. "You can do whatever you feel comfortable with. No one's going to make you participate. But don't shut yourself off to the possibility until you see the place. You may be surprised how things change in that kind of environment— how your mind opens up. They specialize in BDSM, but I'm sure they can accommodate whatever situation or fantasy is most enticing to you."

Her mind automatically rewound to the day in the seminar room—Jace tying her hands and being in control, touching her. She'd accessed that scene in her head countless times over the last two weeks, had touched herself as she filled in the blanks of what could've happened if they'd been alone and had no past to contend with.

And still, despite the constant fantasy rerun, the effect hadn't worn off. Even now, heat built low in her belly at the mere thought. She closed her eyes and pinched the bridge of her nose, a champagne headache starting. "Guys, really, I appreciate what you're trying to do, but I don't need this. I'm fine."

"We've already packed your bag, and there's a car waiting for you outside," Daniel said, causing her head to snap up. "Grant Waters, the owner of the place, has set up a tour for you tonight so you can see it before people start arriving for the weekend retreat tomorrow. We've also reserved you a private cabin."

"Daniel," she demanded, trying to keep her voice low enough so that it wouldn't garner the attention of the people at the other tables. "You can't actually expect me to go to this place."

He frowned. "Look, if you go on the tour and decide not to participate in anything, then take the weekend to enjoy the scenery and the cabin. It's beautiful out there and surrounded by vineyards. Plus, I think they do have a masseuse on staff if you really want to do the spa thing. I think the break will be good for you regardless."

"And Daniel and I are going to be doing press for the next few days. If you're on a 'spa' weekend, it will save you from having to be a part of it," Marcus added.

She kept her eyes on them and gulped the last of her champagne, shocked to find herself actually considering the whole thing.

A weekend away from the press—and the boys, for that matter—did sound kind of tempting. And she hated to admit it, but for some reason, the whole celibacy thing was suddenly driving her mad. Going solo with her vibrator hadn't fixed anything. In fact, it'd only made her fantasize and want sex *more*. It was as if seeing Jace again had tripped some wire inside her.

She blew out a long breath. She could throw herself into her work like she had planned, but deep down she knew this restlessness wasn't going to go away so easily. Wasn't this what she'd really been yearning for? A bit of physical indulgence without all the complications.

And at least at this place the guy would know she wasn't cheating, but doing it with her fiancé's consent. That helped. Felt less seedy to do it under the pretense of being kinky instead of being a lying cheat.

Maybe if she could have a real live man to warm her bed for a few days, she could cleanse her mind of these stupid Jace fantasies. She'd been infatuated with him when she was a teenager, weaving daydreams about what it would be like to be with him. Apparently her mind had gone straight back to that old place—forgetting how awful it had been after she'd actually gotten what she thought she wanted. Stupid.

She needed an exorcism. And this might be just the thing to do it. She grabbed the envelope off the table and nodded at the guys. Resolved.

"Okay, I'll go. But"—she jabbed a finger at Marcus then Daniel—"if this turns out to be creepy or gross in any way, I'm holding both of you responsible. I will seriously dig out all those toys I know you guys have and beat you with the most painful ones."

Marcus snorted. "Daniel might actually enjoy that."

She rolled her eyes.

Daniel ignored Marcus's comment and smiled at her. "Happy birthday, sweets." He lifted his coffee cup. "Here's hoping you have fun. It'll be like losing your virginity all over again."

Oh, God, she hoped not. Losing it the first time had been the worst mistake she'd ever made.

SEVEN

Evan's palms were damp against the arms of the over-stuffed chair as she waited for the owner of The Ranch to meet with her. The limo drive to the place had been long, and as the minutes had slipped away, so had her resolve.

She glanced around the well-appointed sitting room, trying to focus on anything but her reasons for being here. Dark, rustic furniture, wood floors, artwork displaying Texas's varied landscapes, and a large stone fireplace, which she was sure was more for show than practicality in this climate. If she didn't know better, she would've guessed she was in some high-end ski resort and not a retreat specializing in kink.

She tilted her head back and groaned. This was stupid. Ridiculous. She wasn't the type of person to go to a *sex* resort. Was she really that desperate? She'd lived without sex for over a year. Why was it suddenly such a big deal?

There could only be one reason.

Goddamn Jace. He'd always been able to stir up that part of her without trying. Even when she'd first met him and hadn't totally recognized the feeling as desire, she'd been drawn to him, wanted to be in his sphere of attention as much as possible. He had a way of making her feel like she was the only one in the room, and after years of being invisible to everyone around her that feeling had been heady, addictive. She should've been immune to it by now. But after a few seemingly harmless touches on that stage, Jace had flipped the switch and had her engines firing on all cylinders again. Man, she was screwed.

A massive wooden door on the opposite side of the room eased open, and an impossibly tall man with wavy dark hair stepped inside. He gave her a smile that seemed to warm the whole room. "You must be Ms. Kennedy."

The deep twang in his voice matched the cowboy boots peeking out of the bottom of his faded jeans. The image totally didn't fit with what Evan had imagined the owner of this type of resort to look like. She hadn't expected head-to-toe leather or anything, but a handsome cowboy hadn't been on her radar of possibilities either.

She smiled. "That'd be me. But please, call me Evan."

He crossed the room in two long strides and put his hand out to shake hers. "Welcome to The Ranch, Evan. I'm Grant Waters, the owner and operator."

She shook his hand, hoping he didn't notice just how sweaty her palm was. "Nice to meet you."

He held her hand for a moment longer, holding her gaze, no doubt evaluating her, and then stepped back to sit on the couch across from her. He crooked a thumb at the door. "Would you like something to drink? We have everything but alcohol here."

No alcohol? Well, so much for plan A on how she was going to get up enough nerve to do this. She shook her head. "No thanks. I'm fine."

"So, I hear your fiancé surprised you with a membership."

She crossed her legs to keep her knee from bumping up and

down with nerves. "Um, yes. I'd never even heard of this place until tonight."

"Well, we don't exactly advertise." He braced his forearms on his thighs, leaning forward a bit. "Interesting choice of a gift—to give you a membership and not get one for himself. Any ideas on why he would do that?"

The timbre of his voice was low, seemingly casual, but she didn't miss the sharp glint in his eyes. This man was making sure she was on the up and up. She squirmed a bit in her seat. Despite how often she had to do it, she hated lying, especially to someone who looked like he could smell bullshit from thirty paces. She scrambled for some plausible explanation. "I . . . Well, I haven't been all that sexually adventurous in my life, and I think he's worried if I don't sow my oats or whatever, I'll always wonder after we're married."

Grant seemed to chew on that for a moment. "Just because you get married doesn't mean you're locked down to non-adventurous sex. Lots of couples come here for ménage or to switch partners. Or even if they only engage with each other, there are lots of things a couple can do between themselves to spice things up."

She wet her lips thinking of threesomes, couple swaps. The ideas should have appalled her, but instead her body awakened as all kinds of illicit images flooded her mind. "Daniel's not exactly into any of that stuff."

Grant gave a sage nod. "Ah, I see. Vanilla guy marrying a girl who may not be so traditional."

She sighed. "I honestly don't know if I'm traditional or not. I haven't really explored very much."

His lips curved into a kind smile, one that eased the tension that had filled the room a few seconds before. "So what are you hoping to experience here, Evan?"

She twisted her engagement ring round and round on her finger. What *was* she hoping to experience? She'd had naughty fantasies in her life—who hadn't? But what would she actually want if giving carte blanche? "I'm not sure."

He rubbed a hand over his five-o'clock shadow, considering her. "Why don't we walk around the main building? I'll show you some of the activity rooms and we can see what appeals to you. Maybe it'll help us tease out what desires are hiding in there."

She smiled. "Okay, that sounds good."

A few minutes later, Grant led her up a flight of stairs and into a long, quiet hallway. Sconces provided soft lighting, but the maroon walls and dark wood floors gave the impression of entering a secret lair. She had the urge to whisper her question, but the guy was so damn tall he probably wouldn't hear her up there in the stratosphere. "So no one's here right now?"

"No, we close a few days once a month to do general maintenance. Everyone will start arriving tomorrow." He slipped a hand onto her lower back and eased her forward. "Go ahead. Each window gives a view into a different room."

She took a few steps and turned to look through the first large window that flanked the right side of the wall. A dreary, stone-walled dungeon, complete with manacles and a host of other tools she didn't recognize came into view. If not for the little security camera tucked into the upper corner of the room, the place could've fit into any ancient castle. "Wow, this looks authentic."

Grant stepped up next to her. "As I'm sure you can imagine, this is one of the more popular rooms since so many of our guests practice BDSM. We have a number of dungeon areas throughout the resort, including a few larger ones for group play."

She nodded, anxiety twining through her.

"This one makes you nervous."

She peeked up at him, surprised by his spot-on assessment. "A little. Not sure I'd want to jump right into that."

He chuckled. "Fair enough."

They walked past a few other themed rooms—a doctor's office, a classroom, a barn, a decadent boudoir, a strip club scene complete with a pole. The sheer level of detail of each room boggled her mind. They were not fooling around here. Some big money had been spent.

Every scene affected her on some level as her mind automatically placed her in each fantasy. The naughty nurse. The stripper. Her skin had flushed well past the point of comfort as they traveled down the hallway. They crossed in front of the window to the next room, and her heart picked up speed.

She stared at the mock police station setup. The desk. The jail cell behind it with a narrow bed. What would it be like to have a guy play bad cop? To handcuff her and have her at his mercy? To pass her off to his partner to share her?

The vision of two cops hauling her into the room, arresting her with plans for their own satisfaction, filled her head. Two above-the-law officers handling her however they pleased. Bending her over that desk and shoving her skirt over her hips, taking her from behind while the other used her mouth for his pleasure.

Whoa. Where had that come from? She tried to wet her lips, but her mouth had forgotten how to make spit; all the moisture in her body had rerouted much, much lower. Jesus, what was wrong with her? *That* shouldn't turn her on.

Grant's voice was like dark whiskey as he leaned closer to her. "Tell me why this one appeals to you."

"How do you know—"

"Darling, you're breathing faster, your face is flushed, and your nipples are so hard, you're getting *me* hot and bothered."

She ducked her head, wanting to cover her face with her hands, but he put a finger under her chin, forcing her face toward him. "No shame here, Evan. You're not going to get judgment from me or anyone else who comes here."

"It's just . . . I . . . ," she said, stumbling over her words.

"You feel uncomfortable that this turns you on," he said, his tone gentle. "This room is usually used for scenes that involve power play."

"Is that a fancy way of saying 'pretend rape'?" she asked, her stomach knotting.

He frowned. "No, not at all. What's speaking to you is not a rape fantasy. Rape means non-consensual, and I doubt you desire a true loss of consent."

She shuddered. "No way."

"So, it's a dominance/submission fantasy. A cop is a classic role of authority and dominance, the prisoner the counterbalance to that. It's role-playing mixed with D/s—like most of these rooms. Nothing to be ashamed of." He laid a reassuring hand on her shoulder. "As long as everyone is aware of the risks and it's consensual, you can embrace whatever desires you have here. Even the dark ones."

She nodded, absorbing the power of his words, the freedom of such a concept. Maybe this *was* the answer to her present situation. Exploring her most forbidden fantasies in a no-strings-attached, safe environment, while still keeping her comfortable situation at home.

She cleared her throat. "So does this mean I should try the BDSM route?"

"I would say it'd be a good place to start," he said, amusement glinting in his eyes. "The important question is, in your fantasy, which role are you playing? A cop or the prisoner."

Her eyebrows scrunched. Huh. She hadn't even considered being in the cop role. That didn't seem nearly as enticing. She glanced up at him. "The prisoner."

He smiled. "Well, that answers a lot. I think The Ranch is going to be able to provide exactly what you need."

"Really?"

"No doubt," he said, ushering her back toward the door they'd come in originally. "And I already know a few members who could be perfect at providing it for you."

Anticipation rippled through her. This was either going to be the most exciting or the most idiotic decision she'd ever made.

Unfortunately, based on her track record with men and sex, odds weren't in her favor.

EIGHT

Jace tilted back his root beer and watched as other members started to drift into the main room. It would probably be a busy weekend considering The Ranch had been shut down for a few days this week.

Andre flipped through the packet of papers he'd picked up for them at the door. "There are five new female subs tonight. Well, Tessa isn't new. She apparently had a falling out with her boyfriend and wants a new master."

Jace set his bottle on the table. "Are the other four guests or new members?"

"Two guests, two new members. So only two are going through the mandatory public display of submission," Andre replied, still going through the pages. "Are you up for that tonight?"

Jace shrugged. "I'm not a big fan of demanding submission before I've even talked to the chick."

Andre chuckled. "Conversation, then fucking. Got it. You're such an old-fashioned guy, Jace."

"Bite me."

Andre cocked his head, his smile challenging. "That could be arranged. But only if you beg."

"Uh-huh. Why don't you hold your breath and wait for that to happen?" Jace had never been one for limits and labels, so he had no issue being sexual with Andre within the ménage dynamic. But after living a childhood with a father who dictated every damn thing in Jace's life, he didn't do submissive. "Just tell me about our two possibilities."

Andre turned the page. "Okay, candidate number one has been in a D/s relationship twice before, but is currently single. She has very few limits and is really into pain play. Open to ménage. She's hoping to find a long-term master but is fine with short-term things as well."

Jace leaned back in his chair and grimaced. "Ooh, I don't know."

"Yeah, if she wants serious pain stuff, neither of us is the right kind of dom for that."

"Plus, the open-to-relationship ones always have an agenda. Even if they say they don't. I'm not here to spend the weekend cuddling and getting to know each other." He didn't come to The Ranch looking for relationships. He didn't go anywhere looking for that.

Andre smirked. "You know, not every woman here is out to trap you with her white picket fence. You're not that great of a catch, anyway. Now me, on the other hand . . ."

Jace flipped him off. He knew Andre was open to finding a steady relationship eventually, but his friend's bisexuality and penchant for ménage tended to get in the way of any lasting plans. It was only a matter of time before Andre would figure out that the whole "till death do us part" thing wasn't meant for people like them. Plus, why put your heart in someone else's hands and give them the power to crush you?

Jace had learned his lesson on that one and didn't need a refresher course. D/s would never again be anything more than fun and fucking for him. Period. "Just tell me about the other woman, smartass."

Andre turned another page, reading for himself before saying anything. A smile crept to his lips. "Here we go. This woman is a D/s virgin. Shows tendencies toward the sub role and is looking to explore that. Grant wants her to have a master who has gone through the full training here—score one for you. She has a cop fantasy—score one for me. Not seeking anything permanent because she's already in a committed relationship."

"Uh-oh, is she married?"

He shook his head. "Engaged, but it says she's here with her partner's consent."

Jace leaned back in his chair. "Yeah, sure she is."

"What, you think she's lying?"

"If she'd been married for a few years and was doing it with consent, I may be able to buy it. You know, getting bored, wanting to branch out. But engaged? That's when people are shitfaced in love with each other. No dude willingly lets the girl he's engaged to go fuck around on him on her own. Could you imagine Reid sending Brynn out here by herself to fool around?"

"Reid would burn the place down first. But you never know. I've heard some guys get off on that whole girl cheating on them thing. Cuckoldry or whatever it's called."

Jace sniffed. Maybe guys who've never actually had a woman step out on them could get off on that, but he knew there was nothing remotely sexy about the humiliation of the real thing.

Andre lifted his hand at someone behind Jace and waved him over. Jace turned in his seat to find Grant sauntering their way.

"Evening, fellas." The owner shook each of their hands. "Good to see y'all out here. It's been a while."

"Yeah, things have been crazy," Jace said. "But we figured we've earned a break."

"So what can I do for ya?" Grant asked, turning to Andre.

"This new member, Sasha. Her bio says she's engaged but is here with the guy's permission. How do we know that's true?"

The corner of Grant's mouth hitched up. "I don't have them put anything on that sheet that I haven't verified. It's unusual, but the fiancé is actually the one who purchased the membership for her as a gift. Apparently, he prefers vanilla, so he's letting her work a few kinks out of her system before they get married."

Jace snorted, almost choking on his drink. "Seriously?"

"You bet."

Jace set his bottle down. "Is the guy an idiot? If this woman discovers that she truly is a sub, she's not going to want to go back and be vanilla for the rest of eternity."

Grant shrugged. "I know that. And you two know that. But I figure it's better for them to find that out before they take the plunge instead of after."

"Well," Jace said, "you're better than anyone I know at determining it. Is she really a sub or just playing around?"

"She's sub. I'd bet the vineyard on it."

Andre grinned. "Guess we found our girl for the night."

"Ah, fellas, not so fast," Grant said, tapping the papers on the table. "You must've not read all the way down. She checked *no* for ménage."

"You've gotta be freaking kidding me," Jace said, grabbing the packet to read it for himself.

"You could always take her on yourself," Grant suggested, a hint of challenge in his eyes. "She's over there in the back corner chatting with the other available subs."

Jace grimaced, the idea holding no appeal. Since his divorce, he hadn't had any interest in taking on a sub solo. One-on-one just felt too serious, too intense. He came here to have fun and ménage ensured that things stayed light. "We'll just find someone else."

"Have a nice night, guys. Don't do anything I wouldn't do," Grant said, moving away to go talk to another table.

Andre smirked. "I'm guessing that doesn't rule out much."

Jace tossed the papers back on the table in frustration. "Looks like we won't be taking on a newbie tonight."

"No big deal. I saw that Melissa chick earlier, and she was hinting that she'd be interested in joining us later. It'll still be a fun night."

Jace rolled his shoulders, trying to fight the tension gathering there. He wasn't interested in Melissa. She was a pretty girl, but he knew none of it was God-given—fake tits, fake lips, spray-on tan, and enough makeup to put a porn star to shame. That didn't do it for him. He preferred women who had that natural, girl-next-door type of beauty. Girls who you'd never guess had a kinky streak if you saw them out in the world. Unfortunately, that was sometimes hard to find at a place like The Ranch.

"Here we go," Andre said, pointing at the front part of the room.

All the rest of the members had taken their seats around the room—some on the plush couches and others at the candlelit cocktail tables. The lights were turned low except for those shining on the staging area at the front. Grant opened the double doors, and the initiates were led in blindfolded with their arms bound behind their backs.

Even though Jace knew none of the initiates were for him, the erotic sight of women stripped down to the barest essentials and volunteering for submission had his cock twitching in his jeans. The beauty of a woman who knew what she wanted and was brave enough to trust someone else to give it to her was unmatched in his book. He never took for granted the gift the sub gave by putting her trust in his hands. And he made damn sure he thanked her thoroughly for that submission by driving her to whatever heights of pleasure she was capable of.

He shifted in his chair. Damn. He'd been looking forward to indulging that side of himself tonight. Maybe he should reconsider the girl who'd listed being open to short-term even though she was ultimately looking for long-term.

Andre craned his neck, looking toward the back of the room instead of the stage. "Doms are already heading over to the single subs area. I can't see her face, but if the brunette's the one who's open to ménage, we should go for her. She's hot."

Jace turned and squinted, trying to make out the figure in the darkened back corner of the room. Candlelight lit the outlines of the men and women quietly chatting. A petite brunette had her back to them, but even in the dark, Jace could see the delicate curve of her bare shoulder and the sweet column of her uncollared neck. Something about her called to him in a way that no other woman had so far tonight.

"I'm in," Jace agreed. Maybe an Evan look-alike could purge the fantasies that'd been stalking him since South Padre.

Jace stood, a little surge of hope going through him. Maybe the night would turn out to be interesting after all. Andre joined him as they headed toward the back of the room. They weren't the first to reach the brunette, so they stood back a ways as Colby, one of the other doms and a friend of Jace's, talked to her.

The woman was even more enticing close up. Her dark hair spilled forward, shielding her face as she kept her eyes down from Colby's. She was wearing a simple black bra and panty set—standard issue for an unclaimed sub who didn't bring her own fetish wear. Jace allowed his gaze to travel down—creamy skin, breasts that looked to be the perfect handful, and legs . . . *shit*.

"What's your name, sub?" Colby asked.

"Sasha."

Andre cringed and leaned toward Jace's ear. "The no-ménage chick."

Jace's mouth had gone dry as he stared at the faint jellyfish scars that striped "Sasha's" leg. What in the hell was Evan doing here? Then the words from the bio sheet came back to him. *Ah, fuck.* The engaged chick with the vanilla fiancé.

Evan thought she was a sub?

His burgeoning erection turned into a raging hard-on. God, how he'd love to find out if that was the case. Be the first to draw out the submission if it was really in her. But complicated didn't even begin to describe getting involved with Evan. Not only was he doing business with her fiancé, but she'd made it clear in South Padre that she wanted nothing to do with him, couldn't even bear to have lunch with him. And hell if he could blame her.

Plus, even if she had been open to him and ménage, sleeping with her again would be ten kinds of stupid. Especially after how he'd felt when he'd walked away from her the last time. She'd been his first lesson in heartbreak. Even way back then, they'd always had this dangerous vibe between them—one that had scared him shitless. She wasn't a fuck 'em and forget 'em kind of girl, and he was a cut and run kind of guy.

Colby's lazy Houston accent snapped Jace from his thoughts. "What makes you think you could be a submissive, sweetheart?"

Evan dipped her head a bit, like she was afraid to answer the question.

"Answer, sub," Colby said, his accent not hiding the natural authority in his voice. "Now's not the time to be shy."

Jace stepped closer and had the urge to tell Colby to back the fuck off even though the guy was doing exactly what he would've done in the same situation.

Evan cleared her throat. "I've, uh, had fantasies about being dominated."

Jace nearly groaned aloud. He should've been disturbed. At one time he'd seen this girl as a little sister, had promised his parents he would protect her from the dangers of the world and from guys like him. A promise he'd fucked up royally. And there was still a deep protective urge that rose when she was around. A possessive one that had been there from the beginning.

But God, somewhere along the way his view of her had warped into something entirely different. He knew the night she'd come to him at sixteen that his feelings toward her were far from familial. But now that the barrier of the strange situation was lifted all he could see was a beautiful woman there for the taking. A beautiful woman who wanted to be dominated.

Colby glanced up at Jace, noticing him now that he'd stepped next to Evan's table. "Better move on, J. The lady isn't looking for what you guys want to dish out."

Jace's jaw clenched. "Fuck off, Colby."

Evan's head snapped up, her eyes going wide when she saw Jace.

Colby's brows lifted. "What's your problem?"

Jace eyed Colby. The guy was his friend, an excellent dom and one of the trainers here. Evan would be in safe hands. But hell if he didn't want to choke the guy at the thought of him touching her, bending her to his will, drawing out her submission. His fists clenched.

Andre shot Jace a don't-do-this look. "No, Colby's right, man. She's not down with ménage."

Jace clenched and unclenched his fists, an urge he hadn't had in as long as he could remember surfacing. The words were out before he could stop them. "Maybe I'll go solo tonight."

Andre's eyebrows rose, but before Jace could respond, Colby was pulling out a collar and laying it on Evan's table, letting her know that he was offering to take her on. Jace's hand, as if acting on its own accord, yanked the strip of leather from his own back pocket. He squeezed the collar in his hand, inches away from laying it down and making his first solo claim in two years.

Colby stared at him, waiting to see what Jace's move was going to be.

Shit. Shit. Shit. Anxiety rose in Jace like a tidal wave, drowning the surge of bravado. What the hell was he doing? He didn't do jealous or possessive. Not anymore. The fact that he was feeling either was a glaring sign he should back the fuck off. Now.

His good sense screamed for him to bail. To back off. His body and mind warred, but finally, he forced himself to step backward, leaving Evan to Colby, the concession almost physically painful. He had to give her up. Do the smart thing.

But before Jace could take another step back, Evan looked down at his clenched hand and looked . . . disappointed.

NINE

Evan tried to wet her lips, but her mouth had gone arid the minute she'd seen Jace. What in the hell was he doing here?

"Sasha, do you accept my offer?"

Her gaze darted to the man standing closer to her—dark brown hair and hazel eyes, a friendly smile teasing at the corners of his mouth. Handsome. And built like a brick shithouse. The collar on the table meant he was offering to take her on, which meant . . . Her focus returned to Jace and the collar he gripped in his hand. He was offering, too?

No, Jace had stepped back and was half-cloaked in the shadows at the edge of the singles area.

"Jace, what are you doing here?" she blurted out before she could stop herself.

The other man turned to Jace with a questioning look.

"I'm a member," he said, his voice tight.

Oh, fan-frigging-tastic. This was *so* not what she needed right now. The whole point of coming to a place like this was the anonymity, the privacy. And now not only had she run into someone she knew, but Jace, the last person in the world she needed to be around.

The man turned toward Jace. "You've got history with her?"

"Sure do," Jace said, the words clipped.

"So are you making a claim or not?" he asked, his words laced with annoyance. "You know I'm not going to overstep if you have some previous connection to her."

Jace's gaze darted back to Evan and for a moment, she forgot to breathe. His jaw flexed. "No, I'm not."

Evan clenched her teeth together, not sure if she was more relieved or insulted. She reminded herself that this was a good thing. Despite the fan club her hormones were forming just from being near him again, getting naked with Jace was a first-class bad idea.

Mr. Hazel Eyes graced her with a sexy smile. "Guess that means you're mine, darling. That is, if you're interested, of course."

Nerves thrummed through her. The guy was hot as hell and he had kind eyes, giving her reassurance that he probably wasn't some psycho. Always a bonus. But was she actually going to do this? Could she hand herself over to a stranger? Her eyes automatically found Jace again—the only anchor of familiarity in a suddenly fast-moving world of unknown.

Jace shoved his hands in his pockets, his expression softening. "You don't have to choose Colby. You don't have to choose anyone, Ev. You can turn around and go home. Back to the guy you're marrying. This isn't something to mess around with if you have doubts that you can handle it."

His gaze dipped down and traced over the oh so faint scars on her lower belly. Ones that no one else would know to look for except him. Shame, hot and fierce, burned within her.

"I'm not that kid anymore, Jace. I don't need someone to protect me," she said more sharply than she'd intended. She switched her focus to Colby, her anxiety ratcheting up another notch. "I accept your offer."

She caught Jace in her peripheral vision, scowling.

"Thank you." Colby smiled down at her and gripped the back of her neck. "Now stand up, sub. I want to sample what's mine for the weekend and make sure my friend Jace back there knows who you belong to since he seems to be confused."

Her eyes widened as Colby helped her from the stool and to her feet. He had her put out her wrists for cuffs, then locked her arms behind her back. "There, that's better."

He slipped his large hands onto her hips and stepped in front of her, pulling her close. His hard body pressed against hers as Jace glared at her from over Colby's shoulder. Colby dipped his face down until his eyes were inches from hers and his lips only a breath away.

Holy shit. He was going to kiss her. Right away. With Jace watching.

Before she could catch her breath, his mouth met hers, warm and inviting. Her eyelids closed automatically, and she tried to give herself over to the kiss. It'd been forever since she'd really kissed someone, and the sensation was something new again. Soft and sensual, his tongue teased hers, testing the waters. He was a good kisser, not giving or taking too much. But despite his skill, the experience felt empty, vacant. All she could think about was the man behind him, standing there watching it happen.

Colby pulled back and stared down at her, running a thumb over her lower lip. "You have a beautiful mouth. I can't wait to feel it against my—"

Without warning, she was yanked sideways by a firm hand on her upper arm, the jolt nearly causing her to tumble onto her ass. "What the—"

"Get your goddamned hands off her, Colby," Jace said, his voice full of grit.

Colby's eyes narrowed. "Don't be an asshole, Austin. I gave you your chance, and you didn't make a claim. She chose me."

"She can change her mind. You haven't collared her yet." Jace led her a few more feet away from Colby. She didn't know what else to do but let him. "I changed my mind. I'm offering. Let the lady choose again."

What? Oh, shit. Evan's heart jumped into her throat. She pinned Jace with a desperate stare. "What are you doing?"

"Giving you a choice."

No. No. No. She didn't want a choice. She couldn't be trusted with this choice. Especially not after her lackluster kiss with Colby. "Why are you doing this?"

He wrapped his hand around her nape and without any further warning, brought his mouth down on hers. Electricity, sharp and instant, sparked at the contact, waking every nerve ending in an all-encompassing rush. *Oh, Jesus.* The muscles in her legs quivered, fighting to hold her upright position, and pulsing heat radiated down to her clit.

He kiss was hard, hungry, not at all tentative like Colby's. It was a proclamation, a claiming. And God, she wanted to be consumed by it. By him.

But as quickly as he'd started it, he pulled back and straightened. "Just choose me, Evan."

It took her a second to find her voice and her brain. "Jace, I—"

Something flickered in his eyes, and his mouth hardened into a line. "I know you're new at this, sub, but you're to speak only when spoken to. And you need to address me as sir or Master J in public. All you have permission to do right now is choose your dom for the weekend."

She sucked in a breath, the change in his demeanor and stark authority in his voice almost knocking her off her feet. Everything was happening too fast. Her thoughts and hormones were whirling into a firestorm in her gut, and she couldn't process any of it.

He frowned. "Answer the question, sub. It's not that hard. You want Colby or you want *me*?"

Ha. There was the question of the day. Physically, she wanted Jace so bad her arms strained to bust out of the bindings just so she could touch him. She couldn't remember ever having a kiss affect her so intensely. But how could she risk being with him even in a casual way? Nothing with Jace had ever been casual for her.

And after what had happened between them in the past, how could she trust him? Back then he'd had her completely convinced that he really cared about her. She'd opened up to him like she had never done with anyone else, and it had all been bullshit. Just Jace fulfilling a duty. A guy trying to make a messed-up girl feel better about herself.

Too bad she hadn't figured that out before she'd talked her way into his bed one night and taken things too far.

She'd imagined many times that year what losing her virginity to Jace would be like, but being a mercy fuck had never been part of the fantasy.

Neither had getting pregnant.

Though Jace didn't exactly know about that last part.

So why in the hell was he standing here, asking her if she wanted him? He couldn't be serious about sleeping with her, dominating her. Her tongue darted out, wetting her lips with a nervous flick. Despite the warning sirens shrieking in her head, the thought had her hot in all the right places.

No, this had to be about his ridiculous protective streak. He probably just wanted her to select him so he could haul her over his shoulder, stuff her back in the limo, and send her home.

She straightened her spine. "I'm serious about trying this, Jace. Don't do this so you can keep me from participating or give me some edited, half-assed experience. I know you still see me as someone who needs a keeper."

He frowned. "What I see is a girl jumping into a game she knows nothing about just because her fiancé isn't doing it for her in bed.

But if you're really here to find out what it's like, I'm one of the best doms here. I can help you."

Her eyes narrowed. "Thanks, but I don't need another sympathy screw. You already covered that with me a long time ago."

He winced.

"Come on, Austin. You're wasting all of our time," Colby said.

Jace lowered his voice. "Look, I realize what a dick I was to you back then, and I can't even begin to tell you how sorry I am. But I'll make you a deal, *Sasha*. I can leave everything outside these doors as long as you can. I want you. And based on that kiss, you want me, too. So let's keep it that simple. This is sex. The past doesn't exist here. And I promise whatever I do with you, sympathy or pity definitely will *not* be a factor."

She blew out a breath. Could she really block out everything while she was here? Be someone else for a while? She came here for one reason: to feed her physical side in a no-strings-attached environment. Could she do that with Jace? She wasn't a desperate, love-struck teenager this time. Jace didn't mean anything to her anymore. And if they didn't dredge up the past, her secret was safe.

Could she just focus on the fact that he was a sexy man who happened to get her hormones firing faster than any other guy ever had? He certainly stirred up a tempest with a kiss whereas Colby had only left her cold.

Hell, she was a master of compartmentalization. When she'd run away all those years ago, she'd learned very quickly how to lock away painful memories and emotions. It was the only way she'd survived it. And she'd certainly been able to tuck away her libido for the last few years without much incident. So why wouldn't she be able to do this?

There was no reason. She was strong enough, and she'd earned this chance for indulgence. If Jace stuck to those "no past" rules, then so could she.

She glanced at Colby, who nodded at her as if he already knew what she was going to do and understood. She took a deep breath and turned her gaze back to Jace. "I'm all yours . . . sir."

The green in Jace's eyes darkened, clouding the normal humor that resided there. He stepped closer, his intimidating height looming over her as he grasped her elbow and led her away from Colby. Her arms had been bent into L-shapes behind her, so keeping her balance was a challenge, but Jace made sure she didn't tip over. He took the collar he'd been holding and wound it around her neck.

"This will let everyone know you're mine while you're here," he said into her ear. "Don't take it off."

"Yes, sir."

He fastened the lock and ran his fingertip along the hollow of her throat. "And don't worry about half-assed, baby. I'll make sure you get exactly what you need."

She shivered, goose bumps tracking over her exposed skin. This wasn't a side of Jace she'd ever seen. He'd always kept it lighthearted around her when they were younger—quick with a joke or harmless teasing. The guy who hadn't taken anything seriously, including her. Master J seemed to be a whole different animal all together. If she focused on that, this different persona, maybe blocking out the past would be easier than she thought.

He urged her forward, and she tried to find her voice. "Grant said I may have to do something in front of the group."

Jace shook his head as he led her to the side of the room. "Only guests are required to submit publicly. You and I? We need to take care of some things in private first. Now move. Andre, get the door."

She whipped her head around to see Jace's friend from the conference a few steps behind them. Andre shot her a saucy smile, then moved in front of her to shove open the door. He swept an arm in front of her. "After you, *bella*."

They entered a quiet hallway, her hammering heart and unsteady breath the only sound. She looked between the two of them. "Where are we going?"

"Our cabin," Jace said. "And you're not so good at this not speaking thing, Sasha."

She huffed.

They reached the end of the corridor, and Jace grabbed a long silk robe from a hook and draped it over his shoulder. "It's gotten chilly."

Andre pushed open the exit door, and the cool night air rushed over her as they stepped outside. He crooked a thumb at one of the two golf carts lined up next to the wall of the main building. "I reserved one of the cabins next to the lake. It's too far to walk with Evan—er, Sasha—barefoot. We can take one of these, or if you want to go scenic, I can call the stable and have them bring around two of the horses."

Horses? The place had freaking horses? Damn, how much had Daniel paid for her to get in here?

"Let's just take the easy route for now." Jace moved behind her, running his palms along her arms. "As lovely as you look all trussed up like this, I'm going to need to undo these. You have to be able to hold on to the cart."

She warmed under his touch and the compliment, but kept her mouth shut. She would prove that she could stay quiet even though it was killing her not to ask a hundred questions. Jace unfastened her cuffs and slid them off. She stretched her arms above her head and rolled her wrists.

When she glanced up, she found Andre watching her, his gaze hot enough to set the cedar-planked building behind them on fire. He put his hands in his pockets, and her focus was drawn downward where the crotch of his black slacks bulged.

"Your woman's eyes are wandering, Jace," Andre teased.

She quickly looked away, her cheeks heating. "Sorry."

Jace chuckled behind her. "Don't apologize. You have permission to look at Andre all you want. And you're going to have to get used to guys getting hard at the sight of you. You look like a walking wet dream in this getup."

Her breath caught.

"You're surprised I'd say that to you," he said, his voice close to her ear, his body heat warming her back. "Tell me why."

"I've just never seen this side of you. You were always so—"

"Careful? That's because you were my foster sister and didn't need to see this side of me. Didn't need to see how non-brotherly my feelings had become for you."

She stilled.

His hands gripped her shoulders from behind, causing her to flinch. "That's right, Evan. If you don't hear anything else that I say, hear this. I didn't sleep with you because I felt sorry for you. I did it because I'd wanted you so bad and for so long that when you offered, I wasn't strong enough to do the right thing and say no."

She closed her eyes and swallowed hard, the revelation rocking her to her foundation. She wanted to ask why—why had he said all those things afterward, turned her away? But she wasn't sure she needed to hear those answers right now. This was supposed to be free of the past. It wasn't the time for forgiveness or healing hurt feelings. Venturing into that territory was dangerous. "Jace—"

"Shh, don't say anything. I'm going to keep to my promise of no past. I just wanted you to know that before we go any further. Needed you to know that whatever I do with you this weekend isn't to right some wrong or because I owe you for fucking up back then. It's because you're a beautiful woman who's asking to be dominated. I'll give you one guess as to what that does to me."

Her heart began to thump harder. He grasped her wrist and drew it low behind her back. Denim rasped against her fingers as he cupped her hand over his rock-hard erection. Her knees wobbled as liquid heat rushed through her.

"Lack of attraction is definitely not a problem. Never has been," he whispered. "Only now, I don't have to hide it."

Andre cleared his throat. "Unless you two plan to get it on right here in the doorway, we should probably get a move on."

Jace's lips grazed the curve of her neck before slipping the robe over her shoulders. He took her hand and laced his fingers with hers. "Come on, babe. Andre's right. No need to rush. We have a few things to discuss first."

Rushing was exactly what she wanted to do right now because she feared that if she thought this through too much, she'd be high-tailing it out the front gates. But he was right. They probably needed to talk before jumping in, even if it was as two "other people." This whole lifestyle was a mystery to her, and she had no idea what kind of dominant Jace was, what he would expect from her, and if she could, in fact, handle whatever that was.

She followed Jace on shaky legs to the cart. Andre sat in the driver's spot, and Jace joined her on the seat that faced backward. His arm banded around her waist. "Hold on, short stuff."

She stiffened at the old nickname he used to call her when they were teenagers, the little zing of ancient affection stirring within her. It was affection she didn't need to reignite. "Please don't call me that."

He glanced down her, his eyes flashing with regret. "Sorry. It just slipped out."

She turned her head and looked out at the expanse of vineyards flanking the east side of the property, her chest clenching with cold fingers of fear that she was making a big mistake. That she couldn't trust her heart to stay out of it with Jace. "It's okay. Just call me whatever a dom calls a sub. No past, right?"

He nodded resolutely as the cart started moving. "Right, *pet*."

TEN

Jace set his jaw in determination as Andre parked the cart in front of their sprawling cabin. This was a fucking disaster. If he had wanted to venture back into the world of one-on-one, doing it with someone he used to care about was the absolute worst way to go about it. The fact that he was even feeling such a drive to have Evan should've been testament enough that this was a bad move.

But the minute Colby had taken control of her, all of Jace's solid logic had disintegrated into a cloud of testosterone-laced dust. He'd wanted to break Colby's fingers one by one for having the nerve to touch her at all. Then Jace had done the stupidest thing of all. Kissed Evan.

After that, there was no going back. The primitive part of him had staked his claim. She was his. Even if it was only for the weekend. And now he was going to have to deal with the fallout of that decision. The only hope he had left was that maybe she'd become open to the idea of ménage, and Andre could come into the picture and ease some of the intensity of the situation. But right now, Jace was done analyzing it.

Screw it all—the guilt over how he'd fucked up things in the past, the anger at Evan for leaving and making him worry she was dead on the street somewhere, and the fear that he hadn't done the one-on-one thing since Diana. All of it was shit he couldn't do anything about right now.

What he could do something about was the fact that a beautiful woman—one he'd fantasized about for the last two weeks—wanted him to dominate her, to fuck her. *That* he could do. Evan clearly didn't want to dredge up their history, so he definitely was more than happy to go along with that. This was about sex. Plain and simple. That's all he needed to focus on.

He stared past the house to the moonlit lake beyond, channeling the dark part of himself that laid in wait for nights like this, and slipped fully into his dominant role. This is when he felt most comfortable, most free to be himself. Usually he kept it casual and was one of the more laid back doms, subscribing to the belief that fun didn't have to be mutually exclusive of D/s. But with Evan he was going to need all the armor the dom role could offer him. Boundaries needed to stay hard and clear. She'd said she didn't want half-assed. Well, she was going to get her wish.

"Welcome to our humble hacienda." The cart dipped as Andre climbed out. "I'll leave you two alone. I've got a few things to take care of before I head back to the main building."

Jace waited until Andre slipped into the house and then pinned Evan under his gaze. "The Ranch's safe word is *Texas. No, stop, quit* don't mean anything here. *Texas* is the only thing that halts whatever's happening. You can say *yellow* if you need me to ease off some activity but don't want to stop everything. If you're gagged and can't speak, I'll give you a hand signal for a safe word. Do you understand?"

Her eyes widened a bit, but she nodded. "Yes, sir."

"I don't give a shit if your fiancé gave you permission to be here. While you're here, you're mine. And when you go back home, you will not tell him that I'm the guy you were with. My business is important to me. And no matter how okay Dr. Dan may be with you doing this, no guy wants to work with the man who's fucked his woman."

"Okay," she said, her voice wavering a bit, but heat flickering in those pale blue eyes.

The corner of his mouth lifted, his confidence about the situation building. She was already feeling it—the rush a sub got when her dom took control. He stood and hooked a finger in the O-ring hanging off her collar to pull her up to stand. He cupped the back of her neck. "Do you have any hard limits—anything you're absolutely not open to?"

Her gaze shifted sideways.

"Pet, you need to tell me so that I don't push you too far."

She sighed. "Fine. I still have a thing about the dark, okay. Blindfolds will be fine as long as I can tell there is light on in the room."

The admission tugged at him. She'd never told him why she had that fear, but he knew she'd been left alone for days after her father committed suicide before the authorities had come for her. So he had his suspicions and none of those suspicions were pleasant. "Anything else?"

She shrugged. "I've never done this kind of thing, so I don't even know what my limits are."

He nodded. "Fair enough. We'll explore your boundaries together."

She wet her lips. "All right."

He had the urge to lean forward and taste her freshly moistened mouth, but he held back. Patience would make it better for all involved.

"Now, I want you to go into the house, find the sliding glass doors in the back, and go onto the deck. There's a hot tub there that looks out on the lake. It should already be heated, but go ahead and turn on the jets. Wait for me there."

She nodded and moved to head that way, but he caught her arm in a firm grasp.

"Don't get in without me. And don't take off anything. I want the pleasure of undressing you myself."

Even in the moonlight, he could see her cheeks color. And hell if that alone didn't make his cock strain against his zipper. He was used to women who'd been there done that, who weren't shocked by much. How was it possible that after all these years Evan still had that edge of innocence she'd carried with her at sixteen?

Back then, it'd been a glaring warning for him to steer clear, but now . . . Well, now it had him imagining all the things he wanted to do to her to make her skin turn that shade of pink.

Evan stood in front of the bubbling hot tub, steam swirling with her view of the dark night and the black water of the lake a few yards beyond. It was similar to the night she'd stood on the beach in South Padre, except this time, she wouldn't be alone. The water wasn't going to be what caressed her tonight. No, the man who'd haunted the periphery of every fantasy she'd ever conjured was going to take her over. Use her. Give her pleasure.

A shiver stole over her, and she rubbed her arms through the silk robe. Emotions were spinning through her like numbers on a slot machine.

Anticipation. Need. Fear.

She didn't know exactly what she was getting into, and having Jace be on the other end of it was like playing Russian roulette. But she had a feeling the danger of it was adding to the edgy excitement coursing through her.

Hot hands gripped her upper arms from behind, and she gasped.

"Good girl," Jace said against her ear, his voice melting over her like butter on hot cornbread. "You take direction well. That earns you rewards."

She clenched her thighs together as damp heat gathered between them, his words as effective as a stroke. "What happens if I don't follow instructions?"

His chuckle was soft and sensual as he ran his hands over her shoulders and pressed against her back. "Plan on being naughty, pet?"

His blatant and unashamed manner had her normal inhibitions shriveling like grapes in the sun. Jace didn't apologize for what he wanted, and neither should she. If she was going to do this, she needed to really *do this*. She tilted her hips, seeking him, and nestled her ass against the steel length of his cock. "Depends on what happens if I am."

His fingers found her hair and yanked back, catching her by surprise. He ran his tongue up the column of her neck like a cat licking up cream, and she nearly buckled at the knees. "Then you get punished, which can be fun, too. Just depends how rough you like it, babe."

She swallowed hard. Based on how much her sex was throbbing at his tight hold on her hair, she had a sneaking suspicion of which side of the pain fence she would fall on. "Yes, sir."

He released his grip on her hair and slowly stepped in front of her. His gaze drifted down the length of her as if assessing his prize. "Definitely too many clothes on. Take off your robe."

With trembling hands, she undid the tie at the front and let the robe fall open, revealing her scant bra and panties beneath, then slipped the silk off her shoulders. Jace's green eyes turned hungry as he stepped forward and ran a finger along the lace edge of her bra. Her nipple tightened to an aching point.

"So sexy, pet. You're going to test my restraint. I find I don't want to be gentle with you."

"Then don't be," she said, her words coming out before she could stop them. "Sir."

His head lifted, his eyes boring into hers. "How's that fiancé of yours going to feel if you go home with marks on you—*my* marks?"

"He'll deal with it," she said, her mouth going dry at the thought of Jace marking her, of branding her. "He knows what goes on here."

Jace's eyes narrowed. "Is Dr. Dan really vanilla or is he a guy who gets off knowing his woman is being fucked by someone else? Because I'm not here to get him off."

She shook her head. "This is all for me. I swear. This is what *I* want."

"You sure? 'Cause there's nothing pretty or romantic about what I do. It's raw and rough. You're mine to use however I want, you understand?"

Her throat contracted, the words turning her on more than she cared to admit. If he was trying to scare her off, it wasn't working. "Yes, sir. I want that. I didn't come here for flowers and poetry."

"Prove to me how bad you want it, then." He grasped her shoulder, pushed her down to her knees without finesse, and started unfastening his jeans. The discarded robe protected her knees from the wooden slats of the deck, but the bite of discomfort was still there. For some reason, that only dialed up her excitement more.

The rasp of his zipper drew her attention to the view in front of her. Jace pulled his fly wide and released his impressive erection. Lord, help her. She'd thought her mind had exaggerated his size because she'd been a virgin at the time and it had hurt, but damn, he had a pretty cock.

He gave her a predatory stare. "Tell me *exactly* what you're thinking, pet. I like that look in your eye."

She met his gaze, a wave of confidence coming with this new role. "I'm thinking I want to taste that beautiful cock, sir."

His lips curled into a smile. "Well, well, look who has a dirty mouth. May need to keep it busy to silence you."

"Perhaps."

He fisted his shaft and closed the distance between them. With his other hand, he grabbed at her tresses again, tugging hard enough for her scalp to tingle. "Open for me."

She parted her lips, and he moved her head exactly where he wanted it before sliding his cock into her mouth. Slow and easy. She closed her eyes, savoring the salty flavor of his skin, the uniquely male taste. He groaned and titled his head back. "That's right, baby. Convince me what a good girl you're going to be."

He controlled her movements with his tight grip on her hair, taking what he wanted without apology. She swirled her tongue around his length, drawing all her focus to making Jace feel as fabulous as she did being there at his feet and at his mercy. She'd never minded giving a guy head, but there was something so different about doing it this way. Of being used for his pleasure. It was intoxicating.

She boldly raised her gaze to meet his as she pressed the tip of her tongue along the sensitive vein on the bottom and then drew all the way back to lavish attention along the smooth head.

"Ah, shit, that feels good."

She took all of him again, so far to the back of her throat she had to work hard to keep her reflexes relaxed. He pumped into her harder, his careful control slipping a bit, and she closed her eyes to enjoy the rush of feminine power, of knowing that she could unglue him, too. His voice was gravelly when he spoke again. "You're not so sweet and innocent anymore, are you, pet? You've learned some tricks."

She made a *mmm* of affirmation, and his cock seemed to swell against her tongue. Trusting her instinct that he probably liked to take it as rough as he liked to give it, she lifted her hand and scraped her nails across the tender skin of his testicles while increasing the suction around his shaft.

"Holy fuck, Evan." He tilted his head back and his fist tightened on her hair. With one last thrust and groan, the heat of his release jetted against the back of her throat.

She closed her eyes and savored the moment he gave himself over to it. Taking all he had to give her. Quick and dirty and oh so nice.

A minute passed before he pulled his softening cock from her mouth. She pressed the top of her head against his belly, the hard plane of muscles heaving with his ragged breaths. His hand slid over her scalp, gentle where he'd been rough a moment before. "Jesus, that was good. Remind me to reward you for that."

She raised her face to look up at him, but the sound of the sliding glass doors opening behind her had her vaulting to her feet. Jace put a firm hand on the crown of her head, pushing her back down. "I didn't tell you to get up."

"But—"

"Relax." He tucked himself back into his jeans and zipped his fly.

Andre stepped onto the deck, carrying a tray of sandwiches and bottled soda. He glanced over at the two of them, the corner of his mouth curving. "I thought maybe the two of you would want some dinner. Although, it looks like you may have already jumped to dessert."

Evan felt the blush work up the length of her, and her gaze darted to the ground.

Jace put two fingers under her chin, lifting her face to him. "Don't be embarrassed. I don't want you to feel shame with me or Andre. You look beautiful right now. There's nothing sexier than a sub giving herself over to this process and pleasing her master. I like others to see what's mine and wish it were theirs. Andre's just jealous that you're not kneeling before him."

"Damn straight," Andre agreed, setting down the tray and stretching out on one of the lounge chairs that surrounded the hot tub.

Her gaze wandered over to their new companion. He'd changed out of the slacks and into a pair of black cargo shorts and a snug-fitting T-shirt. And damn, the man looked good—all tawny skin and tightly packed muscle, his dark features a reverse image of Jace's light ones. He gave her a wicked smile, and the embarrassment she'd felt began to morph into something else, something far more pleasant than shame.

"Ah, you like Andre looking at you," Jace observed.

Her focus snapped back to him.

"Stand up, pet." Jace put a hand under her elbow and helped her to her feet. "If you enjoy Andre seeing you like this, then maybe you should give him something to watch."

"Wait, what?" she asked, her heartbeat thumping in her ears.

Jace stepped behind her and walked his fingers along her spine until he reached the hook of her bra. With a flick of his hand, the strap unhinged, and he slid the bra down her arms, exposing her breasts to the night air and to Andre.

On instinct, her hands lifted to cover herself, but Jace caught her arms and tucked them behind her back. His mouth went to her bare shoulder and teeth grazed her skin. "Tell me, Andre, you think my little sub likes you seeing her beautiful tits."

She bit her lip, feeling vulnerable, but unable to deny the effect the exposure was having on her body. Every part of her ached to be touched, licked. She was so slick with heat she was sure both men could see it soaking her panties.

Andre sat up on his elbows, the reflection of the hot tub lights flickering in his brown eyes. "I would say those nipples are begging to be tasted. They're so tight and pink."

Jace stepped back around her and let his gaze roll slowly over her. "I think you're right. Hook your arms around the railing be-hind you, pet, and keep them there."

She followed his instructions, the movement causing her small breasts to jut out further. Jace's hands gripped her waist then slid up and over her ribs until he plumped both breasts in his palms. Her breath quickened at his firm touch. She arched back, needing more.

"Tell me what you want, Evan."

He'd used her real name for the second time, but she no longer cared what he called her as long as he gave her some relief. "Please. I need your mouth."

"But Andre will see," he pointed out, his tone filled with feigned concern.

"Let him," she gasped. "Just please."

His head dipped down and his mouth closed over one of her nipples, causing her to cry out. He sucked and licked on one side and used his hand on the opposite breast, rolling the nipple between his fingers and sending shots of pleasure straight to her core.

"Oh, Lordy," she murmured, her head lolling back.

His teeth grazed against the hardened nub, then bit. She jolted at the sharp snap of pain, but then pleasure, hot and wicked, chased the sensation. Holy shit. Her nipples had always been wonderfully sensitive, but hell if she wasn't on the verge of coming from that stimulation alone.

A sound akin to a growl rumbled low and deep from Jace as he lifted his head. "You like being watched?"

"I . . . I don't know."

He smiled and rasped a thumb over her nipple. "I think you do know. How wet did you get for me that day on stage?"

She shuddered at the low, coaxing tone of his voice, the devil inviting her to take his hand for a little walk.

"You know what I think? I think if the lights hadn't gone out, you would've let me slide my hands up the rest of the way under that dress, would've let me fuck you with my fingers while your fiancé and all those people watched." His hand traced down her belly and teased at the band of her panties, but his eyes never left hers.

"I wanted you to," she whispered.

His gaze turned hooded as he moved his hand beneath the triangle of silk and found her wet heat. She hissed, so ready to tip over the edge. Just a few glides over her clit would do it.

"That night I stroked my cock, remembering the sweet scent of your pussy, all slick and ready for me. Imagined how good you would feel coming around me."

She tilted her head back and whimpered as he dipped two fingers inside her. "Shit. Sir, please, I'm so close."

"Well, now, look how nicely you asked. You're a quick learner." In one swift motion, he yanked her panties down and off, leaving her fully naked against the railing. The cool air licked at her freshly shaven skin. She'd made the last-minute decision the night before to shave herself bare, and suddenly she was very, very happy she had made that call. Jace went to his knees, grasping the backs of her legs and lifting them. "Just hold on, baby."

She locked her arms more tightly around the railing behind her, her muscles straining, but she was far beyond feeling pain. Jace spread her thighs wide and guided her legs over his shoulders, putting his mouth centimeters from her sex. Using the tip of his tongue, he traced the delicate folds as if he had all the time in the world, teasing her, making her writhe against him. His hands clamped down hard on her thighs, holding her in place for his painstakingly gentle assault.

"*Mmm,*" he said, kissing the inside of her thigh, so close to where she really wanted his mouth. "You taste so good. I may just do this all night."

She groaned. "I won't survive it. I . . . It's been too long."

The words tumbled out before she had time to think them through, and she wanted to smack her forehead when she realized what she'd said.

Jace's lips paused along the trail he was kissing up her thigh.

"Baby, if that boyfriend of yours isn't worshipping this beautiful cunt every chance he gets, he deserves to have some other guy fuck you because that's a goddamned crime."

His words were coarse, dirty, but the heat behind them had her temperature climbing as high as the steaming hot tub behind him. No longer in teasing mode, Jace ran the flat of his tongue along her pussy, sending tremors through her entire body. Then he locked his lips over her, sucking her clit into his mouth.

The sharp cry that ripped out of her was unrecognizable to her own ears. Jace hummed his approval against her skin, moving his mouth and tongue over her with the skill of a man who knew his way around a woman's body.

Another wave of hot moisture flooded her sex, and the erotic sounds of his mouth licking and sucking against her skin had her mind buzzing and her body quivering. Pleasure, fast and fierce, lashed at her, driving her higher and higher. It had been . . . so . . . damn . . . long. No matter how much she had tried to convince herself, masturbation had nothing on this—nothing on a real man whose sole intent was to send her into oblivion.

One of Jace's hands left her thigh and two fingers dipped inside her. Her inner muscles clenched around him, her body's need turning desperate. *Oh, my.* She arched up, but Jace didn't lose his hold on her. His fingers pumped inside her, while his lips and tongue paid homage to every inch of her sex.

She tried to hold off for another moment, not ready for the mind-blowing sensations to end. But when he sucked her clit back between his lips and nipped at her with his teeth, every cell inside her seemed to split open.

"Oh, God. *Jace!*" Keening cries passed her lips, and her hips rocked against his mouth as her orgasm overtook her. She didn't care that they were outside, that someone was watching, or that the sounds coming from her throat were probably broadcasting her climax for anyone in a one-mile radius. In fact, she kind of liked the exposure—spread and open to this man—offering her pleasure to him. To Jace.

Sweat slicked her body despite the cool evening, and as the remnants of her release coursed through her, her arms begin to slip from the rail behind her. She quickly tried to adjust, grasping for purchase, but her arms trembled and gave out. "Oh!"

She winced, expecting to hit the ground, but her back landed on something hard and warm. Two arms. "I got you, *bella*. Easy."

She blinked, her eyes focusing on Andre, who stared down at her, smiling. He eased her upper body to the ground as Jace gently grabbed her thighs and slipped out from under them. The two of them set her down on top of her discarded robe.

Jace pushed a lock of damp hair off her forehead as Andre stepped away. "You okay, pet?"

She gave him a tentative smile, suddenly feeling shy about her very vocal display. "I can't feel my arms, but I'm pretty fantastic otherwise."

He laughed and leaned forward, capturing her mouth with his. Her eyes fluttered closed, and her hands immediately laced in his hair. This kiss started off soft and gentle, but soon his tongue parted her lips and took possession of her mouth. His spicy flavor mixed with the taste of her own arousal, which still clung to his lips. Despite the rocking orgasm seconds before, desire, hot and heavy, rose anew. Good Lord, the man could kiss.

Just as she was about to be bold and let her hands travel to more than his hair, he pulled back. "I'm going to stop before I haul you off to fuck you without feeding you dinner."

"Maybe I'm not that hungry."

Amusement crinkled the corners of his eyes. "It's my job to take care of you right now. And I know new subs are famous for skipping meals their first day here because of nerves."

She looked down guiltily. She hadn't eaten anything since breakfast.

He ran a thumb over her lips. "Don't worry. The night is young."

With that, he climbed to his feet, bent down, and swept her up into his arms. She let out a little sound of surprise. "What are you doing?"

"I'm going in the house to take care of a few things. You are going into the hot tub to relax and eat something." He cocked his head to the side. "Andre, I'm putting you in charge of her. Make sure she eats."

Before she realized what was happening, he lowered her into the bubbling tub. The heated water enveloped her naked body, and her gaze shot to Andre.

Jace ran a hand over her hair. "Are you okay staying with Andre alone?"

She didn't feel any threat from Andre. In fact, just looking at him made her want to praise God for creating the male form. But what was her role? Was she supposed to please Jace's friends, too? The thought sent a surprising jolt of desire through her. "Yes, I just—"

Jace gave her a reassuring smile. "Andre is one of my best friends. I'd trust him with my life, so I trust him with you. If at any point you want to touch him this weekend, you have my permission. But he won't touch you unless you ask him to. You understand?"

She couldn't tell if it was the temperature of the water or the mind-blowing dynamic Jace had just laid on her, but she felt a bit lightheaded. She nodded. "Yes, sir."

"Now, chill, eat. I'll be back for you in a little while."

She listened to Jace's retreating footsteps as Andre leaned forward and propped his forearms on the side of the hot tub. "So, gorgeous, mind if I join you in there?"

ELEVEN

Evan took a deep breath—as if that would do a damn bit of good—and nodded at Andre. "Sure. Come on in."

He flashed an easy smile and grabbed the tray of sandwiches off the lounge chair and set it on the side of the hot tub. "Start eating, *bella*. I have a feeling Jace has big plans for you, and he won't put up with you skipping meals. Don't want you passing out."

Something about the way he said *bella*—*bey-yah*—made her all fluttery inside. Like her female genes were wired to be a sucker for the way that spice-laced accent rolled off his tongue. Made her want to find out if those lips tasted as good as his words.

She reached over and grabbed one of the sandwiches to give her shaky hands something to do. Her normally voracious appetite had been non-existent all day, but after round one with Jace, she was already feeling a little weak. Sustenance wasn't optional. She bit into the sandwich right as Andre peeled off his T-shirt.

Bad idea. She nearly choked on the first bite.

Hot damn, he was beautiful—hard, well-honed muscles, naturally tan skin, and a faint trail of black hair tracking from his navel down. Her gaze traveled up his torso and paused at silver glinting in the moonlight. Nipple rings. She'd almost forgotten that sexy little detail from the night in South Padre. There was something so darkly enticing about that kind of piercing on a man. A blatant, unapologetic pronouncement of sexuality.

She bit her lip, wondering what it would be like to run her tongue over one of the rings, to tug it with her teeth. She shoved another bite of sandwich into her mouth before she did something stupid. Like give Andre permission to do whatever the hell he wanted to her.

He hooked his thumbs in the waistband of his shorts and then glanced down at her. She must've looked like a deer in headlights; she certainly felt like one. He chuckled. "Sorry. Habit. I'll keep these on."

She didn't know if she was relieved by his decision or damn disappointed. God, what the hell was wrong with her? She already had an equally potent man to herself for the weekend. How could she even be tempted to want more than that? She barely knew if she could handle Jace without melting into a puddle of uselessness.

Andre straddled the side of the tub and then slid into the water, taking a seat on the opposite side from her. "Ahh, that's nice."

Hell yes, it was. She was suddenly very happy for the water concealing her body because she was certain her nipples had hardened as soon as he'd gotten near. Ugh. This had to be a side effect of long-term abstinence.

He stretched his arms out along the edge of the hot tub and sank lower, letting his head rest against the side, but keeping his eyes on her. "Relax, Evan. Jace wasn't kidding. I'm not going to make a move on you."

Unless she asked. He didn't say it, but the rest of the sentence hung in the steam-filled air between them. She set her sandwich down. "So, I'm not sure I get this whole thing."

He cocked an eyebrow. "Define *this whole thing.*"

She sighed, so many questions springing to her lips she didn't even know where to start. "Obviously I'm new to the whole BDSM scene, but I assumed that possessiveness went together with dominance. I guess I'm confused about Jace being cool if I touched another guy when he took me on as his slave, sub, whatever, for the weekend. He certainly didn't seem to want Colby around me."

His lips curved. "Jace would most definitely *not* be cool with you pursuing some other guy. And God help the man who tried to flirt with you while you're here with Jace this weekend. Fists would fly."

Her brows knitted. "Then why—?"

Andre frowned as if trying to formulate an explanation she could understand. "Jace and I are roommates and long-time friends. He trusts me. We share a lot."

Awareness smacked her over the head like a two-by-four. Duh. Why hadn't that possibility hit her before? "You share women."

He nodded. "We do."

Oh, sweet Jesus. Thoughts of the two of them naked, both taking what they wanted from her, assailed her. Her internal thermometer jumped back into the red zone. But at the same time, the idea scared the shit out of her. Jace was already an overwhelming prospect, his dominance promising to send her to a place she hadn't been before. She wasn't entirely convinced she could handle him alone, much less add Andre to the mix. It would be sensory overload.

Although . . .

She snuck another glance at Andre. If she really did want to keep this purely physical with no risk of her emotions getting involved, maybe sensory overload was exactly what she needed. The third person could create sort of a buffer, ensuring no quiet one-on-one intimate moments with Jace. Just carnal indulgence. Her mind whirled with possibilities.

All she managed to say was "I see."

He chuckled. "Don't worry. There's no pressure here. We know you didn't list ménage as something you were open to right now. I think the only reason Jace allowed me out here to watch is he suspects you have an exhibitionist streak."

If her cheeks weren't already flushed from the warm water, she would've turned bright red. She put her hands over her face. "I still can't even believe I did that."

"Hey," he said, bumping his foot against hers under the water and making her look up at him. "Don't be ashamed. You were beautiful, and it was sexy as hell. I feel privileged that you let me stay and watch."

She gave him a small smile, embarrassment still flaring bright within her. "So is that why you like ménage? Because you get to watch as well as participate?"

He moved forward, coming within inches of her as he reached past her for one of the sodas on the sandwich tray. Wisps of his cologne wafted past her—a soft musk with notes of ginger. Her breath caught with the knowledge that she wanted to reach out and touch him, to lick off the beads of water that tracked down his well-built chest, but she kept her hands—and tongue—to herself. He slid back to his spot and took a swig of the drink.

"Yes, I won't lie. Seeing another guy pleasuring a woman, bringing her to the edge, definitely does it for me. As does having someone watch me do the same thing. But ménage is more than that. It pushes everyone to heights you can't get to with just two people. It's intense and edgy. Add in BDSM to that and it's unbelievably hot."

Desire stirred deep within her at the picture he painted. Then another thought hit her, but she wrangled in her next question before it slipped out.

He smiled. "Ask your question, *bella*. I can see it on your face that you just swallowed one back."

God, was her every thought that obvious? Or was it just a dom thing to be able to read people so well? She cleared her throat. "Okay, so, when you and Jace are sharing, do you two, you know . . . interact?"

The idea sent a strange thrill humming through her veins even though it shouldn't. She'd seen enough male-on-male action at home to last a lifetime.

He glanced past her shoulder as if to make sure Jace hadn't come out of the house yet. "It happens from time to time. Things get hot, and boundaries that exist outside the doors tend to weaken. But a woman usually seeks ménage because she wants all the focus on her, so we typically oblige that desire."

She considered that for a moment. "So are you and Jace together outside of here?"

His smile turned wry. "We're not lovers, if that's what you're asking. We keep the sexual play confined to when we're with a woman. Jace is pretty open sexually, but he's primarily straight."

"And you?"

He shrugged. "Not as much."

"Care to elaborate? Or is that too personal of a question?"

He took another long sip from his bottle. "It's fine. And honestly, if I could figure out a hard and fast label for it I would. But I guess most would call me bisexual. My relationships have been exclusively with women. But I do find myself on occasion sexually attracted to a guy and have acted on it . . . within the confines of a place like this. I don't broadcast it. The people in my life wouldn't understand."

"I guess ménage serves a few purposes for you then. The whole cake and eat it too thing."

He smirked. "I wouldn't say I've got the whole cake, but a pretty good slice I guess."

She frowned, something in his tone telling her that wasn't the full story, but it wasn't her business. She grabbed her own soda and uncapped it. "So what happens when Jace takes on someone solo like this? Do you go and find someone as well?"

He shrugged. "Guess I'll figure that out. He hasn't gone solo in years."

She stilled, the bottle halfway to her mouth. *"What?"*

———

Jace paced around the living room. He'd set Evan up to be alone with Andre, thinking that his oh-so-suave friend would open up her mind to the possibility of ménage. This one-on-one thing was crazy. Jace hadn't even fucked her yet, and he was already surging with things that hadn't been in his vocabulary in years—possessiveness, jealousy, protectiveness. He could put a fist through the wall knowing that in a few days she'd return to Dr. Dan's bed—a guy who clearly wasn't giving her what she needed, at least not in the bedroom.

Jace raked his hands through his hair. What the fuck was wrong with him? He should've known better. Something about Evan had always tested his limits, had made him question himself at every turn, and apparently her effect on him hadn't dimmed with time.

Damn, he needed to change this dynamic fast or he was going to end up getting himself in trouble. But the thought of Andre entering the picture had him all knotted up. Sharing a woman was the ultimate turn on for him. It fed all his kinks in the most deca- dent ways. And he could already tell Evan was attracted to Andre. There was no doubt she'd gotten off on him watching as Jace made her come. But now Jace had this ridiculous urge to race back out to the deck, pluck her out of the water, and hoard her away all for himself.

What if he walked out there and she was fooling around with Andre? Would he be turned on like he normally would be or would he want to kick Andre's ass for touching her? He sank onto the leather chair in the living room with a groan. Christ, he didn't know the answer.

Evan's melodic laugh drifted into the house from the deck, hitting him straight in the solar plexus. Andre was making her laugh. Probably laying on that charm that came so easy to him and flirting with her in Spanish, which seemed to get women to drop their panties faster than anything Jace had ever seen. Smooth motherfucker.

Or maybe Andre had already won Evan over and was running his lips along the tender column of her neck, tickling her with his tongue, sliding his hands over those beautiful tits and nestling himself between her naked thighs.

Jace shot to his feet and stormed toward the back of the house. He shoved open the door and steeled himself for what he may find when he stepped onto the deck. But as the hot tub came into view, all he saw was Andre sitting opposite Evan, a broad smile on his face. His friend's eyes darted Jace's way, and Evan turned her head.

Her skin had gone dewy from the steam and her normally straight hair was curling around her face. She looked like a beautiful water nymph come to life. A tentative smile teased at the corner of her mouth along with a definite ripple of apprehension. The combination nearly sucked the air from his chest. She was happy to see him, but was also knocked a bit off balance by his presence. Everything a sub should feel for her dom.

The women he chose to be with these days didn't take the sub thing all that seriously. It was fun and games. Roles played. He kept it at that level now because true D/s stripped down too much, not just for the sub but for the dominant. It exposed people's deepest vulnerabilities, shone light into those ugly corners. He'd learned that the hard way. But Evan had never played this game, so she was coming at it green, with an honesty that he was finding hard to resist.

He leaned against the railing of the deck. "So what's so funny?"

Evan shot Andre a warning look. "Nothing."

Andre grinned. "I'm trying to get Evan to spill the details about her naughty cop fantasy."

She splashed water at him. "Traitor."

Jace couldn't stop the laugh that bubbled out. "Well, you can't blame the guy for asking, Ev. He *is* a cop."

"Oh, my God." Mortification crossed her face. "I'm just going to drown myself now and save myself the rest of this conversation."

"Ah, had he not told you that part yet?" Jace asked, enjoying the fact that she could be naked in a hot tub, talking to two guys who'd seen her screaming in orgasm already, but still be embarrassed about a dirty fantasy.

"No." She shot Andre a glare.

He held up his palms. "You didn't ask. But you should at least tell Jace about it. How's your dom supposed to know how to please you if you don't tell him what turns you on? Everyone has those fantasies that they're afraid to tell others. That's the beauty of a place like this. You don't have to keep them tucked away."

Jace watched as she gnawed her lip, her nerves evident. But he could tell the temptation to open up to them was there, too. He walked over to the edge of the hot tub and propped his forearms on it.

"As my sub, I expect you to be open with me. If you're not, I'll eventually draw out whatever those desires are by other means. You won't be able to hide them forever. But I'm not going to command you to share with us right now if you're not ready." He reached out and cupped her cheek, holding her gaze. "But know that you're safe with me. And with Andre. No judgment. I guarantee that for every dark fantasy you have, we probably have a hundred more sordid ones to match. Especially Andre, he's a sick bastard."

"Hey, wait a second," Andre protested.

She smiled and the anxiety pinching her features seemed to ease as she took in his words. She nodded, her eyes not leaving his. "Thank you."

He had the urge to bend down and press his lips to hers. Just because. But he held off. If they weren't in the middle of a D/s scene, he needed to keep his distance. That kind of casual intimacy was not what either of them had signed up for. "Let me grab you a towel and get you out of here."

The minute he turned his back, her soft voice halted him. "I . . . I have a capture fantasy."

The words shot straight to his groin and snapped him right back to what he was supposed to be focused on with Evan—sex. But he didn't move, knowing that if he faced her she may lose her nerve to continue. "Okay."

"Two rogue cops. Arresting me. Being rough. Taking what they want from me however they want it. Forcing me to get them off."

Holy hell. Jace closed his eyes and took a long breath, his body thrumming from the erotic images assaulting his brain. His cock hardened to the point of agony. She wanted to be manhandled and fucked by two men? The idea set fire to the darkest parts of him— appealed to the primitive core of his dominant streak.

Part of him wanted to whirl around, grab her, and make that fantasy come true for her. Right. This. Minute. But she wasn't ready for that kind of thing yet. He'd never done a capture scene, but he knew they were seriously intense. The pretense of no consent— even with a safe word—was a powerful thing for the psyche to process. For someone so new to D/s, she could get too freaked out to enjoy it. Plus, he had no idea if she was emotionally strong enough to handle that kind of mind fuck. He hadn't forgotten those cuts he'd found on her the night they'd slept together.

A frown touched his lips. There was no way he could take that risk with her. That was the kind of thing you did with a long-term partner, one you'd built total trust with. The type of relationship he'd never have with her, or anyone else for that matter. He wasn't built for trust anymore.

But it didn't mean they still couldn't have a great time tonight doing a whole list of other things. His frown lifted, his darkening mood rallying at the thought.

He grabbed a thick towel from one of the benches and went back to the hot tub. "Thank you for trusting us with that. I know that wasn't easy for you."

She nodded and stared down at the water. Jace ventured a glance at Andre and almost burst out laughing. The guy looked like he was in pain. Probably from the raging hard-on he suspected Andre was hiding beneath the water.

Andre checked that Evan wasn't looking in his direction and mouthed, "Lucky bastard."

Jace grinned, although he did feel a little sorry for the guy. Andre had watched Evan get off, sat with her while she was naked, and had heard about a fantasy that he could definitely help fulfill. All without being invited into their bed for the night.

"Let's get you out of here, babe," Jace said, offering a hand to Evan.

She peeked up at him from under her lashes, but before she took his hand, she slid along the bench of the hot tub toward Andre. Andre froze as she neared him, as if he were afraid if he moved anything, he'd maul her. Lifting out of the water, high enough to give both men a view of the top curve of her luscious breasts, she leaned over and laid a lingering kiss on his cheek. Andre closed his eyes, and Jace could almost see him quivering with restraint.

"Thanks for the chat, Andre. And for being such a gentleman," she said, a shy note to her voice.

Andre cleared his throat. "Anytime, *bella*. Any. Time."

Jace heard Andre's unspoken offer. *I want you. Just ask.* He doubted Evan had missed the intent behind the words.

Something tightened low in Jace's gut, the conflicting feelings boiling over. Seeing the little spark between her and Andre had him hot all over, but also ridiculously jealous. Her cop fantasy proved she at least was a little open to ménage, so he could probably guide her down that path. And Lord, she'd be gorgeous bound and spread for the two of them. But goddamn it, he didn't know if he could share her.

And sharing was what he did. Who he was.

Maybe he just needed to get this first time out of his system with her. Satisfy whatever primal part of him wanted to stake his claim on her before Andre touched her.

Yeah, that had to be it.

Evan glided back to the spot in front of him and took his hand, her eyes like blue fire. "I'm all yours, sir."

The intent in her words and resolute expression made every cell in his body vibrate with anticipation. His concerns melted away under her hungry gaze.

To hell with the psychoanalysis. All he needed right now was Evan.

Alone.

He'd figure out the rest later.

TWELVE

Evan followed Jace into the house, her legs like Jell-O beneath her after the long soak in the hot tub and the erotic overload of sharing her fantasies with the two men. But the wobbly muscles didn't prevent tension from reclaiming her as she mulled over her talk with Andre.

She pulled the towel more snugly around her and took a deep breath. "Jace?"

He stopped in the doorway to the bedroom and turned around to look at her, frowning when he saw her expression. "You all right?"

She had the urge to look down at the floor, but forced herself to keep her gaze. "Why are you doing this?"

He crossed his arms over his chest and leaned against the doorframe. "I thought we already covered that."

"Andre said you never take on a sub alone. That you always do ménage."

His jaw muscle flexed. "Andre has a big mouth."

"So why are you doing this with me?"

He pushed off the doorjamb and pointed to the spot in front of him. "Come here."

Tentatively, she walked the few steps forward to stand before him.

He cupped the back of her neck and captured her gaze. "I told you. I'm doing this because I *want* you. No, I don't do one-on-one a lot—that's why I hesitated at initiation. But when I saw you with Colby, I realized that even if you weren't into ménage, you belonged in *my* bed this weekend."

Her chilled skin warmed under his words and possessive tone. She nodded and swallowed hard, building up courage for her next words. "I'm open, Jace."

His grip tightened on her neck, making the collar dig into her tender skin. "What are you talking about?"

She shifted her weight from foot to foot, her nervous energy fighting to break loose, but kept her eyes on his. "I'm open to what you like—to ménage, to you and Andre."

A storm cloud crossed his face, as if her proclamation both pleased him and pissed him off all at the same time. "You don't have to change your limits for me, Evan. I don't need ménage to enjoy myself. You're more than enough alone."

"But what if I'm curious?" she said, her voice gaining some strength despite her frantically beating heart. "I checked *no* for ménage because I was already freaked out enough turning myself over to one stranger. Not because the idea of two guys isn't appealing."

"And now the thought of me sharing you with Andre turns you on?"

Her body shuddered with a *hell yes* but she kept her response neutral. "Maybe."

"We can both be pretty demanding," he said, his voice darkly sensual as he threaded his fingers through the damp hair at her nape. "What makes you think you can handle us both?"

She tilted her chin up. "What makes you think I can't?"

His lips curled in a wicked smile. "Confident, aren't we? Drop the towel. Let's see how you handle your own master first. Then I'll determine if you've earned the pleasure of being shared. Ménage is not for the faint of heart, pet."

She lowered the hand that was holding the towel around her and allowed the terrycloth to fall to the floor. Unashamed. Aching for him to touch her. "I'm tougher than I look, sir."

"Oh, I have no doubt about that."

He gave her a slow once over and ran his hand down her back until he cupped her ass and drew her against him. She didn't resist. "Good girl. When you're with me, that's all I want to see you wearing. My collar and that pretty flush you get when I touch you."

He seated the crotch of his jeans against her sensitive flesh, sending ripples of pleasure through her. Her fists balled against his T-shirt. "Yes, sir."

He lowered his head, kissing the sensitive spot beneath her ear. "Now, let me show you what happens when you question your master and make unsolicited suggestions."

In one effortless motion, he hoisted her up over his shoulder, placing her face against his back, and smacked a palm against her bare ass. Hard.

"Hey!"

"Quiet." He locked his arm around the backs of her thighs and carried her into the bedroom, leaving the door open behind them.

She bit her lip as the stinging began to tingle. *Oh, my.*

The bedroom was a good bit bigger than the one in her cabin, but looked to be decorated in the same rustic style. Nice cozy bungalow. The only things that alluded to its purpose were the metal rings hanging from some of the walls. She caught a glimpse of the bed in the mirror above the dresser and saw that Jace was carrying her over to the foot of the bed where a long padded table was set up.

He sat her down on the edge of it. "Face down, pet."

She looked to his face to try to get a read on what he was going to do, but his expression was stoic.

"Don't make me tell you again."

Hurriedly, she turned over on her stomach and moved to the end of the table. It was a massage table of sorts, but she doubted he was going to give her a rubdown. She rested her head in the cushioned face cradle, her heartbeat pounding so loud she didn't catch his next command.

"You're earning more punishment by hesitating. I said lift your head."

She followed his instructions and he tied a band of silk around her eyes, blocking out most of the light. Anxiety wound through her.

A hand brushed over her hair. "You have my word that I won't turn out the lights."

"Yes, sir," she said, his reassurance easing her a bit.

He grasped her wrist, drew it down the side of the table, and slid something around it. The clink of metal echoed through the room as he locked the cuff to the leg of the table. She pulled back, testing the hold, but the cuff didn't give at all. She could flex her wrists but that was it. He quickly followed with the same treatment on her other arm. A rush of nerves went through her.

"Jace, I think—"

Thwack! His hand landed on the back of her thigh, making her jolt. "Your job is not to think, pet. Your job is to feel. Trust that I know what you need."

She swallowed her protest, the sting from the spanking sending a bolt of hallelujah straight between her legs. *Whoa.* She wasn't a stranger to pain being linked to relief—her years of cutting had taught her that. But never had she considered it could be arousing.

His finger traced the area on her thigh he had spanked. "You know how fucking sexy you look with my handprint marking you? You look better than the art hanging in my store."

Her hands flexed in the bindings, the words rolling over her like sensual fire. "Thank you, sir."

His tongue replaced his finger as he drew it along the back of her leg, licking her burning skin. Her thighs pressed together as moisture, hot and slick, coated her sex. She had the urge to press against the table, provide some relief to her clit as it swelled to an aching mass. He locked a hand over her other leg to keep her from squirming. "You're not allowed to stimulate yourself without my permission."

"I can't help it."

"Oh, I bet you can." His hand came down on her ass again and she moaned. "You like being spanked, pet?"

"I'm not sure." It was a lie. But she couldn't bring herself to admit how much it was turning her on. If he kept at it, she wasn't entirely convinced she wouldn't come simply from that and the slight brush of the table's padding against her clit.

His chuckle was low and dangerous. "So if I slid my hand between those beautiful legs of yours, I wouldn't find that pussy wet and clenching for my cock?"

His crude words sent a hot shudder through her, and her inner muscles flexed as if punctuating the accusation. Her pulse seemed to relocate and settle directly behind her clit, her body going into full-out begging mode. Unable to fight off the need, she spread her thighs for him. "Why don't you find out, sir?"

He made a *tsk*ing sound. "Such a smart mouth, sub. Need to teach you some manners."

A metallic sound filled her ears and the lower end of the table collapsed beneath her. She gasped. His hands caught her legs before she could fall, and he lowered them until she was standing on the balls of her feet, her arches stretched. The part of the table still supporting her torso angled downward until she was prone in a bent-over position. Totally helpless.

"Spread your legs." Jace nudged her feet apart with his foot. "You want me to find out how wet you are, then show me."

Her heart hammered against her ribs as she followed his instruction, making herself as physically vulnerable as she'd ever been. He could do whatever he wanted to her in this position, and she wouldn't be able to stop him. She squeezed her eyes shut as need railroaded through her. The loss of control shouldn't excite her like this, but hell if she could stop her body from responding.

Jace ran his hand up her inner thigh and palmed her sex, gripping her like he owned it. Like her pussy had been created for him and he'd only leased it to her for a while. He rocked his hand against her, painting her delicate skin with her juices. "*Mmm*. So slick and hot for me already. Good girl."

She whimpered. The pressure against her clit was maddening, pushing her closer and closer to the edge. She moved her hips in time with the motion of his hand, chasing the orgasm that hovered on the horizon. But the stimulation wasn't enough. She needed Jace inside her, filling her, driving into her.

"Stop squirming." He smacked the flat of his fingers against her cunt, sending a rocket of shocking pleasure straight up her spine.

"Please," she panted. "Jace, I need more."

Blessedly, he put his fingers against her again. His other hand caressed her back, her tailbone, drawing lower and lower until his fingertip brushed along the cleft of her ass. "How much more, babe?"

Her muscles automatically flinched, but the position had her spread for his perusal, and there was no escaping. His fingertip grazed the untried opening, the feather-light touch sending bolts through her, making her buck against her bindings. *Holy fuck.* Was that supposed to feel that good?

"*Mmm*, so responsive," he murmured. "Have you ever been taken here, pet?"

She pressed her forehead into the table, the combination of sensations and his suggestion nearly undoing her. "No, sir."

"But you want to do ménage? What if one of us wants to fuck your sweet ass while you ride the other's cock?"

She felt lightheaded and more turned on than she'd ever remembered being in her life. Forming words had to happen between the sharp breaths she was dragging in. "Just because I haven't . . . done it before . . . doesn't mean I'm . . . unwilling. Sir."

"Good answer, pet. Here's to exploring your limits." Cool and slippery liquid replaced his light touch for a moment, eliciting a squeak of surprise from her, and then his finger was back and no longer tentative. He smoothed the lubricant over her opening, teasing her and lighting up all of her nerve endings.

"Jesus, Jace. I'm going to come. Please, I want you inside me."

"No coming until I give you permission. If you go before, I won't give you what you want." He moved his finger against her ass and pushed gently, easing past the resistant ring of muscle, and instantly vaulting her to another level of bliss—the dark, forbidden thrill of it pinging through her.

"Oh, *God*," she ground out, trying to move against him, wanting him to pump forward. To move.

"Hold on, baby, not yet," he said, slowly moving his finger back and forth and removing his other hand from her clit. "Not until I feel you around me."

She could hear the rasp of his zipper, the sound of him tearing a condom wrapper open—no doubt with his teeth since his other hand was busy fucking her ass with a maddeningly slow pace. And then he was against her, the tip of his cock brushing against her pussy.

"Please, Jace. *Please*." She knew she was begging. Sounded desperate. She didn't care.

"Oh, pet, you sound so pretty begging for my cock. I could get used to the sound of that."

Within one blissful second, he was thrusting forward, filling her, stretching her until she thought the sheer onslaught of sensation would kill her. It had been so long since she'd been with anyone and never had she experienced something like this. The combination of his long cock inside her, the slide of his finger in her ass, and the bindings cutting into her arms had her riding an unfamiliar high. One she didn't want to come down from. It was edgy and disorienting . . . and freeing.

Jace groaned as he seated himself fully inside her then drew back, rocking her against the table with each thrust, the movement providing perfect stimulation to her clit. "You're so beautiful like this, Evan. Bound and pleading for release. Even if you didn't feel like heaven around my cock, I could come just looking at you."

Her breaths were coming short and fast now, his words only pushing her higher, her orgasm rushing toward her like a freight train. His pace increased, pistoning into her with the singular focus of launching them into the stratosphere.

She fought hard, clinging to the last vestige of control she had over her orgasm, the double assault of sensation barreling her toward oblivion. She balled her fists tighter, her fingernails digging into her palms.

He moved a second finger inside her back opening as he fucked her hard and fierce. Her senses shorted out—the smack of skin against skin, the scent of sweat and arousal, and Jace inside her all twining into a ball of pulsing light behind her eyelids. She couldn't hold on.

"Now," Jace demanded, his own dwindling control lacing his voice. "Come for me, baby. Let me feel you let go."

"Jace!" A rough scream ripped out of her chest and metal clanged as she reared up against her bindings and let the orgasm sweep her under. Dots of color exploded in her vision and for a moment, she lost all sense of where she was.

"Oh, *fuck* . . . Yes." Jace's groan soon joined with hers as he buried deep and gave her his own pounding release.

His body collapsed against her when he was finished, the two of them a heaving pile of sweat-slicked, shaky limbs.

Seconds passed. Or was it minutes? Evan wasn't sure. All she was sure of was that Jace was draped across her back, his cock still inside her, and she'd never felt so sated in her life.

She'd always enjoyed sex, but this was something unlike anything she'd ever experienced before. She had no idea it could be so intense, so all-encompassing. *So fucking good.*

Jace kissed the back of her shoulder. "You okay?"

"Um, I think so?" she said, her voice hoarse.

He gave a little laugh, his chest bouncing against her back before he pushed up and off her. He slipped off her blindfold. "Let me get cleaned up real quick, and I'll come get you out of these bindings."

He left her alone for a minute, and she heard the sink turn on and off, then he was back at her side, clad in a pair of pajama pants, a smile teasing at the corners of his mouth. He freed her wrists, helped her off the table, and slipped a fluffy terrycloth robe around her before settling her onto the bed.

He sat on the edge of the mattress and stared down at her, looking like he had loads to say but was holding it all in. She reached out and touched his mouth. "Why are you fighting that shit-eating grin?"

He smirked beneath her fingertips. "'Cause I don't want to get all teenage boy, 'wow that was awesome' on you. It could kill my bad-ass dom reputation."

She laughed, suddenly feeling less self-conscious about what had just transpired. This was the Jace she remembered—the quick with a joke, lighthearted guy. "Don't worry, your reputation is intact. And yeah, that was . . . something."

He arched an eyebrow. "Something, huh? As in something you enjoyed or something that totally freaked you out?"

She touched her throat. "I think that answer is pretty obvious. I may not have a voice tomorrow."

He rubbed a thumb over her bottom lip. "I love how vocal you are. It's hot. But I just want to make sure you're okay since you're new to all this."

She shrugged. "Maybe I'm little weirded out that I liked it that much. I'm not exactly a person who enjoys taking orders in everyday life. It's one of the reasons I went into business for myself."

He nodded. "Yeah, you'll find that people's everyday personalities don't always match their sexual ones. There are a lot of CEOs wearing collars around here, not to mention mild-mannered librarian-types brandishing whips. You just never know. You are what you are."

She threaded the belt of the robe between her fingers, staring down at it. "So is that how you see it? You're either built this way or not?"

"Yes, that's what I believe, but . . ." He put his hand over her fidgeting ones. "Don't get stressed out already, okay? Just because you enjoyed what we did doesn't necessarily mean you're a submissive."

She raised her gaze to him.

"It just means you're hella kinky," he said with a broad smile. "And of course, that I'm a kickass lover."

She burst out laughing and shoved his chest. "Egotistical asshole."

"Comes with the territory, babe. I didn't land on the dom side of things by chance." He climbed off the bed and stretched. "I'm going to run you a bath. The rest of tonight is for relaxing."

She yawned. "You don't have to do that. I can take care of it."

He stepped back and shook his head. "No, I've put you through your paces, and it's my job to see that you're attended to. Part of the pleasure of being a dom is taking care of a sub after she's served so well."

She sank back into the pillows and laced her fingers behind her head. "Well then, far be it from me to deny you that pleasure. Get to it, master."

He laughed and saluted her. "Right away, slave girl. And while you're bathing, I'll let Andre know that his infamous charm has worked on you, and he's now invited to play in our sandbox this weekend, too."

She bit her lip, nerves creeping back in. "Right."

He paused, something akin to worry on his face. "Unless you've changed your mind?"

She shook her head. No, this was already feeling too comfortable with Jace, too easy. She hadn't felt this content in as long as she could remember. Dangerous territory. A few nights of this and she'd be in big trouble. She needed to get safety nets in place. Right. Now. "No, you can go ahead and tell him. I'm up for anything."

His expression darkened, something unreadable crossing his face. "Be careful saying things like that, pet. *Anything* is exactly what they specialize in around here."

THIRTEEN

Evan padded out of the bathroom in Jace's oversize pajama top after soaking in the tub for way too long. Her nerves were still twitching like a faulty circuit board. She had no idea how she was going to handle the sleeping arrangements. But as she stepped into the bedroom, relief flooded her. Jace was sprawled out on the left side of the bed, fast asleep.

He'd left a bedside lamp on. The soft light gilded every line in his muscular back and the golden strands of his mussed hair, making him look like a sun-kissed Greek sculpture. Her entire being ached to run her hands along his bare skin, through that hair, to crawl next to him in the empty space he'd left for her, and curl up with him for the night.

But there was no way she could go there. Not tonight. Not ever. So instead, she grabbed a pillow off the bed and the quilt that was thrown over the chair by the window and tiptoed out of the room, clicking the door shut behind her.

The living room was dark except for a few lit candles that were taking the place of logs in the fireplace. She eyeballed the suede-covered couch. It wouldn't be as cozy as that big bed, but it would do. Tomorrow night, she'd let Jace know that she wanted to head back to her own cabin whenever they were through for the evening so she could have her own space.

She stepped around the coffee table, tossed her pillow and blanket onto it with a sigh, and headed toward the fireplace so she could blow out the candles.

"What are you up to, *bella*?"

Her heart nearly hopped out of her chest. She spun around to find Andre leaning against the doorway to the kitchen area, sipping a glass of water.

She put her hand to her chest. "Good Lord, you scared the hell out of me."

He frowned in the dim candlelight. "Sorry. Didn't realize anyone was still awake." He nodded at the couch. "What are you doing out here?"

She shifted her weight from foot to foot, feeling like a kid caught sneaking out after curfew. "I, uh, thought I'd sleep out here tonight. Jace is already sleeping and I just—"

"You're scared to share his bed."

She choked on her attempt at a laugh. "Of course not, I just did a lot more than that with him."

"So I heard." He gave her a wry smile and set his glass down on the dining table before joining her in the living room. He propped a hip on the back of the loveseat, drawing her attention to the fact that along with his T-shirt, he was only wearing a pair of black boxer briefs, underwear that were made for a body like his. She forced her gaze upward.

"It's understandable, you know? To feel weird about it. You *are* engaged."

"Right, 'cause my moral code on that is stellar. I just had sex with someone else."

He shrugged. "Sometimes sex can be easy to keep separate, but sharing a bed overnight is a whole different animal. Especially with someone you used to have feelings for."

She leaned back against the wall and sighed. "I'm being ridiculous."

"Nah, not at all." Andre stepped closer and held out his hand. "Come on, take my bed, and I'll sleep out here."

She waved him off, heading toward the couch. "Oh, no, really, I'm fine. I've slept in worse places." *Much worse.*

"Not a request, *bella*," he said, his tone firm. Her gaze snapped up as he moved in front of her and closed the space between them, his brown eyes flickering with more than candlelight. He braced a hand against the wall, caging her between him and the fireplace. "Jace told me about your invitation. I'm honored. But now you've got two bossy men on your hands. So, no, you won't take the couch."

"Oh." Blood began to thrum against her pulse points, his heady, masculine scent mixing with the vanilla of the candles. She searched for her voice. "I, uh, guess you accepted the invitation?"

Smooth, Evan. Real smooth.

He laughed softly. "I'm making you nervous."

"Maybe," she said, giving him a shaky smile. He must be a force of nature in an interrogation room. She certainly felt ready to confess her darkest secrets to him. "I haven't seen this side of you yet."

"I didn't have any right to show it to you." His lips curved as he reached out and drew the tip of his finger along the edge of her collar. "But feel free to tell me to back off."

She gave a little shake of her head. "Don't want to."

"Good, because you know what I've been trying to do all night?" His tone and touch were soft, hypnotizing, lulling her into some suspended state between reality and dream.

She held his smoky gaze, her breathing loud in her own ears. "What's that?"

"Been trying to make myself go back to the main house and find someone for me to spend the weekend with like I should. Give you and Jace some privacy. But instead . . ." His gaze slid down the length of her, making every inch prickle with awareness. "All I could think about was how the person I wanted was already here. How I'd rather watch you with Jace and listen to your sexy screams tonight even knowing I couldn't have you."

His words snaked over her, stirring urges she thought had been exhausted for the night. Now she knew what it felt like to be truly and utterly seduced. There was no other word for it. "Well, now you can."

His smile was slow, confident, his whole demeanor a shocking departure from the easy-going guy in the hot tub. It was as if she could feel the dominance rising within him, a floodgate being unlocked. "Indeed I can. But you're not sure that's what you want right now."

She blinked, his words not registering for a second.

"What? I . . . Yes, I want . . . But I'm—" Her words came out a jumbled mess. There was no doubt she wanted to pull Andre down to her, feel his mouth on hers, touch him. But there was a tug in her chest, a strange urge to ask Jace first even though he'd already given her permission. She glanced over at the door to Jace's bedroom.

He followed her gaze. "Ah, *bella*. It comes so naturally to you already, doesn't it?"

She turned her focus back to him, her brows knitted. "What do you mean?"

He brushed her hair off her forehead and smoothed her brow. "To be loyal to your dom. To make sure that what you want will please him as well."

She started to deny it, but snapped her mouth shut when the accuracy of his words set in.

"It's beautiful to see. And hard to resist." He bent and put his lips to hers, a gentle press, a taste with a promise of more. She laid her palms against his chest, enjoying the pounding of his heart beneath her fingers and the feel of his mouth on hers. So different from Jace's, but no less potent. He pulled back way too soon. "But I'm going to."

She stared at him in shock. "What?"

He palmed her hip, drew her against him, and let her feel just how aroused he was. "Believe me, there's nothing more I'd like to do right now than lay you out on this rug and taste and touch every inch of you."

She sucked in a breath, her panties instantly dampening as he molded her against him.

"But, you've had a long night, and I don't want you going into anything with doubts." He eased away from her. "I'll wait until tomorrow when Jace can be here with us, too."

"But all night you've been—"

"Tortured?" he asked with a smirk.

"Basically."

"I'll be fine. I've been on stakeouts that lasted for weeks and have interrogated suspects for hours on end, all with just a smidgen of a chance that I'll get what I want." He put his hand out to her again. "So, I can be infinitely patient when the end result is worth it."

There was an underlying warning in his words. She could only imagine what that level of patience and self-control could mean in a D/s situation. A guy who wasn't rushing to get to the finale. One that could erotically torment his sub until he or she couldn't be pushed any further. She took his hand. "Must make you a formidable master."

"Hmm, guess you'll find out," he said, pulling her to his side. "Now, let's get you to bed before I make a liar out of myself."

Knowing it was no use protesting further, she followed him to the other side of the cabin and into his room. It was almost a mirror image of Jace's, except that the bed at the center was bigger than any she'd ever seen before and was half covered with file folders and papers. "Holy crap, that thing is huge."

"Always what a guy wants to hear when a woman walks into his bedroom."

She rolled her eyes.

"It's a custom bed meant to serve the polyamorous of the world. You put two big guys and a woman in a king bed, it gets a little tight."

Yeah, she remembered that from the few times she'd slept in Daniel and Marcus's bed. "Do you and Jace usually sleep all together with the woman you're sharing?"

"No, we use this bed for play, then Jace goes to his own room for the night." He stepped around the bed and started gathering all the paperwork he'd apparently been working on when he'd gone out to get that glass of water. "Once we're outside of a scene, Jace usually likes to be alone. Plus I'm not sure he's totally comfortable with the idea of sleeping naked with his roommate. Like I said earlier, sex and sleeping together are two totally different things."

She frowned. Jace seemed like the most sexually open person she'd ever met. It seemed odd he'd be uncomfortable about that. But it wasn't her business.

Andre grabbed the stack of papers he'd gathered and walked toward the desk in the opposite corner of the room. "Let me get all of this out of the way. I was trying to get some work done since I couldn't sleep."

"Working on a day off?"

He shrugged. "I'm trying to make detective. There are a few people competing for the position. I'm one of the younger ones. Figure I can't out-experience some of them, but I can damn sure outwork them."

He put his hand out to her. "Come on, gorgeous. Let's get you into bed. It's late."

She smiled and let him lead her by the hand to the bed. Andre peeled back the comforter and patted the mattress. She climbed beneath the covers. "You know, I don't think I've been tucked into bed since I was a little girl."

He laid the blanket over her and placed a light kiss on her lips, the latter sending warmth to the best places. His gaze softened. "I feel privileged to be the one to break the dry spell then."

Oh, he and Jace were breaking her dry spell all right.

"Good night, *bella*. Get some rest." He leaned over to click off the bedside lamp.

"Wait."

He paused, his fingers on the switch, looking over at her.

She was going to tell him to leave it on because of her fear, but something else sprung to her lips instead. "Stay."

"What?"

She pushed the comforter back down. This was ridiculous. She spent enough nights alone. Screw that. This was supposed to be her fantasy weekend. And she had no history and mixed-up feelings to worry about with Andre. She just liked him, plain and simple. Enjoyed talking to him, and well, touching him wasn't so bad either. "Stay with me?"

He eyed the bed a bit warily. "Evan, I'll be fine. The couch won't kill me."

"It's not about that. I'm just—" She looked away quickly, biting her lip. What in the hell was wrong with her? She'd almost slipped up and told him she was tired of sleeping alone. "I mean, I was thinking before we jump into the whole ménage thing, this might help me get more comfortable with you, be less nervous."

He arched an eyebrow. "Just how comfortable are we talking? Because I pride myself on self-control, but I'm not dead."

She laughed and raised her hand, remembering his Boy Scout reference from a few weeks before. "Scout's honor. We'll just sleep. I won't even run my tongue along your nipple rings and tug them with my teeth, even though I really, really want to."

He shook his head then peeled off his shirt. "We better be careful around you, *bella*. We may have met our match."

He clicked off the lamp, bathing the room in moonlight, and climbed into bed. Without saying another word, he stretched out behind her and gathered her against him, as if they were lovers who had slept this way for years. She couldn't prevent the little sigh that passed her lips as his arms and heat enveloped her.

It was lovely and sexy and comforting.

Almost perfect.

The only other thing that would make it better would be to have a certain blond stretched out against her other side.

And *that* realization scared her more than anything had in a long, long time.

FOURTEEN

Jace stomped out of the bedroom, squinting through the bright morning light filling the living room. He'd woken up cold, alone, and pissed. Pissed that Evan wasn't in bed next to him and really pissed that he cared.

He should've never given in to his need to claim her last night. She'd responded so well under his hand, thrived beneath the dominance like a daisy in sunshine. The rush he'd gotten from her reactions had left him reeling. So much so that he'd gone and dropped his guard without realizing it. He had joked around with her like he used to, had even wanted her to share his bed overnight, which was something he never did with anyone. He'd let himself *feel* something for her, goddammit.

Which is exactly why last night could never happen again. Even if the mere thought of having Evan all to himself for another round had his dick stiffening in his pajama pants. The only way he was touching her again was if Andre was there, too. End of story.

He glanced around the living room, his gaze landing on the couch, a pillow and blanket spread out on it. *Oh, hell no.* If Evan had slept on that hard sofa instead of waking him and admitting she wasn't cool with sharing a bed, he was going to spank her ass. He'd told her he would take care of her this weekend. Why wouldn't she let him?

But if she had slept out here, where the hell was she? He looked around the room again and noticed an abandoned glass of water on the dining room table.

Ah, fuck.

The answer hit him like a knee to the groin. He knew exactly where she was.

And he should be damn happy about it, but instead he had to breathe through a wave of anger he had no right to have. He'd set this up. Talked to Andre himself last night. Rolled out the goddamned red carpet. This is what needed to happen, right?

Unable to stop himself from confirming his suspicions, he crossed to the other side of the cabin until he was standing in front of Andre's door. He probably should knock.

No, screw that. He needed to see the unedited version and get it through his thick skull that he had no claim to Evan. And she owed him no loyalty either. Gritting his teeth, he turned the knob and pushed open the door.

What lay inside wasn't unexpected, but twisted him up just the same. The comforter was in a tangle, exposing Andre and Evan, both half-dressed and sound asleep. Evan's shirt had ridden up, and Andre had a hand splayed possessively over her bare belly.

He blew out a breath.

So they'd fucked. Without him.

And then Evan had chosen to curl up with Andre for the night— a stranger to her—instead of with him. Well that was just fucking fine. Perfect.

Andre was the one who was better at the romantic, cuddling shit with women anyway. Shouldn't Jace just leave him to it? Mr. Suave had probably murmured sweet words to Evan after they'd had sex. Told her how beautiful she was, how happy he was to be next to her. Kissed away her fear of the dark.

Bitterness burned at the back of Jace's throat.

Whatever.

He resisted the inclination to slam the door and clicked it shut instead. So, problem solved. Let the two of them screw until the sun went down if they wanted. Because each time Jace knew Evan was with someone else, it would help him put another stone back into the foundation she'd rocked by stepping back into his life. Would remind him of what this was. And what it most definitely was not.

He made his way back to the kitchen and put on the coffee, planning to drink a cup on the back deck so he wouldn't have to hear it if Evan and Andre did decide to have a little pre-breakfast action.

But before the coffee finished percolating, Andre shuffled into the kitchen, sniffing the air. "*Mmm*, coffee. Thanks, bro. I'll take one sugar. And how 'bout some pancakes, too? I like mine in Mickey Mouse shapes."

Jace shot him a deadly glare and shoved past him to grab mugs from the cabinet.

Andre smirked as he leaned against the counter. "What crawled up your ass?"

Jace grunted and turned his back to him to pour himself a cup, trying to get a hold on the jealousy, the anger, the frustration that he was feeling either of those things in the first place. "I'm fine. Just need some caffeine."

"You and me both." Andre pushed up from the counter as soon as Jace moved away from the coffeepot so he could get his own fix. "I barely slept last night."

Jace's teeth clenched, but he forced himself to look unaffected. None of this was Andre's fault. The guy had only done what the two of them always did—shared a woman without concerns about jealousy. Jace kept his tone relaxed. "Yeah, well, tough to sleep when you're too busy screwing."

Andre turned around and sipped his coffee. "No kidding, she's got some stamina, that one. Man, so fucking hot. The way she—"

Red clouded Jace's vision as fuming heat flooded his system. He slammed his cup down on the counter. "I don't need a goddamned play-by-play, asshole."

Andre smirked. "Yeah, that's what I thought."

The smug tone made Jace's fists curl. He'd never punched a friend, but there was a first time for everything.

Andre nodded in his direction. "You can stop plotting my murder. I'm just proving a point."

Jace barely heard him over the angry buzzing in his brain. "What the hell are you talking about?"

He shrugged. "I didn't do anything with Evan—well, besides kissing her. She was reluctant to go further without talking to you first, and I wasn't going to go down that road if she didn't feel ready."

"Oh."

Oh. Jace's chest shouldn't have puffed up, shouldn't have filled with a rush of relief and . . . satisfaction. He couldn't stop the idiotic smile that crept to his lips, so he tried to cover it by picking up his mug again and taking a swig of scalding coffee.

"Un-fucking-believable," Andre said, shaking his head. "Don't do this, man. Not with her."

Jace opened his mouth to ask him what that was supposed to mean, but Andre raised a hand to halt him.

"Look, I'm not blind, okay? You're broadcasting 'mine' vibes with a damn bullhorn. This girl means something to you. I get it. And it's good to see you still have that in you. But this is not the girl to do that with. No matter what happens this weekend, you need to remember she's not yours, mine, or ours."

Jace made a dismissive snort, even though Andre's words dug right beneath his skin. "I'm well aware of who she belongs to."

"Uh-huh." Andre gave him a narrow look and then walked around the island to slide onto a barstool on the other side. "That's why you're all of a sudden looking at me like I'm the enemy?"

Jace blew out a long breath, realizing that trying to bullshit Andre was like trying to punk the CIA. "Look, I'll be fine, all right. I just need to get back to what we do best. No more one-on-one."

"That's the smartest thing you've said since we got here. Now just don't try to tackle me the first time I touch her. Because I *am* going to touch her, Jace. She may have developed some sense of loyalty to you, but you're not the only one she's attracted to."

The smooth assurance in Andre's voice had Jace's jaw tightening again, but he gave him a quick nod. "I'm—"

"Please tell me that's coffee I smell," said a hoarse voice, halting further conversation.

Both of them turned to see Evan pad barefoot into the kitchen, looking rumpled and oh so tempting in Jace's shirt.

Jace handed her a mug, determined to prove to Andre—and himself—that he could move past whatever had come over him and make this simply another fun, relaxing weekend with a hot woman. "Good morning, sunshine. Sounds like you swallowed a mouthful of gravel."

She took the cup from him and pushed up on her tiptoes, surprising him with a soft kiss, then a saucy smile. "I swallowed something for sure."

Andre chuckled. "Ten seconds."

Both Jace and Evan turned toward him. She lifted a brow. "What's that?"

"The amount of time you need to be in the room before all my blood rushes south."

She laughed, an open and unashamed sound that did indeed make Jace's cock begin to stiffen. Yesterday, Evan had been unsure, cautious, but now the vixen he'd gotten a glimpse of in his room last night was emerging. They were making her feel safe—free to be herself. The transformation gave Jace some weird twinge of pride.

She looked up at him, those blue eyes and her palm against his bare chest making him forget his train of thought. "I want to kiss Andre, too. You okay with that?"

Choking back the *fuck no* that first jumped to his lips was like swallowing broken glass, but he covered it with a casual shrug. "Why wouldn't I be?"

Some unreadable expression flickered over her features, but then she mirrored his shrug. "No reason. I guess I'm still figuring out the protocol of this whole thing."

He smirked. "I appreciate your diligence, babe, but I already told you I don't care what you do with Andre—kiss, fuck. Him. Me. Both of us at the same time. That's the beauty of ménage. We're all just here to have a good time."

The words weren't charming, but he had to say something to put all this shit back into perspective. Remind everyone, including himself, why they were doing this.

Her lips pressed together, a little crease forming between her brows. "I'm just trying to wrap my head around the no-jealousy thing."

"You're not dating either of us. Can't get jealous over someone who isn't yours in the first place." He nodded at Andre, though it took everything he had to do so. "Go ahead, I think he's been patient enough."

She turned her head to Andre, and he gave her a disarming smile. "I can be as patient as you need me to be, *bella*. I have no doubt you'll be worth the wait."

Jace grunted. *Silver-tongued bastard.* Jace was no slouch in the flirting department, but somehow Andre always knew the right thing to say to make girls go all gooey.

Evan handed Jace her coffee mug, effectively dismissing him, and crossed over to the island. He had the impulse to grab her arm, stop her, kiss her until she couldn't remember her own name, much less Andre's. But instead he kept his hands locked around her cup, gripping it until his knuckles turned white.

She leaned over the counter toward Andre, exposing her little black panties and luscious ass to Jace, probably purposely taunting him after his I-could-give-a-shit-if-you-kiss-him speech. Jace tried to look away, but couldn't help himself from watching.

Andre's gaze met his briefly, as if challenging Jace to stop him, but Jace wasn't going to make any move to prevent it. This is what needed to happen. Andre gave a satisfied smile, then hooked a finger in Evan's collar and captured her lips in a heated kiss.

Jace braced himself against the edge of the counter as the wave of possessiveness enveloped him. The deepest, most primal part of him wanted to lash out, to rip her away from Andre. But as Evan sank into the kiss and the raw need between the two of them became more and more apparent, Jace's fiery anger turned into some other emotion—one it took him a second to identify.

Guilt? Where the hell had that come from? What did he have to feel guilty about?

Then it hit him.

Evan deserved to be happy.

He'd seen how sad she'd looked on that beach in South Padre, how lost she'd seemed. And God knows she'd had it rough as hell as a teenager. Now that same person was in front of him— lighthearted, turned on, enjoying her time with him—and though he hated to admit it, with Andre. She'd come here for a fantasy weekend, an escape from her normal life, not to be caught up in whatever mixed-up crap Jace was feeling toward her.

There. He'd admitted it. There were residual feelings from the past that seeing her again had stirred up. So what. Didn't change a damn thing.

He needed to get it through his head that this weekend was about her. Not him. Not Andre. And certainly not about some pissing contest over which guy she wanted more. Especially when the guy she actually wanted was in some house in Dallas planning his upcoming TV show. Evan was only there for a few days, and Jace was wasting time acting like some insecure teenager. *Stupid.*

No more. She came to them with a purpose, and he was going to make damn sure she accomplished her goal. Whatever fantasy she had tucked away in that pretty head of hers, he wanted to give to her. If sharing her with Andre was one of them, then so be it. Jace could tamp down the useless jealousy and lock it away. Hell, he'd locked away worse.

And God knows he enjoyed seeing her come apart with pleasure—what did it matter if there was an extra set of hands bringing her there?

In fact, he knew how much more sexually intense things could get with someone as responsive as Evan if Andre were added to the mix. It's why Jace preferred ménage in the first place. Some levels could only be reached with a third person involved. And man, if that's where Evan sought to go, he wanted to be the one to take her there. Wanted to watch her give herself over completely to sensation, to submission.

Visions of Evan in the throes of passion assailed him—both he and Andre pushing her further and further, her blue eyes going hazy with bliss, her lips parted in a silent plea . . .

A jolt of desire sliced through his tangle of emotions, dimming everything except the need to see Evan let go again. He wanted to fall to his knees with relief. *Thank God.* Finally a reaction that made sense! *This* he could work with. Screw all the rest of it. He'd shove the other stuff down and grab on to the desire.

Jace set the cup down, his palms suddenly hotter than the coffee inside it, and moved a step closer to Evan, making himself focus on what the kiss was doing for her rather than worrying that it wasn't him on the other end of it.

Andre continued to work her over, the good-morning greeting morphing into a lust so palpable Jace could taste it in the air. His cock stirred to awareness, thickening at the erotic sight. Evan had one hand threaded in Andre's hair, but the other one was gripping the edge of the island as if it were the only thing holding her back from climbing across the counter to get closer. He half wished she'd just let go and hop up there. He couldn't think of anything better for breakfast than Evan sprawled out on that island like a hedonistic buffet.

A little mewl of pleasure escaped her, and Jace tamped down the remaining whispers of hesitation. He stepped up behind her, nestling his growing erection against her backside and sliding his hand onto her abdomen. She tensed in surprise, then softened, not breaking the kiss but melting against him. God, she felt good. Pliable. Trusting. Totally fucking into it.

He moved his hand lower, teasing at the band of her underwear, stroking her bare skin. She rocked against him, fitting the cleft of her ass against his cock. He groaned at the friction and kissed the back of her neck, inhaling the scent of both her apple shampoo and Andre's lingering cologne. "*Hmm*, seems like you want more than coffee this morning, sunshine."

She eased away from the kiss and untangled her fingers from Andre's hair, her movements as languid as a sleepy cat. She peered over her shoulder at him, a wicked glint in her eyes. "I never want *anything* more than coffee."

The halt in action had his body protesting, but he couldn't help but chuckle. "You're a vicious tease, you know that?"

"I've been called worse."

He gave her ass a playful swat, enjoying the flash of lust the move incited from her. "Go ahead. You can have your caffeine. We have all day to taint you with our lecherous demands."

She spun to face him and smiled, her lips tantalizingly swollen from Andre's kiss. "Guess I better make a fortifying breakfast for all of us then."

"Now hold on, *bella*," Andre said, settling back onto his stool, his movements a little jerky, no doubt from a monster hard-on. "Just because you're the submissive in this arrangement, doesn't mean you're the kitchen bitch, too. We've been bachelors a long time. We know how to put a meal on the table."

She moved around Jace and headed for the fridge. "Oh, hush, I'm not offering because I'm your slave or whatever. I'm offering because I enjoy cooking." She stuck her head in the refrigerator and her voice became muffled. "Plus, I've had bachelor fare. I'll pass."

Jace sniffed. "Hey, Andre can make some mean *chilaquiles*. And I can . . . Well, I kick ass at making toast and coffee."

She emerged from the fridge and set her treasures next to the stove. "Have a seat, Iron Chef. I got this."

"Our sub is kind of bossy, Andre," he said as he slid on the stool next to his friend, trying to ease the earlier tension between them.

Andre smirked. "Yeah, but if it involves me getting to watch her flit around the kitchen half-naked, cooking something better than burnt toast, I'm all for it."

"Good point."

Jace watched her as she moved with efficient grace from one task to the other. Breaking eggs, lining up bacon in the pan, stirring a pot of grits, tasting a bit on the tip of her finger before tossing salt into the pot. She was beautiful. And more at ease than he'd ever seen her. Like she felt right at home with them, casually cooking breakfast and teasing them with the easy sway of her hips.

Andre set his elbows on the island, apparently as fascinated by the scene as he was. "So what do you like about cooking?"

She shrugged, keeping her back to them and stirring the grits. "I remember my mom cooking for me. Never anything fancy, but all really good, comforting stuff. Baked macaroni and cheese. Chicken and dumplings. She worked overnight shifts, so she always made sure I had something good to eat before she left for work. I looked forward to that time every day. Watching her prepare everything and having her listen to my chatter."

She paused as if lost in thought, her spoon still. Jace frowned, knowing the story wouldn't end well.

"She died right before I turned seven. And pretty much everything in my life, including those home-cooked meals, stopped." She started stirring again. "So I figured when I got older, I would learn how to do it. Make the people around me feel as well taken care of as I did back then."

The thought of everything warm and comforting in her life disappearing when she was still so young made Jace's chest ache, made his own family drama seem ridiculously petty in comparison. He'd never gotten the full story from her, but his parents had told him Evan's background when she'd come to live with them. Her mother had been killed on her way home from work by a drunk driver, and her father had completely fallen apart after her death. He'd spiraled into depression during the years following, had neglected Evan completely, and had eventually taken his own life, leaving his daughter with no one in the world.

Jace shifted on the stool, searching for what to say. He wanted to pull Evan onto his lap, tell her he was sorry she had to go through that, that no kid should have to experience such tragedy. But he knew she'd resist any attempts at sympathy from them and would see it as pity. He was surprised enough that she'd even shared the story about her mother. When he'd last known her, all discussions about her past had been strictly off limits.

He cleared his throat. "Well, we're honored that you deem us worthy of taking care of this morning."

She glanced at him over her shoulder, giving him a thank-you-for-not-pushing smile. "No worries. I don't get to do this too much lately with all the travel we've been doing. Plus, Daniel's more of a restaurant guy than an eat-at-home person, so it's nice to get back to it."

Just the mention of her fiancé's name set Jace's teeth on edge, but he refused to let his opinion show on his face. Dr. Dan was sounding more and more like an idiot every second. Obviously the man wasn't satisfying Evan's sexual needs. And apparently he wasn't appreciative of her nurturing side. What the fuck did she see in the guy?

Money? Fame?

He didn't picture Evan as the trophy wife type, but what did he know. He hadn't pegged his ex-wife for that either, and it had turned out to be her life's mission. Maybe growing up like Evan had made those things too tempting to pass up.

Andre drummed his fingers against the counter, and Jace could feel his friend's agitation. Uh-oh. Something was on Andre's mind, and he wasn't one to hold his tongue. Jace shot him a warning look, but Andre's mouth was already opening. "I know it's not my business, but do you really love this guy, Evan? It seems like you two don't have a lot in common."

Jace kicked Andre under the counter, giving him a what-the-fuck look.

Evan stiffened, and Jace wished he could see her face. A few seconds passed before she answered. "You're right, it's none of your business. But yes, I do."

Andre frowned. "Shit, I'm sorry. That was out of line. Sometimes my mouth opens before the filters get involved."

She shrugged. "Don't worry about it. Now you just owe me an answer to a wildly personal question of my choice later on."

"Uh-oh. Why don't we just forget I said anything?"

"Not a chance."

Silence fell between the three of them while she finished cooking, and Jace worried that Andre had pushed Evan back into her shell with that ridiculous question. But when she divvied out portions onto plates and turned around, her easy smile had returned. She set a plate down in front of each of them and rolled her eyes as she took in their expressions. "Relax, guys. I'm not going to run out the door because you asked me a question. I'd just rather not discuss my relationship while I'm here."

That made two of them. Jace would rather forget Dr. Dan existed at all, at least for the weekend. "We promise not to tread there again, Ev."

"It's fine. Now eat before it gets cold." She pointed at their plates, and they both obliged her. She joined in, taking a few bites from her own plate as she studied the two of them. Her gaze turned serious. "Listen, I know this is an odd situation, and I'm still figuring things out as I go along here. But I want you both to know that when I'm with you, I'm fully with you. I'm not thinking of anyone else or anything outside of here. Okay?"

Her declaration had Jace wanting to be *with her* again right at that moment, but he forked a bite of scrambled egg instead. If he jumped her every time he had the urge too, they'd never make it through a meal. "Same here, babe. You're our sole focus this weekend."

"Our obsession, really," Andre added, his expression comically solemn. "I doubt either of us could even conjure up the image of another woman if we tried."

She laughed and pointed the piece of bacon she'd lifted off her plate at him. "You're only obsessed because you're the one who hasn't gotten laid in the last twelve hours."

Andre looked her up and down with unabashed appreciation. "Don't sell yourself short, *mamacita*. Me wanting you has nothing to do with a few hours of deprivation. If it were only about a stiff dick, I could've gone back to the main house last night."

Her nipples became noticeable points beneath her shirt—
Andre's words as good as a pinch—and Jace's mouth went dry.
Andre leaned forward on his elbows and peered into her mug.
"Well, would you look at that? Seems you're all done with that
coffee."

Evan licked her lips, obviously registering Andre's meaning. She
peeked over at Jace, checking in with him, giving him the reins
whether she realized what she was doing or not. The rush of power
it gave him was like a needle full of adrenaline. She was stunning
regardless, but when she slipped into the sub role, it tore the air
right from his lungs. He didn't deserve the gift, didn't deserve that
level of submission or loyalty from her. But hell if he was going to
turn it down right now.

He shoved his plate aside. "I think you're done with breakfast, pet."

"Seems so, sir." The corner of her mouth quirked up, but Jace
also sensed nervous energy rolling off her.

Nice. He liked her a little on edge. It would only make things
better for all involved. He opened his mouth to give her the next
command, but Andre's hand landed on his shoulder, stopping him.
"Let me top her this time, J."

Jace choked back the groan of frustration before it made its way
out. Leave it to Andre to immediately push him right to the limit.
Andre rarely asked to be the lead dom in a ménage, so Jace had a
feeling this was more about their conversation this morning than
anything else. Knowing Andre, he'd probably relegate Jace to a
watch-but-don't-touch role just to prove a point.

Jace glanced at Evan, who was observing their exchange intently, and reminded himself that this weekend was about her. He
loosened his fists, which had automatically clenched. "No problem.
Evan agreed to be submissive to both of us, so go ahead."

He said the words with what he hoped was a relaxed tone, even though it was going to be a tortuous test of will to watch Andre dominate her and not be the one controlling the situation. He could do this. He wanted Evan to have the experience of being shared—of knowing what it was like to pleasure and be pleasured by two very different men.

And despite the possessiveness he'd been wrangling with, he knew he could trust Andre with Evan. The guy could piss him off, but he was also one of his best friends and would never do anything out of line. Andre's restraint with Evan up until this point had proven that.

Plus, Jace knew if he could focus on the right things, seeing Evan submit to Andre would turn him on. Beyond the sheer forbidden aspect of watching two people fuck, Andre's method of dominance brought out a different side of a woman than Jace's more in-your-face style. The guy turned it into an art form and it was sexy as hell to watch a girl get worked over by him.

Many women suspected Andre's smoother approach would make him an easier master. But Jace knew better. Andre was velvet-gloved seduction, but he also was filled with unnatural amounts of patience. He'd seen some of the toughest subs break down into desperate tears, outright begging for release by the end of a session with Andre.

Of course, Andre never denied a woman that reward. He just didn't rush to get there.

Though based on the hooded gaze Andre shot Evan, Jace wondered if she had even managed to drive Mr. Slow Hands to his breaking point. Every man had his limits.

Jace just hoped that Evan wouldn't push him past his own.

Andre knew it was killing Jace to not be in charge right now, but he was doing it this way for the guy's own good. Hopefully, this would force Jace to get a grip. Because whether Jace wanted to admit it or not, he looked at Evan differently than he had any other woman Andre had ever seen him with.

And nobody wanted to see Jace open up his heart again more than Andre did. He'd watched Jace's bitch of an ex-wife break down a man who'd had such a hopeful, idealistic spirit and turn him into the guarded soul Jace was now. But Evan couldn't be the one. When Andre had asked her the question about her fiancé, he could feel her honesty in her answer. She was already in love with someone else. Getting attached to her wasn't an option.

The knowledge pained Andre as well. He hadn't done more than kiss Evan and already he was feeling an undeniable draw toward her. There was something about her that tugged at him, made him want to know everything about her life. What made her laugh. What made her toss and turn so much at night. Why she loved some guy who didn't seem to fit her at all.

But it wasn't his right to delve into those areas. He had to be content with the here and now, focus on the physical. It was something he was used to doing. Hell, he'd kept his feelings hidden from Jace well enough all these years. He certainly should be able to keep emotion out of things for a weekend.

Andre turned to Evan, the stark anticipation in her pale blue eyes drawing all his thoughts back to where they should be. He crooked a finger at her. "Come here, *bella*. I want to feel that beautiful body of yours next to mine."

Her teeth tugged at her bottom lip, but after a second's hesitation, she moved around the island and slipped between his and Jace's chairs. Jace swiveled on his stool, bracketing Evan from behind with his spread knees, but not touching her. Evan's eyes widened a bit, the awareness that she was caged between two men obviously not lost on her. Good.

Andre tucked a lock of her dark hair behind her ear, then cupped her jaw. "Any more doubts? If so, you need to tell me now."

She shook her head, her cheeks coloring. But there was humor in her expression. "No, I'm officially a hussy who wants two men."

Jace chuckled behind her. "Doesn't make you a hussy, pet. Just makes you awesome."

"Makes you perfect, actually." Andre ran a thumb along her moistened bottom lip, and her entire body shuddered, causing her pert nipples to strain against the thin material of the dress shirt. Man, he loved that—loved that a simple look or brush of skin could rouse her. He hoped to get the chance to explore that gift to its fullest. Bring her to the edge with the slightest of touches, warm breaths, and sensual suggestion. Have her half out of her mind with desire before he even allowed himself the pleasure of being inside her.

Imagining all the possibilities had his dick throbbing, and he closed his eyes briefly to reel himself in. He prided himself on his patience, but the repeated erotic overload with no release was taking its toll. If he didn't stop weaving fantasies about all the ways he wanted to be with Evan he was going to shoot off like an excited teenager before he even got her naked.

When he opened his eyes again, Evan was watching him, a shy smile teasing at her lips. "I'd love to know what you're thinking, sir."

"How 'bout I show you instead." He leaned forward, unable to resist sampling her mouth for another second. She let out a little sigh as her lips parted, accepting his kiss and then matching his pace when he dialed up the intensity. The earlier kiss had been a test of his restraint, but now he had no more reason to hold back. Right now he was going to indulge in what he'd wanted since the moment he laid eyes on her in that hotel lobby.

He moved his lips to her neck and blazed a trail of open-mouth kisses down her throat and sternum, savoring her flavor. *Mmm.* Like salted caramel—sweet femininity mixed with earthy arousal. He nuzzled her breast, eliciting a shiver from her, then claimed her nipple through the thin shirt, sucking and teasing until the cotton turned translucent. She let out a soft moan and arched backward, leaning into Jace's arms for support.

Andre glanced upward to catch Jace staring down at the scene, green eyes swirling with hunger. Andre's own desire jumped up a notch as he met his friend's gaze. *These* were the moments that kept Andre going. The times when the barriers of friendship and sexuality fell away and he got to indulge in both a beautiful woman and his best friend without worry. Nothing else ever gave him the same feeling of freedom. And he couldn't deny that having Evan between them added a sense of rightness that he hadn't felt before.

"She's beautiful, isn't she?" Jace asked.

"So beautiful." Andre brought his full focus back to Evan's sweet, yielding flesh and tugged at the open collar of her shirt. "I barely slept last night thinking about how good you felt against me. Don't make me wait another second to see you naked."

Her hands lifted to her top button, but Jace grasped her wrists and pulled them back. "Allow me, pet. It'd be my pleasure to undress you . . . for Andre."

Andre could tell those last two words were difficult for Jace to add. Damn. Never before had he seen the guy struggle so much with sharing. Jace thrived on ménage—it was part of who he was, his sexual makeup.

Guilt niggled at Andre. Maybe forcing Jace to play second with Evan was a bit cruel, but there was no going back now. It was for everyone's own good. He couldn't stand by and watch Jace fall for the wrong girl again. He hadn't stepped in when he'd suspected Diana was more manipulator than submissive to Jace. He'd thought his own mixed-up feelings for his friend had clouded his judgment. But then Diana had crushed Jace in a way that Andre had feared could never be repaired.

He wouldn't stand by again—even if Evan's effect on Jace was unintentional—and watch Jace get hurt. Andre would do whatever it took to protect Jace from himself.

"Are you okay with me undressing her?" Jace asked, his voice tight.

Evan looked at Andre, her pupils dilated and her face flushed with heat.

He nodded. "Yes, please do."

Jace lowered Evan's arms to her sides and then reached around her to start unbuttoning the shirt from behind. He worked from the top down, each unfastened button revealing another tempting expanse of smooth ivory skin. And even though Andre had seen her naked the night before, he found himself holding his breath as he waited to see all of her again, knowing that this time he wasn't restricted to keeping his hands to himself.

Evan's eyes became all-consuming as her gaze drifted down his face, to his torso, and finally down to his boxer briefs. He had to suppress his own shiver. Man, she knew how to make a guy feel wanted. For a moment, it was as if she was the dom and he the sub, sitting there waiting for the next command. Her heated perusal was as effective as a tangible stroke against his skin, causing his erection to press so hard against the elastic of his underwear, he worried his blood supply was going to be cut off.

"*Bella*, I don't know what I did in my former life to deserve this. But I must've been a very good boy."

Jace laid a kiss on the back curve of her neck. "And I must've been canonized a saint."

She grinned. "Just so you know, flattery will get y'all every-where."

Andre arched an eyebrow at her. "Everywhere, huh?"

Jace reached the last button and slid the shirt from her shoulders, allowing it to fall to the floor. Andre took his time enjoying the mouth-watering view and the way the flush on her face worked its way down her body, chasing his gaze. She ducked her head in deference, but a wicked little smile touched the edge of her mouth, letting him know she enjoyed him looking at her like this. He shook his head. So sweetly submissive, but so damn spunky all at the same time.

He was starting to understand what Jace was going through. Evan had something about her that got to Andre on more than just a sexual level. Lord, how was he going to be satisfied with just having this one weekend with her? There were too many layers he wouldn't get a chance to explore, too many avenues he and Jace wouldn't get to take her down.

However, now wasn't the time to worry about those things. Not when she was looking so sinfully gorgeous and aroused. Her pert nipples were tight and moist from his earlier treatment, and he was tempted to pay homage to those again. But as his eyes tracked lower, other things climbed higher on the list. The soaked state of her black satin panties for starters.

Boy, she'd probably go off like a rocket with the simplest of strokes.

Too bad he wasn't going to make it that easy.

FIFTEEN

Evan's heart was pumping so fiercely, she had no doubt Andre could see her carotid jumping beneath her skin. But despite her nerves, she wouldn't have chosen to be anywhere else than standing between these two men—even if she did sense a bit of a weird vibe between them this morning.

Andre cupped her face in his large hands, the chocolate color of his eyes almost hypnotic. "*Bella*, I plan to make you feel very, very good, but you will not come before I say so. There will be consequences if you do."

"Yes, sir." In that moment, with his smoky tone and the way he was looking at her, she may have agreed to anything.

She was tempted to pinch herself to double-check that she was awake. She'd always had a rich imagination—the fantasies she could conjure up while pleasuring herself were dirty enough to shame a hooker. But the reality of being surrounded by these two powerful men was blowing all those previous daydreams out of the water. And boy, was she happy she hadn't bailed after things got too comfortable last night.

She'd tossed and turned in bed all night, torn on what to do, but then Andre had pulled her close and whispered, "Let that busy mind rest. I've got you."

After that, Evan had fallen into a sound, contented sleep. She'd also awakened with renewed resolve to enjoy herself this weekend and to stop focusing on how being around the guys was affecting her. So she had a little affection blooming for Jace and Andre. Who cared? It was a natural reaction to sharing some hot moments and a bit of intimacy for the first time in a long while. It wasn't real, but was just another piece of the fantasy that would go away when she returned to reality on Monday.

And until that reality returned, she was going to be fully present with these two men. Not that she could think of much else right now even if she'd tried.

Andre peeled off his shirt, which nearly sent her into full-scale panting mode, and Jace crowded behind her, all warm breath and body heat lapping against her skin. Neither was touching her, and that alone had her body ready to go mad with anticipation. Moisture coated her sex, and the deep throbbing that had begun the moment she'd entered the kitchen this morning turned downright unbearable. She flexed her fingers, fighting the desire to reach out and grab one of the guys and take over.

She could be patient. After all, neither of the guys looked like they planned to wait long, not with the beautifully full erections that graced the front of Andre's boxer briefs and Jace's pajama pants.

Andre tossed his shirt to the side. "Take off your panties for me. I want to see all of you."

Andre's voice glided over her like thick cream, causing another rush of liquid heat to find its way to her pussy. She was sure the moment she took off her underwear, the evidence of her arousal would track down her thighs. How she could be so desperately aroused after her rocking night the previous evening was a wonder.

Usually a good orgasm could keep her satisfied for days, but now it was as if the more she got the more she needed, like crack or chocolate-chip cookies.

She hooked her fingers in the waistband of her panties and slid them down her legs, enjoying the tickle of cool air against her hot skin.

When she returned to a full stand again, she found Andre staring with hungry interest at her newly bared flesh. "Look how sexy and wet you are for us already. I bet you taste as sweet as you look."

"Better," Jace said, his voice soft and sexy against her ear.

Andre slid off his stool and crouched down, laying a hand on her hip and bringing his face to within inches of her. He nuzzled the spot where leg met pubic bone, inhaling deeply, then ran his tongue along her inner thigh.

Oh, Jesus. She tensed and grabbed his shoulder for support, fearing her knees would give out beneath her.

Warm hands palmed her waist and steadied her. Jace. "You can lean into me, pet. Let him taste you."

She relaxed against Jace and focused on simply feeling all the sensations. Andre's touch roamed over her legs, and his tongue traced the edges of her vee—so close to her aching clit, but never actually touching it. She automatically widened her stance, silently asking for more, for some kind of relief. But instead of obliging, he drew the tip of his tongue along her outer folds, making her arch in his direction. Jace held her firm, not allowing her to place Andre's mouth where she most needed it.

"What's wrong, gorgeous?" Andre asked, his tone teasing.

"You're killing me." She let her head tilt back, and Jace took the opportunity to move his hands upward, finding her nipples and giving them a firm pinch. A deep groan escaped her. "Both of you. Absolutely killing me."

Andre chuckled. "I promise no one has ever died from this. I like to take my time to explore." He flicked his tongue against her clit—one sharp, teasing stroke that had her ready to beg. "How else will I figure out what makes you writhe, what makes you get this hot and wet?"

He moved his hands up her outer thighs, tracking higher until his palms found her ass. His fingertips teased along the cleft. She quivered at the memory of Jace's fingers inside her the night before. Her nails dug into Andre's shoulders.

"*Mmm*, so you like me touching you here," Andre said, drawing a finger lightly over her back opening. "Have you let anyone have you here before?"

She shook her head.

"But you want to try it," Andre said, more a statement than a question.

A day ago, she would've said no, but after her experience with Jace, the overwhelming sensations he'd drawn out of her, she was more than curious about how it would feel to take it a step further. "Yes."

"She's not ready for both of us yet," Jace growled, his entire body seeming to turn into marble behind her. Andre sat back on his heels, his eyes narrowing as he looked past her to stare at Jace. She didn't turn around, but some silent, not entirely friendly communication seemed to be coursing between them.

When neither said anything, her nerves begin to rise. "Is, uh, everything all right?"

Andre's expression softened as he brought his attention back to her. "It's fine, *bella*. Jace here is just having a hard time letting me top you. It seems you inspire his selfish side. But, I didn't give you permission to ask questions."

She bit her lip. "Sorry."

He drew his finger down the line of her abdomen, then leaned forward and kissed the spot above her mound. "Guess I'll make you both wait a little longer for your pleasure now."

"Seriously?" she asked before she could stop herself.

Those sensual lips of his curled. "You both need to learn better manners. *Bella*, follow me." He stood and took her hand, then shot a pointed look at Jace. "Stay here. I'll deal with you in a second."

Jace would give Andre one more minute before he charged into his bedroom to see what the hell he was doing with Evan. Jace knew he was being an asshole. He'd agreed to play second, and he didn't make agreements he didn't keep. But he was having trouble relinquishing control even though he was trying as hard as hell to be cool with it.

If he was smart, he'd turn around and walk out of the cabin right now. Being around Evan was bringing up dangerous shit inside him. Old feelings he'd thought had been buried deep enough never to resurface. But he couldn't will himself to move.

He scrubbed a hand through his hair and paced. Another minute passed, and Jace was ready to stalk across the house to bang on the bedroom door. But Andre slipped back into the kitchen, his dark eyes flaring, to intercept him. "What the fuck is your deal, man?"

Jace ignored the question. "Where is she?"

Andre folded his arms across his chest in his take-no-shit cop stance. "I left her in the bedroom so we could talk."

"There's nothing to discuss."

"The hell there isn't." Andre stepped closer, crowding Jace against the counter until he was so close, his body heat radiated onto Jace's bare chest. "I can't believe you're doing this. You're fucking falling for her! Falling for *someone else's* woman, Jace. Are you that much of a masochist?"

Jace groaned. "Calm the hell down. I'm not falling for her, okay? I *used* to love her. The possessiveness is just hard to shake."

Andre put a hand on Jace's shoulder and pinned him with his

gaze. "Well, I'm about to help you shake it real fast because if you keep acting like this, I will lock that door and fuck her alone. She doesn't deserve to be caught in the middle of some stupid tug-of-war."

Jace clenched his fists, the thought of being cut out of the picture making him want to break stuff. But he knew Andre was right about it not being fair to Evan. "Whatever."

"I know you don't want that. And neither do I." Andre moved even closer and his hand went to the nape of Jace's neck. The firm grip and his nearness had Jace's heart picking up speed. He sensed some shift in his friend, and the change knocked Jace a bit off balance. The effect wasn't entirely unpleasant. "But since you can't seem to adjust your attitude on your own, the only way I'm letting you in that room with us is if you give me all the power. You need to see that you're nothing special to her. She'll give herself to me just like she did you. She's here for the fantasy. That. Is. All."

Jace's jaw flexed. "I'm already letting you lead."

Andre gave him a smug smile. "No, Jace. *All* the power. I know you had to bottom when you trained, so I'm sure you haven't forgotten how to take an order."

"*What?*" Jace's jaw went slack. "You want me to fucking *sub* for you?"

"I think the only way to get it through your hard head that Evan isn't yours is to give up complete control. To me." With his other hand, he reached down and cupped Jace, smirking when Jace hardened beneath his touch. "Trust that I'll make sure everyone has a good time, and we'll solve this little possessiveness problem you're having in the process."

Despite the shock of the suggestion, Jace shivered with pleasure at the touch, his hands gripping the counter behind him as Andre stroked the length of him through his pants. He had no idea what had come over Andre—they'd never touched like this outside of a

scene, and Andre had certainly never challenged him for dominance, but he could tell the guy was dead serious.

"I don't take orders from anyone," Jace said though gritted
teeth.

"You will from me if you want in that bedroom. Otherwise, you
can stay out here and take care of this hard-on by yourself."

Jace tilted his head back, the simple stimulation doing more to
him than it should. "Screw you, Andre. I'm not here to feed your
let's-humiliate-Jace fantasies."

Andre stepped back—the disgust clear on his face—and his
hand dropped to his side, leaving Jace hard and sweating. "Yeah,
'cause that's what I do, right—humiliate subs?"

Jace cringed. "No, I—"

"You know, one day you're going to figure out that not everyone
is out to tear you down. I'm trying to fucking help you not make
the same mistake again." Andre turned his back to him to head
toward the bedroom. "Enjoy your morning, asshole."

Jace squeezed his eyes shut, trying to get a hold of the funnel
cloud of conflicting emotions and desires whirling through him. He
hadn't meant to insult Andre, but he'd never given control over to
anyone. Even in training, the domme in charge of his submissive
experience had accused him of trying to top her from the bottom.
Anytime someone tried to direct him, he just wanted to lash out.
His father's talent for humiliation had left him with more than just
a bitter taste for authority.

But was he really going to stand by and listen to Andre and
Evan screw while he sat out here like an idiot, nursing his pride?

"Wait."

Andre looked back over his shoulder, his annoyance obvious.
"Talk fast, Austin. I've got a beautiful woman bound and waiting
for me."

"I'll sub for you."

Andre's jaw ticked slightly, but his eyes remained hard. "Try to top me and I'll kick you out."

Jace inhaled a deep breath through his nose, fighting the urge to tell Andre to fuck off. If Jace wanted his problem solved with Evan, this probably was a surefire way of doing it. "Fine."

"Good." Andre's gaze tracked over him like a beast sizing up its prey. "Now give me your wrists and shut your fucking mouth."

SIXTEEN

Evan flexed her wrists against the leather cuffs binding her arms together in front of her, unintentionally jangling the chain that attached the cuffs to a hook in the ceiling. Andre had left her standing there in front of the bed, her legs spread with a metal bar linking her two ankles, and had given her no further instructions.

She had no idea how long they planned to leave her like this, but all she knew was the longer she stood there, the wetter and more desperate she got. Never had she imagined being so deeply attracted to two different men at the same time, but she was discovering all kinds of secrets about herself this weekend. Including the fact that this whole bound and submissive thing was working for her on a number of levels. Time would only tell if all this self-discovery was a good or bad thing. Some switches may have been better left unflipped.

The door squeaked and she looked up, a gasp escaping as soon as she saw the state of the two men. Andre had his hand around the back of Jace's neck, leading him in, and Jace's wrists were bound behind his head, his fingers laced against the back of his scalp. The muscles in Jace's chest and arms were on full display in that position, the tribal-style tattoos on his bicep like rippling works of art. Evan's throat went dry at the beauty of him. "Oh, my God."

Jace's gaze met hers and then roamed down the rest of her body. "I could say the same to you, sunshine."

"What's going on?" she asked.

"Because Jace couldn't play nice this morning, I now have two lovely slaves to play with." He pushed Jace forward. "Now, go ask the lady to take off your pants. Both of you have lost the right to clothes this morning."

Jace looked like he wanted to throw a barb back at Andre, but he clenched his jaw and walked toward her. When he stopped in front of her, his eyes were green fire. "Would you mind getting me naked, please?"

She looked down at her bindings and the spreader bar at her feet. "How am I supposed to do that?"

"You're a bright girl, *bella*. I suggest you get creative," Andre said, crossing his arms over his chest.

Jace raised an eyebrow in challenge. She yanked on the chain attached to the ceiling, making sure she had enough slack, then eased down until she was able to tilt forward and fall to her knees. The planes of Jace's well-honed abdomen were now eye level with her. He stepped a little closer, and she had the urge to lick him from head to foot. Instead, she leaned forward and drew her tongue along the irresistible v-line of his pelvis, tasting salt and a fine sheen of clean sweat.

He shuddered beneath the treatment and his cock, which was already beautifully hard, twitched against his pants. "He didn't say to torture me, pet."

Andre laughed as he stepped up beside them. "No, I didn't, but

I appreciate your initiative. Feel free to taste him anywhere except that cock I know you like so much. Your mouth is mine today. Got it?"

"Yes, sir."

She looked up at Jace and could see the amount of strength it was requiring for him to stay quiet and still, to let Andre be in control. It was obvious being submissive wasn't Jace's natural state, but she also couldn't miss the heat in his gaze and the response of his body. Natural state or not, he was as turned on as she was.

She nuzzled his navel with her cheek before grabbing the waistband of his pants with her teeth and tugging downward. As carefully as she could, she drew his pants down, freeing his erection and leaving him as bare as she was. He stepped out of the puddle of cotton on the floor, and she lifted her head to smile in victory at Andre.

"Nicely done, *bella*. Now back on your feet."

He helped her to get steady again and then pulled on the ceiling chain, drawing out the slack. Her arms rose in response until they were stretched above her head, leaving her spread and on display for the two of them.

Andre laid a hand on Jace's shoulder and pushed. "On your knees, Jace. Help me thank Evan for being such a helpful little sub."

Jace dropped to a kneel, and Andre stepped behind her, his arms wrapping around her hips and his fingers finding her heat. Andre gently spread the lips of her sex with this thumbs, exposing the evidence of exactly how aroused she was to Jace. Wet and swollen and pulsing with need.

Jace leaned forward and placed a soft kiss against her clit. "So, so pretty, pet."

Goose bumps pricked her skin, Jace's rapt attention and the feel of his breath against her skin almost too much to bear. She couldn't remember ever aching for someone so damn much. The way the two guys made her feel—like she was something to be worshipped, like no other woman had existed before this moment—had more than her erogenous zones tightening.

Jace tasted her again with a patience that belied the hungry look in his eyes. Soft and teasing. Like he was savoring each nuance of her. Exploring which lick and nibble would make her tremble.

She panted softly. Even with the carefully measured strokes, his tongue was a lethal weapon against any control she'd been maintaining. He nipped at her clit, and she arched up, the chains rattling loudly above her. "Holy shit."

"Remember, no coming, *bella*." Andre slipped a finger inside her, while Jace continued to coax her into oblivion.

Pleasure, hot and overwhelming, made it near impossible to follow that instruction, but she held on with every ounce of willpower she had. She forced her eyes open so she could take in the erotic image of Jace bound and beautiful at her feet and Andre's tan fingers working against her pale skin.

"You guys are a good team," she said, her voice thick.

Andre nipped at her earlobe. "*Bella*, you have no idea." He shifted his position, letting his finger slip from inside her, and grabbed Jace's chin, halting him. "Enough. You haven't earned the right to make her come."

Jace backed away, though he looked reluctant to do so, and rose to his feet, clearing the way for Andre. But when Andre stepped around her, he didn't face her. Instead, he locked eyes with Jace. "I'm going to unlock your wrists, but if those hands touch anything without permission, including yourself, I will secure you to that wall and make you watch. You got that?"

Jace's muscles flexed in the bindings, as if he were a lion ready to pounce the minute he was freed. But he nodded.

Andre's smile was wry as he stepped forward and unlocked the link securing the two cuffs to each other. Jace lowered his arms and rolled his shoulders, but otherwise remained where he was standing, his focus on Evan.

Andre walked over to the armoire against the wall and unlatched it. When he turned back around he was holding a riding crop. Evan's heartbeat ticked upward. She had enjoyed her little venture into spanking the night before, but this seemed like a whole different zip code. Andre rolled the thin shaft of the crop between his fingers, his attention on her. "Jace said you seem to like a little edge to your pleasure, *bella*. Is that true?"

She wet her lips. "I'm not sure. Maybe?"

Andre's smile was soft. "Let's see if I can turn that *maybe* into a *yes*. You remember your words?"

She took a steadying breath. "Yes, sir."

Andre closed the distance between him and Jace, and with two quick snaps hit Jace's nipples with the riding crop. Jace sucked in a sharp breath and his cock flexed in response.

Andre smiled with satisfaction as he reached down and stroked Jace's length. "See, it's not so bad. Even a big tough dom like Jace knows how sweet a little pain can be."

Jace's gaze darted down to Andre's grip then back to Evan, concern flashing in his eyes. "I, uh, don't know if Evan's into, um, us. We didn't discuss that limit."

Evan barely choked back her own moan at the unashamed contact between the two men. "Please. Don't censor yourselves for me. I could come just watching how hot the two of you look right now."

Jace raised his eyebrows, and Andre gave her a sly grin. "Jace, I think we have a naughty voyeur on our hands."

"I think we have a naughty everything on our hands," Jace said, giving her a smile that damn near melted the marrow from her bones.

"Indeed. Maybe it's time we make use of that." Andre stopped stroking Jace and handed him the riding crop. "You will hit her until she comes. And Evan, you will not come until I give you permission."

She gulped. "Yes, sir."

"And what are you going to do?" Jace asked, his eyes narrowed.

Andre leaned close to Jace's ear, but Evan could hear the resolute words nonetheless. "I'm going to make her fantasy come true."

Her heart seemed to pause midbeat, but Andre was headed her way before she could fully process what she'd heard. He reached out and touched her cheek. "Why the wide eyes, *bella*?"

"I'm a little scared," she admitted.

"Don't be." He pushed her hair away from her face. "Jace and I would never hurt you. We only want to bring you to the place we know you can get to. Can you give us your trust?"

She swallowed hard, focusing on the sincerity swirling in those endless brown eyes. Trust wasn't something she dished out easily. People throughout her life had shown her time and again that it was a gift to be abused, but for some reason she found the answer jumping to her lips. "Yes. I trust you."

"Thank you." The smile he gave her was tender, not at all like the stern face he'd been wearing since he'd slipped into his dominant role. He brushed a thumb across her lips, then leaned down and tasted her mouth in a sensual kiss, one that made her toes curl into the area rug. Gentle but demanding, Andre drew her out of her busy mind and into another place where her thoughts came slow like honey.

Soon, a second set of hands touched her hair, her nape, and then lips were on her neck. *Jace.* The soothing comfort of having him there behind her added to the dreamlike buzz overtaking her senses. She wanted to dissolve into a puddle between them. Her limbs went liquid and the energy around them seemed to shift. This was supposed to be exciting, edgy, fun. That's what ménage was about. But being between the two of them suddenly didn't feel as scandalous as it did *right*. Warmth was spreading not just between her legs but deep in her chest.

She had never really imagined what it would be like to be the recipient of so much attention. Hell, she'd spent much of her life cutting her own skin just to prove to herself that she wasn't, in fact, invisible to everyone. But this amount of focus and affection was almost too much for her to process.

"God, I love how you taste, your scent," Jace whispered against her skin as he placed open-mouthed kisses along her spine. "You've always been so damn perfect, Evan. Always."

The words and his use of her name were too much, the niggling worry exploding into an all-encompassing surge of anxiety. She yanked against the chains holding her arms above her head and pulled back from Andre's kiss. "Yellow."

Andre's eyes met hers, his concern obvious, and Jace stopped what he was doing behind her. "What's wrong, *bella*?"

She closed her eyes, taking in a full breath, trying to hold it together. She couldn't do this. Couldn't do lovemaking. She wasn't strong enough for that. Not with these two. "Please, nothing romantic. I just want . . . I . . . Just the game. Please. *Sir*."

Andre's frown was deep when she opened her eyes again, but after a searching gaze, he nodded. Without another word, he uncuffed her hands, bringing her arms down to her sides, and then squatted to unhook her ankles from the spreader bar.

"I'm sorry, it's . . ." She let the words trail off, not sure how to finish the sentence.

Jace stepped out from behind her, his face an unreadable mask. He tapped her chin with the flat end of the riding crop. "No more talking, pet. Andre's in charge, not you."

Andre rose after freeing her from the bar and pulled off his boxers. He gripped his erection and stroked his thumb over the glistening tip. "This is what you want, *bella*? No kissing and sweet stuff, just a hard cock ready and willing? 'Cause I can do that, too."

She wet her lips. She wanted all of those things—the sweet and the dirty—more than she cared to admit. But the romantic part was way too dangerous. Her heart always led her down the wrong path. She refused to follow its siren call again. She needed to keep her mind centered on the physical, on the insistent ache between her thighs and not the one the guys were causing in her chest. "Yes, sir. That's what I want."

He moved past her and sank onto the bed, spreading out on his back, beautiful and naked and aroused. "Jace, bring her here and get her head back in the right place. If she's thinking this much, we aren't doing our job."

Jace grabbed the back of her collar, the pressure pushing against the front of her throat. "Come on, pet. Let's get you focused."

Jace led her to the bed and hauled her onto it. Once she was on her knees, his fingers threaded into her hair and gripped tight. "Show Andre what a talented mouth you have."

Without finesse, he pushed her head downward, and she opened her mouth to take in Andre's awaiting cock. Andre let out a deep grunt of appreciation, and between that response and Jace's almost painful grip on her hair, there wasn't any room left for thought. As Jace guided her up and down with unrelenting precision, her jangled nerves faded into the background, and her senses took over— Andre's masculine flavor, the two men's intermingling scents, and Jace's control over her movements.

She focused on giving pleasure, on truly submitting, and on the consuming sensation of that loss of control. There was safety in that mindless state.

"Keep going, Ev. You know what to do." Jace released her hair, and the bed dipped as he adjusted his position. She continued to swirl her tongue around Andre's length, loving the fact that with each swipe his thigh muscles tightened beneath her like he was barely maintaining his own control.

"Now, Jace," Andre ordered.

Before she registered what he'd said, the sharp bite of the riding crop smacked the back of her thigh. She gasped around Andre's cock as the stinging sensation raced over her skin. Jace gave her a second's pause, enough for her to call a word if needed. But when none came, he rained a set of lightning-fast blows against her bare bottom and thighs. *Holy Lord.* Fire lit up her nerve endings and sent luscious zinging heat straight to her most sensitive parts. She hummed her pleasure against Andre's shaft.

Andre rocked his hips forward, guiding her to take more of him. "Ooh, you like the feel of the crop, sweet *bella.* Jace does a good job, doesn't he?"

She nodded as best she could.

"Spread your knees for him," Andre directed. "Give him a pretty little target."

She braced her hands on Andre's thighs and adjusted her position, leaving her knees spread and exposed from behind while she continued to pleasure him.

The riding crop traced along the bottom curve of her ass, slowly, methodically, and then flicked, sharp and quick, against her pussy. She cried out around Andre's cock, the rush of pain and pleasure almost launching her into orgasm.

Andre grabbed her head. "Enough. You're tempting me to finish this way."

She followed his directive and looked up to find him propped up on his elbows, eating her up with his gaze. Her eyes automatically shifted downward. "Sorry, sir."

"Ah, look at you. Not just beautiful but submissive by instinct. You're going to be the fucking death of us both." He reached out and grabbed a condom from the side table. "Come here, *bella.* I've waited long enough."

After donning protection, Andre palmed her waist and she scooted up to straddle him. Jace slid off the bed, his eyes never leaving hers. She bit her lip, the reality that Jace was going to watch her fuck another man settling in. The knowledge came with equal parts guilt and illicit desire. Did they really do this with no jealousy? She couldn't imagine standing by while either one of them had sex with some other chick. The thought made her want to grow talons and scratch the hypothetical bitch's eyes out.

Jace gave her a nod, reading the question on her face. "It's fine, Ev. *I'm* fine. You're not the only voyeur in the room. Enjoy yourself."

Andre's hands traced up her sides, bringing her attention back to the handsome man beneath her. "Blindfold her, Jace. I only want her focused on one thing."

"No, it's okay, I'll—"

"Hush, *bella*. Not your choice."

Jace grabbed a strip of fabric from a drawer in the side table and tied it tight over her eyes, blocking out all but the faintest hint of light. Her heart began to hammer, but she didn't have time to worry further because Andre's large hands spanned her hips and drew her down onto his cock without ceremony. *Oh, my.* The sweet invasion dragged all her attention back to center, to the sensation of her body stretching to envelope his hard heat. *"Mmm."*

"That's right," Andre soothed as he guided her up and down in an impossibly patient rhythm. "Ride my cock. You feel so good around me—so hot and wet."

A ragged breath sounded to her right, and she knew Jace was watching them, listening to Andre's words. Picturing Jace standing there, hard and ready, getting off by seeing her take her pleasure with someone else was beyond erotic.

"You know how perfect you look right now, *bella*?"

She shook her head as she dug her nails into Andre's ribs, keeping the slow pace though she ached to have him fuck her harder, faster. "No, sir."

"So perfect that Jace can't help breaking the rules by stroking his own cock while he watches you," Andre said, his voice like velvet against her ears.

She groaned and another rush of heat flooded her sex, enveloping Andre's already slick shaft. She could picture Jace there—muscles tight, sweat dampening his blond hair, his hand giving slow, firm strokes to himself while he watched her ride Andre's cock. *Oh, God.* Pleasure, quick and urgent, coiled low in her belly, and she had to suck in a deep breath to reel herself in. One touch to her clit and she would go off like a firecracker.

Using her hands to guide her, she leaned down to Andre's chest, finding those nipple rings she'd been fantasizing about and brought her mouth down on one of them. She drew her tongue around the hardened nub and sucked the metal ring into her mouth, tugging in the process.

"Shit, that's nice," Andre said, his muscles going tense beneath her.

The cool touch of leather tracked down her spine as she worked—Jace's riding crop cataloguing each vertebrae. "Don't be shy, Ev. Andre likes the bite of pain with his fucking just like you do."

The riding crop snapped against her upper back in three successive jolts, lighting up her skin in radiant waves. She automatically bit down on Andre and he quaked beneath her, digging his fingers deeper into the curves of her hips and muttering a string of Spanish.

She took that as positive feedback and moved to the other side, pulling the ring with her teeth and clenching her inner muscles around him as she plunged down on his cock again. She loved that she didn't have to hold back, could be as bad as she wanted to be because neither of them was going to judge her. This was nothing like sleeping with the few guys she'd dated in the past where she was always trying to guess what was the right or wrong thing to do. With Andre and Jace, it was all instinct, a primal place where there was no wrong way.

Jace continued with the riding crop, making her feel as if static had replaced the blood in her veins, and Andre finally gave in and picked up his pace, thrusting into her with near abandon.

Their bodies turned glossy with sweat and Andre's grip on her hips began to slide. "Lean back, *bella*," he said, his voice gritty.

She braced her hands behind her on his thighs and tilted her head back, letting her hair tickle the skin that Jace had lit on fire. Andre brought his hands down lower and flicked his thumb over her clit.

"Oh," she ground out, the word catching in her throat.

"Not yet, *bella*," Andre warned. "Not until I say."

Her nails bit into his skin as he continued to strum his thumb over her hot button. She didn't know if she could wait, if she could hold on much longer. Desire wicked through her like wildfire and she could feel the orgasm hovering on the edge of her control. Just one more stroke and . . .

Smack! Smack!

Fire lit up her nipples and she cried out, her voice echoing off the wood floors. Then ecstasy, hot and fierce, slammed her. Jace hit her again and her mind went fuzzy with the sensation of it all. She couldn't even lift her head—all she could do was ride Andre and feel *everything.*

A deep moan ripped out of Andre, and his cock pulsed inside her, giving her his release with the force of a bullet train. But just when she was about to tip over with him, he moved his hand away from her clit. She whimpered in protest.

"Lift up, *bella*. You're not done." He grabbed her arms and braced her hands against his chest. His breathing was rapid beneath her fingertips. "You've earned her, Jace. Take her."

She pushed upward, lifting off Andre's cock, and firm hands palmed her waist from behind. Her mind was still reeling, but the chill of gel being spread over her back opening jerked her back to the present.

Jace kissed the base of her spine. "You're not ready to take both of us together, but you're going to take me."

Andre found her clit again and stroked her with fingers slick with her juices. She closed her eyes behind the blindfold, the delicious pleasure almost sending her straight into orgasm. "Yes, sir."

Jace touched her gently then positioned himself at her back entrance, pressing the tip of his cock against her. "Focus on letting me in, baby. Relax your muscles and push against me."

Andre's fingers didn't stop their ministrations, and she held on to that sensation as she followed Jace's instruction. Her body resisted the invasion, making it feel like there was no way she could ever take him, but she wasn't going to give up that easily. She took another deep breath and focused on relaxing, on accepting him. The first thrust felt like she was going to rip apart, but then he pushed past the ring of muscle and all went white behind her eyes.

"Oh, *God* . . ." Her body turned as taut as a guitar string and every shred of her being seemed to jerk to hyper-awareness. Pleasure wasn't even a fair word for it.

Jace hissed out a breath as he pulled back and eased into her again. "Oh, Evan, baby."

His words stopped making sense and so did her thoughts. Andre's thumb took over her clit, and his fingers plunged deep inside her, stroking her as Jace continued rocking into her.

She felt . . . invaded. In the best possible way. Invaded and utterly dominated by the two of them. Her pleasure was no longer in her conscious control. Her arms began to quiver, and sweat trickled down her neck. Breath started to come in short fits and starts. She felt alive and electric and half out of her mind. The feel of both of them inside her something she'd never forget. "I don't . . . know . . . how much . . . longer . . ."

"Shh," Andre soothed. "You both have permission to come.

Let it take you, *bella*. Let me watch both of you fall apart above me."

With his free hand, Andre yanked off her blindfold and she found his eyes full of stark desire and something else, something far more intense.

Jace's own breathing became erratic, and his tempo went from canter to gallop. "Come for me, Evan. Come for both of us."

Andre's eyes stayed locked with hers as he stroked her clit with increasing pressure. Then his fingers curved inside her, hitting the spot that she'd thought was a myth, and the world around her exploded.

A wretched cry tore out of her, and she thrust against Jace in a mindless frenzy, her entire body seeming to contract around him. She was no longer in control of her muscles—her body was taking what it wanted, pushing her higher and higher into a place she hadn't been before. She was floating. No pain or worry. Just thoughtless bliss.

Somewhere in the distance, she heard Jace's own moan of ecstasy, felt his heat spill against the condom and the resulting softening of his grip on her waist.

Andre grabbed her quivering arms, and she collapsed against him in a boneless heap. Her mind couldn't process anything—emotion, ecstasy, pain—all of it wrapped around her in an overwhelming rush.

Then, she lost it.

Tears—something she hadn't felt against her cheeks in a decade—sprung forth without warning or control. She didn't even realize what was happening until she found herself sobbing against Andre's sweat-slicked chest.

"Oh, *bella*." His hand caressed her hair. "It's okay, you're okay."

The bed dipped and Jace grabbed her hand, running a thumb over her palm. "Are you all right, Ev? Did I hurt you?"

She shook her head against Andre, the sobs continuing to wrack her like she was some delirious lunatic.

Jace kissed her knuckles. "It's okay, just let it out, sweetheart. This can happen sometimes."

Andre rolled to his side, taking her with him, and Jace stretched out along her back, spooning her. With soft caresses and soothing words, both men held on to her, letting her go through whatever craziness had taken her body and mind hostage until she didn't know which was more frightening—that she was crying for the first time in years or that she was happy.

SEVENTEEN

Jace sank onto the couch across from Andre. "She's sleeping."

Andre was sitting forward on the loveseat, his elbows on his knees, fingers steepled. He nodded, though he looked lost in thought. "That's good."

Jace ran a hand through his towel-dried hair. The shower hadn't cleared his mind like he'd hoped. It'd only left him more worried. And Andre looked to be on the same mental path as he was. "Seemed like more than just a reaction to subspace, didn't it?"

Andre sighed. "I don't know. I've seen people get emotional afterward, but it felt like more. Yes."

Well, wasn't that always the theme with Evan? Everything always felt like more. More intense. More important. More special. He glanced at Andre, debating whether or not he should share what he knew about Evan. Share the fear that wouldn't stop tapping at the back of his brain. If they were going to continue doing this with her, Andre needed to know.

Jace blew out a breath. "She used to have emotional problems . . .

as a teenager. Maybe something like this is too much for her to handle."

Andre's gaze lifted. "What kind of problems?"

Jace held his stare. "The night I slept with her, I found healing scars on her stomach. Some old, some new. Deep cuts. All in a perfect alignment."

Andre winced. "Christ."

Jace sank against the couch cushions, the weight of the memory making him feel tired. "I was so freaked for her when I figured out what she was doing, and then I was so fucking pissed at myself for falling into bed with her. We were close then and I should've seen that she needed help, that she was lost. But I was too damn preoccupied with how much I wanted her to realize anything was wrong. Dude, she told me she loved me that night, and I fucked it up completely."

Andre rubbed the back of his neck. "That's heavy stuff to process, especially at nineteen."

"We had this perfect night in bed. The lights had gone out from a summer storm, and the whole evening seemed to bring us to some other world where reality didn't exist. But while we were lying there afterward, the electricity came back on, and I saw her scars. I panicked and backpedaled like a damn coward. Told her that I should've never touched her, that I had drunk too much and made a mistake, that she needed to tell my mom what she was doing or I was going to say something for her." He tilted his head back and stared at the wood-beamed ceiling. "Then my parents came home unexpectedly and found us together, still half-naked. My dad kicked me out of the house for good that night and told me he would report me for statutory rape. Evan disappeared before brunch hit the table the following morning."

"God, man. No wonder you were relieved to see that Evan was okay. It had to be brutal not knowing where she was or if she was all right."

"You have no idea." Jace had spent months not sleeping, always carrying around the knowledge that wherever Evan was, it was his fault. His parents had asked him to look out for Evan when she'd come to live with them, and he'd been determined to show his father that he could be more than the family screw-up. He'd befriended Evan, gained her trust, had made her feel safe in a new place. Then after all of that, he'd still gone and proven his father right. He'd fallen for a girl he didn't have any right to, one who needed a friend not a lover.

"Did your dad actually turn you in?"

He sniffed. "Of course he did. Bill Austin doesn't make idle threats. But I denied it and they couldn't find Evan, so I was never charged."

"She saved you by leaving."

Jace lifted his head. "Yeah, talk about guilt. But jail probably would've been better than the nightmares I conjured up wondering what had happened to her."

"She hasn't told you anything since she's been here?"

"No. We agreed to no past. I'm not sure I want to know." His cell phone vibrated from the spot where he'd left it on the dining room table. He ignored it. "She seems like she's got it together now, but there are shadows behind her eyes. And after the breakdown she had in there, I'm not sure what to think."

"She was exorcising something. I don't think it was a bad thing." Andre propped his feet on the coffee table. "But I can tell you one thing for sure: If Dr. Dan is vanilla, Evan is signing up for a life of frustration. I've never seen someone as green as she is take to the sub role so well. Vanilla is not going to satisfy her."

"Don't give me another reason to want Dr. Dan out of the picture." Jace stood and paced to the window at the front of the cabin. "You're supposed to be the one reminding me why I shouldn't try to shoulder in on another guy's woman. Especially a guy who's about to give Wicked a much needed injection of cash flow."

"Watching me with her didn't break the hold she has on you?" Andre asked, his words measured.

Jace closed his eyes and pressed his forehead against the window. He'd gone into that bedroom anticipating that seeing Evan with someone else would solve his problem. But it had only made it worse. Seeing her give herself over to the two of them, even watching Andre dominate her had gotten to him in a way that ménage never did. He tapped his head against the glass. "It only made me want her more."

The couch squeaked as Andre shifted, and Jace vaguely registered the sound of his cell phone buzzing again. "And having me there, too?"

"Felt right."

Andre released a breath. "So I guess that leaves us with two options."

"Oh, yeah?"

"Yeah. We be smart and walk away now. Save us both the risk of getting attached and then getting our guts handed to us when she walks away."

Jace groaned and turned around. He was already knee-deep in attachment. "Or?"

Andre leaned forward, his expression weary. "Or both of us spend the next two months showing her what she's going to be missing if she goes through with the marriage. Give her a chance to make that decision with her eyes wide open. And accept that we'll probably be sending her a goddamned blender as a wedding gift at the end of the process anyway."

Well, didn't each of those options sound like a frolic in the fucking flowers. Kick in the face now or kick in the balls later? Whichever path he chose, Jace knew Evan would leave at the end of it. It's not like he and Andre could offer her anything permanent even if she decided to renege on her engagement. There was no happily ever after waiting for her here. But at least in the second plan he'd have the chance to touch her again and maybe he could save her from making the marriage mistake like he had.

"I don't think I can let her go yet," Jace admitted, the heft of that knowledge like sandbags on his shoulders.

Andre raked his hands through his hair, weariness clear on his face. "That makes two of us then. Aren't we a couple of masochistic assholes?"

Jace walked over to the couch and perched on the arm of it. "She may not even agree to it. You saw how she reacted when things got too intimate. Maybe this is only a one-weekend, get-the-kink-out deal for her."

Andre snorted. "That's like saying a person can cure themselves of being straight or gay. We know she's submissive. So we need to show her how nice it can be to fully embrace that."

The plan was starting to take shape in Jace's head, sounding more tempting as Andre kept talking. But he knew without parameters, they could all end up in a disastrous tangle at the end—hurt feelings, possessiveness, jealousy, guilt. He'd damaged Evan enough the first time around and didn't want to set her up for more pain. And hell, he needed to keep his own expectations in check. This weekend had proven that Evan could get through the cracks of what he thought was impenetrable armor. They all needed a parachute cord—fine print at the bottom of their agreement—that would allow them to go in with the end in mind.

Jace shoved his hands in his pockets and looked at his closed bedroom door, picturing how content and beautiful Evan had looked when he'd left the room. "At the end of the two months, all of us walk away, no questions asked, no obligation."

Andre frowned. "I don't know if we have to spell that out. What if she doesn't want to leave? What if we don't? A lot of possibilities could open up."

Jace stared at Andre as if he'd spoken in tongues. "Possibilities?"

He shrugged. "Maybe the three of us could work out something less . . . time limited."

"Like be the guys she comes to on weekends to get her off so she can go back home to the good doctor with a smile on her face?" The thought made the muscles in his neck tighten. "I'm not some . . . concubine. Or whatever the dude version of that would be."

Andre's eyebrow arched in a way that rose Jace's hackles. "Oh, right. 'Cause what? Having a woman use you just for sex makes you feel cheap? News flash: That's your fucking MO, man."

Jace crossed his arms over his chest, the dig landing squarely. He knew it was his method—no strings, no commitment, just a good time. But something about having only that tiny piece of Evan while knowing she'd be giving everything else to someone else would be too much to tolerate. "Not an option."

"So maybe we can be the guys she comes to without Dr. Dan in the picture at all. We can offer her a lot more than he can."

Jace scoffed. Now Andre was venturing into the ridiculous. "You've officially lost your mind, *amigo*. We can't compete with all that fairy-tale shit—the dream wedding, the famous husband, the picture-perfect two and a half kids I'm sure she wants. All we are is good in bed. Women fuck around with guys like us, but they want forever with guys like him."

"Don't give me that pile of bullshit, Jace. You know that both of us are more than capable of giving her what she needs even if it's not in the traditional way. And don't pretend this is all about sex. What just happened between the three of us in there felt a hell of a lot different than some carefree fuck."

"You really have been drinking tainted Kool-Aid. What little picture have you painted in your mind, dude? A cute little house in the suburbs where we live together and share Evan? Maybe give her a kid or two and figure out who the daddy is by the hue of their skin? Have the neighbors call us fags and Evan a whore? Yeah, that sounds like a lovely life for all of us."

Andre paled a bit. "No, of course that wouldn't work. And I have no clue where things could lead. But maybe one of us could be with her publicly. No one else has to know what's going on behind closed doors."

Jace gave a derisive laugh. "Right. Because God forbid your buddies on the force find out who you really are."

"That's not what this is about."

"Sure it's not. Those guys know that you share women with your roommate? Or that you like to fuck other dudes sometimes? Cane 'em on occasion?"

Andre winced. "Fuck you, Jace. Don't be an asshole just because you don't have the balls to open yourself up to something real for a change."

Jace's neck muscles tightened, his blood beginning to roar in his ears. "Last time I checked, learning from an utter failure was smart not chickenshit."

The muscle in Andre's jaw ticked, a sure sign his own anger was grabbing hold. "*You* did not fail your marriage, Jace. Diana used you. She manipulated you so well with that fake-ass victim, please-take-care-of-me act that she still has you thinking you're the one who wasn't good enough. She wanted your money and to control you. When those two perks went away, she found someone else to manipulate. End of story. You were just too smitten to see her for what she was—a well-groomed leech. Evan is *not* Diana."

Jace ground his teeth, the images of the day he walked in on his wife packing her bags flooding his brain. Jace had been busting his ass trying to get Wicked off the ground, doing his best to prove to Diana—who'd been categorically against the venture—that leaving his father's business wouldn't alter the comfortable lifestyle she enjoyed. He'd had his first big day of sales and had come home with an armful of roses and her favorite bottle of wine only to find her preparing to leave. A total fucking blindside.

Without a lick of emotion in her voice, Diana had told him she'd been cheating on him with his former co-worker for months and that she was pregnant.

When Jace had asked if the baby was his, she'd shrugged and said, "How could I trust you to raise a child? You can't even take care of me."

The child had turned out not to be his, but he'd felt the loss as much as if it had been. He *never* wanted to feel like he had when she'd walked out his door that night. He'd rather be alone forever than experience that kind of emotional filleting ever again.

"This discussion is over," Jace said, going cold at the memory. "Two months . . . if Evan agrees. We'll be exclusive with her during that time. Then we all wash our hands of it. That's the only way I'm in."

Andre's eyes burned with all the things Jace could tell he wanted to say, but finally he nodded, his jaw tight. "Fine. Two months."

"Thank you," he said, the fight draining from his voice. As insane as Andre was, he couldn't blame the guy for considering more with Evan. She'd opened up an ache a mile wide inside of him, too. But clearly they hadn't had the same effect on her. She hadn't given them any indication she wanted anything more than sex. She was in love with someone else, and they needed to keep that vital fact at the forefront of their minds.

Andre gave a weary sigh and crooked a thumb in the direction of the dining area. "That's the third phone call you've gotten in ten minutes. You may want to get it."

Jace stalked across the room, his mind still spinning from the argument, and grabbed the phone. "Hello."

"Finally! Where the hell are you?" his sister demanded. "I've been trying to get ahold of you all morning."

"I'm out of town . . . at a client's. What's wrong?"

"Mom's in the hospital. They think she had a heart attack."

"Oh, God." All the air whooshed from Jace, and his grip tightened on the phone.

"She's okay," she added quickly. "They've stabilized her, but they're doing a lot of tests to see what the problem is. She may need surgery."

He headed toward his bedroom. "Which hospital?"

"The Baylor in Southlake."

"I'm about an hour outside of the city. I'll be there as soon as I can."

"Thanks," she said, relief in her voice. "And fair warning, Dad's on a rampage about everything—the ambulance response time, the nurse, you name it. He even snapped at *Wyatt*."

"Jesus, the apocalypse must be near." Jace couldn't even recall his dad throwing a firm word in his oldest brother's direction. Wyatt, with his genius IQ and oh-so-responsible nature, had never been able to do any wrong in his father's eyes. Jace had been half-convinced his brother had come out of the womb a grownup. "Tell Mom I'm thinking of her and will be there in a little while."

Jace exchanged good-byes with his sister, tossed the phone on the bed, and grabbed his bag off the floor to start packing his clothes.

"What's going on?" Andre asked from the doorway.

"I've got to head back." Jace explained the situation as quickly as he could while gathering his things and stuffing him into his duffel bag. "Can you tell Evan what's going on? I hate running out like this."

"I'm sure she'll understand."

Jace sighed. The last thing he wanted to do was leave Evan behind after all that had happened in the last day and a half, but he had to see for himself that his mom was okay. At least he knew Andre would take good care of Evan for the rest of the weekend.

"If Evan agrees to the deal, tell her that I want her back here next weekend. No excuses. She has two months before she gets married. I plan to help her make the most of it."

Andre smirked. "And I plan to show her why she shouldn't walk away."

Jace slung his bag over his shoulder and pushed past Andre to go back into the living room. "We're not that good, Andre. Don't make this into something it can never be."

Something Jace could never be.

Good enough for Evan.

EIGHTEEN

Jace climbed out of his Dodge Viper, the only luxury item he hadn't been able to part with when he gave up his financial gig, and checked his watch. He'd made it to the hospital in half the time it would've taken a normal person to complete the trip. Sometimes a fast car and a roommate who could get you out of speeding tickets came in handy.

He hurried up to the floor his older sister, Leila, had told him their mom was on and found her and Wyatt talking quietly in the waiting area. Leila stood when she saw Jace approaching, pushing her hair behind her ears—something she did nonstop when she was stressed. She gave him a tight hug when he reached her. "I don't even want to know how fast you drove to get here."

"Don't ask," he mumbled.

She huffed as she pulled back from the embrace. "Thank God you finally answered your phone. You had me freaking out this morning that something had happened to you, too. Where the hell were you?"

"I had some business outside of town."

Wyatt sniffed. "Yeah, right. Was the business blonde or bru-nette this week? Or maybe both?"

"Fuck off, Wy," Jace said, shooting his brother an annoyed glance. "Not all of us want to spend our time jerking off to Excel spreadsheets."

Leila raised a palm to each of them. "Can it, boys. This is not the time. Here comes Dad."

Jace glanced over his shoulder to find his father stalking toward them. How the man managed to be in a full suit even though it was a weekend and his mother had supposedly been rushed to the ER in the wee hours of the morning was a wonder. Perhaps he'd taken to sleeping in them.

Jace knew the second his father registered his presence because his lip curled in that derisive way that seemed especially reserved for his youngest son. "Well, look who decided to show up."

Jace ignored the remark, as he did most of the things his father said to him.

Wyatt rose from his chair when their father stopped in front of them. "How's Mom?"

"She's tired. Said they've poked and prodded her so much she feels like a head of cattle. They haven't determined what the exact problem is yet, but I'm not sure if that doctor would know an ass from an elbow. I've requested a specialist."

Leila sighed. "Daddy, that doctor was the specialist. One of the top in the field from what the nurse said."

"Yeah, I wonder how much he paid her to say that," his father muttered.

"Can I see mom?" Jace asked.

"Oh, so now you're concerned?" his dad asked. "Seems she ranks pretty low on your list since you couldn't even bother to get here until lunchtime. Wyatt's been here since five and even Leila got here by seven and she had to drop the kids off at a babysitter."

Jace clenched his teeth. "I got here as soon as I found out."

Leila touched Jace's arm. "She's in room three thirty-three."

Jace stepped around his father, trying to keep his smartass gene in check, and headed toward his mother's room. He was here for her. Not to spar with his dad.

When he tapped on the door and peeked into the room, he was met with a view of his mother linked up to a tangle of beeping machines. Her skin was paler than he'd ever seen it and her light hair, always perfectly coiffed, was sticking up on end. The whole scene made his chest hurt. She looked like she'd aged ten years since he'd seen her.

Reid had told him how rundown his mom was looking, but Jace still hadn't rushed over there to see her. He'd been a damn coward. Thank God she was okay. If she had . . .

His mom cracked open her eyes, cutting short his runaway thoughts, and gave him a soft smile when she saw him standing there. "Jason."

"Hey, Mom." His mother had always called him by his given name, insisting that she hadn't gone through the trouble of picking out a name, only for it to be shortened.

"Your father told me you weren't coming."

He rolled his eyes. "Like I would miss the chance to drink free coffee and stare at hot nurses."

She gave a little laugh. "Thank you."

"For what?" He sat down next to her and captured her small hand in his.

"For not coming in here with the doom and gloom face. Your brother and sister are looking at me like I'm going to be playing cards with St. Peter next week. And don't even get me started on how your father is acting."

He gave her hand a squeeze. "They just don't realize how tough you are. I know you're not going anywhere. Anyone who can live with Dad this long can handle way worse than some lame heart attack."

"You realize I'm never going to be allowed back in this hospital after your father is finished with them, right?"

"Guess that means you better stay healthy from now on, then."

"Ugh, I'll probably have to give up bacon. Not sure if that's a life worth living." She adjusted herself to sit up a bit more. "But enough about all this. I'm tired of talking about it. Tell me what's going on with you. You haven't been by in a long time."

He frowned, guilt tugging at him. "I'm sorry. I've just been busy with the store. I landed a big contract and have been working on that."

"Oh? Is that what's got that light back in your eyes?" She nodded in his direction. "You look happier than you have in a while."

He shrugged. "I guess so. It could mean a lot of money for the store."

"*Hmm.*" Her eyes narrowed, giving him that look that mothers had the patent on. "If money made you that happy, you never would've left your father's business. What aren't you telling me?"

He sighed, not sure if he should bring up Evan when his mom was in a fragile state. It was good news but he didn't want it to stir up any of the negative memories of when Evan left.

"Spill it, Jason."

He leaned back in his chair. "You missed your calling as a police interrogator."

Her perfectly manicured brow arched.

"I saw Evangeline."

He didn't think it was possible for his mom to pale any further, but she did. She pulled her hand from his and brought it to her chest. "You found her? Is she—"

"She's great, Mom. Beautiful, successful, engaged." He almost choked on that last descriptor, but managed to get it out. "You wouldn't even recognize her. I didn't at first."

She blinked hard, tears lining her bottom lids. Her voice was barely a whisper. "Thank you, Lord. I thought—"

"I know. Me, too." He grabbed one of the paper cups from the side table and poured her a glass of water, worried that he'd stressed her too much with the news. "Here."

She took the cup from him, her hand shaking a bit, and sipped. "How did you find her?"

Jace explained how he'd stumbled upon Evan in South Padre, but his mom seemed to only be listening with half an ear. He finished the story, and the room filled with the quiet beeping of the machines. He shifted in his chair and cleared his throat. "Maybe after you're back on your feet I can bring her by so you can see how well she's doing for yourself."

She stared down at her water for a while longer, then finally spoke. "I doubt she'd want to see me."

He frowned and leaned forward, bracing his forearms on his knees. "Why not? You two always got along."

His mom looked toward the room's only window, her whole body seeming to sag deeper into the sheets. "Because she has no reason to want to see me. I was just another person who failed her in her life. I knew how much support she needed when we signed up to have her in our home. But when she wouldn't open up around me, I felt useless and fell back to working my crazy hours. I gave up."

"She wasn't exactly an easy shell to crack."

"You managed to get by her defenses." A humorless smile touched her lips. "That was always your gift. Wyatt the brilliant mind, Leila my artist, and you the big heart. You have a way of caring for people that makes it impossible for them to not let you in and love you."

He smirked. "I think I got the short end of the gene pool on that one, Ma. And that superpower definitely didn't work on Diana."

She turned to him, her lips pressed into a thin line. "Don't say that. Diana was a spoiled waste of space. And you think your brother or sister wouldn't kill to have a little bit of your charisma?

You have friends like Reid and Andre who would literally take a bullet for you. You have every woman you meet wanting to be part of your orbit. People are drawn to your kind spirit."

Jace almost said that the woman thing wasn't because of his spirit, but remembered he was talking to his mother. "I think they may have doped you up a bit too much there, Ma. You're getting sappy on me."

"All I'm saying is that when none of us could get through to Evangeline, you got her to let her guard down, to smile. I thought it was a good thing for both of you. You were showing your father and I you were capable of being responsible, and Evangeline had someone to relate to." She shook her head and looked down at her hands. "But as time went on, I knew I'd made a mistake. I saw how you two began to look at each other. I sensed the shift, and I didn't do anything about it."

He sighed. "Mom, stop. What happened wasn't your fault. I was old enough to know better. I should've had the strength to stay away."

His mom didn't say anything for a few seconds and when she lifted her head to face him again, her eyes were full of regret. "You were all she had holding herself together. When we kicked you out that night, the glimmer of light behind her eyes went out. She begged your father to let you stay, that she could go live somewhere else for a while. But your father told her she shouldn't waste time being a martyr for you, that you'd have another girl in your bed by the next night, that she didn't mean anything to you."

Jace sucked in a breath. *"What?"*

She swiped at the moisture on her cheek. "I should've stepped in and stopped him. Or at least stayed up with her that night and talked to her more. You'd made a huge mistake, but I knew you honestly cared for her."

Jace put his head in his hands, his heart breaking for Evan all over again. He'd tried to sneak back into her room that night, apologize for the things he'd said, but she'd refused to open the window for him. Now he knew why.

"In the morning, there was a note tucked into my coffee mug. She told me she was sorry and for me not to be angry with you. She said she'd loved you and had wanted it to happen, but realized afterward that she'd made a mistake. She pleaded for me not to let your father kick you out for good—that you didn't deserve to lose your family, not over someone worthless like her."

His gut twisted. All those things he'd said to her that night and she'd still defended him. "Why didn't you ever tell me about the note?"

She took a deep breath, and set the cup down, the beeping on her heart monitor ticking up a bit. "Because it was a suicide note, honey."

Jace's breakfast threatened to come up. He gripped the arms of his chair.

"I didn't tell you because I couldn't let you bear that on your conscience if she had gone through with it." She shook her head. "You made a bad decision, but Evangeline was a fragile soul. That night was simply the tipping point. We all could've handled things differently."

"So all this time, you thought she was . . ."

"Yes. And I've never forgiven myself for what happened. It was my negligence that started that ball rolling."

Yeah, maybe she had gotten the ball rolling but his stupidity and his father's hateful words had dropkicked that ball over the edge. His jaw clenched, imagining how Evan must've felt when his dad had told those lies about him. "She ran away thinking I'd used her. That everything between us had been a lie."

"Well, hadn't it been?" said a voice from the doorway.

Jace jerked his attention to the door to find his dad leaning against the jamb, newspaper tucked under his arm. Apparently he'd been standing there long enough to follow the conversation.

"Don't think I didn't know what you were doing back then—the kind of crowd you were hanging out with, the types of parties you were going to," he said, stepping inside the room. "You were cycling through women like a chain smoker goes through Marlboros. Evangeline wasn't anything to you except another conquest. She was just so desperate for someone in her life to love her that she read what she wanted to in the situation. I was the only one who had the guts to tell that poor girl the truth."

Jace had spent a lot of his life angry with his dad, but as he stood across from him right then, he realized that the anger had finally morphed into hate. "She could've killed herself."

"And whose fault would that have been?" he asked, his voice as cool as the gray of his eyes. "Whatever that girl has been through since she walked out our door—and I guarantee you the street wasn't kind to a kid like her—has been on you, son. Your fault. Because no matter what we've tried with you, you've always managed to be a fuckup."

His mother gasped. "Bill! Stop it."

His father's words sliced through Jace like a jagged hunting knife, skinning him until everything inside him felt bloodied and raw. He couldn't even form the words to respond.

His father made a disgusted sound in the back of his throat as he headed toward his mother's bed. He tossed the newspaper onto the rolling table, knocking over his mother's empty cup. "I got you your paper, Sherry. Seems our son is now set on humiliating us in front of the whole damn city."

Jace's eye caught one of the headlines on the page his dad had folded: *Councilman Speaks Out Against Suggestive Ads by Local Sex Shop.* A picture of both their local councilman and Jace's store were included.

His father righted his mother's cup and poured a glass of water like he hadn't just ripped his son to shreds. He took a swig of the water, his back to Jace. "I thought if I was hard enough on you I could make you into a man, but all you continue to be is an embarrassment to this family. I'm ashamed to call you my son."

His mother's eyes were wide as she looked between the two of them. "Bill, take a breath. Let's calm down."

"No, don't bother. Let me relieve you of your hardship, *Bill*," Jace said, finally regaining his voice. "Because you don't have to call me anything from now on. For all I care, you can tell people you're the father of two."

"Jason, wait," his mother pleaded.

Jace stepped around the other side of her bed and leaned down to kiss her cheek. "I love you, Ma. I'll check on you later, but I can't be around him anymore. I'm done."

NINETEEN

"He's still not answering?" Evan asked, nervously swirling her spoon in the soup Andre had insisted she eat when she'd woken up from her nap.

Andre tossed the cell phone onto the dining room table and leaned against the wall. "No. I called his sister, and she said he left the hospital over an hour ago after he had some blowout with their dad. Apparently the two have vowed to never speak to each other again."

She cringed. "Guess things haven't improved with Jace and his father. They were always at each other when I lived with them."

Andre snorted. "His dad's a jackass. He has this amazing son who's breaking his back to run a business he's passionate about—with no help from the family fortune, by the way—and all his father can see is that Jace doesn't fit into the mold he's created for him. Jace would never admit it to anyone, but his father's constant digs tear him up."

She looked down at her soup. She'd woken up from her nap planning an escape route. The two men had stripped more than her clothes in that bedroom this morning. Her defenses had been left in a tattered heap on the floor, and she needed time to reconstruct them before facing either of the guys again. But the thought of Jace somewhere alone, feeling worthless in his family's eyes, had her chest feeling tight.

She pushed her chair away from the table and looked up at Andre. "You need to go find him."

Andre's eyebrow quirked. "You want me to leave you to find Jace."

She straightened in her chair, feeling more resolute by the second. "Yes. I'm not going to be able to relax and have fun here if I know he's somewhere else feeling shitty. Go find him, take him out for a beer, do whatever guys do to make each other feel better. I'll be fine spending the rest of the weekend in my cabin catching up on my reading."

The corner of Andre's mouth tilted up and he pushed off the wall. "*Bella*, I agree with you that Jace probably doesn't need to be alone right now, but I'm not leaving you anywhere. You want me to find him, then you come with me."

"What?" she asked, flustered at the suggestion of taking any of this outside The Ranch's gates. "No, I can't. I mean . . ." She scrambled for an explanation that wasn't *I'm afraid I'm falling for the two of you.* "My agreement with Daniel is for here, not—"

He shrugged. "So don't tell him you left. You can stay with us tonight. We have a guest bedroom if you need your own space."

Stay with the two of them? At their place? The whole thing sounded stupid and ill-advised and way too enticing. "I don't think—"

"Come on, *bella.* Let's not pretend this isn't the same thing under a different roof. Being at The Ranch doesn't make what we're doing any less real."

She looked down at her hands. Real. That was exactly what this was. Too fucking real. "We'll find Jace and then I'll go home. I'll tell Daniel I wanted to end the weekend early."

He sighed. "How about we cross that bridge when we get to it? We need to track down Jace first."

She nodded, feeling better now that she had an escape hatch rigged up. "Okay."

"Get your stuff packed up, and I'll call Grant. He's not going to let you leave with me unless he verifies that it's what you want."

"What? I'm a grown woman. I don't need permission to go with someone."

"Here you do," Andre said, crouching down in front of her and laying a light kiss on her lips. "Grant doesn't mess around with people's safety. He'll just make sure that you're going with me on your own volition and not because I ordered you as your dom to do so."

She huffed. "I feel like I've entered an alternate universe."

He nuzzled her neck, sending warmth trickling down her spine and beating back some of the anxiety that had crept in. "And what do you think of the natives?"

I think I've found my home planet. But she didn't share that thought. "I think they're cocky and high-handed."

He laughed softly against her skin.

". . . And pretty damn irresistible." She let herself fall under the spell of his touch and laced her fingers in his hair, enjoying the satiny slide of his dark locks between her knuckles. "Well, two of them, at least."

"That's good to hear. We have a bit of a soft spot for you, too. In fact, I have something to propose to you on the way over." He pulled back to look at her, his grin sly. "But if I don't stop kissing you now, we'll never leave this cabin. Jace will be on his own."

She drew her hands down from his hair to his stubbled cheeks and sighed. It was really unfair for him to be so damn delicious. He made it next to impossible to hold on to her resolve. "All right, call the Grand Poo-bah so I can get permission to leave with you, kind sir."

———

She and Andre didn't have to search too hard for Jace. His little sports car was parked on the side of the building that housed both Wicked and the guys' third-floor loft. Andre entered the code to open the gate for the private parking area and pulled into the spot next to Jace's. "Let's go see what the damage is. My guess is he'll either be a total brooding pain in the ass or—"

"Act like absolutely nothing is wrong."

He cut the ignition and smirked at her. "Hasn't changed much since his teenage years, huh?"

She shrugged. "It always seemed like the harder his dad came down on him, the more devil-may-care he became. Like he was determined to show his father his opinion didn't even make a blip on his radar."

Andre's brown eyes reflected the same sadness she felt for Jace. "Guess we'll just have to go remind him that not everyone thinks he's a jackass." He pushed open his door. "Well, unless he *is* acting like a jackass, then all bets are off."

She laughed. "Right."

Andre led her to the front door of the store. "Let's check his office first. He's been spending a lot of time in there lately."

The bottom floor of Wicked was more a lobby and didn't have any products displayed. Instead, the most gorgeous black-and-white erotic photography Evan had ever seen adorned the dark maroon walls. Soft classical music filled her ears as well, but she had trouble dragging her focus away from the artwork. She touched the corner of one large piece—a collared woman was in the process of disrobing and in the background, two men sat in the darkened corner of the bedroom, leaning back in their chairs, their attention held captive by the display.

The photographer had captured the light so perfectly. The soft curves of the woman's body gleamed, and the dark angles playing over the faces of the men she was undressing for promised wickedness to come. Something that could've looked pornographic under an amateur's camera had been morphed into something stunning and pure. "God, I wish I was this good."

Andre slid a hand onto her lower back. "I have no doubt you are. I can't wait to see your photography."

"I don't do this type of work," she said, looking at the price on the picture and trying to keep a straight face at the astronomical amount.

Evan let Andre lead her up the stairs to the main store. She paused at the glass door leading into the shop, which had poetry scrawled across it in calligraphy. She read it aloud, running her fingers over the lettering:

Where true Love burns Desire is Love's pure flame;
It is the reflex of our earthly frame,
That takes its meaning from the nobler part,
And but translates the language of the heart.

SAMUEL COLERIDGE

Andre smiled. "That was Jace's mission statement when he started Wicked. He wanted a place lovers could come to without shame. A place where desire and sex were simply seen as natural extensions of people's love for one another."

She reread the poem, absorbing the words. "I had no idea he was that much of a hopeless romantic."

Andre pushed open the door. "He used to be, *bella*. Life can tear that out of you sometimes."

Jace turned out not to be in his office so Andre led her to an unmarked door at the back of the building and typed in a code on a keypad to unlock it. "We have to trek up another flight of stairs, but the view's nice."

"No problem," she said as she followed him up, though she wondered why someone who came from gaudy money like Jace chose to live in a walk-up above his business.

Andre peeked back at her and sniffed when he saw her expression. "Don't ever play poker, Evan. You'll get taken for everything you've got."

She frowned. "What are you talking about?"

"You wear your every thought on your face." He started climbing the stairs again. "Jace lives here because he turned away his family's money. They won't give him access to his trust fund unless he returns to the family business."

"Oh."

"It's also why we're roommates. Helps both of us to split the expenses."

She sniffed. "That's not the only reason you live with him."

He paused, looked back down at her again, his posture rigid. "What?"

"Your poker face isn't in place all the time either, officer," she said, her voice gentle. "But don't worry, he has no clue."

Andre shook his head, his expression resigned. "I knew you were going to be the death of me, *bella*."

When they both reached the top of the stairs, Andre swung open the door to find the TV blaring ESPN and two empty beer bottles sitting on the coffee table, but the living room otherwise empty. She peered over his shoulder. "May have some brooding on our hands."

They stepped inside the loft, and she locked the door behind her. The place was much bigger than she'd expected from looking up from the street. High ceilings with exposed ductwork, a solid wall of windows draped with simple white curtains at the far end of the place, and gorgeously aged brick walls flanking the left and right sides of the space. Every area was open to the next—kitchen, dining area, living room—with only a few supporting columns here and there. A metal staircase in the corner of the dining space spiraled up to an open second level where the bedrooms were located.

"Wow, y'all aren't exactly slumming it, Andre."

He clicked off the television, grabbed the beer bottles off the table, and walked toward the kitchen. "Jace worked a good deal for this when he leased the store space on the two bottom levels. Plus, believe me, it didn't look like this when we first moved in. Someone had divided up all the space with cheap sheetrock. Took me a year to tear this thing down to the bones and get it in this shape."

"*You* did all this?"

He tossed the bottles in a trash can and shot her a deviant smirk. "Haven't you heard? All Mexicans know how to do construction. It's like a requirement to be a card-carrying member."

She rolled her eyes. "Smartass."

"Nah, I worked at a Home Depot to get through college and took every DIY class I could. After the crap I see every day at work, sometimes it's nice just to just zone out and hit shit with a hammer."

"I totally get that."

He pointed to the windows. "Jace is probably out on the balcony. You should go out there first. You're better-looking than me, so there's less of a chance of getting your head bitten off."

She blew out a breath, trying to shore up her emotions. She needed to make sure Jace was okay and leave. That was it. "All right. Wish me luck."

She pushed back the curtains and found the sliding door that led to the outside balcony. Jace was perched on the edge of a lounge chair, forearms braced on his thighs, looking off into the greenbelt that bordered the back of the building. His head turned in her direction when she shoved open the door and stepped outside.

His expression remained flat when he saw it was her. "You were supposed to stay with Andre."

"He's here, too."

"Fucking Andre," he muttered, turning back to stare at the view.

She took a tentative step forward. "Your mom okay?"

"Probably going to need bypass surgery, but yeah." His words were clipped, his tone without emotion.

Evan didn't know how to handle this version of Jace. She was so used to the guy who seemed like nothing ever got to him. She risked moving closer and sat on the lounge chair next to him. "It's hard to imagine your mom slowing down long enough for them to even keep her in a hospital bed."

"Huh, no kidding." He laced his fingers between his knees, still only looking out at the trees. A long stretch of silence passed, and she began to feel like an intruder in whatever world he was lost in. It was stupid to think that she could offer him any comfort. What was she to him besides the girl he'd messed around with this weekend? He'd made it obvious that he hadn't wanted Andre to bring her here. She shifted forward, planning to stand up and leave him to his thoughts, but his quiet voice halted her. "Mom told me what my dad said to you the night you ran away."

The statement knocked her back on her butt. "Oh."

He turned toward her, the wear of the day evident in every line of his face. "I need you to know that what he said wasn't true."

She sighed. "Jace, look, that was a long time ago. Let's not—"

"I didn't say the right things to you that night either. I know that. When I saw your cutting scars, I got scared."

She looked down at her hands, her cheeks heating with shame. "You were right to be worried. I was a mess back then."

"You were hurting, and I should've been there for you. Should've seen that you needed a friend, not a bed buddy."

"I'm the one who kissed you first. I wanted it to happen. You had been an amazing friend to me, but I wanted all of you. Wanted you to look at me the way you looked at those girls you dated. To feel beautiful and important. It was a stupid teenage crush."

He reached out and grabbed her hand. "And I should've stopped things before they turned sexual. I was nineteen and knew better. But that doesn't mean it wasn't real for me, too. You were never just some girl to me. I loved you long before you kissed me that night, and I'm sorry I didn't tell you that when you needed to hear it the most."

Her throat tightened with the old grief of that night—the devastation she'd felt when he'd turned away from her. "I was a messed-up kid, Jace. I pinned all that hope on you because you were the first boy who ever made me feel like I was worth something. It wasn't a fair burden for you to carry. Whether you loved me back shouldn't have been a life-and-death matter."

He took a deep breath. "What happened when you left? Mom told me about your note."

She shook her head, the turmoil she'd felt inside back then still branded onto her psyche. "I sat on the edge of a bridge, watching the black water swirl, thinking that if I jumped no one would miss me."

She looked up and caught the pain that crossed his face. "Oh, Ev . . ."

"I sat there for what seemed like forever, trying to get the nerve to just do it already."

"What stopped you?"

Her lips lifted into a humorless smile. "This cocky street kid ambled by and plopped down next to me like I'd invited him to sit there. He told me, 'Ya know, they've done studies and shit. Every person who's survived a suicide jump has said they regretted jumping halfway into the fall. Makes you feel pretty bad for the dumb fucks who don't live to fill out that survey.' Then he offered to share his bag of Cheetos with me."

"Heh. And that convinced you?"

She shrugged. "Made me think of my dad. Made me wonder if he would've changed his mind if given the chance. And suddenly I didn't want to end up like him. I shared the Cheetos and let the kid lead me back onto solid ground."

"What was the kid's angle? Trying to get in your pants?"

She laughed, the thought altogether ridiculous. "No, you would've been more his type than me."

"Oh."

"He took me back to an apartment he was crashing at. Gave me a place to stay and eventually a way to make money. Saved my life basically."

Frown lines appeared on Jace's face. "A way to make money?"

She bit the inside of her lip, not wanting Jace to know the shameful things she'd done, but knowing he deserved honesty. "He knew a guy who owned a dinky little photo studio. The guy paid me under the table, and I learned everything I could about photography."

Jace cringed, too smart not to read in between the lines. "Behind the camera or in front of it, Ev?"

She swallowed hard. "I really would rather—"

"Tell me, Ev. I need to know what happened to you."

"At first, the guy wanted me for photos. His Internet business thrived on underage teens. But all my . . . scars made me unmarketable."

Jace paled. "Jesus."

"I offered to help with the camera work and whatever errands he needed me to run. It made me sick to do it, but it was do that or end up selling more than my photography skills on the street."

Jace put his head in his hands. "God, Ev. Why didn't you just come home? Even if you hated me, why put yourself through that?"

She looked out at the expanse of green, so he wouldn't see the truth on her face. She'd found out shortly after that she was pregnant and knew she'd never be able to go back to the Austins'.

Scared out of her mind, she'd called the number on an adoption ad in the phonebook. The small amount of financial support she'd received through the agency had saved her life, but handing over her and Jace's baby had been like yanking out her soul and setting it on fire.

She let out a breath. "Because I knew if I went back, I would just be sent to a girls' home to wait it out until I turned seventeen before I got turned out on my own anyway. What did it matter? I was so lost in my depression it didn't really matter where I was anymore."

"I can't even tell you how sorry I am, Evan. I feel like I ruined everything for you."

She gave him a tired smile, the sadness over the past making her limbs feel heavy. "We both made stupid mistakes. Mistakes that other teenagers everywhere make every day. The price for me was higher because I was an emotional powder keg. I made you my life raft and that isn't anything anyone should have to be for anyone else. Especially at that age."

"And how are you now, Evan? Really." His green eyes were awash with concern, his tone tender.

"I'm good. Really. When I finally earned enough money to get on my feet, I started seeing a counselor, did the antidepressant thing for a long time. Learned how to channel my need to cut into more productive things. Now if I'm stressed, I go for a punishing run instead of a razor. Or take out my camera. Or maybe spend a weekend with two guys who like to tie me up and have their wicked way with me."

He finally smiled at that. "Is that right?"

"Yes, all that scary stuff is in my rearview mirror."

And had stayed in her rearview because she'd taken the dangerous variables out of the equation. Can't feel worthless if you don't seek anyone else's approval. Can't feel abandoned if you don't trust people to stay. And can't get a broken heart if you don't fall in love.

"So you're happy now?" he asked, his gaze searching her face.

She absently twirled her engagement ring around her finger and sighed, her most truthful response since he'd come back in her life falling from her lips. "I'm happy enough."

He leaned back in the lounge chair, closing his eyes for a moment as if absorbing her answer, then reached out and took her hand. "Come 'ere."

Jace was tired. Too tired to continue thinking about the fallout with his dad. Too tired to be pissed at Andre for bringing Evan here when it was beyond crossing the line. And too tired to continue fighting how he felt about Evan.

His dad had been right on one thing—it was Jace's fault, all the things Evan had gone through after she'd run away. Which meant it was his job to make sure he made it up to her. Fuck "happy enough." That shit wasn't acceptable. If Evan had told him she was truly content, he would've told her to get off his balcony and go home. He'd been prepared to let her go for good if that's what was best for her.

But that's not what her answer had been. So if Dr. Dan wasn't making her goddamned ecstatic, then Jace figured the guy deserved to have some competition. If Evan spent two months in Jace and Andre's bed and still wanted to be with Daniel, then so be it. But Jace was going to do everything possible to show her that she had options. No, they couldn't offer her a fairy tale, but he and Andre could show her all they had to give.

He dragged Evan onto his lap, her warmth a welcome respite from the chill he'd carried since leaving the hospital. The rays of the late-afternoon sun slid over her left side, plunging the other half of her in shadow. Darkness and light. Sweetness with an indelible edge. "You're beautiful, Ev. Really, knock-me-on-my-ass beautiful."

She smirked, though the sarcasm didn't reach her eyes. "You've had too much to drink I think."

He shook his head. "You've never been able to see how amazing you are. It's a terrible habit."

She adjusted herself, sitting astride him, and reached out to run her fingertips through the hair at his temples. "I think we share the same affliction."

He cupped a hand around the back of her neck and brought her mouth down to his. Her lips parted without hesitation, filling him with a tenderness that hadn't been present in their previous kisses. Their tongues twined in a languid and sensual rhythm that belied the burning need that was beginning to pump through his veins. Her fingers tracked through his hair, her nails scraping along his sensitive scalp.

God, she felt good. Like she'd been made to fit against him like this.

Heat spread down his nerve endings, landing squarely in his crotch. His cock swelled against her, the straddling position and her thin cotton skirt leaving hardly any barrier between them. He rocked against her, knowing she'd be able to feel the rasp of his jeans against her pussy. She moaned into the kiss, but he didn't break the connection.

She ground herself against his erection and their kiss turned from tender to hungry. His fingers went searching for more of her. He found the hem of her blouse and moved his hands beneath it, sliding over her ribs and palming her lace-covered breasts. With one quick flick, he unfastened the front hook and freed her from the bra. God, she felt good beneath his touch. Soft and sweet and burning hot.

He wanted to pull the shirt off her, take her pert nipples in his mouth, so he could hear that sexy whimper she sometimes made, but he knew they were already pushing it being out there on the balcony. The back of the building was pretty private with the greenbelt, but not gated.

He pinched her nipples between his fingers and she fell away from the kiss, her head tilting back as a soft cry escaped. The sound wrapped around his cock, beckoning all his blood there.

"I love that you like it a little rough, sunshine."

She brought her gaze down to his, the flame behind those baby blues enough to set his every cell on fire. She reached down and gathered her skirt up to her thighs so that there was one less barrier as she rubbed against his crotch again. "I love that you like to give it rough."

He groaned, her candidness driving him to the edge. "The dirty talk sounds good on you, Ev. No one would peg you for a bad girl."

She shot him a wicked grin and lifted her skirt just a tick in the front, exposing her beautifully smooth cunt pressed up against his denim-clad erection.

"Ah, fuck. A dirty mouth and no panties?"

"Andre forbade me to wear any. Said we were coming here to cheer you up."

"I knew I liked that guy for some reason." Jace's hands tracked up her inner thighs, his thumb reaching out to caress her heat. The pad of his thumb went slick the instant he found her swollen nub. So wet and ready for him.

She sucked in a sharp little breath as he stroked her clit, the afternoon breeze making her skirt flutter around her thighs. "Lord, that feels good."

"I need you. Now."

She walked her hands up his chest, forcing him to recline all the way on the lounger. "So take me then."

He grabbed her wrists and kissed each one. "Out here?"

She glanced down at his hold on her wrists, her voice going husky. "Out here, sir. Please."

Her change in demeanor alone would've made his cock hard if he hadn't already been ready to pound into her the minute she'd climbed on his lap. He pulled her close and turned until he had reversed their positions on the lounger. Thank the gods of sex he'd left his wallet in his pocket when he came home. He reached for a condom.

She plucked the foil wrapper from his fingertips and tore it open with her teeth. He laughed. "In a hurry, pet?"

"Not at all. May I?"

He nodded.

She unfastened the button of his jeans and dragged down the zipper at an impossibly slow pace. Her eyes stayed on his as she spread his fly and wrapped her fingers around his cock. She stroked with just enough pressure to make him shudder. "Looks like I'm not the only one who went commando today."

He rocked into her adept grip. "I had to rush out to the hospital."

"I like it. It's sexy."

"I'll never wear underwear again if this is what I get as a reward." She drew her nails along his balls, adding an irresistible sting to the pleasure. He grabbed her wrist, stilling her. "But if you keep that up, this may be a one-sided quickie."

She laughed, and he released her so she could roll the condom along his length. "Wouldn't want that."

"Definitely not." He hiked her skirt up and positioned himself between her thighs, bracing himself on his forearms. "Tell me now if you're too sore from this morning."

She locked her legs around him. "Bring it on. I'm tough."

Of that he had no doubt. He sank into her, his whole body seeming to groan with satisfaction as her velvet clasp enveloped him. She sighed beneath him, and he wished he could capture that sound in a bottle—so darkly seductive. He could get off simply listening to her take her pleasure.

He canted his hips backward, sliding his cock until only the tip was inside her. Looking down their bodies, he watched as he moved back inside her. In and out, the connection as erotic a visual as he'd ever seen. He glanced up and caught her watching the same thing.

"You like seeing me fuck into you, pet?" he asked, his voice like sand in his throat.

"Yes," she said—no shame, no embarrassment. He gave her a hard thrust, and her teeth pressed into her bottom lip. "Makes me wish I had my camera with me. You're too beautiful not to photograph."

His balls tightened, the idea of Evan taking photographs starring the two—or three—of them an enticing fantasy. "Maybe next time. Or the time after that. Or after that."

Her lips parted on a gasp as he pushed deeper, burying himself to the hilt and grinding his pelvis against her clit.

"Because I'm never going to get enough of you, Evan."

She squeezed her eyes shut and tilted her head back, exposing the damp column of her neck. "Jace."

A simple plea. Maybe to fuck her harder. Maybe to stop making long-term promises. He didn't know. And at the moment he didn't care. He lowered his mouth to her neck and pressed his teeth to the tender skin, eliciting a moan and a buck of her hips.

Fuck. Her response to the roughness sent electricity curling down his spine and winding around his cock. Her cunt clenched around him, and his own groan of pleasure filled the balcony. His hips dialed up the speed without his conscious awareness as he mouthed her throat. The lounger creaked beneath them, mixing with their ragged breathing.

She dug her nails into his shoulders. "Jace, I'm so close. Can I—"

The request rippled through him like fire. She was asking. Asking to fucking come. Without the pretense of a scene happening. Every muscle in his body seemed to coil tighter, her submission like sexual heroin to his already climbing pleasure. "You have my permission, baby. Let me feel you come."

He reached down to give her even more pressure on her clit and stroked. Her torso arched and he claimed her neck again, this time sucking her skin so hard he knew it'd leave a hickey. A proud, visible mark for Dr. Dan and the world to see. *Mine.* The word whispered through him, feeling more right than anything had in a long time.

He held on, driving into her with rocketing need. A freight train without brakes. Sensation enveloped him. Evan cried out in orgasm, calling his name and burying her face against his chest.

And that's all it took. The pleasure pooling at the base of his spine exploded like a sunburst, and waves of bliss rolled through him as his cock pulsed inside her. "Oh, baby. God. Yes."

Mine.

When their breathing slowed, he eased out of her and settled her skirt back down. She didn't open her eyes, simply laid there with a sated smile. He quickly discarded the condom and zipped back up, even those few seconds too long away from her. He settled back down next to her, and she cuddled against him, both of them perfectly content lying in silence next to each other.

As he lay there watching the sky turn to dusk, feeling her heart slowing to a steady beat against his side, he realized that two months would never be enough. That he wanted her to walk away from Dr. Dan. That he'd never stopped missing her. And that he'd claimed her as his long before he'd known what that meant.

There was no walking away unscathed. It was already too late.

"So Andre told me about your proposition," she said long after he thought she'd dozed off.

He traced his fingertips down her arm. "Is that right?"

"*Mmm-hmm.*"

"And?"

Her sigh was weary, but she snuggled closer. "And I can't imagine going back to The Ranch and letting anyone else touch me."

He closed his eyes, letting her statement wash over him. "Glad to hear it, Ev."

"Daniel gave me two months of freedom before the wedding and the move, so I might as well spend it how I want it, right?"

"Of cour—" Every tendon in his body went stiff as he registered the rest of her comment. "Wait, what move?"

She sat up on her elbow to look down at him, her brow furrowed. "To L.A. For the show. As soon as we get back from our honeymoon we're going to start packing up to head west. I thought you knew."

Her words twisted his windpipe into a knot. He tried to clear his throat, but no response came out. Two months and she'd be gone? Like cross-country gone?

She ran her thumb along his forehead, smoothing the creases. "What's wrong?"

He swallowed hard, forcing down the lump. "Nothing, it's just, I'm a little surprised is all. I didn't know. I mean, I knew that we would end this part when you got married, but I was hoping to still be a friend afterward. I just found you again. And now you're leaving."

Her smile held heartbreak. "You think Daniel would've let me do this with someone local, someone I'd have a chance of seeing after we're married?"

He grimaced. Of course not. The guy may be an idiot but he wasn't stupid. "I see your point."

She laid her head against his chest again. "Guess we just need to make these two months count."

Fucking-A he was going to make them count. Screw it all—his rules, his fears, all of it. No way was he letting Evan walk out of his life again. Not without doing everything in his power to stop her.

He curled his arm more tightly around her, his resolve hardening like steel inside him.

Game on, Dr. Dan.

Game fucking on.

TWENTY

"Tuck your tits in more. You have nip showing," Finn advised as he adjusted the lighting on Callie's left.

"Professionalism, Finn," Evan reminded her intern from behind her camera.

"Sorry." Finn cocked his chin up in a haughty pose. "Pardon me, Ms. Jessup, for my crassness, but there may be a wee bit of your naughty bits exposed on top."

Callie giggled and adjusted her boobs in the snug red bustier she'd donned for the first part of her boudoir photo session. "No worries, dollface. It's not like I'm a real customer. But the British accent does sound cute on you."

Finn blew her an air kiss.

"That looks good. Keep the light at that angle. And muss up the pillows behind her on the bed. They look too perfect." Evan adjusted a setting on her camera, then straightened. "You look gorgeous, Cal. You still sure this is what you want to do?"

Callie shot Evan an eager smile. "Definitely. I didn't spend four hundred bucks on lingerie and have you drag an air mattress in here for nothing. I'm going to show Brandon exactly what he's missing if he keeps hanging out in the slow lane."

"You trashy whore," Finn teased.

Callie stuck her tongue out at him. "Says the man slut."

Evan waved Finn out of the shot. "Enough you two. Let's work on some make-your-man-drool magic. Ready?"

Callie smoothed her expression and gave the camera her best come hither look. Evan snapped a few shots, then checked the preview window to make sure the lighting looked as good on film.

"Looks all right?" Callie asked, her voice not quite as confident as it was before.

Evan sized her up in mock evaluation, then smiled. "I'd do you."

She grinned. "Excellent."

Evan spent the next hour and a half snapping shots of Callie and adjusting each background in between Cal's outfit changes. Finn also jumped behind the camera for a small chunk of the session to get some practice. He kept telling Callie to look fierce, which inevitably made Cal laugh instead of looking fierce at all. But even with that, there was no doubt they had gotten some great shots.

By the time Callie had headed out in her street clothes to meet Brandon for a date, it had gotten dark outside. Evan checked the time on her cell phone. Damn. She'd told Jace and Andre that if the session didn't run too long, she'd try to stop by before heading home for the night. But she was going to have to text one of them and cancel.

They'd all gotten in the habit over the last month of stealing whatever time they could together, not bothering with the pretense of going to The Ranch anymore. That home turf boundary had already been crossed the day she went to Jace's apartment and made love to him on his balcony. She'd stayed the night there with the two of them, cutting through every safety net she'd set for herself.

No matter. She could fall for them just as easily wherever they were having their interludes. Her heart certainly didn't care about the location.

But having "the end" looming at the end of eight—now four—weeks had kept her in check. Ever since she'd broken down and cried at the cabin, she'd made sure to hold a piece of herself back when she was with them. It'd taken her a few days to get her footing again once she'd returned home, but now her guard was solidly back in place. Leaving herself that vulnerable again was not an option. Especially after she'd felt the shift in Jace.

Over the last few weeks, he'd morphed from Mr. Distant Dom to a grown-up version of the boy she used to know—playful, sweet, and so fucking flirty that it was hard to believe that when the bedroom door closed, he could be such a ruthless cuss. The combination was the sexiest damn thing she'd ever encountered. Add in Andre with his relentless charm and giving nature, and a girl could completely lose herself.

She wanted to lose herself.

But that's exactly why she couldn't. There was no way she would give someone else that power again—the ability to define if her life was happy or sad. She was in charge of her happiness now, and she would be in charge of it when she got on a plane to California in a few weeks. She'd prove to herself she could survive all on her own when she walked away from Jace this time. Pass the ultimate test and stop worrying that one emotional slip-up would send her spiraling back into dangerous depression. Maybe then she could go forward and live her life without the white knuckles.

Evan turned off the last of the lights in the studio, too tired to pack up the bedding and equipment. She'd take care of it tomorrow. She headed back toward her office in the front. Finn, who'd parked himself in her chair, looked up and smiled. "I've got all the shots loaded onto the computer."

She sat on the corner of the desk. "And?"

"They're almost sexy enough to make me think straight thoughts.

We did good." He clicked a few buttons to send the pictures to a flash drive. "They'll still need some touch-up, but if that stick-in-the-mud boyfriend of hers doesn't jump her bones after this, then he's just after her for her free cupcakes."

"Or maybe he plays for your team," Evan teased.

Finn's expression turned sardonic. "If that were the case, he would've checked out my ass when he stopped in here last week, not yours."

Evan cringed and instinctively glanced at the door Callie had gone through to go out on her date. "Did he really?"

"No doubt. Ogled actually." He rose from the chair and stretched. "But I wouldn't worry about it. Men are pigs, and that skirt you were wearing that day was kind of daring a guy to look."

She scoffed, affronted. "I had just changed. I was on my way out to go . . . dancing."

Well, not really dancing, per se. Not vertically at least. Jace and Andre had sent over a box with a brand-new outfit and a note to leave the panties at home. The V-neck blouse, snug little leather skirt, and matching boots had definitely been a step out of her comfort zone. But driving over to their place, knowing she was bare beneath, had gotten her heart racing and her thighs damp by the time she'd stepped out of her car. The three of them had barely made it out of the foyer before the guys had bent her over the back of the couch, skirt shoved around her hips.

A little flutter of heat tickled her sex at the memory. Finn's eyebrows disappeared beneath his shaggy bangs. "Must've been some night out. You've gone all blushy."

She automatically lifted her hands to her cheeks, feeling the burn beneath her fingertips. "What? No. I—I'm a little embarrassed that Brandon checked me out. Cal's really gone on him. I want it to work out for her."

"I think it's fine. He's a little stiff, but it seems like the guy is treating her well." Finn lifted the flash drive. "Mind if I work on some of these at home? If you don't like my edits, the originals are still on your hard drive."

"Sure. Just make sure to guard the files. The pictures are private. No working on it with your classmates or anything."

He grinned and tucked the drive into his pocket. "No worries. I'll guard them with my life."

A sharp rapping on the main door made them both jump. Evan looked toward the front, but she'd closed the blinds on the front door when Callie had left and couldn't see who was on the other side. Weird. No one would be looking for a photographer at eight at night. It was probably the homeless guy on the corner wanting a bathroom. Or maybe Cal had forgotten something. "Let me go see what that's about."

Finn frowned. "If you don't recognize whoever it is, don't open the door. Callie said one of the shops down the street was robbed at gunpoint a few weeks ago."

She nodded, her stomach tightening a bit. "I'm just going to take a peek. I won't let anyone in. You stay by the phone in case we need to call the police."

She made her way over to the door and discreetly lifted one slat of the blinds. Familiar chocolate-brown eyes met hers, and her shoulders sagged in relief. Unlatching the dead bolt, she called over her shoulder, "It's fine, Finn. It's a friend of mine."

She pulled open the door and had to swallow down her gasp. Andre. In full uniform. Holy mother of God. Black button-up shirt stretched broad across his chest, badge gleaming in the streetlight, pants that fit him in all the best places. But her body's lightning-fast response was thwarted when she took in the worn expression on his face. She lifted her hand, planning to reach out and touch his cheek, ask him what was wrong, but she remembered they weren't alone. She lowered her arm quickly.

"Hey, *bella*."

"Hey." She glanced over her shoulder at Finn, who'd stepped

away from the office area and into the main part of the gallery. "Finn, this is my friend Andre."

Andre gave a cursory nod to Finn. "Nice to meet you." Then he looked back to Evan. "Am I catching you at a bad time? I didn't realize you'd still be working."

"No, we just wrapped up a little while ago. Both of us were about to leave." She sensed a disquiet coming from Andre, something unruffled in his normally smooth exterior. "Finn, why don't you go ahead and leave? I'll finish locking up, and Andre will make sure I get to my car safely."

Finn eyed Andre, wariness in his hazel eyes. "You sure?"

She offered him a bright smile, one that hopefully didn't say *get the hell out of here please*, which is what she'd been tempted to say. "Yes. Go. I've already worked you into the ground tonight. I'll see you tomorrow."

Evan waited until she made sure Finn had driven away on his motorcycle without getting mugged, then dead-bolted the door and turned to Andre, who had sank into one of the club chairs in the waiting area she had near the door. "What's going on?"

"Jace said you weren't going to be able to come by tonight. And I just . . . needed to see you."

"My session ran late and I told Daniel I'd be home by ten." She squatted down in front of him, placing her hands on his knees. "Is everything okay?"

He leaned forward and touched her hair with gentle reverence as if making sure she was really there at his feet and not a mirage. She hadn't seen him in a few days and, since then, bags had taken root under his normally sparkling eyes. "I just needed to see something good after the shift I had."

The simple sentiment tugged at her. She leaned her face into his touch, feeling the warmth of his palm against her cheek and adjusted from a squat to a sitting kneel. "Want to talk about it?"

"Not really. Just working a pretty gruesome case with the detectives. It's what I signed up for. But it never gets easy seeing innocent people die," he said, the words as tired sounding as he looked. "I can't get the images of the crime scene out of my head tonight."

"Oh, honey."

He rubbed away the crease in her brow. "And look at me, laying this macabre shit on you. I'm sorry." He glanced around at her studio. "I shouldn't have even come here. I know this is your job. If I had known your employee was still here, I would've never—"

"Shh . . ." She laid her hand over his. "It's fine. He thinks you're my friend. No harm done."

The corner of his mouth hitched a bit. "Am I your friend?"

She ducked her head. "I'd like to think so."

"Then why does it always feel like more with you, *bella*? Why when I had a shitty day are you the first person I wanted to see?"

Her breath hitched, the naked honesty in his voice catching her off guard. He hadn't said it in that patented Andre seduction tone, but in a way that made her believe he really was curious about her answer. She glanced up at him, her shields flying up in defense. "Because you had a bad day and wanted to get laid."

Hurt descended over his features, making her immediately regret her glib remark.

"You know, you and Jace are way too much alike sometimes." He shifted forward in the chair. "Come on. Do what you need to do and lock up. I'll walk you out so you can get home to Daniel."

"Wait." She put a hand on his thigh and pushed him down before he could stand up fully. "I'm sorry. I didn't really mean that. It's just . . . I can't be that person. For you or for Jace. In a month, if you have a bad day, I'm not going to be here. We can't pretend like this is something more than it is."

"And you can't go on pretending that it's not," he said softly.

She looked down, her eyes stinging. "Won't change the outcome."

He slipped a finger beneath her chin, tilting her face toward him. "So be it. But at least be honest when you're with us. Trust us with the real you. Not some edited version. Do you think you can do that?"

She swallowed hard, the tempting idea sending cold fear through her. "I can try. But this scares the shit out of me."

His hands cupped her face as he leaned down until his mouth was just a breath away from hers. "Join the club, *bella*."

His lips met hers in an unhurried tenderness, one that belied the fierce grip he locked around her hair. She adjusted her legs beneath her so she wouldn't lose her balance. His tongue stroked hers, his taste and scent filling her senses and lulling her down from fear to something far more pleasant. Her fingers gripped his thighs, the durable fabric of his uniform pants making a scratching sound beneath her nails. She smiled against his mouth.

He pulled back, amusement replacing some of the sadness that had been there when he'd first walked in. "You little harlot. The uniform's doing it for you, isn't it?"

Her grin turned sheepish. "Only because you're underneath it. But I did have the urge to break the law as soon as I saw you standing there."

He spread his legs, bringing the erection pressing against the front of his pants into view, and gave her a look that had her toes curling. "I don't know if you want to test me tonight, *bella*. After the day I've had, I've got a lot of frustration to work out. You might get more discipline than you bargained for. Especially after calling me 'just a friend.'"

She bit her lip, the thrill of the game usurping the lingering nerves about Andre's admission of having feelings for her. "I'll take whatever you think is fair, sir."

He cocked his head toward the front of the gallery. "Those blinds leave quite a gap on each side. You have some place more private? Or do you want anyone passing by on the street to know how much you like to get your ass whipped by your *friend*?"

Her lips parted, the combination of his authoritative demeanor and his uniform making heat surge between her legs. "I, uh, still have a bed set up in the back for the photo shoot I just finished."

He gave her an arch look. "A bed for a photo shoot? You taking naughty pictures, Ms. Kennedy?"

"I'd like to take some of you."

He stood, pulling her to her feet with him. "Only if you're in them with me."

Andre stretched out on the air mattress Evan had set up for the earlier photo shoot and kept his gaze glued to her every move. He'd taken off his gun belt and radio, but otherwise had kept his uniform on. No doubt for her benefit. She hadn't thought he was serious about the photos, but when they'd stepped into the room, he'd given her explicit instructions.

She snapped a test shot, the flash filling the room. She hadn't turned on any of the main lights, only one small one. But even with the subtle lighting, Andre looked downright edible in her preview screen. "I should just stay behind the camera. You're an inspiring subject."

"Already breaking the rules, *bella*? You must want to be punished tonight." He pointed at the spot on the side of the bed. "Over here. I'm losing my patience."

She wet her lips and hit the button that would set up the continuous timer. "Yes, sir. It's all ready now."

Before she could lower herself to the bed, he barked another order. "Get undressed."

She did as she was told. Slipping out of her pants and blouse, then divesting of her bra and panties. The camera flashed, startling her though she knew it was set to go off every thirty seconds.

He smiled. "Definitely a moment worth capturing." He leaned

back on his elbows, taking in every inch of her nudity, making her feel both vulnerable and beautiful all at the same time. "Now I won't have to just conjure you up in my mind when I stroke myself. I'll have my very own pictures."

She shivered. The image of him sliding his hand along that beautiful cock, thinking of her while he pleasured himself was enough to make her muscles wobble beneath her.

"That idea pleases you?"

"Yes, sir. Very much."

He unbuttoned his trousers and eased the zipper down. The camera flashed. He freed his cock from his boxer briefs and stroked the length of it. A soft gasp escaped her. The need to touch him making her fingers twitch at her sides.

"What do you think about when you get yourself off, *bella*?"

Her cheeks warmed, and she dropped her focus to a spot on the side of the bed. "Lots of things, sir. Lately, I simply replay my times with you and Jace and just, uh, expand on that."

"Eyes on mine," he said, his tone brooking no argument. She instantly dragged her attention back to his face. His gaze was fierce, predatory. "Expand on it, huh? We're not being hard enough on you? Maybe we need to push you further."

She held his eye contact but didn't respond.

Apparently he took that as an affirmative. "I see. Well, since the cat seems to have stolen your tongue, show me how you touch yourself."

"You want me to—" She glanced at the camera.

Flash.

"I didn't stutter. Punishment doesn't always come in the form of physical pain. Show me, *bella*." He fisted his cock with another rough stroke. "If not, I may just please myself and leave without touching you."

She closed her eyes for a moment. Centering herself. She'd been in every position possible between Andre and Jace. They'd seen her with her ass in the air, striped with their marks. Why should she be embarrassed about masturbating? But something about sharing the intensely private nature of self-pleasure had her heart hammering.

"I'm waiting. If you're not wet, you have permission to skip this punishment." His smile was sly, knowing.

While holding his gaze, she brought her hand to the lips of her sex, the tissues already swollen with need. Her finger parted her folds and rubbed, the evidence of her arousal slicking her skin. A quiet moan escaped her as she put pressure against her clit.

Flash.

"That's right, *bella*. You look so fucking gorgeous right now. Let me and the camera see what pleases you."

His approval washed over her, giving her the confidence to continue. She moved her fingers along her labia, dipped inside her pussy, and massaged her clit, but not directly. Over the last few weeks she'd learned the sweet satisfaction of delayed gratification, of not coming unless one of the guys gave her permission. Her free hand drifted up her belly and she cupped her breast, pinching her nipple hard, imagining it was Andre's teeth instead of her fingers.

A louder, more urgent moan escaped and she could no longer maintain eye contact. Her head tilted back and her fingers increased the pressure between her legs. Her legs felt weak beneath her and she wondered how long she could remain standing. Her knees tried to give out, but she fought to stay upright.

"Don't let yourself fall. Sit on the floor. Legs spread. Don't stop what you're doing," Andre directed.

She didn't know how he and Jace did it, but somehow they were always in tune with her body, her needs. Even the slightest flinch didn't go unnoticed. She eased down to her knees and then followed his instruction, the polished concrete hard and cold beneath her heated bottom. He could've invited her on to the bed where it'd be more comfortable, but this was punishment.

She parted her knees directly in his line of sight, exposing every bit of herself to him. Moisture glistened at the tip of his cock and he rubbed it over the head with his thumb, the move so natural and unashamed, so ruggedly male, that it made her mouth go dry. *Flash*.

"Show me how wet and ready that pretty cunt is, *bella*. I want to know how much you need me inside you."

She buried two fingers inside her channel and pumped once, twice. Her body clenched around the invasion, desperate for something besides her own hand. The scent of her arousal permeated the small room when she lifted her fingers to him, the glossy state of her skin obvious.

He climbed off the bed, tucked his erection back into his pants, and stalked her way. When he stopped directly in front of her, she didn't dare move. He planted his feet, his stance wide, foreboding. He was so close she had to tilt her head back to an uncomfortable angle to look up at him, the effect making her feel even smaller next to his large body.

The camera flashed again, lighting his face in a menacing combination of shadows. "If the three of us are just stroke material for one another, Evan, just people playing out fantasies, then go ahead and make yourself come. You don't need my help to get off. I've already played the role you wanted to cast me in tonight, right? The guy who came here to use you. A guy you can write off because I'm just part of the game."

She winced. "Andre . . . no."

He lifted his hand, palm up. "Then prove me wrong, *bella*. Come over to the bed with me and let me make love to you. *You*. No roles. Only Andre and Evan."

She tucked her knees to her chest, her skin damp from the combination of the lingering arousal and the abject fear of what he was suggesting. "I don't know if I can do that. I'm scared."

"Of what? Letting down your guard and falling for one of us?"

"Or both," she whispered.

He crouched down in front of her, his stern expression softening. His hand landed warm against her shoulder. "*Bella*, I know things are complicated. But the power is all in your hands. If you can fall for us then maybe what you have with Daniel needs a long, hard look. At the end of this, if you don't want to walk away from us, you don't have to. We're not going anywhere."

She pressed her forehead to her knees. They weren't going anywhere, but she was. She had a promise to keep. One she wouldn't default on.

But in that moment she realized her fear was useless. The thing she was most trying to protect herself from had already happened. She'd fallen for Andre. And had been in love with Jace from the moment he'd kissed her again. No amount of backpedaling or game-playing could save her heart from these men.

"Take me to the bed, please." She looked up at him, caught his gaze. "Andre."

The smile he gave her nearly broke her open, but now wasn't the time for tears. Now was the time to let go and be real with one of the men she loved. Something she hadn't done since she'd snuck into Jace's room that night when she was sixteen.

Andre slipped his hands beneath her, carried her over to the mattress, and laid her down with quiet ease. His fingers went to the buttons on his shirt, but she reached out and stilled his work. "May I?"

"I'd love that."

Evan sat up a bit and taking her time, she slipped each button through its eyelet, exposing the hard expanse of his tan chest. The pace of his breathing beneath her fingertips increased with each button freed. She pushed the shirt over his shoulders and down his arms. She laid a hand over his heart, concern swamping her. "No bulletproof vest?"

He pressed his hand over hers. "They're hot. I took it off when my shift ended."

"Oh." She moved her hand and kissed the spot where it had been. "Good. Because I was about to yell at you."

He chuckled. "I have an appreciation for a little pain, but not the getting shot in a vital organ kind."

"*Mmm*, a little pain, huh?" She lowered her head and used the tip of her tongue to play with the ring through his nipple. She sucked the silver into her mouth, tugging none too gently.

He rewarded her with a soft grunt.

Her hand snaked down to his already unfastened pants and pushed past the fly of his boxer briefs. His cock was hard and hot in her hand. She stroked the smooth length of it, wishing that she could have him bare inside her. She knew both he and Jace had to be tested regularly to maintain membership at The Ranch. And God knows she was clean. But both men thought she was sleeping with Daniel, so they had to protect themselves from the unknown. And she certainly couldn't share the truth with them.

She bent down and gave the head of his cock an open-mouthed kiss. Since he'd touched himself, she'd wanted nothing more than to taste him against her tongue, a salty, spice-laced flavor she now had memorized.

He touched her hair. "Hold on, *bella*. These boxers are strangling me."

Momentarily dislodging her from her task, Andre shucked his pants and boxers, took a condom from his wallet, and then tossed the clothes off in the corner of the room. The camera had continued to flash, but she no longer noticed. All she could focus on was the sheer male beauty in front of her. "Better?"

He leaned over and kissed her lips lightly. "Much."

He tried to shift their positions, to take over. But she pushed him back on his butt. "I wasn't done with you yet."

He sat back with a smile, leaning on his elbows, shameless in his nudity. "Well, far be it from me to thwart you from your mission. Go for it, gorgeous."

She drew her knees beneath her and her mouth was back on him, licking, savoring, enjoying the freedom to touch and taste as she pleased. Part of being submissive to Andre and Jace had meant she'd spent a lot of time on her knees, working to pleasure them at their command. Before she'd met them, giving head had just been a fun little foreplay exercise. Something to do to help out the guy. But the experience with these two men had shifted her entire perspective.

Now she relished her ability to give pleasure. To make a strong man quiver beneath her ministrations. Having been blindfolded and bound numerous times had also focused her senses, had allowed her to appreciate the earthy taste of a man's skin, the scent of his body heating up with arousal—clean sweat and soap for Jace, musky cologne for Andre. The experience had been transformed into a sensual immersion she craved. Even the infinitesimal tension that ebbed and flowed through Andre's muscles as she moved her mouth along him registered on her sexual Richter scale.

Deciding to push it a little further than she had in the past, she took him in her hand and licked the base of his cock, then ventured lower. With a languid pace, she drew her tongue along the seam of his sac.

He gripped her hair and his muscular thighs widened, giving her even more access. "That feels amazing."

She smiled. A man who kept himself this clean-shaven deserved to be rewarded. She mouthed one of the sensitive globes of his sac, swirling her tongue around it.

He grabbed her head with both hands, his body shuddering beneath her. "You keep that up, *bella*, and you may get a new form of hair gel."

She moved back the merest of space. "Maybe I'm getting you back for all the relentless patience you've used on me."

Sweat glistened on his forehead when he looked down his body at her. "Oh, is that right?"

She kissed her way up his chest, crawling along his body, and ended with a nibble along his bottom lip. "No, in all honesty, I just love sucking your cock."

His eyes darkened in that way that made her insides coil tight. "You're the most perfect woman I've ever met."

She laughed. "I bet you say that to all the girls."

He cupped her cheek, his gaze as serious as she'd ever seen him. "No, Evan. I don't." He ran his thumb over her mouth. *"Mi alma es tuya."*

Evan parted her lips to ask him what that meant, but he was already pulling her down for a kiss. His mouth slanted over hers and their tongues twined in a heated dance—one that sent every molecule in her body humming. She sensed a fierceness in the embrace, almost a desperation, like Andre was afraid she'd evaporate if he didn't hold her tightly enough. She wanted to reassure him that she was right here, that she wasn't going anywhere. But they both knew that wasn't true. They needed to treat every time like a cherished gift. Because this was an indulgence neither of them would have for much longer.

She pressed her forehead against his. "Please, Andre. I need you."

Hands and legs tangled, the condom somehow made it on, and soon she found herself rolled onto her back, Andre above her. "I need you too, *bella*. So much."

The camera flash captured the second their bodies collided.

Dueling moans mixed with the rustle of sheets as he buried himself deep inside her. She closed her eyes, overwhelmed by the delicious feel of his invasion, but his voice snapped her back to attention. "Don't. Look at me. I want to see all of you."

Her heart pounded as she lifted her lashes and looked at him. She'd thought she couldn't get any more naked, but this—staring into his brown depths as he rocked into her—was as exposed as she'd ever felt.

He grabbed her hand, lifted it to his mouth, and laid a kiss atop it, all the while not breaking his rhythm. She shivered beneath the simple brush of his lips. "Now you can touch yourself, *bella*." He lowered her palm to where he wanted it. "Let me feel you come around me."

She kept her focus on him, but slid her finger along her clit, the little bundle of nerves slick and swollen and desperate for relief. The instant she applied pressure, her sex clenched around Andre and the pleasurable jolt registered on his face.

Oh, my. She'd never watched a lover so intently. Seeing every nuance of sensation cross his features. Beautiful and sexy and beyond intimate.

She swirled her finger as he continued to move inside her, his pace increasing to match hers. Sharp zings of sensation wicked through her nervous system, making every inch of her skin, her soul, feel alive. She wouldn't last much longer, not after all this and not with his eyes fucking her as completely as his body was. But part of her wanted to hang on just a bit longer. Savor this. No. Savor *him*.

She reached up with her free hand and ran her hand along his stubble, his skin hot beneath her touch. "You're pretty damn perfect, too."

The lines around his eyes creased, almost as if the words were too much to hear, and he leaned down to claim her mouth. Her lips parted for him, accepting everything behind his kiss—the desire, the pain, the loss both of them knew was looming. All of it consumed them and the rhythm of his hips increased as they both began to unravel. Her neck arched, pulling her out of the kiss, and a plea escaped. *"Andre."*

"Let go, *bella*. Let everything go. For me."

Her body responded to his command like a well-trained soldier, all the combined sensations crashing down over her in a maddening rush. "Oh, God."

She cried out as the orgasm overtook her, and Andre chased her climax with his own, the two of them riding the high together. She found his mouth again, inhaled his own groan with the kiss, and held on while her body continued to contract around him. The heat of his release was like sweet fire inside her.

The camera continued its methodical flashing as they both eased down from their high. After a few minutes of lying there with only their labored breathing as a soundtrack, Andre pressed his lips to the curve of her neck, the sweat on his brow mixing with the sheen on her skin.

"Not bad for our first time," Andre whispered.

She ran her hand along the damp hair at the nape of his neck. "Our first time?"

He lifted his head to look at her. "You've never been with only me. I've always just been the third for you."

When she'd first gotten involved with Andre and Jace, she'd thought Andre would simply be an extra bonus—a gorgeous buffer to help her keep perspective about Jace. But over the last few weeks, she'd realized her heart hadn't made that distinction. Her heart wanted them both. Loved them both.

She pressed her forehead to his. "Andre, you've never 'just' been anything to me."

He smiled, but the distinct sound of footsteps had them both freezing.

"What the—" Andre said, rolling off her, instantly on full alert.

But before Andre could say anything else, a man stepped into the studio.

TWENTY-ONE

"What the *fuck* is going on?"

Evan hauled the sheet up to cover herself and Andre, her heart ready to burst through her ribs. "Shit, Daniel. You scared the hell out of me."

"Well, gosh, Evan, *excuse* me," he spat out, the sarcasm at full tilt. "Didn't mean to walk into the building *I* pay rent on and frighten you mid-screw."

She gritted her teeth. "Calm down."

Daniel scoffed as he looked from her to Andre, then back. "Calm down? *Calm down?* Who the fuck is this guy?"

Andre shifted, no doubt taking the condom off beneath the sheet. "Not really your concern, bro."

"The hell it isn't," Daniel yelled, then looked at her expectantly. "Evan?"

The goddamned camera flashed again.

"What the . . ." Daniel glanced at the equipment set up, his face getting redder by the second. "Oh, un-freaking-believable! How could you be so stupid, Evan?"

"Hey," Andre barked.

She laid a hand on Andre's forearm, trying to stop him from making a bad situation worse. "Daniel, please. Get out of here and let us get dressed. You and I can talk privately about this."

"Oh, right. So *now* you worry about discretion? A little late for that." He kicked a leg of the tripod and sent her favorite camera crashing to the floor."

Her jaw went slack. "Daniel!"

Andre bolted off the bed, stark naked and *pissed*. Daniel's eyes widened right before Andre grabbed him by the front of his collar and hauled him up against the wall. "Not one more fucking word, asshole. You did this to yourself, so don't you dare try to insult Evan over something you gave her permission to do." He twisted Daniel's shirt tighter in his fist. "And don't think I won't kick your ass—with or without pants on."

A little gasp passed Daniel's lips, and he squeezed his eyes shut. Andre paused, glanced down, and stepped back a bit. "What the hell?"

Evan's gaze followed his, and even in profile, she could see the bulge in Daniel's pants. *Oh, fuck.* Apparently Daniel's body had a very different reaction than fear in response to Andre's naked form and dominant handling of him. Andre let go of Daniel's shirt and looked to Evan then back to Daniel. Once. Twice. She could almost hear the click when the puzzle pieces snapped in place for him.

She stood, keeping the sheet tucked around her. "Andre, please. Just go, okay? I'll be fine. Let me talk to Daniel."

Daniel turned away, his shame at his body's betrayal obvious. "I'll meet you at home, Evan."

Andre stalked to his pile of clothes and got dressed without looking at her. He didn't bother strapping his gun belt back on, just slung it over his arm. The silence between them was thick enough to choke on. He spun back around, all the tenderness he'd held in his face a few minutes earlier gone. "Is it the fame thing, Evan?"

"Andre—"

"Or are you really just money hungry?" he asked, the words as sharp as barbed wire.

She reeled back, the accusation stinging as much as if she'd been slapped. "You can go."

He shook his head. "Yeah, I think that's a good idea."

TWENTY-TWO

The sharp smack of the door slamming reverberated through the loft and almost made Jace drop the beer he'd grabbed. He kicked the refrigerator shut with his foot and peeked around the corner of the kitchen to find Andre storming through the living area, fury on his face.

Hell. Jace had thought he'd had a bad day, but based on Andre's grand entrance, someone had already cornered the prize for shittiest day.

"Um, hey," Jace said cautiously.

Andre threw his keys onto the glass coffee table with a loud clink and collapsed into the armchair. "Hi."

"You look like you need a drink."

Andre looked up, glanced at the beer in Jace's hand. "We have any Jack Daniels left?"

Uh-oh. "Yeah, I think so. I'll grab it."

Jace pulled the nearly full bottle out of the liquor cabinet and poured a shot into a juice glass.

"He's fucking gay," Andre announced without preamble. "Gay!"

Andre stared at him as if he should know what he was talking about. Jace frowned. Considered the glass. Made the shot a double. "Okay . . . who are we talking about? Your suspect?"

Andre's eyebrows knitted. "What? No. Dr. Dan."

Jace gripped the glass. *"What?"*

"Evan's fiancé. She's going to move away from us to marry a guy who doesn't even like girls."

Jace stared at him. Digested the words. Downed Andre's whiskey.

The liquid burned the back of his throat and he coughed. "And you know this, how?"

Andre ran a hand over the back of his hair. "I went to see her tonight."

"At her *job?*"

"I needed to see her. I . . . I had a bad day and, God, I don't know, I wanted to see her."

Jace knew the feeling. He'd been more than disappointed when Evan had texted him that she wouldn't be stopping by tonight. But going to her studio was a big no-no. They'd all agreed to keep their relationship—or whatever the fuck this was—separate from her "real" life. "You shouldn't have gone there."

"You don't think I fucking know that? I couldn't help it."

Jace poured another shot and walked it over to Andre. "So what happened?"

"I made love to her. Not sex, Jace. Way more than that." He knocked back the shot, made an ugly face. "And, goddammit, I know she was feeling it, too."

Jace sat on the other side of the couch, his breath whooshing out of him. "You love her?"

Andre set the empty glass on the coffee table, his expression turning guarded. "What? You're the only one who's allowed that privilege?"

"I don't lov—" Jace scrubbed a hand over his face. "Fuck."

He hadn't shared his plans with Andre when he'd decided to pursue Evan after that evening on the balcony. He'd gone on pretending that this was a two-month deal. To protect them all in case it didn't work out. But he'd never been able to hide anything from Andre. The guy read people as if their thoughts were printed on their foreheads in Sharpie. "You knew."

Andre smirked. "You've been gone on her since the moment she stepped back into your life. And I've seen how much your guard has dropped these last few weeks when she's around. You've been courting her like your life depended on it."

Anger, hot and fierce, welled up in Jace. "Then why did you go and fucking fall for her too? If you knew I felt that way about her?"

Andre laughed without humor. "Oh, right. 'Cause I'm not allowed to feel anything. I'm just dick number two, enter stage left? What the fuck, man?"

Jace groaned and raked his hands through his hair. "No, that's not—God. When did this get so damned complicated? Now she's got three guys fighting over her?"

The couch squeaked as Andre rose and headed to refill his glass. He grabbed the bottle and poured, his back to Jace. Seconds passed, Andre staring down at the glass but not drinking.

"I'm not fighting you for her, J," he said, his voice quiet. "I want you both . . . I *love* you both."

The admission hit Jace in the chest like an anvil, stealing any ability to draw breath, much less respond.

Andre *loved* him? Not like dude-you're-my-best-friend love. He could tell from Andre's tone, the hunch of his pose that this was something much more serious, something he'd been holding back for a while.

Shit. He'd shared women with Andre for years. They'd both enjoyed fooling around with each other during some ménages, but never had he considered that Andre wanted anything more than that. It'd always been . . . casual. Even though Andre was admittedly bisexual, Jace knew his friend had always strived for a traditional relationship. A quick, anonymous fuck with a male sub at The Ranch on occasion, maybe. But being in a relationship with a guy had never been on Andre's radar—not with his job and his very strict Catholic family. It would flip his life on its head.

Jace set his head in his hands. He didn't know what to say. Or even how he felt. He enjoyed being sexual with Andre. And it's not like Jace had any hang-ups about his own sexuality. He was primarily attracted to women but had never believed in restricting himself to some label. But a committed relationship? A true triad with another man and woman.

"Andre, I—" He looked up.

"Don't say anything." Andre drained the glass, his back still to Jace. "It doesn't fucking matter anyway. Evan's going to move to L.A. She didn't make Dr. Dan leave tonight—not after he was a complete ass-hat to her. And not after he got hard seeing me naked. She made *me* leave. Her loyalty lies with him."

"But why would she want to have a sham for a marriage?"

"Fuck if I know, brother." He turned to look at Jace, his eyes a swirl of emotion. "Maybe she's figured out that love is more trouble than it's worth."

With that, Andre headed toward his bedroom and shut the door behind him, the quiet *snick* more deafening than if he'd slammed it.

TWENTY-THREE

Evan stormed into the house, seeing red. How she'd managed to drive home without breaking every traffic rule in the book was a miracle. Her knuckles ached from gripping the steering wheel so hard. *How dare he?* How dare Daniel talk to her like that, break her camera, throw a fucking hissy fit like he was her real lover?

She shoved open the door to Daniel's office, the heavy wooden door hitting the wall with a loud thud. Both Daniel and Marcus jerked their heads up from what they were viewing on Daniel's computer screen. Daniel rose from behind his desk. "Evan—"

"What in the hell was that?" she demanded, cutting him off.

Daniel's fist hit the desk. "You're asking *me* that? You were the one fucking your brains out with some stranger in front of a god-damned camera."

Marcus stepped around the desk and sat in a chair on the opposite side, obviously wanting out of the line of fire.

She threw her hands out to her sides. "And what the hell difference does that make? You wanted me to find a lover. I did."

"At a club. A private club where no one would see you."

"He's from the club. And no one saw us except *you*."

Daniel turned, ripped a page from his printer, and slammed it down on the desk. "Tonight. But what about when you decided to screw Jace Austin? You know who saw you then?" His booming voice rattled her eardrums. "Somebody with a goddamned hi-res camera!"

She stared down at the photo he'd laid out on the desk, her profile coming into focus. Her skirt hiked up her thighs, head tipped back in pleasure, Jace's hand between her legs. Jace's face was obscured by the thin metal railings of the balcony, but there was no denying the clarity with which they'd captured her own visage. She gasped, her hand going to her mouth. "How did you get that?"

"The gossip site that's running the story tomorrow sent me a heads-up. An anonymous source sold them the picture. They haven't figured out who the guy in the picture is yet—though Marcus could tell right away—but there's no denying it's you. They wanted to know if I had a statement." He sank into his chair and pinched the bridge of his nose. "Jesus, Evan. The newspapers will pick up on it after that."

"Daniel, I—I don't know what to say. I thought the balcony was private."

He glanced up. "How could you be so careless? This could blow up *everything*."

Her stomach flipped over as she found her way into the chair next to Marcus. "I'm so sorry."

Marcus put a hand on her knee and squeezed. "Take a breather. Both of you. This isn't a done deal yet. We just have to spin this. Make it work for us instead of against us."

"And how do we do that?" Daniel snapped. "I'm supposed to be the fucking relationship doctor!"

"Calm down, Danny," Marcus said, eyeing Daniel with what Evan now recognized as the look of a dominant giving his sub an order. "People in relationships cheat sometimes. It happens. So we have Evan admit that she's made a mistake. You admit that with all the travel, you've been neglecting your own relationship. And then you both talk about how you are committed to each other and are going to work it out."

"Wait a second," Evan said, her eyes widening. "*I* have to be painted as a cheater."

Marcus's brows furrowed. "Well, of course. There's no other way."

She looked from him to Daniel with disbelief. "Oh, yes there is. Like we have an open relationship. Or, I don't know, how 'bout some honesty for a change and you tell people you've discovered you prefer men."

"Absolutely not."

"No!"

Both men shut her down in unison, and she wanted to knock their heads together.

"Evan, I can't do that," Daniel said, his tone lowering from pissed to pleading. "People aren't going to accept either one of those. I'll lose all but my most liberal of fans. Everyone else will write us off. We'll lose the TV deal before we can even blink."

"So instead we'll just sacrifice my reputation? Make me out to be the whore who cheated on my oh-so-perfect fiancé?"

"I'll take the blame for neglecting you. Talk about how sometimes cheating is a couple's problem, not just the individual who strayed." He reached for her hand across the desk. "Sweets, I know it's a lot to ask, but I need you to go along with this. Don't kill our future before we even get started. Will you do this for me?"

She stared down at his offered hand, her insides twisting into a sickening knot. Daniel had saved her once upon a time. Had protected her with unwavering ferocity when they were on the streets. The reason she'd never been raped, beaten, or killed while they were out there was because of him. The big brother she'd never had.

How many times had he taken a fist to the jaw on her behalf? Or worse . . .

Besides her mother, he'd been the only one who'd ever been truly loyal to her. The only one to always be there no matter what. She inhaled a deep breath and laid her hand in his open palm. "Fine. I'll do it."

Both Marcus and Daniel seemed to sag in their chairs with relief. Daniel laced his fingers with hers. "Thank you, Evan. This means everything to me."

She sighed. "Just tell me what I need to say and do."

"We're not going to make you do the talking. I don't want to make you lie blatantly on camera. We're going to send you to a hotel for a few days until the initial flash of interest burns out." Marcus flipped over the picture, which was still lying face up on the desk. He tapped it. "And you need to let Jace Austin know that his affiliation with this company—and with you—is over, effective immediately."

She pulled her hand from Daniel's, her full attention switching to Marcus. "What?"

He frowned. "We can't very well have him associated with the book or show in case he's identified as the guy you were sleeping with. And you certainly can't continue any contact with him. The press will be watching you like a hawk."

The room suddenly felt twenty degrees colder and like all the air had been sucked out of it. No more Jace? Ever? And his business . . . "You can't pull the affiliation. Jace's store is depending on it."

"He should've thought of that before he fucked my fiancée," Daniel snapped.

She smacked her hand flat against the desk. "You gave us fucking permission, Daniel! He's a member of The Ranch." She wet her lips. "And . . ."

Daniel's eyes narrowed. "And what, Evan?"

"And we have a past."

"What are you talking about?" Daniel leaned forward, elbows on the table.

"He was the one, Daniel. The one I loved. The one I ran from. . . ."

Awareness dawned over Daniel's face. "The guy who got you pregnant?"

She nodded. "He doesn't know about that part though."

"Christ," Marcus groaned. "This could really blow up if the press finds out who he is and digs that far into either of your pasts."

Fear curled over her spine. *No . . .*

"The name change should protect you for now. And your foster care records are confidential. If we can smooth all this over quickly, no one will have any reason to delve deeper." Daniel rolled his chair back from his desk and stood in a huff. "Go pack a bag. And get rid of Jace, Evan. Tonight."

"But his business is going to suffer, and if they figure out who he is, he'll look like a homewrecker," she protested. "He doesn't deserve either of those."

"Karma's a bitch," Daniel said on his way out the door. "Maybe he deserves to hurt a little after what he put you through back then."

She looked back to Marcus, hoping for a different answer, but his expression was resigned. "It's the only way, sweetie. You were going to have to say good-bye soon anyway." He stood and patted her shoulder. "What's the difference if it's a few weeks early?"

She shook her head. No difference.

She'd always known she'd have to walk away from Jace and Andre. But she never anticipated leaving destruction in her wake. And she never expected it to feel quite like this.

Like her stable existence was breaking apart beneath her feet.

Like she didn't want to face a tomorrow that didn't have Jace and Andre in it.

Fuck.

Panic, sharp and bitter, flooded her, turning her skin clammy and damp. No, she wasn't this person anymore. And she wasn't like her father. She didn't have those kinds of destructive thoughts. She squeezed her eyes shut and wrapped her arms around herself, rocking as the panic charged through her system. Her nails dug deep into her arms, the pain a last-ditch effort to center herself.

She would not get this way. Not again.

She was stronger than this.

Leaving Jace and Andre . . . Would. Not. Break. Her.

She slipped her hand into her pocket, pulling out her phone. Her fingertips were numb as she scrolled through her contacts. He answered on the first ring. "Ev?"

She swallowed past the paralysis trying to claim her throat. "We need to talk."

TWENTY-FOUR

Evan opened the door, fortifying herself with a deep breath, and let Jace into the hotel room. The last thing she'd wanted to do was meet with him in such an intimate setting, but she hadn't had many other options. His loft and anywhere in public was out in case anyone was already watching her. And she definitely wasn't inviting him over to the place she shared with Daniel. So her hotel hideout for the next few days had been the only option left.

Jace walked past her, hands in his pockets and expression unreadable. She clicked the door shut behind him, but didn't turn around, her hand frozen on the knob. She could feel his stare burning into her back. How was she supposed to do this? She couldn't even look at him without wanting to break down and cry.

"A two a.m. invitation to a hotel room is usually a booty call, but somehow I'm guessing that's not why I'm here," he said, his voice flat.

Her shoulders sagged. "No, it isn't."

"Andre told me about Daniel."

Ha. The earlier revelation seemed trite compared to what she had to lay on him now. "I figured."

"Why, Ev? Why are you marrying him?"

His tone was as even as the horizon, but she didn't miss the little catch in his throat on the last word. The hurt. She turned to face him, her hands gripping her elbows as if she could physically hold herself together. "He's . . . my best friend. I love him."

He leaned against the desk. "Like you used to love me?"

She jerked her gaze away from his, tears already threatening to fall. "You know that's not the same thing. Daniel and I— It works. Okay?"

"No. It's not okay," he said, his dominant side seeping into his tone. "You won't convince me that you're better off in some sexless marriage. Not when I've seen how you come apart with me and Andre. You deserve everything a relationship has to offer."

She swallowed hard, gathering her strength again and trying to ignore the pang of want his words had caused. "Someone took pictures of us on the balcony, Jace. They're being released tomorrow."

He hissed out a breath. "What? Who?"

She dared a glance at him. "I don't know. But it doesn't matter. I'm the only one identified in the picture. If we end this now, you'll probably go undetected."

"End this?"

"Yes." She wiped her sweaty palms on her jeans and moved away from the door. He had propped himself against the small desk in the room, so she perched on the foot of the bed—as far away from him as possible. "I'm going to admit to cheating on Daniel. Tell everyone we're working it out."

His eyes widened. "You're going to fucking do *what*?" He pushed off the desk and rose to his full height. "Ev, no way. I don't care how good of a friend Daniel is, you're not going to ruin your own reputation just to save his chickenshit ass from stepping out of the closet and owning who he is."

She clasped her hands in front of her, focused on her engagement ring. "You don't understand. I owe him." She peeked at Jace from under her lashes. "He was the boy on the bridge that day. And the one who protected me every day after that."

Jace winced as he collapsed into the desk chair and raked his hands through his already disheveled hair. "Fuck."

"He saved me and I promised myself I would help him achieve his dream. He would've never gotten to where he is if people knew he was gay." She sighed. "And this offers me what I've never had. Stability. A guarantee that I won't ever go back to how things were before."

"Stability?" he scoffed. "At what cost, Ev? Is the money worth giving up a chance at real love? At being with a man . . ." He paused, wet his lips. "Or men who can give you everything you need without all the fine print."

She looked away. "Sex isn't love, Jace."

"Don't throw that bullshit out at me. Believe me, I know the difference." He rose from the chair and crossed the room to squat in front of her. His large hands closed around her shaking ones. "And I know what I feel for you. What I want with you."

Tears welled, and she clamped her eyelids shut.

He continued on. "I can't compete with major TV deals, but it's not like I can't pay my bills. Even if the store were to fold tomorrow, I could go back to a finance job with a simple phone call."

She shook her head. "It's not about the money."

"Then what?"

"I can't turn my back on him. Daniel was there for me." She bit her bottom lip.

His hands slipped from hers, his tone cooling. "When I wasn't? Is that it?"

That wasn't it at all, but she saw the door open, the way to push him away and save both of them. "I need someone I can count on. A sure thing."

Jace stood, his arms crossed and his expression hard. "Right."

"We've had a good time, but I'm just part of a game for you and Andre. One of your dalliances." She almost stopped when she saw him flinch like she'd slapped him, but she forced herself to keep on. "How many other girls at The Ranch have been between you two? How long do you give them before you get bored and move on to the next?"

"You know you're more than that to me," he said stiffly.

She smirked. "You've been with me a month, Jace. One. Month. You're ready to give up threesomes, settle down, have a nice little suburban life?"

His cheeks tinged red. "I don't fucking know, Evan. This is all new to me, too, all right? All I know is Andre and I both . . ."

Her heart squeezed, her breath catching. Andre and Jace both what? She couldn't decide if she longed to hear the words or wanted to stick her fingers in her ears and hum.

He stalked toward her and planted a hand on each side of her on the bed, not touching her but close enough to make her lean back. His muscles bunched with tension beneath his T-shirt as if he were fighting the urge to grab and shake her. He lowered his face level with hers, meeting her eyes. "You know what? Never mind. You're right. Why would you want what we have to offer? Instead you can have your nice little manufactured fairy tale. The successful husband who looks like he dotes on your every word, the money to buy you whatever you want, and the guarantee that you'll never get hurt. Because it's . . . *Not. Fucking. Real.*"

The last three words lashed her like whip strokes. She struggled to catch a breath—his accusation, his hulking presence, God, his heat, all sending her brain into control-alt-delete mode. Her body, despite her mind's protests, responded to his nearness, her nipples becoming tight points beneath her thin T-shirt. "Jace."

His name came out as a plea, but she wasn't sure if she was pleading for him to go or to stay.

His gaze flicked downward, heated. "Take off your jeans."

Her focus snapped back like a rubber band. "What? No, we can't—"

He pushed off the bed, straightening to his full six feet. "I'm not going to ask again, sub. You promised me another month. If you're going to break your agreement, then you at least owe me tonight."

Her tongue turned to sandpaper—the dominant tone, the beauty of him standing before her, the love she felt for him almost too much to bear. She closed her eyes, fighting the pulse of desire beating low in her belly. "Jace, please."

He gripped her arm and hauled her to her feet, causing her to gasp in shock. His fingers found the button of her jeans, unfastened them, then yanked her pants down her legs. His rough handling should've scared her, should've made her want to run. This couldn't happen. But she couldn't will herself to move. Could only watch him. Wanting him.

He rose and grasped her chin in his hand. "If you're going to say it, say it now, sub."

The safe word. She knew what he was asking. But the word wouldn't form on her lips.

He released her. "On your knees."

Her leg muscles seemed to collapse without her conscious will, making her land hard on the carpet.

He sat on the bed and spread his legs wide. She thought he was going to have her go down on him, but instead he dragged her over his lap, belly down. She automatically reached out to steady herself on the floor, but he was quicker. He grasped her wrists and put them at her sides, then banded his arm over her waist, pinning her limbs down in the process.

"You will not move," he commanded, his voice low and dangerous. His free hand jerked her panties down her thighs and then cupped her heat. She knew what he'd find. He moved his hand away and rubbed his slick fingers along her thigh as if to say, *Your mouth may lie, but your body answers to me.*

"Jace, don't do this," she pleaded, knowing that if he started, she wouldn't be able to stop him, that her undeniable response to him would take over her better sense.

His palm came down hard on her ass, sending stinging pain radiating over her skin. She jerked, but his hold on her didn't allow much movement.

"You're breaking an agreement with your dom. There's a price for that." He swatted the other cheek, not sparing her any of his strength. She yelped but he didn't pause. "And I think you need a good solid reminder of what it means to feel something."

He smacked the back of her thigh. "What it means to be vulnerable."

The blows continued, the pain coalescing with the rush of endorphins, making her dizzy and breathless and so desperate for him she had to fight not to beg.

"What it means to not just love somebody but to ache for them." *Swat!* "To crave them." *Swat!* "To think about them when they're not around."

The tears she'd been fighting all night filled her eyes, dripped onto the carpet. *Jace.* She thought she'd whispered it, but realized no sound had come out.

He hit her again, but this blow didn't have any ferocity behind it. His hand stilled against her tingling skin. "I love you, goddammit. And I refuse to let you run away from me, convincing yourself that this was all some meaningless fuckfest. Don't do that to me, Ev. I can't bear it."

No longer able to hold back her rioting emotions, her chest bounced with sobs. "I know . . . it's not . . . I'm sorry."

His tense leg muscles loosened against her belly.

"Don't be sorry, baby." He flipped her over gently and cradled her against him, his own breath coming fast. "Just be honest. We at least owe that to each other."

"I know." She buried her face in the curve of his neck. "I love you, too, Jace. I'm not sure I ever stopped."

His entire body seemed to sigh against her as he ran a hand over her hair. "Thank you," he whispered. "Thank God."

He stood, lifting her with ease, and walked her around the edge of the bed, then set her in the middle of it. Her bottom throbbed against the cool sheets, but that only served to make her body ache for him more. Regardless of everything going on outside of this room, she needed him. On her, around her, inside her. It was no longer an option.

He undressed her with practiced patience, taking care to caress and touch only enough to stoke her embers. A kiss here. A pinch there. Every contact new and different because there wasn't just lust behind it but love. When she finally lay bare before him, her whole being was vibrating like a tuning fork.

She wanted to plead for him to give her more than just a touch, to fall into bed with her, but she was afraid to speak. Afraid to break the spell weaving around them. Tomorrow her world would fall apart, but right now . . . right now was sacred.

He peeled off his T-shirt and shucked his shoes and jeans, allowing her to drink in the sight of him. His blond hair falling over his eyes, the long, lean body of a swimmer, the intricate tribal tattoo wrapped around his biceps—a bad boy archangel who had already claimed her soul.

He climbed onto the bed and nudged her thighs apart with his knees, parking himself between them. "Have you been with anyone besides me and Andre since you've been tested?"

She shook her head. "No."

"Neither have I." He stroked the back of his knuckles over her clit, a whisper of a touch, but it sent shivers through her. "Are you protected otherwise?"

"Yes," she whispered.

His finger traced a path around her navel, raising goose bumps. "I want to feel you skin to skin, Ev. You okay with that?"

She closed her eyes, trying to steady her ragged breathing. She could think of nothing she wanted more.

"Yes . . . sir." She added the last part not because she had to, but because it felt right. She knew she'd never call another lover that. Jace and Andre owned her even if she couldn't give herself to either of them for good.

He slipped his hands under her knees, lifting her legs and hooking them around his hips. His cock nudged her entrance, the feel of the smooth, bare head making her whimper in need. He rocked his hips forward, sliding into her heat with a groan. "Oh, Ev."

His body trembled against her as he held himself still inside her. She was still tender from her earlier lovemaking with Andre, but the feel of Jace filling her, no barrier between them, was like having the sweetest, most luscious piece of chocolate melting on her tongue.

"God, you feel like heaven." He sank onto his forearms, the length of his body pressing against hers, and captured her mouth in a breathless kiss. She tangled her fingers in his hair, letting her ache for him pour into the kiss. His hips slowly began to move, fucking her with his cock as well as his mouth.

Every time he eased his pelvis back in that slow rhythm, her inner muscles clenched, missing his presence the second he was gone. She moved her hands to his shoulders, her nails digging into the honed muscles, a silent plea for him to take her all. To take her hard. To make her forget about tomorrow.

He broke away from the kiss. "You okay, baby? I don't want to hurt you. I know you and Andre . . ."

A hot flash of shame lit up her cheeks at the reminder she'd already slept with one man tonight. Her gaze darted away from his. She mumbled, "I'm fine."

"Hey." He cupped her face, forcing her to look at him. "Don't you dare be embarrassed. I'm not Daniel. I won't make you pay for something I gave you permission to do."

"I've never been with Andre without you there. I didn't know how you'd—"

"Did you enjoy it?"

She bit her lip. "Yes."

"You love him?"

She tried to look away again, but he held her chin firm. "I—I can't love you both."

"Says who, baby?" He ran a thumb over her lips. "We both love you back. Fuck the rules."

She blinked away fresh tears.

"And you know what it fucking does to me thinking of you two rolling around in that studio of yours?" His cock flexed inside of her, answering for him. "I'm just sorry I wasn't there to watch."

She peeked at him from beneath her lashes. "We took pictures."

"*Ah, hell,*" he said, the agony of restraint crossing his features. He thrust into her hard enough to make her cry out. "You drive me crazy, Ev. If you're sore, you better tell me now, 'cause otherwise, I'm ready to fuck you into next week."

"Do it," she begged. "Please."

"Grab the headboard and don't let go," he ordered. He lifted himself to a kneel and shoved her knees toward her chest, spreading her so wide she thought she might break, and then he plunged deep.

She moaned so loud she worried she'd wake those in the neighboring rooms. The position seated him so gratifyingly deep. He planted his palms on the back of her thighs, holding her in place, and fucked into her with erotic brutality.

Her eyelids wanted to fall shut, the wallop of sensations over-whelming, but she didn't want to miss the view. The ferocity burn-ing in Jace's green eyes, the golden skin now glazed with sweat, the muscles bunching in his chest. God, how would she ever be able to go back to not having him? Her fingers strangled the simple square slats of the headboard as she forced all thoughts away and let her-self fall into the moment.

Jace changed the angle, set her ankles on his shoulders, and freed his hands so that he could touch her clit while he continued to move inside her. Her entire being seemed to contract at the first touch to the swollen nub, his cock simultaneously rubbing against a spot inside her that sent a zing through her nerve endings. *Oh, my.*

The corner of his mouth rose in a wicked smirk as if to say, *Gotcha.*

Before she'd met the two guys, she'd determined that the G-spot was a myth. But just like with everything else, Jace and Andre blew what she thought she'd known about herself out of the water.

"Jace," she pleaded as he continued his dual assault, her knuck-les aching from her grip. "Sir, I don't know if I can—"

"Go for it, baby," he said, short of breath himself. "Come for me."

Her breath wheezed out as she let the tide take her under. The feel of his cock, his fingers, her still stinging bottom, the burn of her muscles from the position, all of it swirled into one massive ball of electricity, pulsing through her with relentless force. Then he hit that internal spot again and everything burst through the seams.

Her scream seemed yanked from the core of her being as the or-gasm claimed her body. Words, some intelligible some not, spewed from her lips. She called his name, she called him *sir*, she called to God . . . but when she called out *I love you*, Jace went over his own precipice.

Fluid, hot and sweet, jetted into her, and his groan joined hers as they tumbled into oblivion together.

Afterward, he rolled off her and gathered her against him, spooning her with his large body. Minutes passed and she thought he'd dozed, but his quiet voice slipped in her ear. "Thank you for that. I've never gone bare since I was with you the first time."

Her lips parted. "What? Not your wif—"

"Condoms for birth control." He nuzzled her neck. "I'm so glad you were my first."

The sentiment tugged at her, made her heart ache. How was she going to do what she needed to do? She retreated to the safety of teasing. "Me, too. I thought it was impossible for me to be your first anything, Mr. Experience."

He snorted. "Are you calling me a slut?"

She waggled her rear against his crotch. "Nah, I was thinking more man whore."

He pinched her butt. "Smartass."

"Said the pot to the kettle."

He kissed her shoulder. "How 'bout being my first love? Does that count for something? 'Cause you've been holding that title for a long time, Ev."

She looked away. "I was just a dumb kid, Jace."

"We both were, but that doesn't mean my love for you was any less real." His voice clogged with emotion. "I can't even tell you what it was like when I woke up the next day and realized you were gone—that I might never see you again."

Dread curled in her stomach. He rolled her over to face him, but she couldn't look him in the eye.

He pushed the dampened hair off her forehead. "Ask me to stay, Evan. Ask me to stay, and we'll face whatever tomorrow brings together. Don't run away from me again."

The soft plea in his voice wrecked her. Ripped out her heart and left it beating helplessly in his hands.

She couldn't answer, so she kissed him long and deep, lacing her fingers in his hair, holding him against her, memorizing the feel of him, his scent. Imprinting every nuance on her brain.

Because of all the commands he'd given her, he'd finally given the one she couldn't obey.

An hour later, he was asleep and she was dressed and packed. She took one last look at him sprawled over the bed, his chest rising with steady breaths, his face smoothed of worry. A picture she knew she'd never be able to erase from her memory.

Then she opened the door and walked away. Leaving her heart behind with him.

TWENTY-FIVE

Jace stretched an arm across the bed, reaching for warmth, for Evan, but his hand hit the nightstand before he found anything solid. And without even opening his eyes, he knew. Knew she wasn't in the shower or downstairs getting a cup of bad hotel coffee.

She was gone.

He hadn't been enough to keep her there.

He rolled onto his back, disappointment enveloping him like an oil slick, weighing down his limbs and coating his throat. He'd lost her again.

She'd told him she loved him back. He'd believed her. But she'd left anyway to go take the goddamned fall for a friend, sacrificing her own chance at something true. All to keep a promise? Or was that just an excuse to let Jace down easy? If Daniel wasn't in the picture, would Evan have given something with him and Andre a real go?

He'd offered Evan everything he had—his heart on a silver platter complete with a little sprig of parsley and an I love you. And she'd turned tail anyway.

He stared at the ceiling, the hazy light of dawn shifting across and changing shades as the sun rose higher and peeked through the parted curtains. The jet-engine blast of the hotel's air conditioner offered an ear-numbing soundtrack to his warring thoughts. What the fuck was he supposed to do now?

Every ounce of caveman in him demanded that he get his ass out of bed and go after her. Track her down and cuff her to him until she agreed to give him another chance. Show her he could make her happy. But he'd made the mistake of chasing a woman who didn't really want him. Once.

He wasn't going to have his nuts handed to him again. He'd pursued Diana until she'd given in. She'd played his ego with PhD level expertise—an intricate dance that had hypnotized Jace into believing that he was the only man for her. The only one who could take care of her the way she needed. She'd exploited his need to feel capable, the need to prove he could be someone's hero and not just the family screw up.

Looking back, he could see how manipulative and unstable she'd been. His divorce attorney had called Diana a borderline personality—needy, attention-seeking, emotionally destructive. But Jace had fallen in love and stumbled right into the snare she'd set out for him. He'd spent the marriage like a lovesick idiot trying to be Mr. Ultimate Husband. She'd spent it emptying his bank account and fucking the guy she really wanted.

Never would he let himself be humiliated like that again. If Evan thought her designer imposter relationship with Dr. Dan was what would make her happy, then so be it. Jace was done campaigning otherwise. Evan had proven the mantra he'd been preaching for the last five years. He was just a good time, a fun lay, not anyone's superhero.

And the first rule in life: Stick to what you're good at.

Now it'd be even easier to do that. Because whatever hope for love that had survived after his divorce had officially snuck out of his hotel room without even leaving a note.

Evan sat in the lobby area of The Ranch, fastening and unfastening the clasp of her watch, the rhythm of the repeated clicking like a metronome for her frayed nerves. Breathe in. Breath out. Don't think. Don't feel.

She'd driven away from the hotel with no idea where she was headed, simply knowing that she couldn't stay there and she couldn't go home. Wherever home was anyway. Suddenly she felt like the last "home" she'd had was when her mother was alive. Everywhere else she'd lived after that, she'd been an outsider. A burden in some cases. An accessory in others.

Her car had found its way to the interstate heading out of the city without much conscious guidance from her. She had no idea if The Ranch was the kind of place you could drop into without a reservation, but it was worth a try. At least here she could hole away in some cabin and fall apart without an audience.

The front desk attendant had been nice enough when Evan had dragged her bloodshot self through the front door, her suitcase trailing after her like an I-have-no-place-to-go banner. But she'd also noticed the way the man's eyes had assessed her wrinkled clothes, her hastily finger-combed hair. She probably looked like she should be checking into rehab instead of a resort.

He'd directed her to wait in one of the cowhide upholstered chairs, then had disappeared behind a large mahogany door that seemed to scream *do not effing enter*. That had been a solid ten minutes ago. Now she was beginning to wonder if he was coming back at all. Maybe she should just go. Find some roadside motel.

But the grit scraping her eyeballs every time she blinked reminded her that if she got back on the road, her car would probably end up with a tree for a hood ornament.

The door opened finally and instead of the front desk guy, Grant Waters stepped through. He was in his standard-issue Wranglers and had a plaid work shirt thrown over a wifebeater, but his dark wavy hair was clearly bed-rumpled and he had flip-flops on instead of his usual boots.

"Ms. Kennedy," he said in an East Texas drawl that could probably inspire the panties off a nun. "To what do I owe this pleasure?"

"Hell," she said, getting up to meet him halfway. "I didn't know he was going pull you out of bed. I'm so sorry."

"Not a problem, I was in the military. I can handle an early-morning wake-up call. Especially for one of my members." Instead of taking her hand, he placed a knuckle beneath her chin, tilted her face up to him, and evaluated her expression like a parent trying to catch a child in a lie. "Camden said he thought you could be on something, but that's obviously not the case. What's going on, darlin'? Who put that lost look in your eye?"

She stepped away from his touch, his all-too-knowing gaze. "I just need a place to stay. Is there any room tonight?"

He crossed his arms over his chest and peered down at her, his fingers drumming against his bicep. "We don't actually. There's a big collaring ceremony this weekend. Multiple couples participating. So we're booked through the next few days."

His answer landed like a sack of rocks on her shoulders, making her bones feel like they might snap beneath the weight of all she'd dealt with today. "Oh. I see."

"I'm sorry, darlin'," he said, sounding truly apologetic.

"It's okay. I shouldn't have assumed anyway." She reached for the handle of her suitcase. "I'll just drive a little farther and find a motel. No big deal."

She attempted to lift her suitcase and barely got it off the floor. The bag seemed to be filled with bricks, even though she knew there were only a few changes of clothes in it. Grant caught sight of her struggle and reached down, placing his hand over hers on the handle. "Wait."

She released the bag and straightened. "What's wrong?"

He stared at her for a long moment, his gaze seeming to tunnel into her, unzipping her casing and peering inside. Instinct told her to look away, look down, look anywhere but at him, but the stare held her as captive as Andre's handcuffs would've.

Finally, he broke the eye contact and hefted her suitcase with ease. "You'll stay with me. You're tired."

She blinked, then his suggestion registered. Oh, shit. The Dom with a capital D commanding her to stay with him? Did that mean . . . ? "What? Oh, no, I couldn't. I can't—"

"You will," he said as if he were Supreme Master Ruler of the Universe. "I'm not letting you get on the road and risk killing yourself or someone else."

"But I can't—"

He laid his free hand on his shoulder. "Calm down, Evan. This isn't a sexual invitation. If it were, you would know. I have a guest room. It's nothing fancy, but you can stay there this weekend."

Her muscles loosened beneath his reassurance. "I don't want to put you out."

"You won't be. Now come on, let's get you to bed." He put his arm fully around her shoulders, and she couldn't help but sag against his side, her body's internal battery fully depleted.

Under normal circumstances, she may have put up more of a fight. May have been more wary of sleeping at some stranger's house. But right now, all she wanted was a bed and the oblivion of sleep. Right or wrong, she trusted Grant. On some primal level she sensed his goodness, his honest nature.

Grant led her to a golf cart parked outside the main building and helped her get seated before securing her suitcase in the back. The ride to his corner of the property was blessedly quiet. She'd expected more questions from the ever watchful owner, but apparently he wasn't going to pry. For now. She had a feeling all bets were off in the morning.

The house they parked in front of was a modest version of the cedar-planked cabins that dotted the grounds of The Ranch. Wraparound porch. Views of the vineyards from two sides. Beautifully simple. Much smaller than she would've expected for a man with Grant's kind of money.

"Let's get you inside," he said, climbing out and grabbing the suitcase. "Sun's starting to rise, and I have horses to feed."

The inside of the cabin was as understated as Grant's wardrobe. Comfortable furniture, simple decor. Not even a family photo in sight. The only make-a-Realtor-go-wild feature was the two-story wall of windows in the living room that framed the vineyard and the horizon beyond. "Wow, that's some view."

"Thanks. It's why I picked this spot."

She let her gaze go all the way to the top of the windows where they narrowed to a peak. Not a curtain anywhere. "Sacrificing a little privacy though. Anybody working in the vineyards could totally see you if you decided to have a romantic evening on the couch or something."

He smiled as he led her through a hallway, his large hand like a heating pad on the base of her spine. "Not an issue. I don't bring women here."

She straightened. "Wait, like ever?"

He opened the door on his right and set her suitcase down inside the bedroom. "I have a whole playground at my fingertips. I don't need to bring someone into my personal space."

"Then why are you letting me?"

"Because you needed me to." He flipped on the light switch in the bedroom. She followed him inside. "And because you're the sub of two very good friends of mine. They would want me to keep you safe and off the roads."

272 ∥ RONI LOREN

"You can't let them know I'm here," she said, the words whipping out of her mouth before she could reel them back.

He walked around the bed and folded the comforter down. "Oh, and why is that?"

"I— There's just a lot going on and I need to be away from it all to think. I don't want anyone knowing I'm here—my fiancé, Jace, Andre, none of them. And if any reporter calls—"

He paused in turning down the bed, looked up. "Darlin', no press would even know the number to call. As far as the rest of the world knows, we don't exist."

"Good," she said, nodding. "I need to be alone."

"Three men on your tail. Sounds like you've gotten yourself into quite a bind."

She groaned. "Are you seriously being punny right now? Because if I wasn't so tired, I would totally throw something at you for that."

He chuckled, the baritone sound making his chest bounce. "Sorry, unintentional. Is there anything else I should know? No bodies in your trunk, right?"

"None for now. Though a few people may want *my* head on a stake by the end of the day. It's going to come out in the media that I've cheated on Daniel."

He straightened, pinned her with his stare. "But you didn't. I talked to Daniel myself when he set up your membership."

"Yeah, well, open relationship isn't something that's going to fly with the general public. If I don't take the fall, he'll lose his television deal."

"I see." Disapproval marked his face like a thundercloud rolling over the calm plains. She shivered. His poor subs must fall over themselves trying to avoid *that* look.

Even though he wasn't her dom she found herself scrambling for some way to make it better. "It's the only way."

"It's your life, darlin'. But in my opinion, any man worth his salt would never let his woman take the hit for something that was his doing. His job is to protect you from anything and anyone who may hurt you."

Her I-am-woman-hear-me-roar gene snapped to attention. "I don't need some guy to protect me. I've handled way worse than bad press."

He walked over to her and laid a hand on her shoulder. "Don't get your feathers all fluffed. I have no doubt you could slay the hounds of hell if faced with them. But the question is, should you have to? And would a man who's supposed to love you, make you?"

"You sound like Jace."

His lips hitched at the corner. "That guy's wiser than people give him credit for."

Jace. Her chest ached like she'd been running for miles. "Thanks for the room."

Grant lowered his hand and headed to the door. "Get some rest, darlin'. You have my word that I won't tell anyone you're here. You're safe from it all for now."

Grant closed the door and left her in silence.

Safe. But alone.

Seems she could never be one without the other.

Maybe it was time she accepted that.

She walked over to her suitcase and unzipped it, staring at what she'd tucked in the front flap. Daniel had handed them to her before she'd left, and she'd wanted to toss them back his way. But now the little prescription bottle beckoned her with its promise. She pulled out the antidepressants she hadn't touched in months, rolling the bottle between her fingertips.

She looked at the empty room, her empty bed, and then went into the bathroom for a glass of water. She tilted one of the pills onto her palm and swallowed it.

Time to get on the train back to numb. Living life in 3-D hurt too much.

TWENTY-SIX

Jace sat at a table in the back of the bar, trying to drown his thoughts in beer and rock music. He'd planned to go home and do the same in a more comfortable chair. But when he'd walked into the loft, Andre had been packing boxes.

Fucking packing!

Jace had asked what the hell was going on, but Andre had simply shrugged. "Going to stay with my brother for a while. I'll get the rest of my stuff when I find a new place."

The few remaining bricks in Jace's already cracked foundation had seemed to crumble into dust beneath him. Andre was leaving? The two of them hadn't talked much in the days following Andre's confession. Jace had been knocked on his ass by the one-two punch of losing Evan and finding out how Andre felt and hadn't even known where to start. But the last thing he wanted was for Andre to bail. "You don't have to fucking move out."

Andre had looked up, his expression flat. "Yeah, man. I do."

And what had Jace done? Had he insisted Andre sit down and

talk with him? Had he told him that the reason he'd been quiet was because he had no fucking idea what to do with the stir of feelings Andre's admission has caused inside him?

No. He'd turned on his heel and walked out. Like a fucking coward.

And now Jace had lost not one, but both the people who actually meant something to him.

He swigged another gulp of beer and leaned his head against the booth, the pulsing beat of the music like a hammer against his throbbing skull. He should've never let himself care. He'd promised himself he wouldn't open up to anyone again, but maybe he had a deeper masochistic streak than he thought. Because it seemed his whole life he'd done nothing but fuck himself over and let down the people he loved.

"Adding alcoholism to your long list of vices?" a familiar female voice asked.

Jace's head snapped upward just as Diana slid into the other side of the booth, her cherry-red lips curled into a sneer.

He had no idea why she was there or how she'd tracked him down, but he didn't care. Now was not the time to have a discussion with her—not when he had more anger and alcohol coursing through him than good sense. "Go away, Di. I'm not in the mood to deal with you."

"I don't give a shit what you're in the mood for," she said, her expression pinched. "You're trying to leave me destitute, and I'm not about to sit back and let you."

"Oh, give me a fucking break. Destitute?" He looked at her diamond earrings and the Rolex circling her wrist. "You haven't worked in the last five years, and you're living with a guy who drags in twice what I was making when we were married. I don't think you'll be standing in the soup line any time soon."

"Greg's money is not mine. He doesn't believe in marriage, so our accounts are separate. And after all the hell you put me through in our marriage, you owe me this. I was there when you built that store. It's half mine."

Jace closed his eyes, counted to five. *I will not yell at a woman in public. I will not grab her by her shoulders and shake her.* "Leave, Diana. I don't owe you a damn thing. We'll deal with this through the courts."

She pulled a manila folder from her purse and set it on the table between them. "You're not the only one who can hire a private investigator, asshole."

He glanced down at the folder as she peeled back the cover. On top was the photo of him and Evan on the balcony—the one that had been released to the press.

Red leaked into his vision, blinding him with the flood of rage. He gripped the edge of the table, breathing through all the things he wanted to scream.

"You conniving bitch," he said, his voice low and dangerous.

"Oh, I'm sorry. Does this make you mad?" she asked coyly. "Now that my ex-husband is trying to take my money, I had to go find funds somewhere else. And his slutty new girlfriend was quite convenient for giving the PI fodder."

Jace slammed his fist on the table, the noise blending into the loud music. "You call her that one more time and I swear to God . . ."

Diana flipped the photo to the side, cutting off Jace's threat and revealing another picture beneath. He and Evan at Christmas back when she was still living with his family.

Shit. Diana knew.

Another flip. A black-and-white photo of a teenage Evan standing by a window. Jace frowned. He didn't recognize the location, but Evan looked the same as when she'd run away, her hair just a little longer. His gaze tracked down the picture and froze. Evan's waistline was rounded, peeking out of the bottom of her T-shirt.

He went cold all over.

Diana smiled. "Guess my PI is better than yours. Did you know your little girlfriend was investigated for a pornography ring? They have a whole file on her. Apparently, she learned her photography skills in a not-so-traditional way." She tapped the picture. "And, huh, wonder where that baby ended up?"

Jace barely heard what Diana was saying. The sounds and lights of the bar swirled around him in a haze as things crashed together in his mind. "Why are you doing this?"

She leaned forward on the table, hawk-eyeing him. "The website gave me fifty thousand for that first picture. Imagine what they would give me for these."

No. No way would he let Evan be exposed like that. She'd lose everything.

He pressed his fingers against his temples. "Tell me what you want."

She leaned back, the face he once thought of as pretty looking like a twisted nightmare. "Five hundred thousand dollars. You give me that, I give you all the information I have. And I'll relieve you of alimony."

He stared at her in disbelief. "*Half a million*? You're out of your damn mind, woman. I don't have that kind of money lying around."

"But your daddy does."

His stomach turned, the implication of her words crawling through him like a deadly virus.

She didn't just want money.

She wanted to destroy him. To make him grovel before his father and lose the business he worked so hard to build.

To win.

And with Evan's reputation on the line, he was going to let her.

TWENTY-SEVEN

Andre crossed his arms and sighed heavily as he leaned back against the bar. "How much has he had?"

Eddie, the bartender, checked the tab. "Enough. His ex stopped by, and he switched from beer to whiskey after she left. I was going to call a cab, but figured I'd try you first."

Andre nodded, watching Jace from across the busy dance floor. Jace lifted his glass and swigged from it, his throat working as he downed it. Andre shook his head. Whiskey. Not a good sign. Jace wasn't a big drinker, so anything besides beer meant he was chasing demons.

Andre swiped a hand across his face. He'd hoped to not have to talk to Jace for a while. To give them both some space. Telling him how he felt had been a world-class mistake, and seeing Jace completely shut down around him afterward had damn near killed him. In one swing, Andre had knocked out his chance for more with Jace and irrevocably wounded a longtime friendship. Wham. Done.

But when Eddie had called him, Andre couldn't bring himself

to turn his back and send Jace home in a cab. So here he was. Like some asshole who didn't know when to quit.

Andre pushed his way through the throng on the dance floor and slid into the booth. Jace lifted his gaze from his empty glass and winced when he saw it was Andre.

Perfect. He was cringe-worthy now.

Andre cleared his throat. "Look, I get that I'm not who you want to talk to right now, so you don't have to say anything. But it's time to get out of here. Eddie's cutting you off and sending you home."

"She had a kid," Jace said, his words slurring together.

Andre frowned. Great. Drunk *and* babbling nonsense. Fun times. "Who? Diana?"

Jace shook his head, a slow move that seemed to take all his effort. "No. She had a kid. *My* kid."

Andre blew out a breath. "Come on, man. Let's get out of here. I think the whiskey's talking."

Jace shoved the empty glass out of the way. "I've fucked up everything. I always do."

Oh, Lord. This was going nowhere good, fast. Andre climbed out of the booth and hooked an arm under Jace's. "Enough. Let's go, amigo. Whatever's going on, we'll figure it out in the morning."

Luckily, Jace didn't resist. Andre led him to his car, helped him in, and locked the seatbelt around him. Jace didn't say a word. Just kept a pensive look on his face—like he was trying to do trigonometry equations without a calculator. Andre had no idea what had passed between Jace and Diana, but apparently it had been more than an alimony discussion.

Andre wanted to ask. Wanted to help Jace with whatever was giving him that look. But the gap between them had yawned wide over the past few days. And Andre doubted there would ever be a bridge back to the comfortable relationship they'd had. So he stayed silent and counted the blocks between stoplights.

Twenty minutes later, Andre had Jace back at their loft. *No, Jace's loft,* Andre reminded himself. This wasn't going to be his home anymore.

Jace had sobered a bit on the ride home and was able to keep steady on his feet for the most part, but Andre helped him to his room anyway. He told himself it was because he didn't want Jace falling and cracking his head open. That is wasn't because he simply enjoyed having his arm around him. God, he was fucking pathetic.

He helped Jace to the edge of the bed and then crouched down to pull off Jace's shoes.

"Why are you moving out?" Jace asked, his words less slurred but still rolling lazily off his tongue.

Andre looked up to meet Jace's intent stare. The green of his eyes swirled with so many things, Andre didn't even attempt to try to pick an emotion. *Drunk. That was the emotion,* he reminded himself. "You know why."

Jace put a hand on Andre's shoulder, leaning in with some pressure. Despite the fact that he knew Jace was acting out of his head, the effect of having Jace over him in that position had Andre's cock stirring to awareness. Freaking perfect.

Silence stretched and Jace's eyes narrowed as he evaluated Andre. Andre shifted his position a bit, but Jace's gaze flicked downward, no doubt catching sight of exactly what Andre was trying to hide.

Jace's brow wrinkled. A beat passed and then awareness dawned. "You're a switch?"

Fucking hell. Apparently Jace's instincts didn't dull with alcohol. "You're drunk."

"Possibly. So if you answer me, I probably won't remember." He smiled in that disarming way that came so easily to him.

Andre rocked back on his heels, meeting Jace's stare. "Yes, I'm a switch. With guys. Happy? Now do you need help getting undressed or are you going to sleep in your clothes?"

"I can do it." Jace peeled off his T-shirt, revealing a view that Andre had seen countless times, but that had never failed to stir something in him. Andre swallowed hard, and Jace stood and unfastened his jeans, surprisingly steady on his feet. "I'm not as wasted as you think I am."

Andre's muscles were coiling tighter by the minute, and the air in the loft seemed too thick. If Jace stripped completely, there'd be no way for Andre to tame his hard-on. He needed to get out of here before he made an awkward situation worse. "Good, then I'll leave you to it. My brother is expecting me back."

Andre shoved his hands in his pockets and headed toward the door. *Get out, get out, get out.*

"I don't want you to go, you know," Jace said, halting Andre in his tracks. "Or move out."

Andre shook his head, keeping his back to Jace. "It's for the best. I don't want to lose our friendship. And if I stay here, that's what's going to happen."

The sound of clothes shifting filled his ears, but Andre didn't dare turn around. He didn't need to see if Jace was getting naked. He took another step toward the door, but before he could reach it, breath hit the nape of Andre's neck. "Yeah, that's probably exactly what would happen."

Andre's blood seemed to still. He turned around to find Jace within inches of him. "What are you doing?"

That was a good fucking question. But with everything that had happened tonight, Jace was acting on pure instinct. He knew he'd had too much to drink, but the fresh air and the car ride over had cleared his head enough for him to realize that regardless of everything else, he wanted Andre to stay.

No. He wanted Andre period.

And he had no idea what to do with that urge except to give

himself over to it. Jace lowered his head and cupped Andre's neck, meeting the naked emotion in Andre's eyes. Fear. Sadness. Want for something Andre had already given up on.

Then Jace kissed him.

A cautious kiss, a soft melding of lips that quietly shattered every unspoken boundary between them. Andre's spine stiffened against Jace's fingers, the shock evident, but after only a blink of hesitation, Andre sank into it, parting his lips and deepening their connection.

Instead of awkward—the way Jace would've expected kissing another man would be—everything about being there with Andre felt comfortable, a natural extension of what was already between them. Sure they'd been sexual together, but this was different. Intimate.

Andre pulled away and stepped back, his jaw clenching. "Don't. Not like this."

"You know why I started drinking tonight, Dre?" Jace said, deciding to lay it all on the line. Now or never. He had nothing fucking else to lose tonight. "Because you were moving and I didn't have the balls to tell you I wanted you to stay. That it confuses the ever-loving shit out of me, but somewhere along the way things have shifted between us." He stepped closer. "I can't imagine my life without Evan. But when I saw you packing your bags, I realized even if I had her, something would be missing. *You* would be missing. I need you both."

Andre closed his eyes and took a breath, as if shoring up his defenses. And for a moment, Jace feared Andre was going to walk out anyway. Just like Evan. But Andre's shoulders relaxed. "I swear on everything that is holy in this world, if you wake up tomorrow morning and blame all of this on being wasted, I will fucking beat you with my billy club."

Jace grinned. Tomorrow he would deal with the shit that had descended over his life. Deal with the crushing news he'd discovered. But tonight . . . Tonight he needed to lose himself in something good. "You know, it's a rare day when I can say I've never done this before."

Andre's gaze skated down the length of Jace, making Jace acutely aware of exactly how much things had changed between them. The look was assessing, appreciative, ravenous. How long had Andre been hiding such blatant desire?

All the blood in Jace's body charged southward. Clearly, his cock didn't care that the person standing before him was male instead of female.

Andre moved closer. "How 'bout tonight I just show you how good of a switch I am?"

Jace lifted a brow.

"I won't let you rush into this. Things are crazy in your life right now. When you fuck me for the first time, I want you to be damn sure you're ready for that, and that it's not because you're looking for some escape."

"Dre—"

"That's my limit for tonight," he said, his tone leaving no room for argument. "I want you. Fuck, do I want you. But that's not on the table yet."

Jace nodded, knowing Andre was right. It wasn't fair to cross that big of a boundary when his brain had been blended tonight. "So what do you propose we do, sub?"

Andre's eyes flared with heat and anticipation at the term. "Let me make you feel good."

Blood pounded through Jace's veins, pulsing at his temples and moving lower. They were really going to take this leap. No going back. Jace wet his lips, letting his dominant instincts fill the spaces nerves were trying to edge into. He may have never done this before, but he knew how to be in charge. "Are you going to make me take off these jeans myself?"

Andre glanced down the stretch of Jace's torso to the open

button at his waistband, then back up to his face. "You really want this?"

"Questioning me already, sub?" Jace hooked his thumbs in his pockets. "Find out if I want this."

Andre, never one to back away from a challenge, moved closer and slipped his fingers in Jace's waistband, finding the zipper and pulling it down. His hand closed around Jace's already hard cock, the thin cotton of his boxers the only barrier.

Jace's body tightened beneath the firm grip. Andre had touched him this way before, but somehow the change in dynamic, the intensity vibrating between them, made it feel like it was the first time. He'd always kept Andre at a distance even in the bedroom. Part of that had been because he'd wanted to keep their friendship boundaries in place, but the other part was that he'd always thought Andre to be one hundred percent dominant. Being in the submissive role was never a comfortable place for Jace so starting up something with another dom would've been an exercise in frustration.

Andre stroked Jace's length, and Jace laid a hand on his shoulder to steady himself. "Why didn't you tell me you were a switch?"

"Because it was easier with you thinking I was only a dominant. I didn't want there to be any weirdness."

"Take off your shirt," Jace ordered.

Andre complied without hesitation, tossing his shirt to the floor. Jace gave him a long hard look and flicked his nipple ring—hard—eliciting a sharp hiss from him. "I should've fucking suspected. You've got masochist written all over you."

Andre's smile was wry, but his pupils had dilated from the spark of pain. "Got a problem with that?"

"No. Kind of makes me want to tie you up and see if you can take it as well as you give it." The words tumbled out before Jace had a chance to consider them. And the surprise on Andre's face mirrored the astonishment Jace felt at his own statement. But as he looked at Andre—the quickened breath, the smooth hard muscle, the erection pushing at the fly of his jeans—Jace realized the thought of dominating and fucking Andre no longer felt bizarre at all. It felt . . . enticing and edgy in the best possible way. And he felt honest disappointment that he couldn't indulge in all of that completely tonight.

He pinned Andre with a stare. "On your knees."

Andre went to the floor immediately and in perfect form—not one leg at a time but instead he rocked down straight from a stand to a kneel. Someone had trained him well. Jace grabbed Andre's hair, tilting his face toward him. "It's not safe for me to beat you tonight. I'm not drunk, but I'm not totally straight either."

Andre burst out laughing. "You're definitely right on that last part."

Jace pushed his tongue into the side of his mouth, fighting not to join in the laughter. "Be careful, smartass, or I may change my mind."

Andre pressed his lips together, his brown eyes crinkling at the corners. "Sorry, I appreciate your concern for my welfare, s— Wait, what should I call you?"

Because *sir* was hers. They both knew it. Jace doubted either of them would ever be able to have another sub use that term again.

"Call me J." Jace stepped back and crossed his arms. "Unzip your pants and show me how bad you're aching to please me."

Andre smoothly unbuttoned his pants and opened his fly, then took his thick cock in his hand. The tip was already shiny with desire. Jace walked over to his bedside table and grabbed a bottle of lube. He tossed it to Andre, who caught it with ease in his free hand.

Jace nodded at the bottle. "You have permission to stroke yourself, but you don't get off until I do. Got it?"

"Got it, J." Andre uncapped the bottle and spread the slippery liquid over his cock with a slow, methodical stroke—one that had Jace's own dick begging for attention.

He made his way back to stand in front of Andre, openly watching Andre's tanned fingers slide up and down his erection. Andre kept his focus on Jace—like the thing that was giving him the most pleasure was Jace and not his own hand. *Fuck, that was hot.* He shoved his jeans and boxers down. "You good at sucking cock, Andre?"

"I haven't heard any complaints."

"Prove it."

Andre continued to work himself with that slow, steady stroke, but he opened his mouth and took the head of Jace's cock onto his tongue and closed his lips around it. Jace groaned as the hot hollow of Andre's mouth sucked the head in and then slid down the shaft, enveloping Jace in the decadent, wet heat.

Andre moved back and forth, pressing the flat of his tongue along the base and increasing the suction. Holy shit. Andre hadn't been lying. The world spun a bit. Jace put a hand on the top of Andre's head to keep himself from swaying. "Get undressed and let's finish this on the bed. I don't want whiskey and that mouth of yours knocking me on my ass."

Andre shucked his pants and boxers, and Jace reclined onto the bed. Without further instruction, Andre climbed in between Jace's spread knees and got back to pleasuring him. Jace's head sank back on the pillows and he gave himself over to the moment. The guy he drank beer and watched football games with was giving him head. And it felt good. And right.

The only damn thing missing was the woman they both loved joining in the fun.

Andre's lubricated hand cupped Jace's balls and squeezed with gentle pressure, yanking Jace from the morose thought. Jace's erection swelled. "Fuck, Dre. That's good."

Andre lifted his head. "Can I touch you?"

Jace knew what he was asking. And hell if Jace's whole body didn't tighten with anticipation. "I didn't tell you that you couldn't."

Andre's mouth closed around him again, but those slick fingers cupping his balls moved down further with confident precision, finding his perineum and rubbing. Electric darts of *fuck yeah* blasted through Jace. He arched, nearly lifting off the bed.

Andre's rhythm didn't falter, but no doubt encouraged by Jace's reaction, a lubed finger teased at Jace's back opening. Jace instinctively tensed, but then reminded himself of the instructions he gave subs and forced himself to relax. The domme he'd done his sub training under had used a plug on him and he'd enjoyed it, but it'd been a long time. And there was something about crossing this line that had Jace's heart hammering. Jace sucked in a sharp breath and Andre pushed past the resistance, increasing his pace with his mouth as a finger eased inside Jace.

Jace groaned, his balls drawing up, an orgasm fighting to break free. *Fuck.* He prided himself on being able to last a long time, but there was no way he was going to be able to deny his pounding urge much longer.

Another slippery finger joined the first and Andre stroked along the sensitive spot inside. Jace gripped the sheets, willing himself to hold on for another minute—the sensations ratcheting up his spine and down his legs were too good to cut short. "Damn, you're good at this."

As if he wanted to put an exclamation point on the end of that sentence, Andre took Jace to the back of his throat. All semblance of control flew from Jace's psyche as sharp pleasure, quick and brain-numbingly wicked, went through his system. His fists balled and a choked moan tore out of him as he came, the hot fluid of his orgasm pulsing out of him in blessed release.

Andre swallowed without a flinch and eased his fingers out of him, leaving Jace sweating and panting. Andre moved off his knees and to the other side of the bed.

"Where are you going?" Jace asked.

"To get a towel to clean the lube off you."

Jace sat up on his elbow and glanced down at Andre's slicked-up cock. "I'm not done with you yet."

"Tonight was about you. I can take care of things on my end."

"And last I checked, I'm the one in fucking charge right now. Get on your hands and knees."

"Jace. We agreed—"

"Don't make me get your cuffs out."

Andre hesitated, but only for a moment. He rolled over and got in position. Jace climbed into place behind him, his legs still shaky from his orgasm. He ran a hand along Andre's spine from tailbone to the back of his neck, enjoying the slight tremor Andre's muscles gave in response to his touch.

"I'm not going to betray your limit, Dre. But I'm also not going to let you get yourself off. Your orgasm is mine tonight." Jace draped himself along Andre's back and wrapped an arm around him to take Andre's cock in his hand. He gave him a strong stroke, taking his time about it.

A soft curse passed Andre's lips.

Jace's own cock nestled against Andre's backside and stirred to awareness even though he'd been fully sated a minute before. "It's a good thing you set your limit early, my friend. 'Cause right now, I'm real tempted to lose my last vestige of virginity."

Andre rocked against him, rubbing himself against Jace's shaft. "I'm not going anywhere unless you tell me to. I won't turn you down next time."

Jace twisted his hand a bit, gripping and stroking Andre firmly enough to remind him it wasn't a chick jerking him off. "You want to come, Dre?"

"Fuck yes," he said between gritted teeth.

Jace slowed his stroke to what he knew to be a tortuous speed. "Ask me nicely."

"Cocky bastard."

Jace bit the back of Andre's shoulder and sucked, tasting the salty sheen glazing Andre's skin. Andre groaned and his cock seemed to swell in Jace's fist.

"That wasn't very nice, sub."

Andre's head lolled forward between his shoulders, the muscles in his back as tight as bowstrings. "Please, J. Let me come."

"That's better. Go ahead." Jace increased the pace and rubbed his own cock against Andre's ass.

Andre bowed up and with a shout, spurted onto Jace's fingers and the sheets below.

When Andre's muscles went slack, Jace rolled them both to the other side of the bed. Neither of them said anything for the longest time. They simply lay there on their backs, breathing hard and absorbing the impact of what had happened.

"You okay?" Andre asked, finally breaking the heavy silence.

Jace kept his gaze on the ceiling. "Yeah, you?"

"That was great." He paused, as if positioning his thoughts. "It's what I've wanted for a long time."

The sentence hung in the air, as if there were a second half to it. "But?"

Andre released a breath. "I miss her, man. I want this. But . . ."

Andre didn't have to explain. Jace knew exactly what he meant. What was happening between the two of them was great, but if Evan wasn't with them, would any of it ever feel truly complete?

Jace climbed out of bed, reality settling down on him like a wet blanket. "I know. Believe me. I know."

Andre sat up on his elbows. "We can't just let her go."

Jace grabbed two fresh towels out of his laundry basket, tossing one to Andre. "She's never going to want to be with me."

"You don't know tha—"

"I got her pregnant, Dre. I took her virginity, and I got her pregnant." He shook his head, his lungs' capacity seeming to shrink. "She didn't even trust me enough now to tell me I have a kid."

TWENTY-EIGHT

Jace watched the fountain in the center of the building's lobby get smaller and smaller as the glass elevator climbed to the top floor. The panel dinged, announcing he'd arrived, and Jace briefly considered punching the button to go right back down. He didn't belong here anymore. He didn't *want* to belong here.

But after looking at every possible scenario, including selling everything he owned, he'd come to the same damn conclusion. If he wanted to protect Evan, he had only one choice.

He stepped off the elevator and into the busy but quiet hallway. Men and women in expensive suits politely nodded at each other as they made their way in or out from their lunch break. Jace's stomach turned.

He'd worked here for years, doing all he could to prove to everyone that he was worth something. That he could be as successful as his father. And Jace had managed to put a dent in that goal. Three years out of college, he'd been one of the top five earners in the company. And he'd been completely fucking miserable.

All the slick smiles, the false handshakes, the endless small talk. Like you actually cared about your client's golf swing.

The whole thing had been like one endless role-playing game where everyone had a script to read from and a cue to follow.

And now Jace was going to step back into that hell.

He straightened the tie he'd dug out of the back of his closet, straightened his shoulders, and headed down the hall that led to his father's office. Might as well get it over with. A kick in the nuts wouldn't hurt any less later.

He passed a couple of open doors, but kept his attention forward. One step in front of the other. The muffled sound of hard-soled shoes on ugly gray carpet mixing with the faint click of keyboards. Jace imagined that's what a death march sounded like. *Click. Click. Tap.*

He turned to round a corner, but a voice held him up.

"Jace?"

Jace glanced behind him to find his older brother leaning out of one of the offices. Great. Just what he needed. An audience to witness his humiliation. "Hey, Wy."

Wyatt gave Jace a head to toe once-over, a crease forming in his forehead. "What are you doing here?"

Jace pulled at the knot of his tie. "Don't ask."

Wyatt cocked his head toward his open doorway. "Come in here a sec."

"Wy, I really don't have time—"

"Come on, little brother. You've got time. Dad's in a meeting." He disappeared back into his office.

Jace shoved his hands in his pockets and followed him. Wyatt probably wanted to gloat and tell him what Jace's assistant duties would be. Good times. He stepped into Wyatt's posh office and sat on one of the two leather couches.

Wyatt propped a hip on the edge of his desk, evaluating Jace with cool blue eyes. "You're here to give in to Dad."

Just the words made Jace want to heave. Give in. To Dad. "Can we talk about something else? Don't you have a new award or something to show off?"

"Don't give me that shit, Jace. You know Dad's the one who does that. Not me." He shrugged. "I know you couldn't care less about all this stuff or what I do."

Jace pressed his lips together, a hint of guilt poking at him. "Hey, if this does it for you, that's great. Honestly. I sometimes wish you'd been born after me instead of before. Trying to live up to your level of success is a bitch."

Wyatt scoffed. "Yeah, my success. I've got millions in the bank and don't have a damn second to spend any of it. Or anyone to spend it with. I'm on top of the world, little bro."

Jace stared at him, shock stealing his words. Wyatt—wunderkind financier and golden child—wasn't happy? Sure, Jace knew the guy didn't date or spend a lot of time on the social scene, but he'd always figured that was how his brother preferred things.

Wyatt ran a hand through his short-cropped dark hair. "Look, just tell me what's going on. I know if you're coming to Dad, things must really be in the shitter."

Jace leaned back on the couch, resigned. What did he have to lose by telling his brother? Wy would know soon enough anyway. No doubt his father would tell anyone in shouting distance how right he'd been, how his wayward son had come groveling back to him for help.

"Diana's blackmailing me. If I don't pay, she's going to ruin the reputation and career of someone I care about." He looked down at his hands. "My store is stable and I know I can grow it, but I don't have the money to pay Diana off right now. So here I am."

Wyatt released a whistling breath. "So you're going to give up your dream to save someone else?"

"She's more important than my store. I figure I can suck it up and work here again for a few years. Get your coffee and type your e-mails—whatever the hell an assistant does. Then save my cash and maybe try a business again one day."

Wyatt laughed, a big and hearty one that almost didn't look right on him. Jace realized he hadn't seen Wy laugh like that since they were teenagers. "I admire your selflessness. But you would be the worst assistant ever."

Jace couldn't help but grin. "What? I can type."

"Look, bro, I know things haven't been great between us for a while. But the only reason I get pissy with you is because I'm damn jealous sometimes."

Jace smirked. "Right, jealous of me."

"Yes, of you, smartass. You're the free spirit of the family. The one who shoots the bird at every rule and expectation and does your own thing. The guy who the girls wanted and the boys wanted to be friends with." His expression turned serious. "I don't want Dad to break you of that."

Jace blinked and stared at Wyatt as if he were seeing his brother for the first time. How had he never noticed how isolated and over-worked his brother had become? While Jace had been busy find-ing every way he could rebel, Wy had been left with the burden of shouldering all of their father's highest expectations.

"Wy, I appreciate what you're saying, but I don't know what else I can do. I can't let Diana release the information she has."

His brother crossed his arms. "How much does she want?"

"Half a million."

"It'll be in your account tomorrow with an extra hundred grand to put toward your store."

Jace stood, waving him off. "No, dude. I can't take your money. It's not your place."

"Pay me back when the store expands," Wyatt said, standing as well. "I'll consider this an investment in a good business."

Jace couldn't believe what he was hearing. Wyatt was going to trust him with that much money? Just like that. And put money into Jace's business? "You want to invest in Wicked? Have you ever even been in a store like mine before?"

Wyatt's smile was droll. "I don't date a lot. But I'm not dead, moron."

Jace raised his palms. "Sorry, big brother. I wasn't sure if you'd lost your V-card yet."

Wyatt punched Jace's shoulder. "Fucker."

Jace stuck out his hand. "No, but seriously, man. This is . . . Well, just thank you. Really. It means more than you know."

Wyatt took Jace's hand in a firm shake, then pulled him in for a gruff hug. "Happy to help. Now get your ass out of here before Dad catches your scent like a dog on the hunt."

Jace stepped back. "I'll find a way to repay you. Not just the money but the favor."

"Don't worry about it."

"No, I already have something in mind." Jace turned and headed out the door, hiding a smile. Once everything settled down, Mr. Workaholic was getting a first-class ticket to a nice big ranch outside the city limits.

Because Jace wouldn't need his own membership anymore.

Being there without Evan was a form of torture he refused to sign up for.

TWENTY-NINE

Evan leaned against the trunk of an ancient oak tree as she scanned through the photos she'd taken of the vineyards. The little digital camera wouldn't have been her equipment of choice, but she hadn't thought to pack one of her own cameras when she'd left the house.

Grant had asked her to take some pictures for a new brochure he was developing for the official winery side of his property. Apparently, in his free time he offered tours and tastings for the public. He'd given her his camera to use even though she'd protested that she'd never get good enough shots with it.

He'd told her to take some test photos to give him an idea of what she could do. Evan suspected he was just being kind and giving her something to focus on while she was holed up at his place. But she'd done the work nonetheless. And it had distracted her. For a while.

But she knew she'd have to head back to town soon. She'd read the Internet stories over the weekend. The cheating scandal had broken and the press was not being kind to her. It didn't help that

Daniel was playing the role of the poor, wronged fiancé a little too convincingly. The media had heaped praise and sympathy on top him like he was some sort of self-help sundae.

He'd called her a number of times, but she couldn't tolerate talking to him yet. She'd texted him that she was somewhere safe and she'd be home soon. Maybe once her medication kicked in more she could walk back into his house and play fiancée without wanting to either sob or punch someone in the face. Right now, she was still too raw.

She hit the delete button on a few shots that had captured too much of the late-afternoon sun and had thrown off the lighting. Her cell phone buzzed in her pocket and she accidentally deleted a photo she'd wanted to keep.

"Dammit." She set the camera down and pulled her phone from the pocket of her jeans, expecting it to be Daniel calling yet again. But instead, Andre's name lit up the screen. Her chest contracted. How could she talk to him without losing it? She could barely think of his or Jace's name without wanting to do tequila shots with a Xanax chaser.

But she'd walked out on the both of them like a yellow-bellied coward. Hadn't even told Andre good-bye. She knew he deserved better than that. By the third ring, she'd built up enough nerve to hit the button. "Hello?"

A breath. Then: "Hey, *bella*."

She bit her lip, just the sound of his voice, the way he said her pet name, making her bones ache. "Hey Andre."

"You doing okay?"

"Been better," she admitted. "Andre, I'm so—"

"Shh, *bella*. Listen. I want to talk to you, but I'm calling because of Jace."

Her breath caught. "Is everything all right?"

He sighed. "A lot's happened. Where are you?"

She looked out at the peaceful rows of grapevine stretching out in the distance, the scene in direct contrast to the riot of emotions beating her raw on the inside. "I'm at The Ranch."

A long pause.

She cringed, realizing too late how bad that sounded. "Grant gave me a place to stay. I'm just . . ." *Avoiding. Hiding. Wallowing. Hating my life.* "Resting."

"You need to come back to town and talk to Jace. He knows about the baby," he said, his voice so quiet, she almost thought she'd imagined what he said.

She gasped, the words like a fist to the sternum. Jace *knew.* "Wh—How?"

"His ex-wife hired a private investigator to get dirt on you so she could use it against him. Apparently, the PI has been posing as your friend Callie's new boyfriend so he could get close to you."

Evan's nails dug into the soft earth beneath the tree, trying to find a grip in her spinning world. Jace knew. He knew she'd betrayed him in the worst possible way. "Oh, God, he must hate me."

"*Bella*, you need to tell him the truth. Can you come to the loft tonight so we can all talk?"

She leaned her head back against the bark of the tree, tears filling her eyes. "Yes. I'll be there."

THIRTY

Evan wiped off the sweat that had formed on her forehead after making the trek up the stairs to Jace and Andre's loft.
She hiked her purse up higher on her shoulder, gripping the strap
as if it was the only thing holding her upright. On the long drive
here, she'd gone over and over how she could have this conversation. But there was no way to make it any easier. She'd had Marcus
meet her a few miles before she hit city limits to give her something
she needed to pass along to Jace, but other than that, she had no
plan.

The fact was Jace knew a secret that should've never been kept
from him.

And he probably hated her. Deservedly so.

And now it was time to tell him the information she should've
provided him with all those years ago.

Her hand shook as she raised it to the door, but she managed to
knock and not run back down the stairs. A few seconds passed and
she thought maybe they weren't home, but then the door swung
open. Andre stood there in track pants and a standard-issue Dallas

PD T-shirt, his tired eyes lighting when he saw her standing on the other side.

She almost imploded with the need to throw her arms around his neck and bury herself in his comfort. But that wasn't what she'd come here for. And she had no idea where she stood with Andre. She hadn't betrayed him like she had Jace, but she had walked away from his love to go to Daniel.

"*Bella*," Andre said, the word so soft, but landing heavily against her. His gaze traced over her face.

She automatically touched her cheek, knowing her face was probably puffy from crying. "Hi. Is Jace home? I— We all need to talk."

Andre extended the arm that was holding the door, pushing it wide and giving her a view of Jace sitting in the living area behind him. "Come on in."

Jace looked her way when she stepped inside, pain marching across his face at the mere sight of her. He turned to the news on TV, his voice coming out hollow. "Andre called you."

She swallowed hard. "Yes."

Jace sniffed.

Andre's large hand cupped her elbow as he stepped up beside her. "Come on, *bella*. Sit. You two need to talk."

He led her to an armchair then sat down on the couch next to Jace, leaving her alone to face the both of them. Andre took the remote control from Jace's hand and clicked the TV off. Jace didn't stop looking in that direction. "You don't have to worry about the information going public. I took care of things with Diana."

Meaning he'd paid that wretched woman. Which made Evan feel even more like shit. "Thank you."

Quiet filled the room, the airy loft filling with the thick sludge of silence.

She set her purse on the floor and then laced her fingers in front of her in her lap, staring at her hands like they held the script on how to say the right thing. They didn't, so she went for the only thing she could say. "I'm so sorry I didn't tell you, Jace."

He winced, closed his eyes. "You told me that night you were on the pill. I would've never—"

She shook her head. "I *was* on it. I didn't know you had to take it longer than a month for it to be effective."

He looked at her finally, grief not anger shifting his features. "Why didn't you come back to me, Ev? I would've helped you. Would've given you . . . and our baby whatever you needed."

The hurt in his voice was like tiny particles of glass digging into every vulnerable spot inside of her. "You were nineteen. And you were . . ."

His lip curled. "Go ahead. Say it. I was what? Irresponsible? A fuckup? The guy who took advantage of you because he didn't know how to keep his dick in his pants? Believe me, it's nothing I don't already know."

"No," she said, her voice sharper than intended. "I loved you, dammit, and you were on your way to being something. I wasn't going to be the person to screw that up."

He scoffed. "Yeah, 'cause look how great I turned out, right?"

She held out her hands. "You did turn out great! Look at what you've built for yourself, the man you've become."

"I'm a guy who owns a sex shop, Ev. Who's been disowned by his family. And who is apparently a deadbeat dad who didn't even know I had a child out there. Yeah, some man. No wonder you'd rather marry Daniel."

"No, Jace. My choices were mine. Sleeping with you. Running away. I knew you wouldn't have turned your back on me if I had come to you pregnant. But"—sadness choked her—"my whole life since I went into foster care was about people pretending to care about me. Out of obligation. Because there was paperwork and money exchanged. I couldn't bear to have you be one of those people."

"God, Evan, it wouldn't have been like that—"

"You know that pregnancy saved my life," she said, cutting him off. "My depression was out of control long before I slept with you. You were right to be worried when you found my scars. There wasn't a day that passed back then that I didn't cut. Not a week went by without me wanting to end it all." Tears finally made it past her resistance and tracked quietly down her cheeks. "Knowing that baby was growing inside me kept me putting one foot in front of the other. Gave me a reason to stick around."

The green in his eyes went shiny. "What happened to our baby, Ev?"

"I found an adoption agency. Lied and told them I didn't know who the father was. They helped me with my doctor bills and some of my living expenses. It's what allowed me to save up money to escape the guy I was taking photos for." She swiped the moisture from her cheeks and leaned over to pull an envelope from her purse. She sat it in her lap, smoothing a folded edge. "Her name is Dahlia. And she's gorgeous and smart and . . . happy."

The sound of his daughter's name reached into Jace's psyche and sliced through all the tethers holding his emotions in control. He choked on the knot of grief that filled his throat. He had a *child*. One he'd never know. Never get to hold. Or tell he loved.

The knowledge swamped him, leaving him speechless, gutted.

Andre laid a steadying hand on Jace's shoulder, a silent pillar of support.

Evan pushed forward when she saw Jace wasn't going to respond, her voice as shaky as her hands. "I placed her with a couple who lives in Oklahoma. They never adopted any other children, so she's the center of their universe." She wet her lips and set the envelope she'd been holding on the coffee table. "They send me pictures every few months."

Jace couldn't move. There was no way he could handle look-ing at a photo of his daughter right now. He raised his gaze to Evan, who looked bruised and battered with her own emotions. He wanted to be angry with her. To lash out. She'd taken away his chance to know his child.

But all he could feel was sadness over the paths they'd taken, over the too harsh consequences for a simple mistake of youth. "Does she have everything she needs?"

Evan's throat worked as she swallowed. "She has love and safety. Her parents are middle class, so they have the same financial concerns any family would. I've been saving everything I've earned over the past few years and have put it into a college fund for her. It's not much, but I figured once Daniel's show started, I'd be able to put enough in there to cover her through all her schooling."

He frowned. "So your arrangement with Daniel was more than just obligation to him."

She touched her left ring finger, that fucking engagement ring still encircling it. "I'd never be able to earn enough money in time on my own."

"Dahlia's college will be covered," he said, his tone leaving no room for her to argue.

"What? No, Jace. I know your business—"

"I have the money," he said, cutting her off. With Wyatt's boost, no doubt Wicked would be fully back on its feet in no time. And there was no way he was letting his kid go without something.

"Thank you." She looked down at her hands. Took a breath. "I'm sorry, Jace. I know you must hate me."

Her assumption was like a kick to the ribs. Did she really think that was possible? That he'd hate her over mistakes she made when she was a teenager? "You don't have much faith in me, do you?"

She wiped her palms on her jeans, her whole demeanor going into retreat mode. "I need to go."

"You don't have to," Andre said, leaning forward, forearms on his thighs. Jace could tell it was taking every ounce of Andre's restraint not to scoop up Evan and comfort her.

Her gaze flicked to Jace.

But Jace couldn't muster up the words to say what he wanted to. He loved her. Couldn't imagine his life without her in it. But how were they supposed to start something meaningful when she believed he'd bail at the first sign of strife?

The kind of relationship they'd be entering into would require the ultimate trust—not just the D/s aspect, but a triad to contend with. A setup that would dissolve into jealousy, mixed feelings, and insecurity if all three partners weren't completely confident in the bond they had. Right now, she wasn't ready for that. She'd sabotage it. They'd destroy each other.

And the realization of what that meant he needed to do just about killed him.

"Tell us what you want, Evan," Jace said, authority underlining his tone.

She glanced from him to Andre, then back to him, the turmoil behind her eyes like a raging spring storm. "I love you both. I want to be with you, but—"

Jace raised his hand, blocking the rest of her statement. "That's enough."

Andre sent him a what-the-fuck-are-you-doing glare, but Jace ignored it. Evan might walk out the door and never look back, but this was a risk he had to take. Otherwise, the three of them were going to build something on a foundation of silt. A little rough water and they'd go under in a blink.

Jace stood. "We all deserve better than 'I love you, but.' When you can take the qualifier out of that sentence, you let us know. And we'll talk. Until then, I think it's time for you to leave."

Part of him wished she would dispute him. Stomp her foot and tell him there was no qualifier. They could sweep her up, kiss away her tears, and make her forget the pain of the last week. But the sag of her shoulders told him he hadn't read her wrong. She wasn't ready to give herself over completely to this, to them. Maybe would never be.

And that flayed him. Made him want to chain her to his bed and spend the night convincing her otherwise. But he'd learned that love couldn't be forced or commanded or even won. It was something that shouldn't take convincing. It just was or wasn't.

And for her, for now, it wasn't. At least not fully.

So what could he do but let her leave?

Evan rose from the chair, her gaze on the floor. "I'm sorry, you're right. You both deserve better than what I can give you right now."

"*Bella*," Andre protested when she headed toward the door.

Jace put a firm hand on Andre's shoulder. "Let her go, Dre."

Andre didn't say anything else as they watched Evan walk away.

The front door shut behind her. She hadn't looked back.

She'd let them go.

THIRTY-ONE

Today was the big day. Evan adjusted her dress for the umpteenth time and then touched the twist in her hair, making sure everything was still in place. Her heart was pounding so hard it could've substituted for the bass in a death metal song.

She'd never liked being in front of a crowd like this. One misstep or wrong line and it'd be splashed all over every gossip website. She'd rehearsed her part in her head, going over and over the words last night.

The man who'd been acting as her handler this morning stepped into her dressing area. "He's ready for you, Ms. Kennedy."

She nodded and took a deep breath, smoothing her dress once more. "Thanks, Eric."

Eric smiled. "You look beautiful. No need to be nervous."

Yeah, right. The biggest decision she'd ever made in her life, but no need to get the jitters. "Let's do this."

He took her arm and led her out of the room and into the hall-way. She focused on breathing in and out and not tripping in the completely indulgent heels she'd gotten for the occasion.

Eric eased her around the last corner and into the main area. Daniel smiled at her when he caught sight of her. If he shared her nerves, he didn't show it. His suit, hair, and expression were as nonplussed as ever. In that moment, she'd never loved him more. This was the right decision.

Eric guided her to the edge of the stage, adeptly keeping her out of the way of the bustling crew and the cameras. "As soon as Daniel welcomes the audience back from commercial, he'll call you up."

"Right. Got it."

"Good luck." He patted her shoulder and then put his headset back on.

They cued Daniel, and he gave a smile to the camera that was the perfect mix of welcome and reverence for what he was about to discuss. The audience, when this pilot premiered, was going to be eating out of his hand. Women and gay men everywhere were going to want to comfort him—the handsome relationship doctor who was going to announce the dissolution of his engagement on national television. The man who was going to wish the woman who was leaving him all the best and assure everyone that they would stay the closest of friends.

The execs who'd freaked when Evan's affair had hit the news were now drooling like men at a titty bar over the chance to launch the show with Daniel as the ultimate sympathetic hero. The no-such-thing-as-bad-press cliché had proven golden.

And thank God for that because she'd realized when she'd left Jace and Andre's apartment that even without them in her life, she couldn't go on playing a role for Daniel. The last few months had been like biting that Garden of Eden apple. No amount of antidepressants or denial were going to let her "un-feel" what she'd experienced with Jace and Andre. They'd tattooed themselves onto her bones, shifted everything inside her to the point where she'd never again be satisfied with "good enough."

So even if she had to go through her life alone, at least she'd be authentic about it. Her mother and father had both died too young and continuing to live her own life on autopilot seemed the ultimate insult to the both of them.

Daniel had done decent damage control for her in the press, saying that they'd both figured out that they were better friends than lovers. Ha! If the public only knew how true that was. Daniel still didn't feel comfortable coming out yet, but she hoped after he grew more secure with the show, he'd take that step as well.

"And now I'd like to welcome my best friend to join me, Ms. Evan Kennedy," Daniel announced, dragging her from her thoughts.

She took one more deep breath, put on a nervous smile, and walked on stage to publicly break up with the boy she'd plan to marry.

THIRTY-TWO

Jace cracked open the beers and distributed them around the living room to Andre, Reid, and Grant. Then he handed Brynn a glass of wine. His friends had supposedly come over to celebrate Jace's birthday, but somehow he'd ended up serving them. Lazy bastards.

"You don't prefer wine, Grant?" Brynn asked. She had her legs draped over Reid's lap and was looking downright mellow after two glasses of Chardonnay.

Grant took a pull off the beer and smiled. "I don't trust these Neanderthals to have anything decent."

"Well, maybe if you'd bring over some free bottles every once in a while, we would," Andre said. "Your shit ain't cheap."

"And waste it on your untrained palates?" Grant said, somehow managing smug with that twangy accent of his. He looked to Brynn. "Darlin', if you'd like some, I'll package up a case next time you and Reid are at The Ranch and send you home with some."

Reid rubbed circles at the base on Brynn's spine, an unconscious possessive hold on his woman while she was in a room full of dominant men. Jace couldn't help but feel hollow at the sight. His own hand filled with nothing but a cold beer bottle.

Two months. Evan had been gone two fucking months. It felt like a century.

He should've never let her walk. His instincts had been wrong. Once again.

Reid smiled. "Sounds good. I plan to take Brynn out there next weekend. She's got a bit of a voyeuristic streak that we haven't indulged in a while."

Brynn gasped and smacked Reid on the chest. "Reid!"

Reid chuckled. "You're in a room full of guys, who, except for Andre, have seen you naked and bound for me. You've been on your knees for Jace. I think we're beyond pretending you're Ms. Innocent."

Her cheeks stained pink, and she took a dainty sip from her wine. "Well you could've at least left Andre with that illusion. Give me some shred of a chance to have someone think I'm a lady."

Andre smiled. "If it makes you feel any better, I've been on my knees for Jace, too."

She tried to maintain her composure, but an indelicate snort escaped. Her gaze went between the two of them. "Damn, that's hot."

Jace grinned, the melancholy mood that seemed to chase him no matter where he was lately easing a bit. At least he had good friends. And Andre. Jace didn't know how he would've made it through the last two months without him. Exploring the new relationship between them had been one of the few bright spots in an otherwise depressing reel of film. Though both he and Andre were all too aware, even in the heated moments, that there was a vital component missing. A sense of incompleteness neither could shake.

Reid rolled his eyes. "See. Dirty voyeur. And don't get any ideas, sugar. I'm not sucking Jace's dick no matter how much it would turn you on."

"Word." Jace shook his head. He was about as attracted to his childhood friend as he was to a swarm of wasps. And though he'd enjoyed the ménage with Brynn, Jace knew it'd been a one-time only deal. Reid and Brynn were kinky as shit, but they were built for one-on-one.

Grant grabbed one of the remaining slices of pizza sitting in the open box on the coffee table. "So when are you two going to come back to my place?"

Jace grabbed a chair from the dining room and straddled it, the little lift in his mood flatlining. The thought of going to The Ranch and dominating any other woman besides Evan made his beer turn bitter in his mouth. "I've been busy with the store."

"Been working on a big case," Andre mumbled at the same time.

Grant took a bite of pizza, considered them. "She's doing well, you know. I've seen her."

Jace straightened in his chair like he'd been pinched, his possessive gene going on full alert. "She's been in L.A. What do you mean you've seen her?"

Grant rarely left his business, so when he'd "seen" someone it usually meant he'd seen them naked.

"She came back after she taped that first show. I hired her," Grant said, his tone as casual as his worn jeans. He tore off another bite of pizza.

Andre looked horrified. "As a submissive?"

Grant smirked. "Look at you two. Like a pack of dogs ready to tear me apart. I'm not that big of an asshole. She needed a place to stay while the media attention died down and while she searched for a new apartment. I gave her a cabin to use in exchange for taking some commercial photos for the winery."

Jace's mouth had gone so dry he was surprised he was able to speak. "She's living at the fucking Ranch?"

The unattached doms would be hunting her like lions stalking a gazelle.

"She handles herself just fine," Grant assured. "Colby's been looking out for her."

"Oh, I just bet he has," Jace seethed. "I bet he's been looking quite a lot."

Reid coughed over what sounded suspiciously like a laugh, drawing Jace's attention. Brynn seemed to be fighting a smile.

"What are you two grinning about?" Jace snapped.

Reid shrugged. "Someone I know once busted my ass to stop whining about not having the girl I wanted and to go get her already. What are you two idiots doing sitting around for? You're both obviously gone on the girl."

"Doesn't matter if she's not gone on us," Andre said, setting his untouched beer on the coffee table. "We left the door open."

Grant groaned and stood, pulling something from his back pocket. "Damn, you two are a pitiful bunch." He handed Jace a small square envelope. "Happy birthday. She told me not to give you this until we finished your party, but despite reports otherwise, my sadism only goes so far."

Jace's pulse raced. She'd sent them something?

Andre was across the room and at Jace's side so quick, Jace was sure he'd teleported. "Open it, man."

Not caring that everyone was there to witness whatever was inside, Jace tore the thing open.

The simple note card inside was filled with her neat script.

Where true Love burns Desire is Love's pure flame;
It is the reflex of our earthly frame,
That takes its meaning from the nobler part,
And   translates the language of the heart.

Andre read it aloud, mostly to himself, but everyone could clearly hear it.

Warmth tracked from Jace's chest, radiating outward and enveloping him. The corners of his mouth lifted into a broad smile.

"Isn't that a Coleridge poem?" Brynn asked.

"And it's the quote on the door to Jace's store. But what the hell's it supposed to mean?" Andre asked, plucking the card from Jace's fingers and staring at it. "Now isn't the time to be all cryptic. Why would she send us this?"

Jace looked up at Andre. "It's not the *exact* quote, Dre."

"What do you mean?"

He tapped the card, the little blank space in the last line. "It's missing the 'but.'"

THIRTY-THREE

Evan turned up the volume on her car radio and rolled down the windows, enjoying the bite in the late-autumn air. The drive out to The Ranch after working all day in her studio was a bit of a jaunt, but she was starting to enjoy the empty stretch of road and the decompression it provided at the end of the day.

Soon she'd be back to fighting city traffic daily when she chose between the two apartments she'd found this week. Both options would meet her needs, but she was having trouble deciding, not truly excited about either of them. Probably because each was just empty walls and empty rooms—exciting but terrifying reminders of this new path she'd chosen.

Secretly, she'd hoped that her note to Jace and Andre would open up the door with them again, at least to talk. But Grant had told her he'd given them the card three days ago and neither of them had reached out to her.

She'd been too chicken to go there in person and risk getting shut down. Over the last few months she'd worked hard on getting her shit together. Had gotten herself fully off the antidepressants.

She now knew she could survive fine on her own—even if not having Jace and Andre in her life had left this yawning gap inside her like a bad toothache, a dull pain that was never far from her consciousness. But losing them hadn't sent her into a spiral of depression.

She would never take a day in this world for granted again. The girl she used to be was buried. Reborn.

But that didn't mean she wanted to subject herself to them sending her away face-to-face.

They'd probably moved on. Maybe it *had* been only a dalliance like she'd told Jace. Maybe once they'd stepped away from the intensity of it all, they'd realized a relationship with her wasn't what they really wanted. She'd been a mess the last time they'd seen her. How could she blame them for not wanting to get involved with her? They'd known she wasn't ready to be with them even before she did.

And really, if they'd moved on. If it had only been a tryst. Then better to know that upfront. She wouldn't go back and change what had happened between the three of them. It had saved her.

The opening bars of one of her favorite love songs drifted from the car's speakers, and she promptly changed the station to hard rock, kicking up the volume. The guitar-heavy track filled the crammed corners of her mind, shoving away her ruminations. The late-afternoon view along the open highway was too pretty to waste thinking about things she couldn't change.

She tapped her steering wheel in time with the music and found her foot pressing on the accelerator a little more aggressively. Her hair whipped behind her as the wind blew through the car. Roads like this made her want a sports car. Like Jace's Viper.

She shook the thought from her head and belted out the chorus to the song, her off-key voice thankfully drowned out by the lead singer's. The last note left her breathless and in the snippet of silence between tracks, a high whining siren pierced her ears.

Oh, shit.

She glanced in her rearview mirror and, sure enough, a flashing red light was quickly closing in from behind. She checked her speedometer. Almost eighty. In a sixty-five.

"Dammit!" She eased off the accelerator and made her way to the soft shoulder of the highway. This was going to be an expensive ticket. Just what she needed.

She put the car in park and watched in the rearview as the cop pulled behind her in an unmarked car and turned off the siren. The setting sun reflected off the windshield of the police car, not allowing her to see inside. Damn. She hoped it was a male cop. In her experience, she had no shot of getting out of a ticket when a woman stopped her.

Evan would fight for feminism to the death, but she was not above using a smile and a nice "I'm so sorry, officer" to get out of a ticket. Though, she did draw the line at tears. Callie had used that method once and Evan had almost died from trying not to laugh. Callie had gotten a ticket anyway.

"Keep your hands where I can see them and stay in your car."

The loudspeaker voice startled her. Hell, she'd only been speeding. Evan kept her face forward and put her hands on the steering wheel as the cop stepped up beside her car. He put his palms on top of the car and leaned down to her half-open window. "Roll down your window, ma'am."

The silky authority in the voice had every molecule in her body freezing in suspension. She turned toward the window, coming face-to-face with a pair of aviator sunglasses, dark hair, and a smirk she'd know anywhere.

Oh my fucking God. She tried to say something but a puff of air was all she could manage.

Andre straightened, the hard body outfitted in his full uniform coming into view. "Get out of the car, ma'am. Now."

Her limbs couldn't process requests. Her hands stayed cemented around the steering wheel. The moment of hesitation didn't go over well. Andre yanked her car door open, leaned over her to unhook her seatbelt, then hauled her out of the car with a firm grip on her upper arm. "I said *out*."

She stumbled, but he held her upright. "I'm sorry. What's . . . What's going on, Andre?"

"So disrespectful." He dragged her around the front of the car to the passenger side, blocking them a bit from the view of the road. "You call me officer or sir, you understand?"

Heat zapped through her like lightning. *Oh.*

He shined a small flashlight in her eyes. "Have you been drinking?"

She winced at the bright light. "No, of course not."

"So you're just driving like a fucking maniac because you think you're too good to follow speed limits?"

His grip on her arm tightened, and he crowded his body against hers, trapping her between him and her car. Her body trembled. She knew what this was. But damn if he wasn't convincing enough to have a thread of fear lacing through her. "I'm sorry, officer. I wasn't paying attention. I—"

"Yeah, you know what I think?" he said, his voice low and threatening. "I think that's exactly your problem. You don't know how to pay attention. You think a nice expensive speeding ticket is going to fix that?"

She wet her lips, letting herself slide into her own role. "I can't afford a ticket, Officer. Please, just let me go. I promise I won't speed anymore."

"Look at you, you can't even look me in the eye when you promise that. You think I don't know you're lying?" The disgust in his voice dripped off the words. He turned his attention toward the rear of the car. "I don't think a ticket is going to do shit in changing her attitude. What do you think, Austin?"

She sucked in a breath, but Andre clamped her chin in his hand, not allowing her to turn her head and see Jace.

"Keep your attention on me," Andre commanded.

"As soon as we take off, she'll be driving like an Indy racer. I think this one's used to talking her way out of stuff with that pretty little mouth of hers," Jace said. "Maybe we should put those lips to better use. I may be able to be convinced to forget about that ticket."

His voice was like sunshine on chilled skin. She closed her eyes, breathed. They were here. Wanting her. Giving her the fantasy she'd only dared speak aloud once. Showing her with action instead of words how they felt. *Where true Love burns Desire is Love's pure flame.*

"*Hmm*, I may be able to be swayed as well." Andre's free hand drifted down her body and then cupped the juncture between her thighs, the heat of his palm searing through the thin material of her skirt. "So, Ms . . ."

"Kennedy," she gasped.

"Ms. Kennedy, how 'bout we work out some other form of payment?"

Under normal circumstance, she may have thought the moment comical. A silly role-play. But the intensity of his gaze, his tone, his touch had dragged her down from fantasyland and into some elemental place where lines between real and pretend blurred. He wasn't fucking around. His dominance was as real as the car pressing into her back.

But that didn't mean she was going to make it easy on either of them. They'd let her believe for all those days since she'd sent the note that they'd given up on her. Her heart had broken every time she'd looked down at her empty voicemail.

They wanted her submission again? Well, they'd have to earn it.

"Go to hell," she said, trying to wriggle free. "You can't do this. I'll report you."

"Oh, look how cute, Austin. She thinks she has some say on what fucking happens to her." His laugh was dark and menacing as he shoved his hand beneath her skirt and into her panties. Without any preamble, his fingers plunged into her pussy, her already wet heat bathing his hand. She let out a whimpering cry and pushed at the solid wall of his chest. He didn't move back an inch.

"Screw you," she bit out, the sharp sound echoing down the empty highway.

His brown eyes turned savage as he moved his hand out from under her skirt. He grabbed a fistful of her hair and yanked her sideways, splaying her stomach down on the hood of her car. Her cheek pressed hard onto the warm metal, and he kicked her legs wide with his booted foot.

The rumble of an oncoming vehicle filled her ears and she tried to jerk upward, but Andre planted a palm between her shoulder blades and pushed her back flat. "Add resisting arrest to your charges, Ms. Kennedy."

"But . . . a car," she protested. She'd never forgive herself if Andre got himself in trouble over this.

He grabbed her arms, securing them behind her, and parked himself between her spread legs, his erection hard against her ass. "You think we fucking care? Or are you embarrassed that anyone who passes by will see how bad you've been?"

The rumble turned to a roar and an eighteen-wheeler whizzed by them, kicking up some of the dust on the side of the road in its wake. She let go of the breath she'd been holding. "I haven't been bad."

Jace stepped into her peripheral vision, but she was afraid to attempt lifting her head. "No fucking remorse. Forget bargaining. Just take her in. Maybe a cell block will do her some good."

Cuffs snapped around her wrists.

"No!" She squirmed, the metal clinking from her struggle. "No, don't arrest me." She softened her tone, attempted to sound placating. "I'm sorry. Just tell me what I need to do."

Jace grabbed her by the hair, lifting her head at an uncomfortable angle and forcing her to meet his eyes. He was dressed in one of Andre's black Dallas PD shirts and dark jeans. Tattooed and badass and so fucking sexy it almost wasn't fair to expect her to resist. No gentleness resided in his face. "You want to play nice now?"

She tried to nod. Couldn't. "Yes, sir. I'll do anything."

White teeth glinted in the rays of the setting sun. "I like anything." He leaned in closer to her, his grip tightening against her scalp. "Until the sun comes up tomorrow, we *own* you, Ms. Kennedy. Every inch of this sinful body of yours. You be a good girl for us and maybe we can forget any of this ever happened."

Her body melted against the hood like car wax, his heated words and cocky smile enough to have everything going liquid inside her. Owned. By the two men she couldn't imagine loving more. "I'm all yours, officers. For as long as you want me."

Jace closed the distance between them and overtook her mouth in a kiss that told her he'd missed her as much as she'd missed him. His lips and tongue staking claim in a way that words couldn't. When he pulled back, she was panting. He nipped at her lip. "You know what you can say if you need to, pet."

She gave him a vixen smile. Nothing they could do to her would coax *Texas* from her lips. For the first time in her life, she needed no training wheels, no safety net, and no fucking safe word. Her trust in these two men had grown to be as natural as breathing. "You won't hear it. There will never be any other 'buts' again, sir."

The hard glint in his eyes softened for the space between seconds. "Get her in the car, Medina. Time we give that smart mouth of hers something to do."

Andre pulled her to her feet, checked her cuffs, and then smacked her ass hard. "Move it."

As she headed toward their vehicle, a black car came into view in the distance, heading in their direction. She picked up her pace. No need for more random strangers looking at her like she was a criminal. Jace opened the back door and Andre put a hand on her head and ducked her into the car. But before she could find a comfortable position with her hands cuffed behind her, Andre leaned inside. "On your stomach. Knees underneath you. Ass up."

She blinked, looked back toward the car that was getting closer. "What? Here?"

"*Now*, princess. I'm not going to write you an instruction manual."

Her already hammering heart kicked up to a deafening rhythm in her ears, but she rolled to her side and positioned herself as best she could. Andre grabbed her hips and helped her get her knees beneath her. He reached beneath her dress and ripped off the panties, the material splitting like it had been made of tissue. The nip of the fall air coasted over her slick skin, inspiring another rush of wet heat.

God, would the people in the other car be able to see what was going on when they passed?

The side of her face pressed into the leather of the backseat, her breathing coming out in sharp little pants. The rumble of the oncoming car grew louder and then slowed, the distinct sound of rubber hitting the dirt shoulder nearly sending her into a panic. The car was stopping!

Crap, crap, crap. She tried to reposition herself, get upright, but the angle and the cuffs had her completely off balance.

A heavy door slammed, muffled footsteps, and then voices. Jace and Andre and . . . another voice that had become familiar to her recently. The molasses tone of Grant Waters. Her breath whooshed out of her—a combination of relief and *oh, shit* twining through her. She was glad it hadn't been a stranger, but what the hell was Grant doing here? Would the boys try to push her that far? Bring in someone else? Maybe she'd been stupid to think she didn't need that safe word.

Grant had been nothing but kind to her the last few weeks, but she sensed under that good ol' boy politeness and gentlemanly concern was an utter ruthlessness. A depth of dominance that intimidated the bejesus out of her. On some molecular level her body recognized the predator and knew she wasn't built for whatever Grant served up behind his bedroom door.

No. She only wanted the sexy dominance of her own men—brash and cocky and laced with a sweetness that made her heart feel too big for her body.

The voices grew louder and a hand palmed her ass through the thin material of her dress. She jolted and a squeak jumped from her lips.

"Easy."

Jace. The tension in her shoulders eased.

"You boys need anything else?" Grant asked. "You've got yourself a fine little prisoner there."

Evan held her breath. But instead of her nerves rising, the fear slipped away like the receding tide. *Trust.* A shining light of warmth deep inside her that was burning bright for the first time in her life. Jace and Andre would only put her through what they knew she could handle. They would push her hard but not shove her over the cliff.

"Nah. She put up a decent fight, but we've got her under control. The keys are in her car," Andre said. "Appreciate your help."

Grant was here to pick up her car. That's all. She smiled and shifted to turn her head the opposite way to try to see the men. The fine sheen of sweat coating her skin had her cheek sticking to the seat. Jace lifted his hand from her ass then replaced the pressure with a swift smack.

"Hey!" She writhed from the surprise and the sharp dart of pain.

"Did I say you could move?" Jace asked.

"You didn't say I couldn't."

He spanked her other cheek, eliciting a moan from her. "Trying to see what's going on, pet? Can't stand to be left in the dark?" He shoved her dress to her waist, exposing everything. "Well, let me tell you what's happening then. Our friend Grant here is now looking at the nice red handprints on your pretty ass because someone can't follow instructions."

"*Mmm*, very nice," Grant said as if he were appraising a show horse.

Embarrassment burned through her like wildfire, growing in intensity when the telltale rush of arousal chased the humiliation. Fuck, what was wrong with her? She didn't want Grant to touch her, but knowing someone besides her lovers was seeing her like this made every soft part of her tingle.

Jace palmed her ass cheeks and spread her. "You like looking like our whore, Ms. Kennedy? Like being put on display for our pleasure?"

She managed a firm "no." But her hips canted toward Jace, betraying how desperate she was for his touch, for some relief for her aching clit.

The leather seat creaked and then Jace was at her core, his tongue teasing along her spread pussy. She cried out from the wicked snap of pleasure, and he huffed with soft laughter, his breath tickling the neediest parts of her. "Baby, you're so wet, all three of us could get in line and fuck you twice and you'd still have some to give."

She squeezed her eyes shut, the aching bad enough to make her consider begging Jace to take her. To do something. Right now.

"Too bad for you, Grant doesn't go for brunettes," Jace said, backing away from her.

"But don't worry," Andre added. "Officer Austin and I certainly do."

She should've been offended by the way they were talking to her. But somehow it only added to her arousal, shoved her deeper into her role in this game.

Her men exchanged good-byes with Grant, all the while leaving her bared and exposed. Anyone could drive by and get them all in a crapload of trouble. But she had to trust that the boys were watching out for anything that could go awry.

She adjusted her legs beneath her, trying to squeeze her thighs together and offer some relief to her throbbing clit. But firm hands clamped around her legs, spreading them again. "We're not done, pet. Don't try to sneak anything the minute we turn our heads."

"Please," she begged. "I need . . ."

"We know exactly what you need," Andre said. "Hold still."

Large hands spread her again, but this time something probed at her back entrance. She flinched, the instinct to reject whatever it was impossible to fight.

"Move again and I might forget to be gentle," Andre growled.

She whimpered but focused on stilling her body, relaxing her muscles. She could take it. They'd each taken her there before. The invading object nudged her again. Pressure. Discomfort. Jace touched her clit and stroked with confident ease, sending her nerve endings alight. "Let us in, baby. Show us what a good prisoner you can be."

She hummed her gratitude at the stimulation, the pleasure loosening the wound-up ball of tension inside her. The plug slipped past the resistance—cool, smooth, and slick—filling her snug passage and stretching her. Then it started to vibrate.

"Oh!" The unexpected sensation touching off electric sparks inside her. *Holy hell.*

Though Jace didn't change his stroke, the feel of his roughened finger on her sensitive nub intensified tenfold, as if her entire pleasure system had been kicked into a higher gear. She moaned and rode his hand, shameless.

He laughed, pulled his hand away, and kissed the base of her spine. "Not yet, baby. Save it for when it's me fucking that gorgeous ass later."

The words shuddered through her, making her feel anxious yet desperate for him all at the same time. How was she supposed to hold off coming? Edgy heat curled like smoke low in her belly, rising and infiltrating every inch of her. With the slow vibration of the plug, all she needed was a few more stokes along her clit and she'd go over. "Please, Jace, sir. I can't—"

"You can and you will. Now, up you go," Andre said. Her skirt slid back down and both men lifted her and settled her into a sitting position, making her acutely aware of the invasion still tucked inside her. They'd turned it to a low setting, a soft humming that was making her pussy ache for its own stimulation. Jace slid out of the backseat, making room. Andre unlatched and repositioned the cuffs in front of her, then pulled the seatbelt across her chest and kissed her mouth. "God, we missed you, *bella*."

The soft words were like balm for her soul, smoothing away any remaining rough spots. She blinked, a flash of tears lining her lids.

But he was back in character before she could respond. He hiked her skirt to her thighs and parted her legs, then unbuttoned the top two buttons of her shirt, exposing the curves of her breasts. He tucked a hand inside her bra and gave her nipple a firm pinch, making her arch. "That's better. Gives us a nice view in the rearview mirror. Come without permission and that vibrator will be all you get tonight."

"You two are dirty bastards," she said, trying to sound petulant, but she could hear the grin in her words.

"Oh, Ms. Kennedy, I think you better not throw rocks in that glass house of yours," he said, his smile sly.

She stuck out her tongue, earning a deep laugh from him before he climbed out and got into the driver's seat.

The ride to The Ranch was a tortuous test of her will. With her hands cuffed in front of her, she could've easily touched herself if she'd tried, provided some relief to the winding rope of desire coiling tighter and tighter inside her. But Andre's threat kept her in check. A beating she could handle, but going to bed without having these men inside her tonight might kill her.

Jace and Andre chatted about sports on the way, not inviting her into conversation—as if she wasn't worth consulting. She was simply the vessel for their use tonight. She recognized the subtle mindfuck, but still found herself growing huffy. "If you want me to cooperate, you should at least talk to me. Plus that guy is the best first baseman the Rangers have ever had. You two don't know what you're talking about."

Jace peeked back at her with a gaze that promised extensive plundering and pillaging to come. His focus traced up her parted legs, over her belly, lingered on the exposed rise of her breasts, then homed in on her mouth. Fucking her with his eyes. Like he was going through a checklist of every part of her he planned to use and abuse before the night was done. By the time he met her eyes again, she was near irrational with the need for him to touch her.

"Do you think it's wise to make demands on me, pet?" His voice was like liquid sin with a splash of menace. "To push me?"

Her lashes lowered in instinctual deference. "I'm sorry. It's just . . ."

"You're undisciplined. I know. We're going to fix that," he said, smug male arrogance wafting from him. "And we didn't pick you up to hear your misguided opinion on baseball. So keep your comments to yourself. I'd hate to have to gag that pretty mouth."

She pressed her lips together and glared, but didn't say another word.

"Good girl, you're learning." He turned back around and resumed his conversation with Andre, leaving her stewing alone in the backseat. *Hmph.* Thoughts of tying *their* arrogant asses to the bedposts and torturing *them* flitted through her head. That might not give her sexual satisfaction but it sure would wipe those overconfident smiles off their faces.

Andre pulled into the half-full parking lot at The Ranch and found a spot. Evan peeked out the window at the large main building and her heart did a cha-cha behind her ribs. They were really going to do this. Were Jace and Andre going to bring her to the police station room she'd seen on her first tour of The Ranch or were they going to go to their cabin? How would it feel to be handled by these men where everyone could see? The thought sent a blush tracking over her from cheeks to painted toenails—shame edged with some illicit thrill.

A thrill? Good God, she was careening off the kinky deep end.

Jace and Andre had figured out the combination to that forbidden lock inside her and once trust had been added to the recipe, her fantasies were spilling out like water from a newfound spring.

The door on her right opened and Jace clamped a hand around her arm. "Come on, pet. Time to pay your debt to society."

She scooted out gingerly, the vibrator moving inside her with every jostle, sending a pulse of need straight to her clit each time. When she planted her heels into the gravel, her legs wobbled, but Jace helped her to a stand.

Andre unlocked her cuffs and grabbed her shoulders. "Turn and face the vehicle. Palms on the car."

"Yes, sir." She followed his instructions and he nudged her feet wide, leaving her completely vulnerable to them. The vibrator continued its steady humming and her arousal threatened to track down her thighs.

Hands locked around her ankles, a pair on each. Jace and Andre at her feet. "You have any weapons on you, Ms. Kennedy?" Andre asked.

"No, sir."

Their hands traced up her calves, caressing, kneading, then slipped below the hem of her skirt. Hot palms against her already burning inner thighs. Each of them massaged, inching closer and closer to her wet heat. She let her head sag forward between her shoulders as she silently begged them to give her some relief.

Roughened fingers slid inside her, deep and without preamble. She bowed up, a cry escaping her lips. "Oh, God, please."

Another hand found her clit. She couldn't tell if it was Jace or Andre, but just that one was inside her and one was sliding along her folds. Pleasure, sharp and intense, whipped through her. She rocked against their busy hands. So, so close.

Then, right when she could feel the first threads of that orgasm waiting in the wings, they backed off. "No!"

Jace kissed the curve of her neck and bit. "You don't get to say no, sweetheart. Strip her, Andre."

"Wait. Here?" She glanced around the parking lot, a shred of panic winding through her. Exhibitionism in her fantasies got her going but suddenly she wasn't so sure if she had the guts to follow through.

"Yes, here. You have to earn these back. Your behavior so far has proven you don't deserve modesty." Andre dragged her skirt down and off then wound his hands around the front of her to unfasten the rest of her buttons and remove her bra.

The edge of coolness in the fall air danced over her, tightening her already aching nipples and raising goose bumps on her skin. Instinctively she lowered her arms to cover herself but Jace caught hold of her wrists and guided them behind her back again, refastening the cuffs. The move made her breasts jut out further and graze the chilled metal of the car.

She wriggled in their grasp. "You can't expect me to walk around like this."

"We can and you will," Jace assured her. "Everyone will see what a pretty prisoner we've got. And how wet and pink you get knowing everyone is looking at you." He positioned himself behind her, the hard ridge of his cock pressing against her ass and the flared base of the plug. "You don't fool me, sweet pet. I know you'll get off on being displayed just as much as we get off by showing you off."

He splayed his hand over her mound, giving delicious pressure and drawing a mewl from her.

"I fucking love knowing how everyone who sees you will want you, but only we get to have you. You're *ours*, pet. Always."

She squeezed her eyes shut, the overwhelming deluge of emotion interweaving with her desperate desire for them. "Yes, sir. Always."

Another hand brushed her hair away from her face and Andre's voice tickled her ear. "Trust us to know what you can take."

She nodded, her fears falling away like dead leaves. She would follow these men into the dark, knowing they would be there to save her if it was too much. "I want to please you. I'll do whatever you think is best."

Andre's smile was like a laser of warmth slicing through the cool air. He laced his fingers in the hair at the nape of her neck and leaned in for a kiss. His tongue slid over hers, and Jace joined in, pressing his lips to her shoulders, her spine, the curve of her ear. Tingles having nothing to do with her hyper-aroused state raced through her like fireflies, lighting any remaining dark corners within her and filling them with the shine of love she had for these two men.

How she had lived so long without this feeling she didn't know. Her black-and-white life had gone Technicolor in the best possible way. Standing in the middle of a parking lot, cuffed and as naked as the day she was born, she'd never felt safer or more content.

Andre eased away, leaving her breathless. He smiled. "We'd better get going before you tempt me off my plan. Despite evidence to the contrary, my patience isn't limitless."

She laughed, and Andre pulled something from his pocket. Black material, but not a blindfold. Her lips parted to ask him what it was, but before she could, she had her answer. Andre pulled the tight spandex mask over her head, blocking out the last glimmer of dusk and muffling the sounds around her. Only a space for her mouth remained open to the air.

What the hell? She sucked in air through her nose, verifying the material was still porous enough to breathe through.

Jace squeezed her shoulder. "We don't want you distracted. All you need to focus on is what we're making you feel."

She nodded, the panicky feeling settling down to a fine electric buzz running over her skin. "Yes, sir."

Hands clamped over her biceps, and the guys made sure she was steady on her feet. They nudged her. "Walk."

She stumbled on the first step, but they kept her upright. "Should I take off my heels?"

"Don't talk crazy now," Jace said. She could picture the naughty schoolboy smile he was probably wearing. "What kind of guys would we be if we made you walk barefoot on gravel?"

"Yeah, uh-huh. You're all heart," she said, letting the sarcasm drip off her tone.

The boys led her through the parking lot and onto pavement. The disorienting feeling of not knowing what was around her had her focusing on putting one foot in front of the other and on trusting the strong men flanking each side of her.

The squeak of a heavy door opening filled her ears and warm air cascaded over her, the contrast in temperature making her shiver. They were going inside. The built-in urge to shield her nudity, to feel shame, rose within her. She inhaled deeply, trying to center herself.

Jace and Andre wanted to show her off, to strip away the remaining bricks and expose the soft vulnerable core of her trust. To push her. If she gave herself over completely to their wishes, she knew the reward would be hers. But that didn't stop her heart having a grand mal seizure beneath her rib cage.

Her footsteps softened as she hit thick carpet. No other sounds filled her ears. The rooms in the main house were soundproof, so she assumed they'd gone in the side door and were walking down one of the hallways. At least they hadn't walked her through the lobby.

But the quiet solitude was short-lived. They tucked her into the elevator and when the doors dinged and opened again, Evan's ears perked at the gentle murmur of voices in the distance. Good Lord, how she must look—naked, masked, and in heels. Not to mention escorted by two gorgeous men in cop uniforms.

"*Mmm, bella*," Andre breathed against her ear. "When you blush it's not only your cheeks that get pink. So sexy."

He thumbed a nipple and the ebb in heat that her rush of anxiety had caused quickly fired up anew. How could she be so turned on yet so fucking terrified at the same time?

The voices shifted, now both in front and behind, people milling around her in a busy room. *Oh, God*. Her muscles threatened to lock in place and fasten her to the floor even while the familiar kernel of desire sizzled within her. "Wait. I don't know if I can do this."

Evan halted in Jace's grip, her muscles stiffening beneath his fingertips. He frowned and glanced at Andre, whose expression mirrored his. They'd anticipated this. But after Evan had done such a good job in the scene so far, Jace had thought maybe she'd already arrived at the place they needed her to be—that zone of absolute trust. But obviously they hadn't won her full heart and submission quite yet. And if the end of the plan was going to come to fruition, then this piece was non-negotiable.

Jace scanned the large open room that made up the top floor of The Ranch's main building. The center of the space was filled with couches for lounging and watching the antics, while the perimeter was set up with every kind of BDSM equipment you could imagine. A few scenes were taking place behind the slim red ropes that cordoned off each area, and two people with yellow T-shirts—The Ranch's safety monitors—were walking the floor.

Heads had lifted when he, Andre, and Evan had stepped off the elevator. The sight of a beautiful submissive stripped and cuffed between two doms dressed as cops was not something most people saw every day. Even at The Ranch.

Electricity had wicked through Jace's veins at the attention. He'd break off someone's hand if anyone but Andre touched Evan, but he couldn't deny that exposing her this way didn't make his cock press even harder against the fly of his pants. He'd never seen a woman look so stunning in her submission. And she was theirs. She loved them back.

But now she just had to know what it meant to trust them.

They had only planned to walk her through the main room to give her a sense of exposure before going into a private area, but now she'd earned herself a tougher punishment. Jace tightened his grip on her arm. "Step to the right and get on your knees, sub. You're blocking the walkway."

"Jace, I can't do—"

Andre smacked her bare ass. "Move it. And it's 'sir.'"

Jace held his breath. Evan's whole body remained taut and, though he couldn't see her face, he saw her wet her lips, part them. *Fuck, she's going to safe word.* They'd read her signals wrong and pushed her too far too fast.

But then the stiffness went pliable beneath his fingertips, and she stepped to the side, her head dipping in deference. She lowered to her knees. "I'm sorry, sir."

Her voice quavered, but her nipples had gone hard and dusky pink, and the illicit scent of her arousal swirled through his senses. Sweet mother of God he'd missed her. He leaned against the wall behind him, overwhelmed by the sight of her, by her compliance. He ran a hand over her head, the smooth spandex material warm from her body heat, and then yanked off the mask. "You're so fucking beautiful, baby. I want to look at you while you take my cock."

She blinked up at him, adjusting to the light, then tried to look over her shoulder to see where she was. Andre grabbed a handful of her hair from his position behind her and held her in place. "Where we are or who's watching is of no concern of yours, *bella*. All you need to worry about is showing Officer Austin how eager you are to suck him off."

Her gaze flared. Anger laced with wicked desire.

Jace unfastened his pants and freed his straining erection, stroking it once in front of her. "You see what you did to me, pet?"

"I'm sorry, sir."

He grabbed her chin and grazed her lips with the already damp tip of his cock. "Take care of it."

Those soft lips of hers closed around him and he damn near lost it at the first graze of her tongue. *Ah, fuck.* These last few months he'd craved her like a drug. Her sweet femininity, the feisty edge to her submission, those soulful eyes gazing up at him. His dreams had been haunted by her face, the memory of her never leaving his subconscious even when he tried to push her from his mind and shore up his heart again. And now she was here, at his feet, giving him the gift of her body, her trust, her everything.

He didn't know if he deserved such a wondrous gift, but hell if he wasn't looking forward to spending every day of the rest of his life doing his best to be worthy of her.

Her mouth slid down his shaft and she took him deep, sending currents of pleasure-laced lightning through his cock and up his spine. His balls tightened, and he sagged against the wall with a moan, letting Andre guide Evan's head back and forth over him.

His gaze tracked up to Andre and Andre smiled, the heat in his eyes enough to scorch the wood floors beneath them. "You two are a sight to behold."

Jace reached out and slid a hand around the back of Andre's neck, pulling him closer. "No, the three of us are."

Andre took Jace's mouth in a hard kiss, one that spoke to how much Andre was fighting to keep his own control. Evan hummed against Jace's cock, no doubt catching sight of he and Andre kissing above her. A little knot of anxiety ran through Jace. What if Evan didn't like the change in dynamic that had happened between him and Andre while she'd been away?

Shit. Evan had just left a relationship where she was the third wheel with two men. How had Jace not thought to warn her before they went into this scene? Stupid. He couldn't bear to have her think she was anything but the center of their universe.

Jace pulled away from the kiss. The panic on his face must've been evident because Andre's eyes widened, no doubt having his own *doh!* moment.

Jace eased back from Evan, tucked himself back into his pants as best he could, and then knelt to take her face in his hands. He didn't want to break scene and screw with the fantasy they were trying to give her, but he had to make sure she was okay. "Baby—"

She smiled, tears glimmering in the low lighting of the room. "You guys are so goddamned beautiful."

He laughed and Andre squatted down next to them. "But you're our focus, *bella*. This doesn't change how we both feel about you."

She looked between the two of them. "I don't always need to be the center. Believe me, I'm not that selfish. I'm just seriously disappointed I haven't been here to watch y'all figure each other out."

Jace's lips curled. "Dirty, dirty girl. We promise you'll get to see anything you want. And know that we want and need *you*. Neither of us has felt whole since you left."

"Nothing's felt right without you, gorgeous," Andre said, brushing his knuckles over her cheek.

She nuzzled against Andre's hand. "I know the feeling."

"Then why did you wait so long to come back to us, Ev?" Jace asked, his voice cracking a bit under the memory on those long months without her.

She bit her lip, looked up at him with her old soul eyes. "I had to make sure I was strong enough. That I was whole all on my own. To know that I wouldn't fall apart again if one day you guys decided to leave."

Her words tore straight through Jace's gut and prodded his dominant core with a red-hot poker. He pinched her chin between his fingers, his demeanor shifting from soft to steel in half a second. "Seems we haven't quite gotten our lesson through that head of yours yet. Andre, get her up."

Before they walked off these grounds, Evan was going to understand that they weren't going anywhere, that she could trust them.

If he had to turn her hide red and flog his way through that last wall of hers, then so be it.

THIRTY-FOUR

Evan yelped as Andre hauled her to her feet then draped her over his shoulder like some caveman claiming his kill for the evening. She wasn't sure exactly what she'd done to piss the two of them off, but she had a feeling they were going to make it abundantly clear before they were done with her.

Those in the room who weren't mid-scene turned to stare at the spectacle they were creating. She pressed her face into Andre's back, her cheeks hot. She couldn't tell if she was ashamed about being carried naked through a crowded room or the fact that everyone knew she'd somehow displeased her doms. She suspected the latter.

Jace grabbed her hair and slipped the mask back down over her face, blocking out the onlookers. "You need to focus, pet, and listen only to us. If I have to repeat myself, I'm going to be very angry."

"Yes, sir," she said, her voice jumping with Andre's brisk pace.

The air shifted and the noises of the room faded behind her. The mask was thin, only softening the sounds around her, but she still found herself straining to hear the smallest of hints as to where they were going. Muffled footsteps. Andre's heart pounding against her ear. Then a grind and a click. A heavy door being opened.

Andre pitched his weight forward, and she went careening through the air. Her cry of surprise ripped through the room, then ended in an *oof!* when her back hit a mattress and knocked the wind from her. The cuffs dug into her skin as she rolled to her side.

The door slammed shut and the scent of . . . vanilla filled her nostrils. Which room had they taken her to?

"On your knees." Andre's tone was like flint against her nerve endings, sparking both fear of what was to come and the sharp arousal of being handled by her two men.

She scrambled to follow the instruction, intent on righting whatever she'd said to upset them. After she was in position, one of them unhooked her cuffs and then planted a hand between her shoulder blades, pushing her down. "Forehead on the bed, ass in the air, pet."

Each took one of her already tender wrists and stretched her arms above her head. Soft leather twined around each one, securing her to the wall or headboard—she couldn't tell. She instinctively yanked on the bindings, but there was only an inch or so of play. Her pulse drummed like a frenetic marching band in her ears.

"Wider." Jace tapped her thighs. She carefully spread her knees, making sure to maintain her balance. Leather cuffs wrapped around her ankles and metal jangled. "Good girl. That's a spreader bar. Now you won't be able to draw those legs together when we work you over."

Work her over? She flexed her ankles and found she couldn't close her legs or spread them further. She was at their mercy in a way she'd never been before. Bound and trussed and exposed for whatever they wanted to do to her. She probably should be frightened. But those fight-or-flight signals never fired. Instead, need swept through her like a firestorm, igniting every erogenous point in her body. She pressed her forehead against the bed and rocked against the bindings, willing herself not to beg them to touch her.

Jace chuckled and walked his fingers along her spine, sending shivers over her. "Look at you. You can't even sit still, can you? What's wrong, baby? Need something?"

She gritted her teeth. "You know what I want, sir."

"*Hmm*, what you want and what you need may be two different things right now." His fingers reached the cleft of her ass and teased around the plug, which thankfully they had turned off when they'd taken her to the main room. He wiggled the vibrator and she couldn't stop a moan from escaping. "I'm not fucking this luscious little ass of yours until I know you're really mine."

She tensed. Did he doubt that? "I am yours, sir. You and Andre's both. I love you."

His warm hand moved away from her. "We love you, too, Ev. But your trust is sorely lacking."

The sound of something slicing through the air filled her ears a millisecond before something smacked against her right ass cheek with a stinging thud. Thin stripes of pain-laced pleasure zipped up her spine. She bowed up against her bindings as a gasp wheezed out of her. *Oh, my.*

Whatever Jace was using came down again on the opposite cheek then again and again—providing both sharp and blunt sensation simultaneously. Her breath came out in short puffs as she absorbed each impact and her clit pulsed in time with the blows.

A hand touched her head. "You like Jace's flogger, *bella*? He took out the braided one just for you."

"Yes, sir," she whispered. Jace didn't pause in his treatment.

"Do you know why you're getting punished?" Andre asked.

Her mind struggled to grab on to her thoughts, the blinding pain and pleasure sensations overloading her neurons. "Something about trust, sir?"

Jace smacked the flogger against her exposed pussy, and she

bucked against the restraints, nearly careening right into orgasm. "Oh, God."

"You know what it does to us, pet, to hear you suspect that we might just walk away from you one day?" Jace asked.

"I'm sorry, but I have to be prepared. I can't ever be weak like I was before." Her voice sounded desperate even to her own ears.

"You are not weak, Ev. Opening yourself up to us fully won't make you that way." The flogger thudded against the back of her thigh. "Submission with contingency clauses is not acceptable. We want all of you, not just your body. Your heart, Ev. Your trust."

She shook her head, tears building beneath her closed lids. "But what happens if I do that and you walk away?" If her life had proven anything to her it was that everyone leaves eventually.

The flogger tumbled against the wood floor. "Take off her mask, Dre."

The blackness gave way to the flickering warmth of candlelight when Andre pulled the material off. She turned her head, resting her cheek on the bed, tears leaking down. Both Jace and Andre kneeled next to the bed.

Andre reached out and swiped the moisture from under her eyes. "Sweet, sweet, *bella*. Don't you get it?"

More tears escaped. "Get what?"

Jace sifted his fingers through her hair, the tender look in his eyes undoing her. "Listen to me, Evan. If you don't hear anything else I say to you tonight. Hear this: When we say we want you, that we love you. We don't mean for this week or this month or until something else comes along."

A fist seemed to close around her vocal cords. "But—"

He shook his head. "No more buts, remember? We're not going anywhere unless you send us away yourself." He brushed a thumb over her forehead, smoothing the creases. "I can't promise that this is going to be easy. But I will promise that I'm not going to give up on you if things get tough. This isn't foster care, Ev. I love you. *We* love you. We want to be your forever."

The knot in her throat seemed to swell until she thought she may stop breathing. *A forever family.* That's what the caseworkers used to call it when kids were adopted. When you were special enough that people wanted you for real, not just for a while. No one had ever wanted that of her.

And now these two beautiful, kindhearted men were looking at her like no other woman existed on the planet. No fine print or contingency clauses. Just love. Pure unadulterated love.

She blinked away the tears and took a deep breath, swallowing past the emotion knotting her vocal cords. "I want that, too. So much."

Andre smiled, his own eyes glinting with moisture. "Can you take the leap, *bella*? Have faith in us and give us your whole heart?"

Leap? She's already plummeted off the mountain. Her heart was theirs now . . . and always. "Yes."

"Thank you, Ev," Jace said, his whole demeanor sighing. "Now let's get you out of these bindings. You've had enough punishment. Now I just need to love you."

Andre and Jace made quick work of releasing her and both stripped out of their clothes. When they flipped her over onto her back, she was able to take in the whole room. White candles lit every corner of the cozy bedroom and rose petals had been strewn over the floor and bed. She smiled. "Rose petals and candles? Who knew you boys were the romantic type?"

Andre climbed on the bed behind her, and Jace got in front of her wearing a wicked grin. "Lie back on Andre, pet. I'll show you how romantic we can be."

Jace positioned himself between her thighs and bent down to taste her with a long, languid glide of his tongue, while Andre kissed along her shoulder. *Oh, sweet Lord.* She murmured her satisfaction—the unending assault on her senses shutting down her capacity for speech. She'd been revved up and brought down so many times, her body was like a land mine—one perfect move and she'd detonate.

Jace swirled his tongue around her clit and nipped at the swollen nub. She whimpered and writhed. Andre held her in place. "Your orgasm is ours, *bella*. No coming until we tell you. Close your eyes and relax."

Relax? That was like telling the ocean to stop moving. She let her eyelids fall shut and clenched her fists, forcing the threatening tsunami back, fighting to keep it in check.

Jace's mouth continued its erotic assault, and he slid two fingers inside her. Her cunt clenched around him, begging for more, for all of him to be inside her. He adjusted the pressure along her inner wall, teasing the sensitive spot inside.

Her head tilted back as the rush of sensation thundered through her. *Fuck*. There was no way she was going to be able to hold on and—

Searing heat spilled across her chest and nipples, cutting off her thoughts and nearly launching her off the bed. *What the . . . Ohhhhhh, God!* The initial burn of pain morphed into an intense, overwhelming surge of pleasure. The smell of vanilla wrapped around her.

"Candles are for more than romance," Andre whispered, drizzling more wax down the line of her belly. She cried out and Jace held her fast against his mouth, the strokes increasing in intensity. "Come for us, *bella*."

The fiery wax splashed right along her navel, pooling in her belly button and running lower, and Jace sucked her clit between his teeth. A scream that didn't even sound like her own tore from her lungs, and she arched toward the ceiling, feeling as if she might levitate right off the goddamned bed.

Sharp, vibrating bliss fanned out through every cell, launching her up and over any place she'd been before. Her body rocked with the waves of it, the combination of orgasm-soaked sensation wrapping around her and holding her tight in its grasp. She didn't want it to release her.

But before she'd even had a chance to catch her breath, the boys were turning her over, hardened wax tightening her skin and flaking off her at every move. Andre slid beneath her, moving her boneless legs to straddle him, and Jace ran his hands over her quivering shoulders.

"Neither of us has been with anyone else besides you or each other since we've last been tested," Jace said in her ear. "Have you?"

She shook her head. "No."

"Then we're going to take you barebacked. Both of us. You understand?"

She nodded, the implication cutting through the afterglow of orgasm and firing up her desire anew. Both of them. They hadn't tried before to take her simultaneously. Had told her they wouldn't do that until they decided she was ready. A zip of fear and drenching need went through her.

Andre smiled up at her, his gaze enough to liquefy the wax still clinging to her nipples. He fisted his beautifully stiff cock and ran a thumb over the dampened tip. "Come 'ere, *bella*. That orgasm was just a warm-up."

She laughed. "You two may kill me with the next one then."

His large hands palmed her hips, drawing her over his cock. "We're going to take good care of you. Promise." He lowered her down to him, inch by delicious inch, sliding into the hot clasp of her core. Skin to skin. "Oh, *bella*."

Ribbons of sweet awareness snaked through her, the snug fit of him inside her stretching her and tightening the plug in her backside. She splayed her hands over Andre's chest to balance as he guided her up and down. The full feeling pushed all her naughty buttons, but how the hell was she going to handle both of them at once? She hadn't seen the plug, but she'd guess Jace had to be twice the size.

"Keep your eyes on me," Andre said, slowly rocking into her. "Trust that we're here to make you feel good, not hurt you. Let go for us."

He stroked a thumb over her engorged clit as he pumped into her, dragging her back into her senses and away from any worries. She was theirs. They loved her. They wouldn't harm her. This was her always.

She tossed her mental parachute from her back, closed her eyes, and gave into the free fall, knowing the two of them would be there to catch her.

Heat blanketed her back as Jace pressed his chest against her. He stroked her hair, kissed the rim of her ear, nibbled her neck. "You look so beautiful right now. I can't believe you're finally mine."

She reached back and circled her arm around the nape of his neck, sliding her nails through his hair, relishing the feel of him, the scent. He'd always had on her on some level. She'd known it since the first time he'd ever touched her. That piece of her heart had never returned. But now she knew what it really felt like to surrender it all. Without fear.

"Lean forward, pet," Jace whispered. "I need to be inside you."

She followed his directive, bracing her elbows on each side of Andre. Andre stilled his hip motion and lifted his head to catch her lips in a long, sensual kiss. His finger continued to stroke along her slick folds, grazing her clit each time, tightening the coil of need low in her belly again.

Jace's palm pressed against the base of her spine and she felt the wiggle of the plug. She sucked in a breath and in one quick second, Jace had slid it out of her. She whimpered into Andre's kiss, the ripple of pleasure followed by the strange ache of emptiness it left.

Cool liquid slid along her back opening and Jace dipped his fingers inside her, spreading the lubricant. Andre increased the pace of his stroking, keeping her on the edge of orgasm, but not quite there. Making things that would probably feel uncomfortable under normal circumstances feel unbearably fantastic.

"Okay, baby," Jace said, his voice as smooth as glass. "Just relax and let me in. Push against me."

Andre deepened their kiss, keeping her muscles like putty, and she focused on not tensing. She didn't want to undo the work the plug had probably done for her. The blunt head of Jace's cock pressed against her opening, feeling impossibly huge, but she did as she was told and pushed against him.

Oh! The ring of muscles seemed to fight against the invasion, and pain/pressure mixed in with the pleasure of Andre's continuous attention between her legs. She blew out a breath and pressed back against Jace again. The head of his cock breached the resistant ring and then slid in, her body giving up and opening to Jace.

But he wasn't all the way in. Another thrust and her body seemed to stretch to capacity. Their cocks pressed against each other through the thin wall separating the spaces. Filling her. Making her gasp. They were both inside her, taking everything she had to give them.

Jace groaned, his fingers digging into her hips. "You feel so goddamned good, baby. Jesus."

She pulled away from Andre's kiss, her senses on overload. She couldn't move, her body pinned between the two of them. But she also couldn't stay still. The energy building inside her looking for a way out. "Please."

Andre pinched her clit and she cried out. "Please what, *bella*? You okay?"

"Please move," she panted. "Please. Fuck me."

One of Jace's hands tracked up her belly, palmed her breast, caressed it. "Baby, don't worry, we're going to fuck you. Very thoroughly. But why rush?"

A pitiful, unintelligible plea passed her lips. She wouldn't survive if they dragged this out. Her blood had already turned molten beneath her skin.

Andre smiled and drew his hips back, sliding along her sensitive tissues and brushing along the pressure of Jace's cock. Then, as soon as he plunged back deep, Jace eased back in a perfectly timed alternating motion. Slow and steady, the glide of the two men inside her enough to shove her to the brink of madness.

Her nails dug into the sheets. She couldn't help or control the pace no matter how much she attempted to. All she could do was take it how they wanted to give it. If they wanted to drag it out for the next hour, she was at their mercy. But God, if they did that she may never recover.

Her soft pants became moans. "I can't. I need. Faster."

"You want us to fuck you hard, pet?" Jace asked.

"Yes, sir. Please. I'm begging you."

Jace's grip on her hips turned bruising and Andre's tucked something between their bodies and against her clit. It buzzed. *Holy. Fucking. Shit.* Blinding darts of pleasure shot through her and she yelped. Andre's hands tangled in her hair, and the pace of the two men's thrusts turned relentless.

Her body electrified as every molecule pulsed with a sanity-threatening energy. The sounds bursting from her no longer felt as if they were a part of her. The boys pistoned into her, their own male grunts and groans mixing into the soundtrack of skin smacking skin and unadulterated sex.

Sweat dripped from her as she fought to stave off her orgasm, but it was like trying to fend off a pack of lions with a twig. The sensation of being taken so fully—two cocks, Jace's and Andre's hard bodies surrounding her—and the insistent hum of the vibrator against her clit all coalesced into a volcanic mass inside her.

"Go ahead, *bella*," Andre said, his own voice strained. "Go over with us."

The words blew the top off her mountain. Her back bowed and a guttural scream raked over her throat and exploded out of her. Pleasure, edgy and intense and absolutely maddening, lifted her to some other plane where nothing else existed but the three of them. The screams went on loud and long as she came so hard her bones seemed to rattle with the power of it.

Andre's own moan filled her ears, quickly followed by Jace's as both men chased her orgasm with their own release. They pulsed into her, their sweet fluid heat filling her while she continued to ride a wave of ecstasy that seemed to only increase with each passing second.

Every system in her body seemed taken hostage as her orgasm refused to relent. Tears sprung forth and though she was anything but sad, she began to cry. Her chest racking with the overwhelming need to literally let everything out.

Vaguely she registered Jace slipping out of her, and she collapsed against Andre's chest. Andre wrapped his arms around her and whispered soothing things to her as her body finally began to ease down from its high. "It's okay, *bella*. Breathe. You're okay. We have you."

Jace was back in a matter of moments, and Andre rolled her to his side, sliding out of her while Jace climbed into bed and tucked her against his chest. Andre flanked her back. Hands brushed away her hair, wiped her tears, caressed her face.

After a few minutes, her sobs quieted and her head stopped spinning. She nuzzled against Jace, sniffling. "Why is it I can't help going into the ugly cry when you guys get a hold of me?"

She could feel Jace smile even though she couldn't see his face. "You and I have very different ideas of what's ugly."

Andre ran a hand along her hip. "Did we hurt you?"

"No, it was . . . amazing," she said, trying to put it into words.

"It was like there was too much energy and my body had to release it however it could, which apparently meant weeping. I'm sorry. Didn't mean to ruin the moment or freak you out."

Andre's chest huffed against her back with a soft chuckle. "Ruin it? That was the most beautiful thing I've ever seen. You were flying, *bella*. And we were right there with you."

A smile lifted her lips as she snuggled against them, arms wrapping around her from both sides. Safe. Content. Loved.

She'd gone flying.

And they'd caught her.

They would always catch her.

Turn the page for a look at

fall into you

the next book in
the Loving on the Edge series
by Roni Loren
Coming soon from Heat Books

Charli Beaumonde adjusted her rearview mirror, wondering, not for the first time, if she should've stopped in one of the small town motels she'd passed thirty miles back. The deserted highway seemed much more jeepers creepers now than it had been this morning on her way out of the city.

She hadn't planned to be out in boondocks Texas this late at night, but the chance to see who was coming and going from the family home of Dallas University's top quarterback recruit had been too good to pass up. Who knew so many men in suits had business in such a little Podunk Texas town?

She hadn't gathered enough damning evidence to put together a story for the station yet, but she was getting there. If she could get one of the players to slip up and talk, give her some names, she could blow the cheating scandal wide open and virtually secure her promotion to the on-air sidelines reporter for the Texas Sports Network.

Her boss had already told her she was one of the final candidates. Charli didn't know how many other people she was up against, but she knew that she could go toe-to-toe with anyone on sports knowledge. Plus, she felt like her screen test had gone well. All she needed now was the one big story under her belt to show that she had the reporter chops as well.

She smiled, picturing herself on the sidelines of the college football games—microphone in hand, the smell of fresh-cut grass and sweaty athletes, the deafening roar of the crowd cheering for their teams. She couldn't think of anything that would make her happier or any place she'd rather be. All the years of working her ass off behind the scenes would finally pay off.

She adjusted in her seat, but the faint flash of light in her rearview had her glancing in the mirror again. Distant headlights pierced the black vortex behind her. Her shoulders loosened a bit, her grip on the wheel easing. For some reason, knowing she wasn't the only person on this lonely road made her feel better. She turned the dial on her radio to find her favorite sports talk station and settled in for the last hour of her drive back to Dallas.

But a few minutes later, the glare of the headlights became blinding in her rearview as the driver flashed his high beams on and off. Squinting, Charli grabbed the mirror, turning it away from her. "What the hell?"

She slowed down a bit, thinking the driver must have some emergency and wanted to get past her. But when she slowed, he didn't go around, he just got closer. *Flash. Flash. Flash.* The lights created a strobe effect in her car, disorienting her. She grabbed the steering wheel and jerked it to the left to move into the other lane, but the other car stayed on her rear as if it were tied to her bumper with rope.

"Shit." She tried again, going back to the right lane, but the car followed, nearly clipping her back bumper. Her creeping unease turned into panic.

Whoever was in the car wasn't trying to get past her—he was trying to get *to her*. She slammed on her gas in an attempt to put some distance between them so that she could regain her vision, but her four-cylinder Toyota was no match for whatever was behind her. The rumble of a bigger, more powerful engine drowned out the quiet hum of her own.

She looked for her cell phone, but the damn thing had clamored to the floorboard when she'd made the hard lane change. Keeping her hands firmly on the wheel and watching her speedometer slide into a zone it'd never ventured to, she tried to bump the phone closer with her left foot. Once it was within reach, she attempted to make a grab for it, but a hard jolt sent her head hard into the steering wheel and her world into a spin.

The sound of screeching tires was the last thing Charli heard before everything went black.

Grant liked the quiet of the night. His resort, The Ranch, didn't slow down until three a.m. most evenings. So after spending his time over there, supervising and making sure everything was running smoothly, he relished the walk over from the main resort area to his private cabin on the far corner of the property.

Not many things could match the calming effect of the breeze blowing through the fields of grapevine, the night bugs singing, and the kind of rich silence that could only be had this far out of the city. In fact, there was one other thing that could trump it— having a beautiful woman fully surrendering under his hand.

That's what he'd really been hoping to find tonight. And every night for the last six months since he'd handed off his last trainee to her new dom. But even with The Ranch at his fingertips, finding a woman who appealed to him and his particular wants was proving near impossible. His tastes had grown refined, specific. The brief, one-off play sessions could sometimes meet his immediate desires. But it was like a carnivore living on a vegetarian diet. He was never truly satisfied.

So instead of clearing his mind with the all-encompassing experience of D/s, he was left to rely on the sound of the crickets and the blanket of the night to soften the edge of his thoughts. It was really the only time of the day his brain would shut down and simply be.

But when he made the turn around the last bend in the path toward his home, a faint screeching sound sliced through the thick night air. He stilled, his ears and body going on full alert—a skill he'd never shaken from his years in the army and CIA. The distant sound of an engine followed the screech and then faded.

He frowned. Probably a driver stopping suddenly to avoid an animal in the road or something. The car had sounded like it'd driven off, but Grant didn't want to assume that. The highway his ranch sat off wasn't heavily traveled. So if someone had gotten in an accident, they wouldn't find help quickly.

He jogged the rest of the way to his cabin and instead of going inside, he headed straight for his pickup truck. His boot hit the gas before he'd even shut the door completely. The drive up to the main road only took a few minutes at a normal pace, but when Grant saw twin beams of light in the distance, he kicked into overdrive, his truck bouncing along the dirt road like an off-road racer.

By the time he got to the main gate, he could see the front end of a car peeking out of the ditch on the opposite side of the road. The soft whine of the dying horn filled his ears. "Shit."

He threw the gear into park and jumped out of the truck. The gate was chained with a padlock, but he didn't want to waste time getting it unfastened, so he planted a foot on one of the bars and vaulted over it.

"Hello?" he called out after landing with a thud on the other side. Only the fading horn and the smell of burnt rubber greeted him. He hurried across the road and peered down into the wrecked Toyota. The tail end had slid into the ditch, the runoff rainwater from yesterday's storm rushing past the back tires. Grant squinted, trying to see into the front seat. The headlights were the only illumination besides the moon, and all he could make out was the outline of a person in the front seat.

"Hello?" he called again. "If you can hear me, I'm here to help you."

No response.

Grant hurried around to the other side of the car and carefully worked his way down the muddy embankment to get closer to the driver. His boots hit the bottom of the gully and water sluiced over his feet. Even this close, it was still too dark to see much. He grabbed his cell phone out of his jeans pocket and hit the button to illuminate the screen, holding the phone out toward the closed driver's side window. The faint light from the phone spilled onto the profile of a woman, head slumped against the headrest, eyes closed.

His stomach flipped. *No. Come on. Be okay.* He wedged open the door, the soft earth only allowing him to get it halfway open, and leaned into the car to put his fingers against the woman's neck. The strong *thump, thump, thump* of her pulse touched his fingers.

"Thank God." He touched her clammy cheek. "Ma'am, can you hear me? You've been in an accident. I'm going to get you some help."

Though, with the nearest hospital forty-five minutes away, he wasn't exactly sure when that help might get there. He hit another button on his cell phone.

Marc, one of his managers, answered on the first ring. "Hey, Grant, what's up?"

"I need you to find Dr. Montgomery. I think he was playing with Janessa tonight in a cabin on the west side."

"You want me to interrupt a scene?" Marc asked, the surprise in his voice evident. "Is everything okay?"

Grant quickly explained what was going on and told him to also put in a call to the hospital to at least get an ambulance headed this way. Once he'd given Marc his marching orders, Grant returned his focus to the woman in the car. He'd learned first-aid skills in the military so he knew not to move her neck or try to get her out of the car. But he checked her breathing to make sure nothing was obstructed.

Her seatbelt was on, so she'd had some protection in the crash. But based on the swelling knot on her forehead, she'd hit her head on something—most likely the steering wheel. With gentle fingers, he brushed her hair away from the tender spot to examine it closer and make sure it wasn't bleeding. He leaned in to get a better look, but a low moan had him halting.

He turned his head and the woman's eyelashes fluttered. Another garbled sound passed her lips.

"Shh, easy now," he soothed, using the tone he employed when dealing with skittish horses. "Try not to move, darlin'. I've called for help."

Her entire body went rigid, and her lids flew open, her eyes going wide with fear.

He backed out of the car a bit, so as not to freak her out more, but put a hand on her shoulder. "It's okay. You're okay. You've been in an accident. I need you to stay still until the doctor gets here to check you."

She blinked, her lips parted as if to say something, but then she cringed and her hand went to her head. "Dizzy."

"You've hit your head. Try to take some nice, slow breaths." Grant kept his tone soft as he watched her follow his directions. "Can you tell me your name, darlin'?"

She squeezed her eyes shut, continuing to take deep breaths. "Uh . . . Charlotte, no . . . Charli."

"Okay, good, Charli," Grant said, happy to hear that she still knew her name. "Do you know where you are or what happened to you?"

"I'm . . . I . . ." A crease appeared between her brows as if she were trying hard to find the information. "I can't remember."

He squeezed her shoulder. "That's all right. We'll worry about that later."

The sucking sound of feet hitting wet earth drew Grant's attention back toward the bank of the ditch. Dr. Theo Montgomery was making his way down, wearing a pair of pajama bottoms and an open oxford shirt, and holding one of the well-stocked first-aid kits from The Ranch. Red marks, no doubt from Janessa's flogger, still marked his bare chest.

"Status," Theo said, all business.

"Name is Charli. She just woke up. Breathing is fine. Probably concussed—can remember her name but nothing about what happened. Contusion on her forehead. I haven't moved her."

"Good." Theo moved in when Grant stepped out of the way. He introduced himself and then started his examination.

———

An hour and a half later, the sun was starting to peek over the horizon as the EMTs checked Charli over one last time and discussed the situation with Theo. Grant stood off to the side, watching as the beautiful redhead tried to stay focused on the conversation these people were having about her.

"Looks like it's only a mild concussion. We can bring her back to Graham General and keep her for observation," the EMT told Theo.

"I don't want to go to the hospital," Charli said, her voice low and hoarse. "I just want to go home and rest."

The young guy frowned down at her. "Ma'am, do you have someone at home who can keep an eye on you for the next twenty-four hours?"

She closed her eyes. "Uh, Farmer Ted."

The EMT's head tilted. "And who is that? A neighbor?"

"My cat."

The ever-serious Theo smiled a bit at that. "Charli, I don't think your cat can call 911 if you go unconscious again."

"He's very smart," she said, not opening her eyes, but her mouth twitching at the corner. "Could probably . . . figure it out."

Her voice was fading a bit, her exhaustion evident.

"No, I think you better let them take you in," Theo said. "You need to have someone with you for a little while. And you can't drive home right now, anyway. It's not safe and your car is trashed."

She raised her gaze then, a flicker of fear passing through those green eyes. "Please, don't make me. I hate hospitals."

The underlying quiver in her voice hit Grant square in the sternum. He prided himself on being able to read even the subtlest clues in people. It had served him well when extracting information from people in his days in the CIA and made him quite the formidable dominant now. And what he was sensing was honest fear in this woman. It was more than not wanting the inconvenience of a hospital—she was genuinely freaked out at the thought.

Before he could think it through, he stepped forward. "If the lady doesn't object, she can stay here for the day. I have unoccupied cabins at my vineyard. She's more than welcome to use one, and I can check on her every few hours."

Charli raised her gaze to him, her eyebrow lifting beneath the knot on her forehead. "You have a vineyard?"

He chuckled. No doubt his muddy jeans and plaid work shirt didn't scream that in addition to his covert side business, he ran one of the most successful wineries in Texas. He held out his hand. "Grant Waters, owner and operator of Water's Edge Wines."

She took his offered hand, and Grant felt the slight tremble go through her fingers, caught the quick-as-lightning glance at the open collar of his shirt, the slight hitch in her breathing. *Well, well.* His body warmed in a wholly inappropriate way at her subtle signs of interest. He quickly dropped the handshake and stepped back. *She's had a blow to the head, horn dog. Reel it in.*

Theo crossed his arms and nodded in Grant's direction. "I can vouch for Grant. I'm a guest at his . . . vineyard cabins all the time. You'll be comfortable and safe here."

"And I can drive you back to town tomorrow," Grant offered, trying not to sound as eager as he felt. "I have to go into Dallas for a business meeting anyway."

She smirked and the faint freckles on her nose twitched. "You're not some serial killer rapist, right? Because I've had a shitty enough night already."

The unexpected comment made him laugh. No, he wasn't a serial killer rapist. But the way she bit her lip after making that comment had his less-than-pure thoughts driving up to an NC-17 rating.

"Nope. Just a rancher and winemaker." And owner of the most elite BDSM resort this side of the Mason-Dixon. But that wasn't something she needed to know about him.

At least not while she was concussed.

But later . . . Well, later was ripe with possibilities.

He'd always had a thing for freckles.

ABOUT THE AUTHOR

Roni Loren wrote her first romance novel at age fifteen when she discovered writing about boys was way easier than actually talking to them. Since then, her flirting skills haven't improved, but she likes to think her storytelling ability has. Though she'll forever be a New Orleans girl at heart, she now lives in Dallas with her husband and son. If she's not working on her latest sexy story, you can find her reading, watching reality television, or indulging in her unhealthy addiction to rock stars, er, rock concerts. Yeah, that's it. Visit her website: www.roniloren.com.